# Praise for *The Key to My Heart*

"*The Key to My Heart* is a simply beautiful book. A Lia Louis novel always leaves me feeling warm and uplifted, and this is her best one yet."

—Beth O'Leary, internationally bestselling author of
*The Wake-Up Call*

"*The Key to My Heart* is a warm, relatable journey through the bogs of grief to living life again."

—Abby Jimenez, *New York Times* bestselling author of *Yours Truly*

"The sweetest, most romantic book. It was a pure delight to read."

—Marian Keyes, internationally bestselling author of *Again, Rachel*

"Gloriously romantic and very funny, this delightful book is not to be missed."

—Louise O'Neill, author of *The Surface Breaks*

"Heartwarming, hope-filled and hilarious, *The Key to My Heart* is wonderful. I loved this tender story about opening your heart and letting love into your life. Reading a Lia Louis book is like hanging out with your very best friend and drinking a whipped cream hot chocolate with extra marshmallows, pure joy."

—Lindsey Kelk, internationally bestselling author of
*The Christmas Wish*

# Praise for *Eight Perfect Hours*

"I read *Eight Perfect Hours* in one sitting, in four perfect hours, because I couldn't bear to put it down without knowing the ending."

—Jodi Picoult, #1 *New York Times* bestselling author

"Depending on your reading speed, *Eight Perfect Hours* also might describe the time you spend with this novel . . . a poignant rom-com about two strangers and the power of fate."

— *The Washington Post*, "Best feel-good books of 2021"

"Delightful. A gorgeous, romantic tale about fate and second chances."

—Sophie Cousens, *New York Times* bestselling author of
*The Good Part*

"Eight perfect hours of escapist, romantic, life affirming bliss."

—Gillian McAllister, internationally bestselling author of
*Wrong Place, Wrong Time*

"Louis (*Dear Emmie Blue*) fills this sweet romance with twists of fate and rich emotional considerations . . . Witty moments and a delightful supporting cast . . . Fans of clean contemporary romances will find plenty to enjoy."

—*Publishers Weekly*

# Praise for *Dear Emmie Blue*

"A swoon-worthy British rom-com with big heart and a heroine worth rooting for."

—*The Washington Post*

"This book is f\*\*king perfect, buy it now."

—Julia Whelan, critically acclaimed author of *My Oxford Year*

"*Dear Emmie Blue* is the new Eleanor Oliphant. Deftly crafted descriptions and characters who jump off the page and drag you into the story. I loved every moment of it."

—Bella Osborne, author of *The Promise of Summer*

"Like *My Best Friend's Wedding* plus an unfairly gorgeous Frenchwoman, mixtapes, and miles of inside jokes . . . *Dear Emmie Blue* will resonate long after readers turn the last page."

—*Booklist*

"Ebbing and flowing with the ups and downs of life, *Dear Emmie Blue* is a delightful read that fans of *Bridget Jones's Diary* and *Eleanor Oliphant Is Completely Fine* will enjoy."

—*BookPage*

## Also by Lia Louis

*The Key to My Heart*

*Eight Perfect Hours*

*Dear Emmie Blue*

# Better Left Unsent

a novel

## Lia Louis

**EMILY BESTLER BOOKS**
—
**ATRIA**
New York   London   Toronto   Sydney   New Delhi

An Imprint of Simon & Schuster, LLC
1230 Avenue of the Americas
New York, NY 10020

First Emily Bestler Books/Atria Paperback edition May 2024

**EMILY BESTLER BOOKS / ATRIA** PAPERBACK and colophon are trademarks of Simon & Schuster, LLC

Simon & Schuster: Celebrating 100 Years of Publishing in 2024

For information about special discounts for bulk purchases, please contact Simon & Schuster Special Sales at 1-866-506-1949 or business@simonandschuster.com.

The Simon & Schuster Speakers Bureau can bring authors to your live event. For more information or to book an event, contact the Simon & Schuster Speakers Bureau at 1-866-248-3049 or visit our website at www.simonspeakers.com.

Interior design by Erika R. Genova

Manufactured in the United States of America

1  3  5  7  9  10  8  6  4  2

Library of Congress Cataloging-in-Publication Data has been applied for.

ISBN 978-1-6680-0129-5
ISBN 978-1-6680-0131-8 (ebook)

*For my lovely, gold-hearted Mum.*

*Thank you for daydreaming with me on windy Leigh-on-Sea walks.*

*It will now forever be our place.*

Hello! Good morrow to you, Jack! Just "dropping you a message before you leave" like you said to. You did say that, didn't you? (I'm pretty sure you did, but also, we both had a LOT of those awful custard-yellow "Boss Man Michael" cocktails at the party and I personally feel like those drinks changed my biochemistry forever. That instead of blood, I'm now somehow eggnog and rosemary and nostril hair and whatever else we suspected was in them?! I STILL feel disgusting.)

Anyway, I just wanted to say I had such a fun time hanging out with you at the party, and how laughable is it that we've worked together this whole time and chose to hit it off the WEEK before you leave the company for the foreseeable!? And . . . . . . . . . ahhhhhhh, I'm so not going to send this, am I? Of course I'm not going to send this. I really thought I might, but of course now I'm too scared to because you are cool and I am a turnip. A coward. Turning into a bit of a wallflower these days, actually. And I suppose because I'm not ever, ever going to send this and nobody will ever, ever see it, I can say what I like now. So! Jack Shurlock, you are really hot. Like, *really*. And were we going to . . . kiss? OMG, I feel like we were!? That moment in the dark, sitting in that booth. When we both stopped speaking and you sort of shifted closer to me, gave that slow smile. Just a millisecond before drunken Cherry sat up between us, retched, and said simply, "I just swallowed loads of sick." I *think* we were, weren't we? And I wish we had. I even had a truly cinematic, Definitely Not Safe For Work dream about it last night—interrupting drunk colleagues excluded—and I keep thinking about it. Seriously. 10 out of 10, Jack Shurlock. Five stars. 100% on the Tomatometer.

(OMG, LOLLLLLL, definitely never ever, ever sending this now.)

Best wishes and happy travels to the man who will never read this!

Millie x

## chapter 1

*I* am going to vomit. I'm going to have a heart attack right here, on a scratchy office chair and in Boardroom Two, which, for some reason, always smells faintly of Pecorino cheese. Perhaps I'll even—*die*? I mean, that's surely possible given the circumstances and that my poor heart is thumping so hard, so quickly, my body must be convinced I'm running a marathon completely untrained. Deaths happen all the time at marathons, don't they? It's why I don't run. (That, and the fact that sweating always turns my face to the color of a shiny, embarrassing, prize red cabbage.)

But now—now I'm *seriously* considering running. Running and not stopping. Running until this stuffy boardroom is nothing but a tiny, unidentifiable speck in the distance. Running until I get to the border, until I meet a nameless man in dark sunglasses who'll shove a fake passport into my hand, along with a false beard and a one-way ticket to a tiny, hidden-away desert town in the Outback somewhere.

Because—God, this is awful. My worst, worst, *worst* possible nightmare. Probably anyone's worst nightmare, for that matter, but most definitely, beyond a doubt, mine—and it's happening. Right now. To me. Actual me. *Millie Chandler.* Live, and in stereo.

Nobody's even said it out loud yet either; why on a totally normal-seeming, run-of-the-mill Thursday morning at nine fifteen I find my-self summoned here, in a boardroom of people mere receptionists like me only ever see when redundancies are announced (or when they're drunkenly tightrope-walking the sexual harassment border-line at after-work drinks). But I already know. Without anyone utter-ing a single word, I know why I'm sitting here in front of three of my bosses, plus Ann-Christin, our incompetent but sweet HR manager whose blank face stares through a laptop screen like a *Star Trek* villain. I knew almost the second I walked into the room a few moments ago, trailing behind Petra, my boss (and, I hope, still my friend), and saw my name projected from a computer onto the screen on the wall. A uniformed stack of them. *Millie Chandler. Millie Chandler. Millie Chan-dler. Millie Chandler.*

Because it seems, somehow, emails that shouldn't have been sent, *have* been sent.

Lots of them.

*So, so, so many of them.*

Emails *I* wrote, but never sent. And "never sent" was how they should have always, always stayed.

Oh my God, I really am going to be sick. Or pass out. Or both. (But then—passing out would *definitely* get me out of this, wouldn't it? And I want, so much, to get out of this.)

"We're just waiting for Paul to arrive," sighs Michael Waterstreet, more hard-hearted cop than managing director, and although I man-age to nod, let out a shaky little whimper of an "OK," I'm so rigid in this chair, it's hard to tell if I actually moved at all or if I've perhaps, due to all the shame and terror and utter *embarrassment*, turned to stone like a petrified fossil.

How has this even happened? *How?* Five years I've worked here at Flye TV, a small, slightly disorganized (but mostly successful) TV sports broadcasting company. Five whole years I've given it my all, like an agreeable robot, a considerate, smiley yes-woman, full of nothing but "Sure!" and "Oh, absolutely!" and "Of *course* I'll send your parcel overseas and pretend I totally believe you when you say it's for the company, and not for your auntie in New Zealand again, who collects what looks and feels like monster truck tires." Yet here I am. *Here I am*, at what I can only imagine is about to be a disciplinary and perhaps what will go down as one of the worst moments of my entire twenty-nine-year-long life.

"Could you, um, please t-tell me what this . . . this is about?" I ask wobblily, even though I am, of course, 99.9999 percent certain what this is indeed about. "Is it about emails? Is it about . . . *my* emails?"

But Michael holds up a large, corn-beefy hand. "We'll discuss it once everyone's arrived."

Oh, it's bad, isn't it? This feels really, really, really, undeniably bad.

I should have known today was going to have a shade of disaster to it too. The signs were all there, and I'm so skilled at looking for signs these days; little whiffs of bad things approaching on the horizon that I might need to dodge. Today, though, I missed them. *Completely.* The traffic that was unusually horrendous this morning (a tiny hint). My favorite work mug—enormous, sloth-shaped, so amusingly funny-faced—that wasn't in the office kitchen cupboard (a bigger hint). And the fact that when I'd asked Chatty Martin in Finance if he'd seen it, he *blanked me.* Yep. Chatty Martin, the man who during a bad bout of tonsilitis carried around his laptop, open on a text-to-speech website through which he spoke to us like an expressionless AI robot, ignored me. (The very biggest omen of them all.)

And now, I'm here. Staring at this screen on the wall.

At my drafts.

*My email drafts that are no longer just 'drafts'.*

All those things I want to say but I'm too afraid to. All those things I type instead, to get them off my chest, to release them, without anyone knowing, without any . . . well, *collateral.*

Oh, God, this really is like a terrible dream. One of those dark "what if" situations you dream up at 2 a.m. when you're feeling sad and alone in the world. Except this is not a "what if" or a dream. This is happening. This is real life—*my* real life.

The boardroom door clicks shut behind me, and my heart drops to my feet. Paul Foot, our director, stands in front of it in a pin-striped suit two sizes too big. He slowly looks at me, to everyone else, and then to the screen on the wall—to that shameful, shameful Jenga tower of "From: Millie Chandlers," each a little window into who I really am. Rants, complaints, my stupid inside jokes, my truths, my . . . *secrets.*

"Righty-o, folks," he says, and—*ah.* There it is. The sloth, smiling judgmentally, in his chubby hand. My favorite mug, now symbolic in its own right.

Because this is it.

This is "The Moment." And how do I even get out of this? The damage is already done. The worst has already happened.

All my email drafts have somehow been sent.

Every single last one.

**From: Millie Chandler**

**To: Michael.Waterstreet@Flyetv.com**

**Subject: Re: millie, set up meeting room asap**

Ummmm, an empty email and an instruction in the subject

without a <u>single</u> please or thank you?????? Not that I expected anything else of course, because I hear how you speak to other people who work here. YOU ARE THE RUDEST MAN ALIVE!!!!

Kind Regards,
Millie Chandler
Reception
Flye TV, Progress Road, Essex

**From: Millie Chandler**
**To: Alexis.Lee@TTMedTech.com**
**Subject: re: sorry, can't make dinner, clients over from Sweden, can't go home until I've closed the sale!!!**
Good. I'm sort of relieved to be honest, Lex. The cinema last week was hard-going. I wish it hadn't been but it was and I felt like you were mad at me the whole time. You were so contrary and argumentative!? It was like you had a problem with everything I said. And lately, it really feels like we're drifting apart, and I hate saying this, but sometimes I think that's a good thing.

**From: Millie Chandler**
**To: Owen.Kalimeris@Flyetv.com**
**Cc: All Office**
**Subject: re: Update from Team India, week 16!**
It's been four months since we broke up, and I still miss you so much, Owen. So much sometimes that it physically aches. I just don't know how to forget you.

## chapter 2

*M*illie, last night, you sent a large number of emails," says Paul, my boss, opposite me at the boardroom table, "and we'd very much like to discuss this."

Paul seems calm and matter-of-fact as a miniature, panicky battle takes place inside my chest. My worst nightmare: confirmed. Verified. And I know some people might see having their email drafts sent as nothing more than an irk, at most an "Oh, bloody hell, that's going to ruffle a few feathers, isn't it? Ha-ha-ha" drama they could do without. But I am not some people. Because my email drafts are *not* just email drafts. For the last couple of years, my drafts have become—my *diary.* A confessional. A haunted crypt of unsaid things; things I wish I could say, things I really, really *want* to say but don't, in pursuit of a peaceful life. No drama. No risk. No eyes on me. No *heartbreak* (and that one's very important). A life where I just take thoughtful, destinationless walks with my friends, cook, (try to) crochet, and get far too emotionally invested in reality TV. A little under the radar. Some might even say "private," especially nowadays.

But now, or at least from what I can only assume from the screen on the wall emblazoned over and over with my name, it's . . . out there. All of it. Everything I think and feel but keep locked up. All my email drafts, *sent*, to real people. And yes, some to colleagues, but worse than that are—*the others.*

Oh, the others.

The emails written to important people in my life. People who I really care about; *love.*

Fuck.

And now I have to explain it. Somehow, I have to explain the whats, the whys, the hows (and the *hows* is what I can't for even a second begin to understand) to three silent bosses and sci-fi-head-in-a-jar Ann-Christin.

"I know sometimes emails *do* get sent in error," continues Paul. "A reply-to-all, instead of a reply to a single recipient, for example. But this—you have sent very many, Millie, and various company-wide emails also. Some of which are . . . *personal.*"

"The—the thing is," I start. *Must. Not. Cry.* "I—I didn't actually send them."

"You didn't send them," Michael repeats slowly, raising a single bushy eyebrow. He's gone full cop. Full army commander. I should've known he might. Michael once arrived at a company winter mud run dressed in animal furs and covered in lard while everyone else ran in waterproof jackets and inadequate sneakers. He's that type. Plus, I have *definitely* bashed out a stupid, snarky email draft or two to Michael in my time, so he's probably seen them and now understandably despises the very bones of me. "They came from your email address, Millie."

"Yes, y-yes, I know, but—"

"And you *do* recognize them?" He cocks his square head toward the screen, at the strings and strings of emails, and suddenly this seems ridiculous. That this has happened at all—because *how* does something like this just happen?—but more, that they're all staring at me, my colleagues of five-plus years, like I've just been found with a corpse sewn into my mattress. "Please know I really am a nice person!" I want to shout. "Your nice, normal, diligent, slightly chaotic receptionist who just wanted to come to work and go home again (and maybe buy a fancy prepackaged prawn sandwich for lunch because that's as risky as she gets)!" But it's like I'm suddenly a criminal. A corporate criminal in smart trousers with a reusable (*Love Island*) water bottle.

"Yes," I wobble. "I do. I do recognize them. And I'm so, so sorry. I'm—I'm . . . totally *mortified*."

"Mm," Michael grumbles, and I can barely look at Petra, who sits, rigid and wide-eyed, as if she's been taxidermized.

"But they were just drafts," I carry on, barely a space between my tiny, quivery words. "I . . . I wrote them, but they should have never, ever been sent. And I—I *didn't* send them, and I wouldn't ever *want* to send them, so I don't understand how they even *were* sent because—" My voice catches and I swallow, look over at them, like a silly, scolded, lost puppy. "I'm sorry. I'm just . . . really nervous. This is all so serious and formal, isn't it? Like . . . like, *Hawaii Five-O* or something." And I laugh now. Totally motorbike-like, totally fake. And not a soul laughs, or even smiles. And now I want to melt into tears and sink to the floor. Perhaps even fall through it to a lovely dark void?

"Millie," sighs Paul, and I like Paul. Paul is kind, like a jolly postman; like someone duped him into a job as company director by telling him it's just chats and nice lunches, and he stays only so as not to leave anyone in the lurch. "You understand we just want to establish officially that you recognize the emails on the screen. That you wrote these."

"Yes," I say. "I do. I did."

"And you were in work as normal yesterday, at your desk, working on your designated company laptop . . ."

"*Yes*," I say, nodding madly. "Yes, yes, that's right, everything as normal. I was at my desk, *as normal*, all day . . ." Except. Oh. The *servers. Yes!* There was an enormous Flye TV server outage yesterday. The worst we've ever, ever had. "Like the Battle of the sodding Boyne, up there," Steve in IT had said as he'd passed the reception desk, cheeks flushed and hair on end.

"The servers were down all day!" I blurt at Jolly Postman Paul. "Could . . . could something have happened with that? Clearing drafts and outboxes? *A surge?* That . . . that makes sense, doesn't it?"

"We don't know, Millie," Paul replies measuredly. "IT rallied and stayed until late last night to fix that particular issue," and there's something about the beat of silence that follows his flat, too-professional tone that makes my stomach drop like a bowling ball.

Am I going to be . . . *fired*? Cut loose from a job I've religiously shown up to for five whole years like the human equivalent of a robot hoover? The last time I saw this many people in a room was last month when Gareth in the warehouse got fired (his giant skate shoe— somehow—got thrown through a production truck's windscreen). I'd felt *so* sorry for him as he left the boardroom, gangly and hunched with shame, Jack Shurlock, the operations manager, walking him to his car. Will that be me? Is it about to be *me*?

Although—Jack isn't here, right now, is he? So, maybe that's a good sign. Since Jack got back from backpacking, he does *seem* to be in fewer meetings than he used to be, but—well, all the same, it's surely good he isn't here. (If only for the fact that worse than getting repri-manded for something like this is getting reprimanded in front of the hot, assured operations manager you once had a crush on. And—oh my God. Did I ever write an email to him? To *Jack*? After that Christmas party. *Did I?* Oh no no no no.)

"IT will look into any sort of red flag." Michael sighs, looking like he would rather be *anywhere* but here, with me and my sad, strange, bewildering email issue. "Something being compromised, hacked, and so on? I'll rehighlight the company-wide server issue too. But just so we're clear . . ." He looks up at me then, a green ballpoint pen in his shovel hand, hovering. "These emails. They were written by you."

". . . Yes."

"And you often take your work laptop home. Yes?"

My cheeks get hot now, because yes, I do often take my work laptop home. Officially, because I have a few extra things to do, mostly if Petra asks me (but unofficially, because I sometimes like to use it as a little TV I can follow YouTube tutorials on or to watch *Married at First Sight Australia* as I cook dinner). But what is he getting at? That *I* sent them? *On purpose?*

"Yes, that's correct," answers Petra for me, and oh, Petra. Lovely, lovely Petra. I wish so much we could communicate with each other in this moment—telepathy or something. A touch of Morse code. What's Morse code for "OMG, Petra, it's worse than you think, because I'm afraid I have inadvertently set my whole life on fire, do you copy? PS, will you still be my friend?"?

"Millie often works more than her agreed hours," Petra continues. "And so takes her laptop home under my instruction. She also recently shadowed Marshal Chandra on camera crew, too, at the darts final? He was very impressed with her."

"Look," interjects Jolly Postman Paul. "I think we can all agree that everything else aside, the bottom line is it's simply unprofessional. Issues you could have officially, *responsibly* raised with colleagues, or even HR."

"I know," I say, swallowing down tears. "I know, and I am so, *so* sorry. They were honestly never, ever meant to be read."

"I see." Paul ponders.

"It's like—it's like something I do to—get things off my chest, you know?" Be human. Right? If in doubt, be honest and human, and you'll appeal to the human in everyone. (I heard that once, on *DIY SOS*, I think it was, and my flatmate Ralph had sniffed emotionally and said, "Tradesmen really are the people's philosophers, aren't they?") "And I know it doesn't excuse anything at all," I carry on, "but the emails . . . I would never want to upset anyone. I don't even mean it. Not a word of it. I just . . . type to . . . *to let it out*?"

"Yes, Paul," says Head-in-a-Jar Ann-Christin, as if I, and my *DIY SOS* wisdom, have simply vaporized. "According to policy, we're not quite in the gross misconduct area, and Millie has secured her laptop adequately, also in line with policy, so unless we get formal complaints from other members of staff . . ." And then her face freezes on the screen, before her head is sliced into two Pac-Man halves. And thank God, because . . . *complaints*? I don't even want to contemplate the idea of there being complaints. About *me*.

"Yes," says Petra stiffly. "I think this is just a case of having some adult conversations. I mean, who hasn't perhaps wanted to say certain things to colleagues, to friends . . ."

"Mm," hums Michael.

"Right," says Paul.

And the silence that follows then is like a big full stop rolling into the room. Paul sips his tea from the smugly smiling sloth. Michael extracts a nose hair between two fingers with aggression. Petra nods.

It's finally over. And all I can think about now, as nervous sweat studs my back, is that my work, really, is the least of my worries, because . . . *what*? And *who*? What have I written over the last two years? Who in my life is currently, in this exact precise moment, opening an unexpected email from me?

Michael gets up, sighs as if disappointed the meeting didn't end in my arrest, and opens the boardroom door. I follow Petra, who follows Paul, who's flanked by Michael, all of us gradually trailing each other, like some sort of messed-up wedding procession.

And on my way to the bathroom, across the thin, ribbed carpet, through the fug of coffee and the hot plastic of machines, I hold my smile. When I get into the toilet stall at the end, I lock the door behind me and, finally, burst into tears.

**From: Millie Chandler**
**To: Steve.Hycott@Flyetv.com**
**Subject: Re: Sponsor me!**
Dear Steve,

I would happily sponsor you, but word on the street is that you said my arse was "fat but flat" as I walked by (WTF?) and that the lovely new temp "should look after herself if she wants to stay married," which is rich coming from a man who looks like a celeriac. You didn't think I heard, but I did. All of us do, by the way, when you make your obnoxious laddy comments. So it's a no from me, mate. I'll donate separately, away from your sponsored bath of sexist beans. :)

Kindest regards of the highest order,
Millie (and FBF arse)

**To: (Dad) Mitchell Chandler**
**From: Millie Chandler**
**Subject: Re: Email not delivering to your Gmail?**
So sorry, Dad, I did get your email, I thought I replied on the day! Was just a tad confused because I wasn't with

Mum on Good Friday? I was in Suffolk with Cate. I dragged her to a beekeeping experience day (she screamed a lot, ha-ha.) Are you sure Mum said it was me she was wit—

*From: Millie Chandler*
*To: MsCateMG@gmail.co.uk*
**Subject: Re: Thanks for last night! Sorry I had to rush off and leave you!**
Oh, Cate, I love you so much. You are my best friend and the best and kindest and most amazing person in this whole entire world. But I hate how nervous Nicholas makes you. I hate how you pretend he doesn't. I hate how he second-guesses you. I hate that he makes you go home to him before you're ready and all under the guise of "I just worry about you." I hate how he checks up on you. (Tracking your phone to "check" you are where you say you are!?!) He doesn't deserve you, and you deserve everything. And I could never say this out loud, but I wish so much that you'd leave him.

chapter 3

One hundred and *seven*. I'm pretty sure that's how many emails were sitting in my drafts, at last glance, meaning—and I *still* cannot believe this—that's how many emails have been sent without my permission. Whizzing off into the world like fireworks. My quiet and mostly harmonious life changed in an instant. *Ruined*, last night, as I stood in the little kitchen at the flat, happily and obliviously pleating little gyoza dumplings from a meal kit I'd ordered on Instagram. I'd even *talked* about my emails before I went to bed, which feels cruelly, right now, like I may have conjured this whole nightmare myself. An accidental spell or something, during a rare moon phase I keep trying to learn about from all those cool and attractive YouTube astrologers.

"I just hope the servers are fixed by the morning," I'd said casually to my flatmate and landlord, Ralph. "It was nice at first. Bit of an extended lunch break for everyone. But then people got grumpy and bored, and it dragged and dragged. I can't do another day like that. No internet. N*o email.*" And it was around that same time last night, apparently, that the servers had surged back into life, causing what I can only assume to be some sort of—surge? *Glitch?* A technical hitch that did something a little weird and funky, and simply . . . upended my entire life as I know it? (And all while I washed my face and obliviously brushed gyoza out of my teeth at home.)

I groan to myself now, in the echoey upstairs office bathroom, having spent the last five minutes sitting on the toilet seat, shaking, my head in my hands, like a poor, sad cartoon.

How has this happened?

*My emails.*

My private emails.

Waiting in other people's inboxes. Oh God, I cannot bear the thought to sit in my head for even a second. Because yes, some emails have been sent to unkind, piss-taking colleagues who may have deserved it a little bit, but—there were others, too, and they're the ones haunting me, spinning-topping around my head, like ghosts. The emails to all the people *not* at work, the people *not* in this building, landing in their lives like grenades full of words. To my lovely friends, to family, to . . .

The smell of lemon bleach hits the back of my throat as I gasp in the silence and—no. No, no, I *cannot* be sick, this isn't an ITV drama, for goodness' sake. I need to hold it together. No more crying. No vomit. What is it my dad always says? *A bad day is just one bad day, among thousands and thousands of others.* Like towns on a world map, he says. "One bad town doesn't make for a bad world, Millie." And this is what this probably is, right? Yes. A bad day. A tiny speck of a dodgy, horrible, frightening town I'm having to pass through. Just until I'm out of the other side.

My phone vibrates in the pocket of my trousers. They're new. Wide-leg, belted, dark khaki. Something I'd never pick for myself, but my best friend, Cate, had convinced me to buy them after I'd had a whopping fail of a work-clothes ASOS order arrive. I'd WhatsApp'd her a mirror photo of me in them this morning. "You continue to be an effortless fashion prodigy, Cate Mancinelli-Grant," I'd typed, and she'd sent back seven flame emojis and "you look amazing!" Oh, I wish I could go back. Turn back the clock to life before that meeting. I had no idea this was waiting for me. This—*mess.*

I pull my phone out, hands shaking.

Three missed calls.

Dad. Cate. A mobile number I don't recognize that feels extra ominous.

I stare at them. *What do I do, what do I do?*

Ralph.

I'm going to call Ralph. Sweet, sweet, sweet, sensible Ralph. He'll know what to do; he *always* knows what to do. He's logical. Optimistic. And so, so ridiculously smart. (Although I'm unsure whether his cleverness quite extends to what to do when your private emails have accidentally been read by the world as much as it does mushroom species, but cleverness is a transferrable skill, isn't it?)

Ralph answers the phone, whispering down the line, like someone hiding during a holdup at a bank, "Millie? I'm about to go into work."

"I know, but—"

"We're not allowed our phones once we've passed through the shop floor, remember. My boss, the one with the hip replacement—"

"Ralph, it's an emergency," I blurt. "Like . . . huge. *Giant.*"

A pause. "Gosh, really?" In the background, I can hear a deep, hollow dog's bark. (Ralph works as a cashier at a huge pet shop with its own on-site groomers. He calls the dogs themselves customers. "Walter, one of our customers, really enjoys the pigs' ears . . .") "Millie, are you all right?"

"No," I say. "I really don't think I am OK, Ralph, and I don't know what to do." I imagine Ralph's round, bespectacled face on the other end of the phone now, his troubled forehead scrunching up, his shiny windbreaker peppered with rain, done up, as always, right to the Adam's apple. Oh, poor Ralph. Moments ago, plodding along to work, probably listening to that *Tea and Fungi* podcast he listens to, then along I come, steamrolling into his simple, sensible life of swimming groups and neat Tupperware lunches, firing flares into the sky. "Ralph, it's my emails."

"What, is it all still offline?"

"No. No, the servers came back on, but—my emails. They're gone. They're all *sent*."

"What?"

"When the servers came back on, all my emails somehow got sent. All my . . . *drafts*."

"Your drafts? Your—*oh*." The penny drops, and Ralph makes a doomy-sounding noise—a mini death rattle that makes me gasp an "*I know!*" down the line. Ralph is one of the only people on earth who know about The Drafts. Well. Besides Lin on the sales team. It was originally Lin—unconventional, principled, girl's girl Lin Kye—who had casually suggested the whole thing two years ago. "Try writing an email, and just don't send it to the fucker," she'd said after finding me puffy-eyed in the work kitchen a few weeks after Owen had broken up with me. "Something about writing *to* them. Tricks the brain, you know? Helps you process it all."

And after a few weeks of writing them, I'd proudly told Ralph about it. I hadn't long moved in with him as his lodger, and it was one of the first late-night, bonding conversations of our friendship. I'll always remember it. Me, Ralph, chatting standing up at the breakfast bar with midnight cups of tea, the soft, barley sugar glow of the low, pendant lights, Ralph smiling sleepily, me feeling a weight starting to lift. And I'd told him because writing them *had* helped, and I was so relieved something had. It felt like progress. These emails, quietly contained in that safe, going-nowhere folder. And yet, here we are. Here. We. Bloody. Are.

"How many?" Ralph asks simply, now.

"So many."

"How many is so many?"

"One hundred—" I swallow, scrunch my eyes closed. "One hundred and *seven*, *Ralph*." And the numbers rush out like a last-minute confession on one of those daytime murder mystery series my dad loves. *It wasn't Father Frederick who stole the church's money. It was . . . me!*

"Christ, Millie. *Shit.*"

"I don't know what to do," I say, and tears pool now, wobbling at the edges of my eyes. "I'm in hell. Like, absolute hell, and I don't even know how or why this has even happened. I mean, I'm a good person, right? You always talk about karma, and giving out good energy, and I . . . I smile at dogs. I try to never gossip. I . . . I rinse my recycling!"

And on the loo seat as an extractor fan rattles on the wall above me like wind-up chattering teeth, I give Ralph a slightly hysterical capsule version of what happened this morning. From walking into work and going upstairs to make a cup of tea to that sinister "Millie, can we speak to you, please?" and the agonizing, embarrassing boardroom meeting with the nose hair and sighing and disappointed, pin-striped Paul Foot.

"All right, Millie, listen to me," says Ralph, calmly. "Everything . . . everything is going to be OK."

"*Will it?*"

"I . . . I mean, *yes*," says Ralph, flustered. "As a matter of a fact, it already sort of—*is*? You were sent away by your bosses without consequence, yes?"

I nod, pointlessly, from the loo seat.

"And Petra is quite correct. Who hasn't wanted to say certain things to colleagues?"

I groan. "But it's everyone else, Ralph. It's everyone *outside* work I'm worried about. Plus, wanting and doing are different things, aren't they? We all think things every day that we would sooner die than actually say. And I've just . . . said it. All of it. At once. Like that. *Bleugh.* Out there."

"Yes," says Ralph. "Yes, Millie, I understand." And I can tell even Ralph's wondering how on earth I've ended up here; running it all through his mind, observing it methodically, like he does when one of his plants isn't doing what he expected. This would never happen to Ralph. He's too sensible to have drafts full of unsaid things; too autonomous and straightforward. Unproblematic. It's probably why I've never written an email to him. I might have known Ralph only two years, but he is one of the greatest friends I've ever had. One of those people who feel so "meant for you" that you're convinced the time before you met them was just time spent getting a bit lost on the way to finding each other.

"Tell me what to do. Seriously, Ralph, tell me what to do. I'm really freaking out."

Ralph blows out a long, thoughtful breath down the line. "Well, firstly, let's try *not* to freak out. And I think one step at a time is always a sensible approach, in any situation."

I nod, hanging desperately on to his every word, Ralph, the mountain ranger, me, the idiot lost in the wilderness.

"I say allow management to continue to investigate, consider apologizing where needed, and until you're told otherwise, I suppose all you can do is . . . complete your working day?"

"Oh, but Ralph, how can I?"

"Well, you're going to have to, Millie," he says calmly. "Take a minute, make a cup of tea, and go calmly back to your desk . . ."

And I peer now to the ceiling, as if I'm who? Tom Cruise? What do I think I'm going to do instead? Push a tile upward and worm my way into the vents?

"I know this is unpleasant, Millie," continues Ralph. "But you must act accordingly. You've told the truth, right? And they have accepted the truth—"

"Until a member of staff makes an official complaint and I am sacked forever and blacklisted."

"Conjecture," states Ralph, as if he isn't going to dignify my catastrophizing with an answer.

Someone comes into the bathroom now, heels on tiles, and locks one of the other cubicles, as my phone bleeps in my ear like a little siren. I glance at the screen—*Cate Calling*. Again. And her name sits on top of a selfie of us both, and I want to cry once more.

Cate. My maternal, witty, hopeless romantic of a best friend. We took that photo last year, on the annual holiday we always take with our other friend Alexis (this time, it was in a yurt in Gloucester, which was freezing and disastrous and ended in Cate having to go to the toilet in a Sainsbury's bag, which definitely didn't make it onto Alexis's pastel-y Instagram page). And I *know* I've written her emails. About her boyfriend, Knobby Nicholas, who micromanages her, controls her, all under the caveat of "But it's because I love you!" Cate'll hate me. How could she not hate the best friend who secretly—or not so secretly now—hates her boyfriend?

And as for Alexis. Oh, I can't even think about Alexis . . .

"Listen," says Ralph as a hand dryer bursts into life on the other side of the door. "I'll be home when you get in. We can sort this then. But this is just a . . . a hiccup, Millie. A blooper, if you will. Certainly not life-ending."

"Really?" I cling to his optimism like a buoy. "Do you really think?"

"Yes. A *blunder*."

"A blunder . . ." I repeat with a wistful sigh. "Oh, I really hope you're right."

A blunder. A blooper. *Is* Ralph right? Is this just a blunder? Because it doesn't feel like a blunder as I stand here, washing my hands. It feels like the end of the world. The end of *my* world as I know it. Like everything is upside down and it'll never be the same again. That the whole universe is watching me; that I've passed through the looking glass. Forever.

I dry my hands. Twice.

OK.

OK, one step at a time, Ralph said, didn't he? And I suppose step one would be: get to desk. Get. To. Desk. I can do that, can't I?

I take a breath, and—here goes nothing—I push open the door to the main office. Low, mumbling chatter, ringing phones, computer keyboards clacking, the smell of coffee and burnt toast.

*Get to desk. Get to desk.*

I walk quickly, and as quietly as possible, across the office floor. Ten strides, that's all it is, or thereabouts, but oh, fuck. *I can feel it*: this heavy, awkward atmosphere, slowly seeping into the room like steam as I walk. Heads turn in my peripheral vision, voices stop, and as I get to the exit, place my hand on the cool, metal handle . . . I just can't help myself.

I glance up.

Just the tiniest, tiniest of glimpses, and . . . I wish I hadn't. Because people are watching me. Most are watching and pretending *not to* from behind partition screens and computer monitors, but some are just plain *looking*, as if I'm some sort of tragic art installation they've paid good money to see, thank you very much.

And as embarrassed heat sweeps up my back, and my eyes drift back to the exit, they land, firstly, on Leona from IT, who just stares at me, hard-nosed, and then, beside her, Jack. Hot Jack Shurlock, who stands against a desk with an iPhone to his ear, his broad shoulders relaxed and square, white shirtsleeves rolled up. And his serious eyes, for just a second, flick up to look at me too.

Someone whispers. Another person laughs.

I push through the door, speed down the spiral staircase.

They must know. They must all know by now. Even if they didn't get an email themselves, emails can be shared and forwarded and even printed and used to wallpaper a bloody room if the mood takes someone.

A blunder. This does not feel like a blunder, Ralph Nobleman. A blunder is a fumbled ASOS order. A blunder is spotting a naked by-stander accidentally filmed in the background of a *Married at First Sight* episode. This is *so much* more than a blunder.

"Oh, there you are!" Petra stands at my reception desk, as always willowy and beautiful and safe, her glossy brown curls like something from a *Vogue* full-page ad. I could cry at the sight of her. "I was starting to worry."

I get to the ground floor. "Oh, Petra," I say.

But there's something about her face. She looks worried. Her brown eyes, concerned circles, her lips, parted. Almost how she looked the morning after finding that flirty "petra's great but isn't u" sent message on her ex, Maria's, phone when they'd been together a whole entire *year.*

"Have you . . . have you had a chance to see everything that's been sent?" Petra asks quietly.

"No. No, I haven't even turned my computer on yet. God, Petra, how the hell did this even happen?"

Petra's eyes close then, and her hand lands softly on my arm and I don't even have the time to prepare for things somehow, amazingly, getting worse before Petra speaks. "Millie, there's a reply you wrote to Owen's engagement announcement," she says. "And it was sent to everyone. The entire company. Including Chloe."

**From: Millie Chandler**
**To: Owen Kalimeris; all UK office**
**Subject: Re: Some Personal News**

Dear Owen,

I can't believe what I've just read. You're getting married. You and Chloe are getting married. And to think, weeks ago, you told me it was nothing serious. And then you asked me out.

I started typing this in the hopes it would help me work out how I feel, to make sense of this sad, dark tornado in my chest, but I still don't know. I don't know how to feel. I just know I cried. I tried not to, tried to keep it in, swallow it down, but it happened almost instantly, the second I opened the email and saw the announcement. Two whole years we've been broken up, and I cried just like that—ran into the work loos, like a perfect cliché, and wore sunglasses inside like bloody Bono in a maxi dress until home time. I blamed a migraine. But everyone at work knew because they got your email too. I hope nobody tells you. I'm embarrassed. Argh, and I'm so bloody ashamed.

It's midnight now, and I can't sleep. I just got your old T-shirt out of my wardrobe to see if it still smells like you. (The black Vegas one you left me to wear when you went away, when we first met? The one I took the piss out of, but never gave back.) It doesn't. It smells like . . . nothing. Ha. A metaphor if ever there was one. And God, what am I even doing? WHAT am I doing? Typing to you in my pajamas, alone, while you are mere miles away, tucked up, oblivious and happy with Chloe. Your fiancée, Chloe Katz from the production team. Of course, Chloe. She always made you laugh.

It was getting easier too. The shitty, ironic thing was that it was finally getting easier. FINALLY. I was thinking about you less, dreading getting those work updates from your team in India less. Missing you less. And then Petra said the channel launch in India was done, and I was braced. Braced because I knew it was only a matter of time before I saw you again—that you popped into work.

And then, there you were.

And it wasn't horrible, like I imagined it would be. It was . . . nice? Like it used to be when we first met. But the way you spoke about Chloe, Owen. That's why this email felt more like a bomb landing on my desk, because two weeks ago you said it was "nothing serious." You said her family were weirding you out and "too heavy." And then you asked me out. *Me*. Your ex-girlfriend. The woman you dumped at your leaving dinner—I still can't believe you did that. Can *you* believe you did that?—before you pissed off to India with a new job and a new life.

And I wondered if the lunch date was just a pleasantry or something. But then you emailed the next day suggesting a time, a date, and that new Thai place in Westcliff, as if it was the most normal thing in the world. And I'd been so confused. But mostly, and I feel SO ashamed about this, I wondered if we might be one of those couples. The types who break up, go away for a bit, grow up, and come back to each other. A story of "meant to be." (Like Jen and Ben. Peyton and Lucas. Nathan and Cara from *Love Island* series two.)

And then . . . this. This lands in my inbox. I keep reading it, checking it's actually real, because you book us a table, we text, and then this!?!?! Not just an engagement announcement, but a whole *wedding date*. But then that's just so you, isn't it? You were always so nought to one hundred. It's the reason I fell in love with you. It's the reason you left. I didn't have that drive, you said. That ambition.

And I'm so thankful you'll never ever see this. I'm glad you'll never know how angry I am at you for hurting me. For discarding me so fast. For falling in love again, even faster. I'm glad you'll never know I miss you. And that I still love you, Owen. I do. And I know I can safely say that here, because you'll never see this. These words will only ever be for me and my stupid, naive heart. This email will never be sent.

Always,

Millie x

*chapter 4*

"Oh, Ralph, I can't do much more of this."

"You need to know how the land lies, though, Millie," says Ralph. "Thirty-one left to read, then you'll have no surprises. Knowledge *is* power. Especially in these sorts of incidents."

"*These sorts of incidents?* Ralph, there's never *been* an incident like this. Name me a single comparable incident."

Ralph says nothing, just taps on the next "sent item" as, beside him on the sofa, I down my red wine and groan into the bowl of the glass.

When I got home from work and flopped through the flat door two hours ago, I had a plan: cry in bed. *A lot.* A big, ugly, snotty, wailing, woe-is-me, my-life-is-over cry. Cry and cry, and then do something totally immersive that would leave no room for thinking. Cook something new and involved, until the sink was brimming, and the fridge was so packed full of food that Ralph would start worrying about "overloading the fan system" again. And maybe even submerge myself into an hour of the Duolingo German course I've just started, discover perhaps what the German is for "I have ruined my life and require a new identity, please." Definitely no *Love Island* tonight, though, or *Married at First Sight*. I never want to look at anything love-y ever again after today. Right now, I hate love. Love has duped me today. Love has snared me, fucked me well and truly over, ensured my dark, bitter heartbreak was seen by my *entire workplace*. I still can't believe everyone has read it. Knowing everyone has seen that whole, massive email to Owen, that *Chloe* has seen it, feels like the world has seen me without clothes on. Without a shred of *skin* . . .

And although I did follow through with my crying itinerary, I've instead cried on the sofa, beside Ralph, who had already preempted my sad, lonely plan and had lured me here, as I walked through the front door, using my favorite stuffed-crust pizza as bait. My knackered heart bloomed at the sight of it. My favorite pizza with one of my favorite people, in my cozy flat share (with the most perfect view in Leigh-on-Sea there is, in my opinion), is just what I needed. But that was until I'd seen Ralph's laptop on the coffee table and two flickering candles, as if it were being blessed before being opened to a huge stampede—one hundred and seven, to be precise—of email demons.

That's where we've been sitting for the last hour and a half: at the coffee table on Ralph's ludicrously regal chesterfield sofa—an unwanted and unsolicited gift from his rich parents, who own this flat—going one by one through my smoking wasteland of a sent items folder. I've lost count of the number of evenings I've spent here, in the last two years, on the sofa with Ralph; TV and takeout and midnight Christmas present wrapping. But nothing—and I mean *nothing*—has ever had the vibe of tonight. Me, mostly swearing, sometimes convulsing, sometimes staring at the ceiling, like someone stunned, all while Ralph reads out my emails and watches me like I'm a fire that's about to engulf the whole town.

And thankfully, some emails have been totally and euphorically benign. Like opening some sort of dark Advent calendar and finding a chocolate instead of a raging ball of fire. Harmless ones I'd started and never finished ("Hi, this sounds gr—") and emails that didn't even get delivered, like the confession I discovered I absolutely *did* write to Jack Shurlock after we'd had that flirty, zingy chat and was-it-an-almost-kiss at the Christmas party before he left to go traveling. (He's a Shurlock *dot* Jack now, and I have never been more grateful for a "this email address is no longer in use, please email this address instead" message.)

But some emails—oh, *some*. Some have not been benign at all.

There are emails to Cate, mostly frustrated emails about Knobby Nicholas, including one telling her I wanted to put a picture of him on a bag of rolled oats and whack it with a shovel; that I wish she'd leave him, turf him out of the house they live in together, throw his belongings on the driveway like he deserves. There are stupid barely one-liners to my (fake) sweetness-and-light cousin Rhiannon, which are literally just "zzzzzz" and "lolllllll, why is this compliment so shady and backhanded?" which will definitely upset my mum and snobby auntie Vye. There's also one calling Prue in Accounts a "dangerous bigot" too (she is, though).

The worst of the lot, though—well, except for the agonizing Owen engagement email that has shaved years off my predicted life span, of course—are the multiple scathing "I'm starting to dread seeing you" emails to one of my closest friends, Alexis, all of which made my heart plummet (and screech into a cushion). And I love Alexis, I really do. I've loved her since the day I met her seven years ago, when it was like I was suddenly introduced to a rocket. I'd started waitressing at a lively, cheap-beer-and-curry-nights pub in Southend and she worked at the bar (a second evening job for her, after interning at a medical technology company in Canary Wharf all day). I'd just dropped out of university and moved back home, Mum's disappointment like a heavy shawl around my shoulders, and Alexis was just . . . *energy.* A walking lit firework, sparking with hungry, nothing-to-lose, determined energy that seemed to rub people up the wrong way, or rub off. To me, it was only ever infectious. Alexis is empowering. A genius. Entirely self-governed, but so loyal. Lie-down-and-die-for-you loyal. But lately, she's been—well. *Not.* At all. She's been argumentative. Spiky, for no reason, regardless of whether I'm talking about work, or recipes, or even Owen being back. She's been the same with Cate too. Almost . . . *mean*, and I keep asking if she's okay, but after I see her, I'm just left wondering what we've done wrong. (Except this time, I've actually *done* something horribly wrong, and thinking about what Alexis's reaction might be makes my heart ache and accelerate in panic all at once.)

"Ralph, can we please stop?"

"Millie . . ."

"Please," I say, my face buried in a cushion. "Just for a little, Ralph. Or a lot. Or forever? Our secret." My only secret, considering I apparently now have *zero.*

"But this one's mild," Ralph continues, his voice ever calm, his kind, green eyes fixed interestedly on the laptop, like a teacher marking essays. "This is just you telling Mark M. in Sales that he should not have stolen your lunch because the Tupperware was marked with your name. Valid, I say."

"Valid, yes, Ralph, but he will now hate me," I sigh, face-planting into Ralph's cushion again; a black-and-blue tie-dyed mushroom print, of course. "I think that's the only email I have *ever* sent him."

"And this is one to your mum that simply says, 'I just had to ask.' "

I peel my face from the surface of the cushion and look at him. "Really?"

"Yep. Just that. See. And this next one," says Ralph optimistically, "says . . . *Oh.*"

"*Oh?*"

His Adam's apple boomerangs in his throat. "It's . . . it's to your mum again, and it says I just had to ask . . ."

"You've already said that."

"No, this . . . this one has more. It says, 'I just had to ask . . . Mum, do you love me despite having nothing to share about me at brunches with your friends or in Auntie Vye's conservatory? All those things my brother does that you seem so bloody delighted by—' "

"Oh no. Stop."

But of course he doesn't, because Ralph knows we have to do this. *I* know we have to do this. I just don't want to. I want the before-life back. Life B. E. *Before Emails.*

" 'Because I don't know if I will ever be like Kieran, or if I will fall in love again, or have children, or know what my credit score is, or even pay off my student loan. Hashtag unfinished art degree.' "

"Why did I say hashtag?" My voice sounds part helium balloon now. "Anything else?"

"Just . . . 'You make me feel like a failure. LOL.' "

"*LOL.* Right. Of course."

Ralph puts a gentle hand between my shoulder blades and settles back with me, on the sofa, which squeaks beneath us like a leather jacket. He's wearing the *Stranger Things* pajamas he asked for on his last birthday—pajamas his parents had handed over in a stiff, luxury gift bag, their faces etched with bewilderment like they had been forced to hand him, their son the ghoul, a human liver. (They, of course, later gifted him a £500 smartwatch he didn't want too.) And as much as everything seems to be slowly and rapidly going to shit, I'm so glad for Ralph right now; that I answered the ad for a room to rent in his— well, technically, his parents'—flat, two years ago, when I was utterly heartbroken and half a person after Owen broke up with me. Ralph and this flat at Four, the Logans, have become a safe constant for me since then. Ralph is simple and calming. Someone who could have gone into the family business (cruise ships worth multimillions) but decided he wanted a quiet, straightforward life instead because small, straightforward things are what make him happy. His job at a pet shop. His hobbies, like swimming and karate and puzzles and mushroom plants. Living with Ralph and his dependability is like good feng shui or something. He's an anchor. A safety net. An extra brother, of sorts.

"What am I going to do, Ralph?" I say into the dim, quiet living room. All the lights are out, except for the television on the wall, and Ralph's gold floor lamp shaped like a palm tree. "I know I keep asking that, but I'm fucked, aren't I? Totally fucked. You can say it. I can take it—well, I can't, but say it anyway."

"Certainly not. You are not fucked."

"But I feel it. Today was just—it was dark, Ralph. Nobody would even really look at me. It was like . . . like I was a naughty dog who'd mauled the furniture or something, and everyone had been given strict instructions to not make eye contact or *she might do it again, and worse still, she could shit on the carpet!*"

"It'll blow over, Millie," Ralph says gently. "Everything always does eventually."

"Yeah. *Sure.*" I lean forward to the coffee table, tip the last dribble of wine from the bottle into my glass.

Everything looks the same; smells the same; the TV even plays the same cycle of weeknight soaps and news items. But everything *feels* out of place. Scary. As if my life has been shaken like a massive snow globe and now everything needs fixing. Just when it was all trundling along so seamlessly, so *quietly* until this morning at work. Petra, God bless her heart, had given me the world's most banal filing task to do in the almost-always-empty-and-used-for-document-storage office next to reception, and I stayed in there all day, scurrying out only to greet visitors and deliverymen, and wanting to completely melt into the floor like slime every time an email reply dropped from random recipients (ranging from "???????" and "lol wtf?" to "Millie, answer your phone NOW").

And my phone. I *never* have my phone off. If I'm not texting, I'm on Instagram, or TikTok, or Reddit, or I'm googling "*90 Day Fiancé* where are they now?" But it was all too much, and my phone, lighting up and lighting up, like a portable disco ball, was only further tangling the huge, twisted ball of wool that is "today." My life. After emails. (A.E.) So I panicked. This morning, I sent a message to Cate and Alexis, simply saying, "I'm so sorry, I'll explain soon" and turned it off, and that is how it has stayed. A dead brick in my handbag. And it's not really helped. It's made everything feel even scarier actually. Not knowing what I'll be met with when I turn it back on. *If* I ever turn it back on. Maybe I could just be like those people—the ones who denounce all technology, grow beards, and live in a little stick house with a bonfire outside and clanky, metal camping crockery.

I pick up my glass and settle back down next to Ralph. "I think some people will actually think something's going on between Owen and me, too," I say. "Because people at work will think he asked me out when he was with Chloe and we actually met up? And, I mean, he *did* ask me out. I wasn't lying, Ralph."

"I know. The man is brazen."

"But it's like . . . nobody has heard from him, just me. You know? It's just my words out there, for everyone to see, and therefore *I'm* the villain. And women always get the brunt of these things in rumors like this."

Ralph nods gently in the quiet. A property program is on TV. A couple, holding hands, grinning at a scaffold-covered terraced house. I wish I were them. Or the cameraman. Or the bloody scaffolder. Anything. I'll take *anything.*

"They all know I love him now, too," I groan. "And I don't even know that I actually *do*, Ralph, but *they* think I do, regardless. That while he's been off getting engaged, launching brand-new TV channels, I've just been . . . missing him and writing saddo emails with my life?"

"That's not true," says Ralph.

"Isn't it?"

"No," he replies. "You've been learning German too."

And that makes me smile. The first genuine smile of the entire day so far.

"And don't forget the accidental cervix I crocheted," I add. (It was meant to be a peony.)

"*Exactly*," Ralph agrees, with a little balled fist. "And look, for what it's worth, I still think something good might come of all this."

I look up over my glass at him. His kind, obliviously hopeful eyes, the boyish peach-seam cleft in his chin. "I really am struggling to see that, Ralph."

"You'll just have to trust me then," he replies, giving an apprehensive, lopsided smile. "We're really not far off finishing them now. And once we've read them all, the sort of . . . dark mystique will be gone, because you'll know. You'll know exactly what got sent to whom, who to apologize to, and, heck, who *not to*."

"*Heck*," I repeat, amused.

"Because far be it from me to judge," carries on Ralph, "some of these emails have been very much warranted."

"Fine." I tip my head back and scrunch my eyes shut, like I'm about to be waxed. "*Fine.* Let's do it. Let's just get it done."

"Good. One step at a time, remember? Emails faced today. And then you can face your phone tomorrow, with knowledge and, therefore, power."

I nod. "Yep, yep. Knowledge, power, into the fucking fire we go."

"And shall I light some incense?" Ralph asks, bouncing up from the sofa, slapping his thighs. "I got some from that interesting little shop in the town."

"Sure." I shrug. "Why not? Can't hurt."

"Which scent shall we have?" asks Ralph. "*Dragon's Blood* or . . . ooh, how about *Positive Vibes*?"

# chapter 5

**To: all LEIGH ESSEX office**
**From: Millie Chandler**
**Subject: Sorry**

To all,

I just wanted to say I'm so sorry to anyone who has recently received or been affected by any emails from me. These were sent in error—due to both a server error and an error of my own judgment. Please erase and pay no mind. I meant <u>nothing</u> said in them. I'm so sorry again. I hope we can all move forward from this, and if anyone wants to chat, my door—well, my reception desk, lol—is always open.

Lots of love,

Millie xx

*To: all office*

*From: Ann-Christin Johnsson*

*Cc: IT team, Paul Foot, Michael Waterstreet, Jack Shur-lock, Petra Kairys*

**Subject: Safety**

We would like to assure members of staff of the safety and security of the Flye TV computer systems. They are regularly serviced and monitored by the relevant teams, in line with company policy, and the security and privacy of data remain of the utmost importance to us as an organization.

Thank you,

Ann-Christin and management

Human Resources

*From: Owen Kalimeris*

*To: Millie Chandler*

**Subject: Re: Sorry**

Millie, I've read your email reply to our wedding invite. I don't know what to say. I'm super confused. Did you mean what you said? Tried calling. Is your phone off? Or have you blocked me? We need to talk.

O x

I am hiding.

I am a grown woman of twenty-nine years old, and I am *hiding* at work, and no, this wasn't part of the plan at all. Well. The *loose-ish* plan Ralph and I put into place this morning as we drank warm drinks in our pajamas, the golden, late-summer light glowing through the kitchen blinds, both of us slightly hungover on the great email dredge of the twenty-first century. (And a whole bottle of wine.)

"What, ideally," Ralph had asked softly, "would you like to happen now?" and for a beat, just a split second, the fresh slate of a new day in front of me, I felt like I had permission to say anything. Say something wild like, "Leave, actually!" Or get on a plane. Do something uninhibited and new. Sign up to a yoga retreat in Bali or a cookery course in Corsica. Hand my notice in. Learn to play chess. Take a job in Brazil. *Abseil.* Because once everything you ever wanted to say is said, once the quiet life you've done your best to craft the last couple of years is suddenly the opposite, once things can't really get much worse, there's a way of looking at it that feels like . . . freedom.

But instead, I'd taken a long sip of sugary tea, looked around at our little kitchen, one of my favorite work skirts drying on the airer, the paperweight I made from a kit Alexis gave me last Christmas (which I ended up somehow crafting into something that looks like a sweet potato) on the mantelpiece. All these things from my life B.E. (Before Emails). And I'd said simply, "Ralph, I want to forget this ever, ever happened."

And it was all going relatively well, all things considered.

Until just now, when I'd spotted Owen pacing quickly across the Flye TV car park, toward my desk after lunch. Lean and loping, that smoky-black hair, sunglasses on, car keys in his hand, everything about him, as always, perfectly clean-cut and turned out. And I . . . well, totally panicked. Shit myself. Jumped up, rounded the desk while hunched over like a human shelf bracket, as if that concealed me at all, and scurried in here, to the little document storage office behind my reception desk. Because—what will I even *say* to him? Plus, what if people see us talking? Most of them are already acting weirdly with me, avoiding me, whispering, giving me pained, awkward smiles, side-eyeing me, like I'm *that* villain. I don't want to give them even more reason to think I'm a horrible person. Plus, say if *his fiancée* turns up? What if Chloe *sees us*?

So, here I am.

Hiding from Owen, from my feelings, from everything and everyone, crouched in the gloom, squatting behind a promotional World Cup cardboard cutout of a microphone-holding Gary Lineker. I really don't know how Ralph can say something good might come of this. I don't think hiding from your ex-boyfriend at work ever falls into the "something good has come of this" category.

I peer around Gary's cardboard arm. Owen is standing there, in front of my reception desk. Why is he still waiting? Why hasn't he just assumed I'm on my lunch break? Does he *want* people to notice him standing there, waiting for me? And of course, I *will* speak to him. Eventually. Just . . . when I've worked out what I want to say, beyond just: "sorry" (and "Please, please ignore that email and pretend it never happened so everything can go back to its quiet, unproblematic way and nobody thinks I'm some sort of horrible homewrecker." Although, I admit, I'm feeling "pretty confused" too now.).

I blow out a long, shaky breath onto Gary's cardboard waist. I wish I didn't, but I always feel wobbly at the sight of Owen, like my fight-or-flight has been engaged or something. It's because it's like he sees right through me; that no matter what I do, no matter the resolve I construct, how much armor I wear, I'm made of glass. Glass he can shatter with just a few words, with a single knowing smile. Because that's how it feels, isn't it, with someone you've been vulnerable with? Being vulnerable with someone is like handing them a map of you. A map of every hard edge, every weak spot, every pressure point, and eventually they memorize every turn, every twist, until they know you, can navigate you, break you open with their eyes closed.

"All right, mate?" I hear on the other side of the glass. Someone else is out there.

"Yeah, good, bro, yourself?" Owen replies, and then some inaudible, deep-voiced chatter.

My ears whoosh with the galloping of my own pulse. Is that . . . Oh my God. Someone is . . . *No.* The door handle squeaks as it's pushed down. Someone is coming in. *Someone is coming in!*

"Yeah, I'm leaving around Christmas—"

And as my eyes drift from the smart, brown shoes to the straight, pressed black trousers, to the fresh, gray-blue shirt, the round, muscular shoulders . . . I literally swallow, a massive gulp, like a Simpsons character.

It's Jack. It's Hot Jack Shurlock.

Oh God, I want the ground to collapse beneath me and suck me into nothingness. Especially when Jack's eyes drop to the floor and meet mine.

"Um. So, yeah. Anyway. Better get on, mate," he calls out to Owen, his eyebrow lifting just a fraction, eyes still on me.

He's covering for me. Hot Jack of Christmas Party and Sexy Dream fame is covering for me. I'd be touched, if I didn't want to die of embarrassment. What on earth must he be thinking? That I'm having some sort of meltdown? A breakdown. First, a mass email send-out. Now, hiding behind a cardboard cutout during the working day . . .

Jack moves into the room, tall, authoritative, pushes the door to, leaving just a crack, and I watch as he strides across the floor. He slots his hands into his pockets, scans the shelves, clicking his tongue. Then a tiny half smile lifts the corner of his mouth.

"Afternoon, Millie," he whispers gruffly, still not looking at me. "And Gary."

"Hi," I whisper. Embarrassment creeps hotly up my neck.

"Am I . . . interrupting something?" Jack asks deep and low. He meets my eyes then, remains poker-faced, but the corner of his mouth dimples again, just slightly.

"Probably best not to ask." I wince, and Jack gives a singular nod.

"Understood," he says, and for what must be only a few seconds but feels like much, much longer, I stay here, crouched on the floor, my knees aching, my calves starting to bloom with pins and needles, as Jack scans the files on the shelves. It's quiet in here, except for Jack's slow footsteps and my breathing. I can hear Owen's distant voice, talking again now to someone else outside. Fundraising Steve from IT maybe? Oh, please nobody else come in.

"I was actually hoping to get some information from you," whispers Jack. "Missed your meeting. Had something tedious to sort."

I nod. "Yes, well, as long as you don't write this down," I say quietly. "Hiding behind cardboard cutouts of Gary Lineker won't exactly go in my favor. After . . . everything." I give a smile, and worry I'm smiling like someone at gunpoint, because all I can think about is what Jack must be thinking of the whole thing. The woman on reception whose emails all got sent. That woman who is currently squatting on the floor by his feet?

"Can't imagine I missed much," Jack says softly, slowly pacing, eyes on the files. "Paul being all sweet uncle?"

I nod. "Um. Maybe . . ."

"Lots of management speak, and Michael being . . . a prick?" His eyes drop to meet mine then, a playful, glinting hazel . . .

And this. *This* is why I liked talking to Jack at the party the Christmas after Owen had left me. This is why I spent that whole weekend thinking up excuses to talk to him again after our flirty drunk chat. We'd found ourselves at a table together either side of Cherry, one of our sound engineers, who'd fallen asleep after too much mulled wine. We hadn't really chatted much until that point, but that night Jack and I talked for a whole hour, our faces strobed by disco lights (and Cherry's passed-out head on the tabletop between us like a Christmas centerpiece).

And although I can't recall exactly what we talked about, I do remember just how much fun I had; how often his hand had lingered on my arm, how a button on the hem of my puffed sleeve kept unfastening, and when it had happened *again,* I'd rolled my eyes, and he'd laughed and fastened it gently, carefully, for me, bottle of beer, still, in his other hand. I remember how much he'd made me laugh, too, which surprised me. Because Jack—he's sort of coolly unreadable. The type of guy who arrives at work in immaculate shirts, gets his head down, and is unfussed about making meaningless small talk by the kettle, because *work is just work.* But there's something in the stubble, the slightly ruffled, messy hair, the tiny smiles he sometimes gives as he's texting on his lunch breaks, that hints at a life lived looser the second he leaves. Like hearing your straitlaced geography teacher listening to rap music; seeing the hint of a tattoo under a surgeon's scrubs.

"Drop me an email or something before I leave," he'd said hotly into my ear, over music and drunken cheers. And of course, I did (well, not *technically,* as per My Email Drafts Law), and then he went traveling across the globe. Gone. *Poof.* Until he came back as temporary maternity cover a couple of months ago. And there hasn't been an interaction between us since, really, beyond good mornings and polite passing smiles. Until now.

"Huh," mulls Jack, sliding another file from the shelf. "So, does the silence mean Michael was . . . *courteous*?"

"Oh. No, no," I whisper. "Definitely not."

"Ah."

"I'm just . . . after yesterday, I'm just a bit too afraid to speak right now or have an opinion that isn't endorsed by, like, the Bible or something?"

Jack lifts a round-shirted shoulder to his ear. "Nobody's listening," he says. "It's just you and me. And Gary Lineker." He smirks over at me then, and I stifle a laugh.

Silence again, just the sound of Jack leafing through a file that's open on his palm. I don't know if he's eking this out for my sake, or if he's genuinely looking for something.

"Petra says your work computer was definitely here that night."

I nod.

"Hm," he continues, deep and low. "I left at six. IT aren't very insightful either. They just say all work laptops have VPNs on since the hack last year?" He paces slowly. "That glitches of all kinds happen, that it simply looks like you sent them . . . " He glances down at me. "I'm just relaying what I've been told."

I nod again. "I know," I say as a sudden breeze from the lobby closes the door with a click, shutting us both in. The room falls silent, and I imagine a camera zooming out, snapshotting this moment, sending itself to Ralph, with the caption "Plan of forgetting it ever happened is going very well, as you can see (smiley-face)."

"I'll speak to a mate of mine, Matt—about the server thing," mutters Jack. "He's a coder." Jack is good at this. At being whatever *this* is. Discreet. Deft.

"There's no need."

"I can send you the protocol to formally complain to HR too. Course, they'll swear they're all about the employees, but. . ." He smiles to himself, crooked, cynical. "They're obviously all for the comp—"

"Jack," I interrupt, and he pauses, lips parted, mid-sentence. He slowly turns his face to me here, on the floor. "I really appreciate it, I do, but . . . I sort of feel like I've dodged a bullet with, you know—not getting fired."

Jack says nothing.

Distant, muffled laughter comes from the other side of the door.

"I think I'd just rather move on," I whisper. "Pretend it didn't happen?"

Jack hesitates, cocks his head to one side, like he's trying to work a crick out of his neck, and then his eyes move to the window. "Hm. Right." He looks older since he left to go traveling. Of course, not in a bus-pass-and-tinned-sardines way—Jack must be only around thirty-two, thirty-three—but in that intangible, refined way; the mature and wise and seen-the-world way. And—yes, OK, maybe also the *sexier* way. He has stubble now. Hair, lightened to maple-y brown by the sun; a little longer and messier. (And I say a little silent thank-you now to the universe, that my email to him never got delivered, because imagine the *embarrassment*.)

"He looks like he's about to leave. Owen," Jack clarifies.

"Does he?"

"Unless you were hiding from Steve. Or—me?" His gaze drops to mine then—his eyes glint with amusement.

"Oh. N-no," I fluster. "Not Steve. Not . . . you."

Silence again. And then, "He's—yep, he's gone."

"Really? Like, definitely?"

Jack nods again. "Well, give it a few seconds," he says, "but yeah, I'd say you're safe."

"Right."

"Steve seems to have gone as well," adds Jack, walking across the floor closer to me.

"Oh. Good."

"Bonus . . ." Jack mutters, as if to himself.

"Yes. Well, best get back to work, I sup—" I stand. And oh my God, my legs. My legs are suddenly swarmed with a warm numbness of fresh pins and needles that—"Shit!"—I buckle, wobble, and grab onto Gary's flimsy cardboard frame to steady myself. He bows, his poor head bending right back, his cardboard neck snapped. And I fall, smack bang on my arse. Gary, amazingly, stays upright, head bent in a solemn bow.

"Shit. Are you—*OK*?" There's a hesitant chuckle in Jack's voice.

"Oh, I'm fine!" I say, dusting my hands pointlessly. I am *mortified*. "Just the worst pins and needles of my whole *life*, but—fine. *Fine*. Ha."

And once again, I am face-to-face with Jack's shoes, his long legs. I slowly glance up at him as he shifts the folder to under his arm.

"Try again?" And as he slowly extends an open hand, I flush, like I've just been lowered into a hot bath. Hot Jack Shurlock is offering me his hand to hold.

"Oh. Thanks," I say, placing my hand in his. He closes his fingers, warm and slightly rough, around my palm and pulls me to standing. Thankfully, my legs, although covered in that prickling static, don't betray me this time.

"Stable?" he asks, and the smile he gives me feels like wordless solidarity. Or . . . pity? Oh, please don't be a smile of pity.

"Yes. Just about, thank you." He releases my hand. "And thank you. For, you know, pretending I wasn't in here and everything."

"Sure," Jack says, and as he pulls open the door, I call out, "And sorry for snapping Gary's neck!" and immediately, I wonder why I've decided to say *that*, of all the things I could say to the operations manager who has not only covered for me while hiding during my working day, but also unjudgmentally listened to my strange, rambling reasoning behind not wanting him to look into the emails *and* helped me up off the floor. And yet, my mouth keeps moving. "I sort of sacrificed him there. In the name of survival. Like . . . like, Jack in the *Titanic* or something. Gary. My very own floating door."

Jack pauses in the doorway and laughs, as if surprised. "Well. I'm, uh, sure he was more than happy to help." Then he turns, walks out, and as he strides up the lobby stairs, I hear him answer his phone. "Yeah, sorry, mate," he says. "Got caught up in something."

I pull Gary's head up, meet his oblivious cardboard eyes. "Sorry about that," I say. "Appreciate it, though."

**From: Alexis Lee**
**To: Millie Chandler**
**Subject: wtf**

I cannot believe the shit you've said. You won't answer my texts. They're not even fucking delivering???? Do not contact me anymore, Millie. I mean that.

**From: Petra Kairys**
**To: Millie Chandler**
**Subject: (no subject)**

Stuck in meeting but wanted you to know in case you hear from someone else gossiping. Rumor has it Chloe and Owen have broken up. Trying to get more details, but she apparently moved out and went to her parents' last night. Please don't panic/internalize. One text broke Maria and me. If it took one email to break off Owen and Chloe's engagement then you probably did them both a favor.
Xxxxxxx

*chapter 6*

$\mathcal{T}$onight, I finish up at Flye later than I think I probably *ever* have, as someone who always scurries out of the door at 5:31 at the very, *very* latest. But after Petra's bombshell of an email about Owen and Chloe actually—oh my God—*breaking up*, how on earth could I have just gone home and enjoyed a usual Friday night of binge-watching and baking? I feel I've hardly breathed since I read it. "Don't panic/ internalize," she'd said, but how can I not?

I stayed behind, firstly, to wait for Petra to get out of her meeting, which overran, hoping she'd somehow emerge from the boardroom saying, "False alarm! I have more info and Owen and Chloe are still together and completely understand your email issue and it turns out you haven't ruined everyone's lives and relationships at all! In fact, you've only made them stronger!" But when I landed no such luck, I decided, nervously, resignedly, bloody *nauseatedly*, that I'd stay to talk to Owen, who Petra told me was "still in with Michael"—even if I didn't want to. Even if I really didn't know what to say, I knew I had to look him in the eyes, as agonizing and as nerve-racking as that is, and . . . *apologize.* Try to put it right.

Now, at 6:20 on the dot, seconds after seeing both Michael and Owen leave, Owen hanging back outside, for a cigarette maybe, or to talk to someone else, I step through the glass doors of Flye's exit. I see him. He's standing at the edge of the open warehouse. There's another hour until the early September sun is due to set, but the weather is so gloomy this evening, the sky sagging with thick, indigo cloud, it feels like an atmospheric deeply autumnal night. The car park is mostly barren, the reception area of the square, flat-roofed Flye TV building is darkened now that the spotlights are off until morning, and the small scatter of night workers are starting their shifts deep inside the warehouse, the shutter up, the lights inside creating a golden square amid the murk, like a dollhouse.

Owen stands, shadowed. I'd know him anywhere: that lean frame, the angular slope of his shoulders, the assured lift of his chin. And there's a part of me that wants to keep walking, pretend not to see him, dive into my car, hurtle off into the night. Because what exactly is my plan here? This is Owen. I have *feelings* for this man. Owen Kalimeris is the only person I've ever been in love with. And for two years, I've carried what feels like a gazillion painful, disoriented emotions about him around with me in a heavy, confusing balloon, and it has now burst in front of him. In front of *everyone.* Covered us all in its goo. And I'm to pull him to one side and say what, exactly? Because despite practicing what I'd say for the last hour, puffing myself up with faux confidence, in the hope I won't turn to jelly when I see him, like I always do, I've gone . . . blank. Like someone's just rubbed a cloth across my brain and swept it clean.

*Sorry.*

I guess sorry is a good place to start, right, with someone who has just broken up with their fiancée because of you? (Yes, Petra, I said it: *Because. Of. Me.*)

"Ah. Millie," Owen says as I arrive in front of him, and instantly the sound of his voice, the familiar sound of "Millie" from his mouth, causes a tiny fist to clench around my gut.

"Hi, Owen."

"Staying late?" he asks. His angular face is half-lit by the warehouse lights, like a mask. He doesn't quite *appear* heartbroken, or furious with me. Maybe it *is* a rumor, a bit of office gossip gone awry? "What happened, then, did you oversleep? Start late this morning, making up the time?" A twitch of a smile.

"Ah," I say. "No, not quite. I needed to, um, talk to Petra about something. No oversleeping over here."

"Oh yeah?" Owen's wide mouth presses into an impressed arc. "Hm. I guess things do change, eh, Mills?"

*Mills. Argh.* A tiny chink in the armor. The familiarity, the intimacy of knowing he knows how much I like to lie in, of how I look sleepily reaching for the snooze button in my underwear on a Saturday morning for the third time in a row.

A spit of rain dots my forehead. For a beat, neither of us speaks.

"Owen, I'm . . . so sorry about the email. I—"

"I waited for you by your desk earlier," he says, one hand slotted in his jeans pocket, one arm dangling casually at his side, holding his phone. "I wasn't here yesterday. I've been in Manchester. With work. Cricket."

"Oh. Right."

"Emailed. Tried calling."

"It's off," I say quickly. "My phone. It's turned off." *And I wish I never had to turn it back on*, I don't add. Because I really am *dreading* turning it back on.

Owen raises his own phone at his side. He's wearing all black. A slim-fitted short-sleeved black T-shirt, straight-legged black jeans, a fraying tear in one of the knees, a peep of tanned skin. He looks healthy. Skin, golden. Limbs, wiry. A runner's physique. "And this," he says. "I get this. This email. *Emails.*"

I nod, rigid in the thick, humid air, as rain starts to fall in a haze. And now I can't even look at him. Embarrassed doesn't even come close. Ashamed is how I feel. *Guilty.* There he was, in Manchester, directing an entire televised cricket game, living this adult, "I'm at the top of my career game and I'm getting married like a real grown-up" life, while I was being read my own emails and convulsing around my home as my flatmate burned incense that smelled like bad shepherd's pie.

"Owen, I really am so sorry. And I'm *so* sorry if I've landed you in anything, with Chloe too. Th-that was never my intention. Just . . . Forget you got it. Forget I said anything. It was a mistake."

Owen stares at me in the gloom; hooded, treacle-brown eyes, un-blinking. "What?"

"Ignore it," I say again, my voice verging on warbling now. "Both of you, you and Chloe, just . . . ignore it. Discard it, or whatever. It's just—it's *stupid*, you know? *I* was stupid. It was a draft, it wasn't even meant to be sent, and I was a bit drunk and feeling sorry for myself and—you know when you just do something stupid? Something stu-pid and *silly*—"

"Are you . . ." Owen grimaces, two tally marks etched between his eyebrows. "Hang on, so, what, the whole thing was a . . . *joke* then?"

"No, no—"

"Someone said they got sent when the servers went down—"

"You just weren't meant to see it, is what I mean. I was *emotional.*" Our voices tangle, and both of us fall silent. Light rain stipples us, like dust.

"Emotional," repeats Owen. "About the wedding?"

I shrug from within my raincoat, which sticks with cold sweat to my arms. "I . . . I don't know. Yes." I'm nervous; *really* nervous, espe-cially under Owen's dark gaze. He did this to me, in the beginning.

When we first met, when he'd come in for planning meetings back when he was a live-match producer, make excuses to talk to me at my desk, I could hardly bear to look at him in the eyes.

Owen is attractive in that clean-cut, almost Waspy way. Dark, Mediterranean eyes, hair always short and neat, sharp and after-shaved from head to toe. But it was more his . . . *air*? Alexis once said, about Owen, after we broke up, "The bloke is an only-just-six-out-of-ten without all the bollocks and bravado," and it was *that* I found intimidating when we first met, and charming too. "The bravado." Owen's demeanor. The . . . *way* of him. Confident and sure of himself, but also infectiously, surprisingly warm. Affable. Genuinely interested in you. Like the boy at school who wound up the teachers and who you tried to ignore, but who always somehow managed to get a genuine smile out of you.

We were a contradiction really. Owen, charming and polished. Me with my out-of-control cinnamon waves, the chaos of freckles all over my skin, T-shirts with silly emblems on he seemed to always be baffled by. Emotional. Clumsy. And I feel that now, as we stand opposite each other. Me, flapping, sweating in the rain, post–massive life blunder, Owen, put-together, baffled, in the middle of something he didn't ask for, or would never plan for, in his perfect, seamless life.

"It's just an email," I say, finally meeting his eyes. "And I'm sorry it made its way to you, Owen, but it was never meant to. Just—I don't know. Pretend you never got it? Tell Chloe the same; t-tell her I'm sorry. I can tell her, if you like?"

"Millie . . ."

"Is she coming in at all? Monday?"

"Millie, seriously, can we just . . ." Owen holds up his palm, eye-lids dropping closed for a second. "Can we just pause for a minute? This . . . I feel like I'm being bombarded."

And I wish I could just disappear from here. The sky dimming fast, a blue haze from Owen's phone in his hand lit up with my own words, glowing between us. God, those old versions of us . . . I can't even imagine what they'd think, if they could see us now. They'd be bewildered, I think. Sad. Because Owen and I went so fast. Well, *Owen* went fast. From one date to huge weekly flower deliveries at work, to "I love yous" and surprise weekends in Prague and meeting the parents. "Maybe a little too fast," my friends said, grimacing as if the bouquets filling my room were severed heads.

And maybe they were right. Maybe it was too fast. Because it didn't exactly end how we both planned, did it? Talking outside the same building we met in, tonight, the ominous bleeping of a forklift our only soundtrack, and a haze of rain misting us, turning this whole scene to a grainy old videotape.

"Chloe wants to cancel the wedding," Owen says, pushing his phone back into his pocket, and shame covers me like a hot rash. "Says it's over. She thinks something happened with us. Stayed at her parents' last night. Five fuckin' grand I've sunk into it as well."

"Owen. I . . . I'm so sorry . . ."

"We've got two months to pay the remaining half to the venue, or it's done. Game over. Venue gone, date gone." Owen brings his arms up and over his head, lacing his fingers together behind his neck. "And . . . Jesus, Millie, this whole thing is crazy. We've just moved into a new place. Cost me a fortune, too—the old Corona cinema? Been converted into flats. And now . . ."

His words taper off, and I don't know what to say; whether I should apologize again or congratulate him on his new flat. New things are important to Owen. Expensive things. Things that make a statement. "Is it pathetic that sometimes I want all these things and achievements just so my piece-of-shit dad will one day see them all and regret pretending I didn't exist?" he asked me once, and so much about him—that Owen bravado—suddenly made sense. Owen is the result of an affair his mum had at work. His father has a wife of forty years, children, grandchildren, and he denies Owen is his; that he exists at all. And my heart always broke for him every time he talked about it.

"I'm sorry, Owen," I say. "I really am. I'll . . . I'll speak to her. I'll fix it."

"You'll *fix* it?"

"Yes."

"What, and that's it?"

"I don't know what else to say?"

*"Millie . . .* fuck, this is . . ."

Owen steps forward then, the soles of his sneakers scraping on the wet pavement, and I step back away from him, but he closes the gap again. He's close to me now—there isn't even two feet between us. I can smell him over the earthy, tea-leafy scent of the rain. The same washing detergent, the same stupidly expensive wax he always used on his hair. Something happens inside me now—an uneasy rush of something that feels like nerves and nostalgia all at once.

"I don't know how to feel," he says, his voice low now, his hand grazing my forearm. Thunder rumbles in the distance, and rain mists our faces, so fine it's like static. "And . . . fucking hell, Millie, I can't stop thinking about it. About what you said."

"Owen—"

"Do you still really have my T-shirt? Did you—" He stops. "Did you mean it when you said you still loved me?"

And there it is. Oh no, *there it is.* And I'm totally unprepared. I might've wished for this, daydreamed this up hundreds of times over the last two years like a stupid movie scene in my head, but I am completely caught off guard. Because the absolute truth is: *I don't know.* I don't know if the reason I couldn't move on is because we *are* meant to be. I don't know if all the pain and longing mean we are absolutely *not.*

For so long, I used to imagine that after he came home from India, his job done, promotion obtained, we might just—put it right? Somehow.

But Chloe. What about Chloe? I know what it is to be heartbroken, and I wouldn't wish that on even the most insufferable person on earth. Not Fundraising Steve, not Sly, I-Secretly-Like-Other-People's-Failings Cousin Rhiannon. Plus, he left me. Quite easily, in fact, so what about *that*, Millie Chandler, what about *that*?

"It . . . I don't know."

And his shoulders sag as silence expands between us. "Right. You don't know. Yet *you* said those things, Millie. *You* typed them."

"It was never meant to be read."

"But it was."

And I open my mouth to reply, but nothing—I have nothing. And it seems, as silence encircles us, like a cloud, neither does he.

I step back, away from him. "I'll speak to Chloe."

Owen gives a dark, flat chuckle. "Oh. Yeah, well, good luck with that one. She's . . . not a fan. Always had a hang-up."

"A *hang-up*?"

"Knows how much you meant to me, I guess," he says, and I find myself shaking my head then, as if to flick off his words, like mud, because I don't know what to do with any of this. I'm at sea. A bottle-shaped woman bobbing, lost, in the ocean.

"Still," I say. "I'll talk to her."

"Right." Owen runs a hand through his dark, short hair and slowly steps back. "Look forward to hearing from you, then, Millie."

And he turns, strolling into the bright box of a warehouse, as a fork of lightning darts through the sky, like a vein. The fire door in the dark slams.

"Fuck," I whisper to myself as hard, wet footsteps tread past me. "*Fuck.*"

"Good night, Millie," comes a deep voice, and as I turn, my eyes find Jack in the fuzz, all unbuttoned collars and quiet confidence. He continues walking, but his eyes flick over his shoulder to the warehouse, to Owen, and then to me, inscrutable, for just a second, before he gets to his car. It bleeps twice.

"Night," I call out as he gets inside his car and shuts the door.

*chapter 7*

*From: 89beastmode.Simon@gmail.com*
*To: Millie Chandler*
**Subject: re: re: send me your tits dirty girl**
Errrr, what the fuck u emailing me back now for? I barely
remember u Millie. But for the record I was trying to have
a bit of fun after our date yet you make it personal about
my breath? It was side effects of vitamins I was taking. It
doesn't normally smell like that??

    ugly bitch. Delete my email. delete my number.

**iMessage from Alexis:** MILLIE??????
**iMessage from Alexis:** wow.
**iMessage from Alexis:** If you felt that way, why not tell me to my
face? Instead of bombard me with emails?

**iMessage from Alexis:** I stood you up and I'm sorry about that but to call me a bad friend?

**iMessage from Alexis:** That you're relieved I canceled?

**iMessage from Alexis:** I'm so sad.

**iMessage from Alexis:** I'm not perfect, but wtf?

**iMessage from Alexis:** I'm so done

**iMessage from Alexis:** I'm too busy for this shit.

**WhatsApp from Dad:** Please call me, Millie. Urgently if poss. Both Mum and me OK, not dead.

**WhatsApp from Dad:** Would like to talk to you asap if possible darling

**WhatsApp from Dad:** Just slightly confused

**WhatsApp from Dad:** Your email insinuated that on the Easter bank holiday you weren't with your mother, but she said you stayed the whole weekend and you went out together.

**WhatsApp from Dad:** When I called her at the time, she didn't pick up. She said she was with you.

**WhatsApp from Dad:** Was she?

**Missed WhatsApp video call from Dad**

**Missed WhatsApp video call from Dad**

**Missed WhatsApp video call from Dad**

**WhatsApp from Dad:** Ignore that. Not sure what I pressed, not wearing glasses.

**iMessage from Cousin Rhiannon:** Millie, I don't know what you meant by your emails? I just received a lot of LOLs and zzzzzs and one saying, "give your head a wobble." Have you been hacked? X x x

**WhatsApp from Cate:** Millie, I've read your emails.

**WhatsApp from Cate:** I just walked out of work.

**WhatsApp from Cate:** Fuck.

**WhatsApp from Cate:** Millie?

**WhatsApp from Cate:** Millie, please answer me.

Cate sits at the breakfast bar, bewildered; like someone who's just been picked up from her sofa by a giant claw and dropped in the middle of an unknown century. But at the sight of her, I practically combust with relief.

*She's here.*

My beautiful, dependable friend is *here*, in my kitchen, which means she doesn't hate me so much that she's blocked me and never wants to see me again. Unless, of course, this is it. Unless this is like a mafia movie, and I'm being lured here, over to the breakfast bar, to be handed a stallion's head—an emblem of a severed friendship. And who knows? I wouldn't be surprised by anything anymore. In fact, a stallion's head would be a fitting end to a nightmarish day of hiding in storage offices and dark, humiliating conversations in the rain with ex-boyfriends.

I stand in the entrance of the kitchen, tightening the cord of my dressing gown. Ralph stands, polishing a wineglass, subtly observing.

"Oh, Millie. I've been ringing your phone off the hook." Cate stands, the bar stool's legs squeaking on the tiles beneath her. "I've emailed you, left you voice notes, *texted* . . ."

"Oh, Cate, I know, and I'm *so* sorry. My phone's been off."

"Ralph said you'd not long been in from work; that you were in your room . . . switching it on or something?"

I'm searching Cate's face like it's one of those computer games where you have to scan a scene and look for evidence and clues, and all I can deduce is, she looks . . . tired? There are puffy, pillowy crescents under her eyes, the same sort that sit under mine. "He said your personal emails were sent? Jesus, Millie, why didn't you call me back?"

I pad slowly toward her. "I was scared," I say wobblily. "You've . . . you've read the emails, then."

Ralph slides a glass of wine across the counter toward Cate, who softly nods a thank you and sits back down on the stool. "Yes. Yes, I did read your emails, but—seriously, are you OK?" Her eyes soften, the outer corners wilting, like she might cry, and now *I* might cry. "I feel like you need to sit down, have something to drink? You look ill. Sort of . . . *loony.*"

Relief floods my body like morning sunshine. *Cate doesn't hate me.* Everything else might be a total mess, but my best friend does not hate me, even though I barreled into her inbox and told her I secretly hate her boyfriend. She cares whether I've had anything to drink; that I look "loony," which I most definitely do. After getting home from that loaded, rainy conversation with Owen a couple of hours ago, I've tried desperately to get back on an even keel, but nothing has worked. I feel out of body. Perpetually shaky. I've turned my phone on, began to slowly face multiple (horrible) notifications, I've taken a hot shower, washed my hair, cried a bit (a lot) into a bowl of Super Noodles Ralph made me. I even sat on the balcony for a little while in my pajamas, with my favorite view—the dark sheet metal of the sea, Canvey Island twinkling in the distance, the smell of fishing nets and the sweet, burnt sugar of cut wood from a flat renovation below. But even that didn't settle me tonight. Cate, though—seeing Cate has, instantly. Like pain relief. Like a cup of tea, like a hot water bottle.

"Oh, Cate, I can't tell you how relieved I am to see you." I cross the floor, fold my arms around her. It feels so wonderful to hold her close, to know she's still here. This tiny kitchen with Cate and Ralph, a remnant of life before.

"Oh, me too."

Behind her, Ralph slides over yet another glass, full of wine, meant for me. It's the color of old tights. His homemade mushroom wine, of course. Utterly disgusting, but—sod it. I release Cate, take a seat next to her, and glug a massive mouthful of it as Ralph says, "I'll, er, leave you two to it, shall I?" and steps out of the kitchen.

The room falls quiet. The fridge whirs. A solar-powered plastic flower dances on the windowsill, squeaking from side to side.

"Cate, I'm so, so sorry."

"Millie, please—"

"No, I really, really am," I say pleadingly. "To get emails like that, and about Nicholas, you must think I'm such a bitch. It must have—I don't even *know*. I've been a shitty, shitty friend—"

"*No.*" Cate shakes her head, a quick shudder, her brown, beach-waved hair brushing her shoulders. "No, Millie, you are not a shitty friend." Her eyes look dulled under the glow of the pendant lights, like bulbs that have dimmed. Like she hasn't been sleeping, and Cate Mancinelli-Grant *always* sleeps. She takes sleep seriously. Her phone left out of the bedroom, an old-fashioned alarm clock to wake her up in the morning, no TV, no blue light—oil diffusers and thick paperbacks only.

"No, Millie," says Cate again quietly. "I mean . . . I was shocked, of course I was, when I read them. I felt *sick*. Walked out of work, faked an illness, was wandering around like a bloody lost Sim. Asim was fine with it, thankfully. He'd far rather lose his PA for the day than risk catching any sort of cold that might land him in bed . . ."

"Oh, Cate, I'm so sorry."

"Please don't be." Cate gives a sad smile, drinks her wine. "And shit, this tastes like . . . I don't know. A burger or something? Like *beef*. Should wine taste like beef?"

"It's made from mushrooms," I say.

"*Oh*." She sips again and shrugs. "In for a penny, in for a pound, I suppose."

"And, Cate, I . . . I didn't mean a word of anything I said. It was just . . . I was just ranting, you know?"

Cate hesitates, the silver C-shaped pendant sighing at her chest. "Really, Millie?" She reaches over and places a delicate, warm hand on mine.

Cate has always had this maternal vibe; this strong, calm, mature way about her. She was two years above me at school, and we met on sports day, when I fell and grazed my chin—yes, *my chin*—and she was nominated to escort me to the school matron. I kept harping on, as we walked, about how embarrassing the whole thing was, and Cate had said, "It was an accident, though. There's a whole department dedicated to it at a hospital, so if you're embarrassing, so is the rest of the world." Then she'd said, calmly, of the (horrid) school nurse, "Sometimes I think I'd rather die than be treated by her, you know? Just to make a point, because how hard is it to care about *actual* sick people?" and I was sold. All in. Fell in friendship-love, if you like.

"Millie," Cate carries on, her voice gentle and reassuring, like warm tea. "I think you did mean what you said. And I didn't want to agree with any of it at first. My first emotion was . . . anger. Like, I was *proper* fuming. But then something just clicked. Because I knew I agreed with every single word you said." Cate sniffs, dabs the tip of her index finger to the corner of her eye. "You know when something is so true, almost too true, that it's unbearable to consider? Like it's . . . *blinding*? And you can't bear to look at it?"

I nod slowly. Because I do. I really do.

"It was that, Millie," she says. "That's what it was."

"Cate, I'm so sorry—"

"So, I walked out this afternoon," she announces in one gust. "I've left Nicholas. I think?"

And as Cate downs a huge mouthful of wine, my heart plummets through my body, like it's been suddenly pushed from a plane and is falling, falling, falling. "Are you . . . *What?*"

"I know."

"Oh my God?"

"*I know.*" She downs even more of her mushroom wine, wincing, like she's forcing down medicine. "And I can't believe it really, the more I think about it. I mean, last year Nicholas actually *admitted* to signing up to a dating app. Because I'd been going out a lot and he thought I didn't *want him anymore*? And yes, he apologized, said he'd have never done anything, that it was just to *have a look*, that he was feeling insecure." Cate scoffs, a sharp snort, puts her glass down on the granite counter with a harsh ding. "But he blamed the relationship, he blamed *me* for doing too much yoga, seeing my sister in the evenings too much, and I just . . . took it? I even said *sorry*? Like, what was I thinking?"

Something hot opens in my chest as Cate speaks, an angry, bubbling orb. "But Cate, he's manipulative," I say. "And he's so good at it. Dresses all his possessiveness and distrust as this protective, romantic, caring, insecure boyfriend who just loves you *too, too* much."

Cate nods, her eyes shining. "I know," she says. "I know. And I kept thinking it would get better. That he'd change and relax a bit when his work got easier, or we'd been together longer, or his mum was out of hospital, or . . . insert delusion here." Her beautiful, heart-shaped mouth lifts a fraction at the corner with sad amusement. "And I feel like . . . *me*. Single? Seriously? Solicitors and a house halved down the middle and who'll get the sodding DFS sofa, blah, blah, blah, but—I also feel . . . *lighter*? I mean, OK, I feel absolutely wired, and I have no idea what I'm going to do or where I'm going to go, and of course, classic Cate, I can't stop going to the toilet." She gives a small, tearful laugh. "But . . . I just walked out, Millie. I got home, he didn't even say hello or ask why I was home. He just went straight into *Why didn't you answer your phone?* And *Swear to me you didn't see my messages* and when it should have been scary, like the end of something huge, it just felt like . . . waking up?"

And as Cate's watery eyes meet mine, I feel everything. *Everything.* Relief and pride and love; but God, so much shame, so much worry and disbelief. And it gathers in one big, hot, forceful storm inside me and . . . I burst into yet more tears.

"Oh, Millie! Don't cry."

"No! No, I should be comforting *you*." I reach for the roll of kitchen towel on the counter, tear off a square. It's patterned with a border of oblivious happy dancing green and purple teapots. I blow my nose into it. "Are you . . . are you *sure* about this? I know the things I said about Nicholas were scathing and—"

"Truthful," says Cate, squeezing my hand. "*Truthful.* And so kind about me too. Do you know how lovely it was to read that stuff about me, Millie?" Cate tears off a sheet of kitchen towel for herself. "He doesn't say it, and *I* don't say it anymore, and I can't believe we just *got* to a point where that was OK, but I trust nobody as much as I trust you. And you say it, you know? You know everything about me, and you say it. So it must be true. Just like I see you; know everything about *you*."

And at those words, a lightning bolt of guilt zigzags through me. Because . . . does she? Does anyone know everything about me anymore? Cate definitely did once upon a time. I told her everything; from bowel movements ("just a courtesy text to say I'm back on an evening poo schedule, thought you should know") and midnight philosophical realizations, to what I was eating for lunch and existential "Just queuing for a KFC and wondering if I'm living enough" worries.

But slowly, over time, it's like I've subconsciously held things back. Squirreled things away. A gradual retreat, I suppose you'd say. Especially since Owen. There's something about giving your whole entire heart to someone, saying, "Here I am in front of you, no barriers, no masks, prepared to do whatever it takes, to make this work, because I love you" and having that someone look at it, at all you are, and saying no that makes you hold things back. Keep things closer to your chest. That just in case it happens again, you still have parts of yourself that you never exposed to the elements.

Cate stands now, circles the breakfast bar, sandals on tiles. "He panicked," she says. "Nicholas. Like, crying and begging, and I was almost doubtful. You know? Then he turned it on me. Like a switch. Without a fucking *breath*. And then it was all —*I knew it. I could just tell. What's his name?*"

"Jeez. What an arsehole."

"Total arsehole!"

And Cate may be tired, wrung out, sad, but she still somehow looks immaculate, as she always does: wide-legged, light-blue jeans, a white tucked-in tank top, an oversize baby-pink shirt half-undone, half off one shoulder. A shirt that would make me look like I riffled through a lost-and-found box to get dressed. Cate always looks nice, always smells nice. She makes sure of it, because she really enjoys it. She likes her outfits, her diary, her home, all carefully curated. And a pang of sadness surges through me thinking about Cate and Nicholas's house. Because I know it's just a house, but she *loves* that house. Three Christmas Lane. I remember how excited she was about the address alone. And she's lost it. Because of me.

"Cate, maybe . . . maybe you could keep Christmas Lane?"

She shrugs. "I don't know, Millie."

"And you share a car . . ."

"Fuck cars. Honestly, I don't care about any of that at the moment."

Cate glances around the kitchen. "God, where did that sweet little man put the bottle of weird meaty wine . . ."

And I know she says she wants this, that she feels lighter and empowered, but I feel—*responsible.* I do. Almost sorry for her, watching her rummage through our kitchen on a Friday night when she'd normally be at home with her own things. Her own cupboards, her own normal-tasting wine, plucked from that integrated wine-cooler fridge she loves so much. Cate was so excited when they bought that house. Bought a candle for every room, would change her bedsheets every Tuesday, following a cleaning schedule from Instagram. And now what? She's walked away from it. Because of my email.

"You can stay here," I say. "Live with us."

"You do not want me in your bedroom—"

"We have a third room," I insist, "and Ralph wants to rent it out, but we hate everyone who comes to interview for it, so . . . let me speak to him?"

Cate's face softens, sad, tired eyes brightening, a deep dot dimpling her cheek. "Are you sure?"

"Completely."

"Oh, thank you." She reaches across the counter for my hands. She lowers her voice. "Did your emails really all get sent?"

"Yes."

"*Fuck.*" Cate's eyes close and she bends, half groaning, half laughing, her delicate bracelets jingling against the worktop. She looks back up at me. "How bad is it?"

"Oh, so bad," I say. "So, *so* bad. Emails to rude people at work. Mum. Alexis, which . . . Jesus, she's so mad at me, Cate. I think she's blocked me. But—I dunno. Because she *has* upset me recently. I just wish she hadn't found out just how much like this. I was so cutting, and . . . It's Alexis, you know? *Alexis.*"

Cate nods knowingly. "She'll come around, Millie."

"Oh, and there was a massive email to Owen, too," I announce. "But sent to *all*. So, that was good."

"Holy shit."

I nod, teeth clamped together, like that little emoji who always looks like he's just walked into a train carriage to find two passengers shagging in the shadows. "I know. I know, I'm an awful, awful monster."

"I mean, it sounds like a fucking nightmare, mate," Cate says carefully. "But you are not the monster."

"Oh, I am."

"No, you're not. We all say shit we feel like we shouldn't have, right? Like, *every* human being on earth can relate to that. Who hasn't drunk-texted their ex? Or, I don't know, been shitty with some knob at work?"

I gaze at her and shake my head. She's talking like someone who hasn't been affected by all this, like she isn't collateral damage herself. "Why are you so nice?" I ask her. "Seriously. Are you going to be OK?"

She offers a tired smile, a tiny smudge of mascara at the corner of her eye. "Always am. And don't beat yourself up. The emails . . . everyone's done something like that at some point. I swear it."

"Hm, yes, well, I'm petrified of my own phone, and even my bloody dad has gone all 'your mother's whereabouts aren't adding up,' so it doesn't *feel* too normal at the minute, Cate, I've got to be honest. Plus, you're here and Owen's wedding's off—"

"S-sorry." Ralph stands in the doorway. He's wearing his glasses, the square, black-framed ones he wears specifically for watching TV, and he's holding an iPad at his midriff, like a little squirrel clutching a hazelnut. "Sorry, I don't mean to disturb you both—"

"*His wedding's off?*" exclaims Cate, still looking at me. "Because of one email?"

"Yes," I say shamefully. "Well, I think more that he asked me out, and *that* was in the email."

"Well, that's Owen's fault, then, isn't it—"

"Sorry," interrupts Ralph, again, clearing his throat. We both turn to look at him. "Millie. Your friend Alexis. Alexis Lee?"

"Yeah?"

"I, erm, I have her as a friend on TikTok? Since your . . . birthday meal?"

"Oh. Right?"

"I wanted to tell you, but I also don't want you to worry." *Oh God.* "It's just—she's posted a short video about your, um, situation," he says. "She doesn't name you. It just has her face, and the text says something like, when your so-called best friend sends you emails you were never meant to receive—"

"*What?*"

"*Best friend,*" scoffs Cate, brown eyes lifting to the ceiling. "Some best friend she's been lately."

"She . . . she doesn't have *too* many followers," says Ralph quickly as I dive across the kitchen for his iPad. "And I wasn't going to tell you, but, well, I thought it might help you stop beating yourself up. She's not exactly acting like a respectful friend right n—"

"What are people *saying*?" I ask hysterically.

Ralph holds the screen to his chest. "It only has eleven likes."

"Are they dragging me?" I reach for the iPad, like a cat batting a moth, and missing. "Are they saying horrible things—"

"*Millie.*"

I freeze, and Ralph and I slowly turn, in unison, toward Cate.

"*Stop,*" she says firmly. "Seriously. You don't even have TikTok, do you? Plus, she's been standing you up. She's been saying things about your job being dead end, stuff about your life being too simple and boring, or whatever it was. Did she not *deserve* the emails?"

I stare at her. "Maybe? I dunno, Cate, I just feel like everything's a *mess.* It's out of control, I don't know where to begin."

"And we can talk it out," Cate replies warmly. "You can listen to my mess, and I'll listen to yours. We'll even make a list. You know how much I like lists. But meantime. *Halt*, motherfucker. You know? Breathe. The worst is over. And all we need to do now is . . . well, I know what *I* need. Right now anyway. A cuddle and a sandwich." She gives another tired smile. "Anyone here up for a cuddle and a sandwich?"

"Duly noted." Ralph nods, a single bow, then goes wide-eyed. "Well. Th-the *sandwich*, of course . . ."

And as Cate snuggles up next to me on the sofa in our cozy, lamp-lit living room and Ralph makes slow, careful cheese sandwiches in the kitchen, I wonder if they're right. Maybe the worst is over. And if it is, how, in a sea of gossip and TikTok cautionary tales, do I move on?

### The Millie Chandler Is Not a Monster To-Do List

- *Have a social media break*
- *Switch iPhone for basic phone? (One of Ralph's bricks from the garage lockup)*
- *Bake cakes and cookies for work*
- *Speak to Chloe*
- *Message Petra about working extra hours/helping out on game days to show work I am not a drama-making liability*
- *Speak to Dad*
- *Apologize to Mum for snarky email about brunches and not loving me*
- *Send Alexis sorry letter (and her fave brownies?)*
- *~~Or just forget all the above and move on anyway?~~ LOL, nice try, Cate*
- *The Cate Mancinelli-Grant OMG So What Now? List*
- *To do: whatever the fuck I like* 😊

chapter 8

**Text message from Millie:** Hi Dad, I have a new phone and
no longer have WhatsApp, so it'll be texts or calls from now
on. I got your messages about Easter. Sorry for confusing you.
Massive glitch at work and all my emails got sent at once, so it
was an old one!!! Tell Mum I'm sorry, too, about her email. But
I'll call you both soon (are you on the rigs this week?). Love
you both x

**Text message from Dad:** OK, darling. I'm on the rigs on
shift until next Sunday. So you weren't with your mum on
Good Friday? Probably an old man moment LOL but
don't mention it to Mum please.
Dad xxxxx

*From: Millie Chandler*
*To: All Leigh Office*
**Subject: Cakes**
Hi all,

Just to brighten your Monday, there are home-baked cakes and cookies (gluten-free and non-gluten-free variations are clearly labeled) in the kitchen. Please help yourself!

Millie x

Reception

Flye TV

Petra plonks herself down next to me at the reception desk and smiles in the way a teacher might smile at a child she suspects might, at any moment, throw themselves to the carpet and cry, all pummeling fists and feet.

"Afternoon, my dearest Millie," she says tentatively, shrugging off her denim jacket. "And how have we been? How was your weekend?"

"Afternoon, my dearest Petra," I parrot with a smile. No carpet cries for me today. Not now that I have my to-do list. "And I *think*—and bear with me because I recently learned such a thing could change at any moment—I might be fine."

Petra grins widely, her lips shiny with clear gloss, and pulls a gigantic bottle of chilled coffee from her handbag. "Oh yeah?"

"Oh *yes*," I reply, and I really think I might be. I'm feeling productive. I'm feeling *determined*. I'm feeling a little bit . . . hopeful even. (Although I'm not sure how much of that is the faux validation of having Chatty Martin finally actually *smile* at me again like he did ten minutes ago, and all because I made him sultana-and-date flapjacks, his favorite. He often talks at length about how much he likes roughage.)

Nevertheless, though, it's a relief to be *here,* and not *there,* in "last week," which was, of course, a total, stone-cold disaster. The weekend was better, a slow crawl from the pits of despair to "maybe things might be OK," and in the end, it even had an air of back-to-school energy. Cate helped me make a list (most of which she didn't agree with), and yesterday, I baked and baked, as Cate went with her mum, Shanice, to pick up some things from her and Nicholas's house, officially moving in to our flat, and Ralph used all manner of strange tools and gadgets to set up my new (old) phone: a very slow but usable 2010 Nokia, one of the favorites of his collection. And it's *so* strange being without an iPhone. At first, I spent a lot of time checking it, my new brick: for signs that Alexis wanted to talk, for messages from Owen telling me the wedding is back on (or still off), for Dad telling me he's found Mum in bed with Andy Hilary, the handsome, gray surgeon who lives opposite them (who Alexis calls "Doctor Zaddy"), or that Chloe was on her way over with two sumo suits and a stripy-shirted referee. But eventually, my brain started to get the memo. There is nothing to check. If my new (old) phone isn't bleeping with a call or text, nothing is happening, and there are no apps I can check, no little alibis I can make up from scraps of last-seen statuses and Instagram Stories updates. There's something quite . . . liberating about it too. Not knowing what my cousin packed in her husband's lunch box, not having to read motivational quotes on Sunday mornings from my bed that make me feel like a lazy pork scratching in a pair of fleece pajamas.

"So, I got your message," Petra says, shaking her coffee like a mixologist. "About helping out at more events?"

"And what do you think?"

"And what did you mean about the phone also?" Petra continues, ignoring my question. She's just got back from a meeting about next year's Wimbledon. Flye broadcasts it most years, and everyone, for a short while, loses themselves to temporary insanity. Strawberry and cream queues are discussed like natural disasters that simply must be stopped, and tennis players are spoken of like Christ's disciples. There are three types of people who work here, I've come to realize. Those who are utterly fanatical about sports, those who are fanatical about making TV (and often talk about it with the sort of affectionate jaded irritation you do about a younger, annoying sibling), and those who simply . . . work here. And I fit into that category like a glove. I started here as a temp, and I've been hoping, deep down, I might start to slowly merge into one of the other categories, by osmosis or something. That I'd somehow see what they see—people like Owen. That *meaning* they find in it. That fire and excitement I've always been a bit jealous of. (I'm still waiting, although I do know by now at exactly which point to tut, or sigh, or say, "What a fantastic serve that was, eh?")

"Oh, yes, my new phone," I say.

"I was confused." Petra frowns. "A Nokia? As in, you've changed phones permanently?"

"That's right," I reply. "I wanted a break from having an entire world in my handbag. You know, on account of everything terrible that's happened."

"Has anything else happened, then?"

The reception desk phone rings and I answer, transfer a call to the Accounts department (one for Bigot Prue, who is still pretending I do not exist) as Petra watches me, drinking more of her coffee like she hasn't had anything to drink in several weeks.

"Does anything else *need* to happen?" I ask, hanging up the phone. "The last time I checked, everything had already happened."

"Yes, but . . . getting rid of your phone? And nominating your free time for . . ." She lowers her husky voice. "*This place.*"

"I'm just trying to lift the curse," I tell her.

"*Millie*. There is no curse."

"I'm afraid there is a bit of a curse, Petra," I say. "But I'm determined to fight it," and Petra sighs, giving me a resigned look that says, "I love you, but fuck right off." I have loved Petra Kairys for almost the entire time I've worked here. She was who hired me at Flye TV, way back when I came here as a temp, and she has acted, ever since, like I'm the best deal she ever got. As if she put an ad out for a receptionist but got some sort of oblivious genius who should be out somewhere, saving the world instead of packing up and returning faulty boom mics. I'd been delighted, though—I wanted something more than waitressing at the pub, and a temporary, no-pressure contract, especially at a cool-seeming TV broadcasting company, seemed perfect at the time.

"Are you sure?" Petra had asked when I accepted the job, and I'd found it the strangest question. But now I see, it was just a very Petra Kairys question. Petra is a cynic and a skeptic, with a "Well, it's too late for me, but it's not for you, so run while you can" air about her that would be more suited to a woman of one hundred and six than a thirty-five-year-old like her. She is also quietly selfless. She loves hard (but only if you're lucky enough), which is why when she'd found that text on her ex Maria's phone, it blindsided her worse than it would most. But Kira—her girlfriend now—has breathed life back into her; warmth and color. They are the sweetest, loveliest couple I've ever known. Petra often jokes Kira must've been made in a factory. "She's just too lovely, too unproblematic to be human."

"And the cakes went down well, I see," Petra says now smilingly. "They're almost all gone."

"And what about the gluten-free cookies? Michael Waterstreet's gluten-free, isn't he?"

"My love." Petra is Lithuanian, and her accent makes everything (especially "my love") sound extra romantic. "Do you need Michael Waterstreet to like your cookies? To like you?"

"Well . . ."

"Please think about this for a second, Millie," she says. "How *dark* that question really is."

I groan into my hands and slowly, like something deflating, lie flat with my forehead on the desk. "Yes," I say. "Depressingly, in the absence of a time machine, Petra, I do need Michael Waterstreet to like me. I need *everyone* to like me and for them to know I am not a bad person and that I want to keep my job. Because I have debt and bills to pay. Oh, and I need to live and eat, et cetera, and what else am I exactly going to do if I don't try to keep this job because I don't really have much of a plan for anything else right now and I'm not sure I have the energy for an existential crisis on top of everything else?"

"OK, love, *breathe*," Petra says warmly. "And you are not a bad person. Plus, you have a job. It's not gone anywhere."

"Until people complain. Then shit might get realer. So . . ."

"Give them cake?"

"Yes. Exactly. Cake." I lift my head back up and look at her, my mess of waves dangling over my eyes, like a living mop. "Thank you." I give her a smile. "For not judging me."

"Obviously."

"And can you get me on broadcasts? Helping on game days?" It's what the "good" people here do. They volunteer their free time, nominate themselves to assist at events, such as football games or cricket matches, because there are never enough pairs of hands or crew members. (Even if those hands are inexperienced and fumbling, like mine.)

"Mhm." Petra nods, setting down her coffee and peeling a brown hair tie from her wrist. "I've already emailed Jack about it." She scoops back a plume of caramel curls with her hand. "Shurlock?"

And the tiniest of sparks kindles inside me, because Petra says his name as if I need reminding. As if Jack didn't kindly cover for me, get shut in an office with me (and broken Gary Lineker), and pull me to standing with one of his tanned, hard-to-not-notice muscular forearms. "And look," Petra continues, "I am never going to say no to you helping out, because I'm selfish and I love working with you, but . . . are you sure?"

I shrug. "I mean, it seems like the sensible thing to do. Show willing, demonstrate to management that I'm not some troublemaker—"

"Yes, I know, but . . . is it what you want to do? *You.*"

I give a firm, ask-no-more-questions nod. "Yes."

"Leave it with me, then," she says, tying her hair back, and pulling two shiny twists of hair to dangle at the sides of her face. An effortless updo executed with no mirror.

"Oh, and is Chloe in this week?" I ask. "I want to speak to her." Yes, a secret, unspoken part of my plan of getting everything back to how it was. Get my ex back with his ex. Yes, the ex I am absolutely not over nor healed from but I cannot and *must not* be seen as a villainous heartbreaker because heartbreak is the worst possible thing I've ever experienced, and how can *I* be behind it for someone else? Yep. Isn't it great here in the scrambled brain of Millie Chandler?

Petra sighs at me then, but says, "Tomorrow."

"I just want to apologize."

"Yeah, well, there're a lot of people who should be apologizing to you, if you ask me," she says. "Michael for being rude and entitled. Steve and his bloody comments. *Owen.* And he should've been apologizing every day for two years. Oh. And the bloody server company . . ."

"Yeah, well, so far the only people who've apologized are a sanitary towel factory I emailed and complained to because the pack I bought were all split. I received a giant box of maxi pads because of that. Shaped like a bouquet."

Petra cackles. "Oh, that's *amazing.*"

"Yup. So, you know. If you want artily arranged hygiene products, just have your life ruined. Small price to pay."

"Millie Chandler, you have not ruined your bloody life—"

"Oh yeah? Look at my amazing sanitary towel bouquet and say that to its face."

Petra bursts out laughing as a deep voice says, "Interesting."

When I look up, Jack is standing at the bottom of the stairs, an eyebrow slightly raised.

"Way to a woman's heart these days, is it? Or just yours?"

I laugh; a sudden, machinelike burst. "Oh. Hi! Erm . . ."

"Noted." His eyes drop to the phone in his hand, a tiny curve at the edge of his mouth.

And before I can think of a witty response, thrown by Jack's sudden appearance, and that glint—that bloody unreadable hazel-eyed glint—a woman I have never seen before pushes through the office doors in sunglasses, an oversize denim shirt dress, and a huge, gleaming, toothpaste-model smile. She's carrying a large duffel bag, which she drops at her feet.

"Shurlock!" she exclaims. "Oh my *Lord*, you weren't wrong about that parking. It's dire, babe. Horrendous. Like parking a bus in a cereal box or something."

Jack's face softens. He laughs, a slice of straight teeth. He shoves his phone into his pocket. "Yeah, well, you do insist on driving those huge tanks."

Giggling, she's suddenly throwing her arms around him, and he's pulling her into him and he's grinning—wide, genuine, delighted— and I don't think I've ever seen him grin like that. Who *is this*? His . . . girlfriend? She definitely looks the type who would be Jack Shurlock's girlfriend. Unabashedly cool. Confident. Makeup-less from what I can tell (or maybe BB cream and lip gloss at a push), but just naturally, symmetrically holiday-faced levels of pretty.

"How are you, babe, all right?" she's saying, muffled into his chest, and he's holding her, strong arms across her tiny back.

"Yeah, I'm good, Jess, really good. And *you.* You look—incredible. Seriously."

"It's the collagen supplements," she says smilingly, looking up at him. "And seeing you. *Obviously.*"

And my face. My face is on fire, and I can't swallow. *Why can't I swallow?*

Jess pulls back and beams up at him, her arms still looped around his waist. "Got you a Starbucks. In *the tank.* Couldn't carry it all. Oh, and—Christ, I'm so rude." She turns to us then, Petra and me, and releases Jack, strides over, a hand to her chest. Her fingers are covered in chunky rings, silver bands mostly, some holding the occasional (huge) purple stone. "I'm Jess. One of the, uh, new Liverpool office guinea pigs, I suppose you'd say?"

"Jess Rizzo?" Petra stands up as Jess gives a smiling nod. "Oh my God, I can't believe we've never met. I'm Petra!"

"Petra, as in Kairys?" shrieks Jess. "Oh my days, at last!"

Petra shakes Jess's hand across the desk, and Jess places her other on top of hers, enveloping Petra's, clasping it. "Such a pleasure." Petra beams, her wide-set eyes twinkly. "Millie, this is Jessica Rizzo. She's worked freelance for us for ages, mostly up north. And we've just hired her for the new Liverpool office."

"Oh. Hi." I smile, extending my hand now. I can feel Jack watching us. "I'm Millie. Reception. Leigh office. Ha."

"Oh!" Jess shakes my hand, her rings pinching my skin, and then she stops dead. "Millie . . . Millie *Chandler*?"

And for a moment, I'm totally endeared that she knows my name, feel sure somehow that I've been such a *fantastic* receptionist at the Leigh office that it's reached the sunny climes of Liverpool, one of the new managers pointing at my portrait with a big pointy stick, saying, "This, receptionists of Flye TV Liverpool, is who you should be striving to be!" But then, the way Jess's cheeks pinken, and her ice-blue eyes stay open for far too long without a single blink, makes my heart still. Because—*ugh*. She recognizes my name for only one reason, and we have both realized that at the exact same time . . . The emails. Of course, the emails. Sent to *sodding all.*

"Nice to meet you," she rushes out, unblinking, before bounding back over to Jack like an excited Labrador. "Come with me to the tank, Shurlock," she says, placing her hand between the muscles of his shoulder blades, which jut slightly through his shirt. "I was a good girl and got you an espresso this time. A double. See? I can remember things."

Did she just say *good girl*?

Jack gives her an amused smirk. "You trying to buy me, Rizzo?"

"Always." Jess grins, stepping out to the sunny car park as Jack follows her, but turns around, pauses in the doorway. A breeze ruffles his hair, those tidy but wild waves, and he says, "Millie?"

"Yes?"

"I'll be emailing you about Sunday rugby. A match? Might need you in a couple of weekends."

"Sure!" I beam back at him. "Great! OK!" And he gives a dip of his head and leaves.

"Jeez, Millie." Petra puts the back of her hand to my cheek and says worriedly, "Do we need to turn the thermostat down? You're really, really hot."


**To: Millie Chandler**
**From: Forester Braun Wild Holidays**
**Subject: Complaint**
Dear Millie,

   We are so sorry to hear of your disappointing stay at THE GREEN-GRASS YURT and thank you for your honesty and feedback. Your experience of no water and no heating is not an experience guests should encounter, and we take pride in every single one of our properties. We would like to arrange a time for our manager to call you, and we are delighted to offer you a complimentary night's stay in one of our tier-two properties (<u>here</u> is a link to all those available) on an off-peak weekday of your choosing. Please respond with a contact telephone number and a time that suits you.

Kind Regards,

Sara

Forester Braun Wild Holidays

*Sleep among the treetops in our three new treehouse self-catering properties here!*

*(20% off when you book using code AUTUMN20)*

**To: Alexis Lee**

**From: Millie Chandler**

**Subject: Fwd: Re: Complaint**

Lex, I complained about the Sainsbury's bag poo holiday (something good came out of my awful horrific email blunder!) and they've offered us a free night. How is 5th November for you? Please come. Me, you, and Cate, as we always do?

I'm so sorry for everything that happened in the way that it did, but please, please, let's talk. I know we both have things to say and address and apologize for. And I really do wish you hadn't posted about it to TikTok. But I really do want to make this right if we can?

Millie xxx

## chapter 9

**Text message from Owen:** Keep thinking about you. Chloe wants to talk. She's coming over tonight. Our wedding favors were delivered today. Flat's full of them. Delivery person was called Millie. Can't make this shit up. O x

The following day, the Flye TV building is heaving, as it often is before a match day—TV crew arriving in dribbles, picking up equipment, OB production trucks being prepped, site passes being organized, call sheets being passed around—and I have spent most of this day so far trying to find an opportunity to talk to Chloe privately, something that is looming large on my list. The *largest*. Especially since Owen's text about the favors. (I do wish he hadn't said he kept thinking about me, though, if only for my own silly little doesn't-know-what's-good-for-it heart's sake. It did nothing for all the shame I feel too.)

And just a few moments ago, the perfect chance to talk to

Chloe—or so I thought—presented itself. As Petra asked me to pop out and grab her a sandwich for lunch, and two freelancers helped themselves to water at the dispenser in the lobby, gossiping loudly (and purposely) about "the wedding cash Chloe's lost, poor cow," I'd seen Chloe herself, out of the window, heading for the tiny café a few buildings down, alone, stretching a hood over her neat, blond head.

So, despite the rain, despite not having so much as a cardigan with me, let alone a jacket, I headed out in it for my break.

But then it all sort of . . . went a bit wrong.

And now I find myself outside that tiny café, in what is now *pouring* rain, as trucks and cars thunder by, spraying the pavement with miniature surf waves. Because Chloe is not alone.

When I pushed open the steamed-up, wooden-framed glass door of the café, Chloe was *right there* in the bustle, but sitting at a table and surrounded by her friends. Leona in IT (Chloe's old colleague) and Samira in Sales, and all three looked up at me as I walked in, like I was a pigeon who'd managed to fly in through an open window and shit all over the saltshakers. I froze, rushed out a takeaway order for Petra to the busy, flustered man behind the counter, and told him I'd wait outside. And with what felt like a whole stadium's worth of eyes on me, I scurried out.

And it is taking forever for the sandwich to appear; be brought out to me here, in this downpour. So long that I'm starting to wonder whether they've forgotten me. I wouldn't blame them. I'm standing as far from the café itself as possible without standing in the middle of the road, shivering and wet, heavy hammering drops of rain stinging my scalp. I must look more like a dog in an abandoned and abused pet charity ad than a woman waiting for her lunch.

Cars speed by behind me, tires sizzling through the rain.

I watch the café door—steamed up from all those full tables, from all the cooking, all the warmth. They'll be out soon, Chloe and her friends, surely. Or maybe Chloe can see me out here. Maybe she'll hold back, wait till I've gone, before she ventures out. I would do the same if I were her. Because, God, she looked *sad*. Pretty, because Chloe Katz just *is*, but also sad. Like someone running on the last 10 percent of their battery.

That's the face I need to remember. Whenever my relentless, stupid heart strikes up, starts thinking about Owen and bloody meant-to-bes and our sleepy Sunday morning lie-ins, how happy my mum would be; how *relieved* she'd be I was doing something she could talk proudly about—that's the face I'll remember. Because I caused that face. And I know what it's like to walk around wearing that face, like a scar. To feel what she's feeling. That awful, awful ache that drains the warmth and hope and life from you.

I fidget. I open and close my phone, which, of course, in Old Nokia fashion, is a quiet screen of nothingness. I check the time. *Where* is Petra's sandwich? If I didn't love her so much and she wasn't already having a bad "balls to the wall" day, as she put it, I'd leave, let them keep the £5.95, return to work, make up a lie about broken toasters at the café, or something, use my wet-through blouse as proof I'd waited and waited for it. But I've ordered now, and I've already waited ten minutes—

Oh. *Great.*

Coming toward me down the street now is a tirade of huge, royal blue, Flye TV–branded umbrellas and a mass of suited and stockinged legs marching beneath them, like a scene from *Reservoir Dogs*. A crowd with a lunch break in their sights. And although I pretend not to look, gazing down at my pointless, sleepy, soaking-wet phone, I spot Paul Foot, his wife, Martha, who always visits on Tuesdays, Ann-Christin, Fundraising Steve, and . . . Jack.

"You watering yourself to grow a couple of inches?" cackles Jolly Postman Paul as they approach, and I laugh, make weird noises that sound a bit like "ha-ha, something like that, yes, yes, that's me!" but my teeth are chattering a bit and raindrops are sliding down my face onto my lips, like tears, so it just comes out like a load of waffle. Painfully, Ann-Christin and Fundraising Steve don't acknowledge me.

The whole group continue walking, semicircling around me on the pavement, like I'm a manhole they need to avoid, but Jack stops.

"Catch you guys up," he says, and he moves to stand opposite me, holds the umbrella above us, casting us in a shadow. He's wearing a slim-fitting, dark khaki green jacket, a crisp, white shirt, and a black tie visible in the slice of his open zip. And, whatever aftershave he's wearing . . . he smells amazing. Something ripples in my tummy at the scent of him.

"Ah. Thank you," I say, eyes lifting to the umbrella above our heads, and then to him. "I didn't—bring a jacket."

"I can see that."

"I didn't realize it was going to rain like this."

"Hm. UK for you," Jack replies gruffly. "And what am I missing here?" He reverse nods, a jut of his stubble-covered chin, toward the café.

"Um . . ."

"What are you . . . queueing for a table or something? Donny Osmond in town?"

I pause. "Donny Osmond?"

Jack laughs—a deep, throaty chuckle that transforms his serious face. "Just wondered if you were waiting for someone to emerge. Someone worth getting this soaked to the bone for?"

"But . . . *Donny Osmond*?"

Jack gives a shrug, a lazy shoulder to one ear. "My nan would queue in a war zone for Donny Osmond. Rain? Child's play."

And that makes me laugh. As soaked, as cold, as hungry as I am, it makes me genuinely giggle. "I'm afraid I'm not waiting for Donny today, no," I tell him. "It's a . . . sandwich."

"A *sandwich* . . ." He ponders, the corners of his eyes crinkling a little.

"Tuna. And it's not even for me," I tell him, crossing my arms, rubbing a hand against my damp, chilly shoulder. I am so uncomfortably cold. "I forgot to order something for me. I just ordered Petra's."

"And you're waiting out here," he says curiously, although it isn't a question.

"That I am, Jack," I say.

"For a sandwich that isn't your own . . ."

"Correct again."

"Petra's tuna sandwich . . ."

And it's then that the café door opens, and there they are—Chloe, Leona, and Samira. Jack gives them a nod, a small dimple of a smile, a casual "hi," and they do the same, their eyes darting between us, but pretending that I'm not actually there. That I don't exist, the pigeon intruder, the wedding wrecker.

And it falls out of my mouth before I've even thought it over. "*Chloe?*"

All three of them stop on the wet pavement, rain sheeting down, and I stride away from Jack, from beneath the safety of the umbrella.

Chloe takes a tiny, tentative step toward me, her two friends standing behind her, staring at me. *Ugh.* If they had lasers for eyes, I would currently be barbecued—charred and overdone.

"I just . . . I wondered if we could talk?" I say as rain pelts my face.

Chloe pulls up the hood of her gray raincoat, her fingers holding the sides of it at her cheeks, painted red nails, chipped. "I—don't think we should, Millie," she says, and her voice—it's sweet really. Musical. Familiar. She'd leave Owen voice notes sometimes, when she'd moved to his team on production and they started working together. Owen would listen smilingly as we cooked dinner or wandered the aisles of Tesco. "Nice girl," he'd say, phone held in front of him in a clasp, as if it was on display. "Up with the lark, always the first on-site, driven. She'll go far, I think." I remember the pang I'd feel in my gut, like a guitar string pulled and twanged. The sting of jealousy and inadequacy that I'd shake away, telling myself off, that Owen was right; how could I *possibly* say I was in a solid, trustworthy relationship if I got jealous when my boyfriend spoke nicely about other women, and team members at that?

"I spoke to Owen," I tell Chloe, over the loud bleep of a reversing truck, the white noise of rain. "And he said—he said about the wedding? That you'd . . . stayed with your parents, and I just want you to know that I didn't mean *a word* in that email—"

"Can we not, please?"

"Nothing happened," I say, my words rushed and desperate. "Honestly, it didn't. It was one silly chat by my desk, and I sent such a stupid, drunken email—"

"I . . . I really don't want to talk about this, Millie," says Chloe, her cold, blue eyes dropping to the pavement. She can't even look at me. "This is . . . this is all really raw for me—"

"I understand. I really, really do—"

"I just—"

"Nothing happened. I just need you to know nothing happened."

"Come on, Chlo," calls out Samira, three clipped, protective words, an invisible shield spoken into the air, and Chloe gazes at me for a pained, resentful, heartbroken second, and I recognize it. That drained, nothing-left dullness in the eyes. Heartbreak. What's left once you've handed your fresh, full, hopeful heart to someone, and it's been returned, like old end-of-day picnic food.

Leona takes her arm. "Come on," she says, and they turn,

hooded heads hunched, walking quickly away in a line like paper dolls.

I feel shame flood my face. My heart feels as though it falls to my ankles.

Jack appears beside me, raindrops falling on my head, and then suddenly not, as he positions the umbrella over me.

"And that's also why I was out in the rain," I say, watching them walk away. "Like a bit of a loser."

"Nobody here's a loser," Jack replies calmly.

Rain spits against the taut fabric above us, and there's a beat of silence.

"You hungry?" he asks.

"Me?" I ask pointlessly. "I . . . I dunno . . ."

Jack raises his eyebrows, just a dart of them—up, then down.

"Yes," I admit. "OK, yes, I am. And cold. Hungry and cold. A rubbish combo."

And his hazel eyes drop to his jacket, just for a fraction of a second, and I think he might offer me it to wear, but he doesn't—*of course* he doesn't. I'm a rained-on, bedraggled receptionist, and he is one of my bosses. He's simply doing what any good chief operations manager would do for a down-on-her-luck, weather-beaten, sad member of staff. Right?

"You ever been to BackDonald's?" he asks.

"Have I ever . . . *What?*"

"Strange diner place around the corner," he says. "My mate who works just over there in the timber yard? He calls it BackDonald's. Back-alley McDonald's?"

I smile despite myself, despite how embarrassed I feel that Chloe wouldn't speak to me; that her friends ushered her away like I was a school playground bully; that it happened in front of cool, together Jack Shurlock. "And does it taste how it sounds?"

"Better," he says. "Like a . . . Big Mac with a criminal record."

I nod. "Like a . . . Big Mac you wouldn't want to take home to your mum?" I offer, and Jack gives a slow smile.

"Exactly," he says. "They might just let you in with a vision like that." And as a waitress dashes out of the café holding Petra's sandwich in a white paper bag high in the air like a flag, Jack says, "Let's drop this first. Then . . ."

"Dark Web Big Mac."

*chapter 10*

*B*ackDonald's (or Bob's, as it's really called) is like stepping into a time warp. It's a tiny little slice of a café, between a bathroom showroom and a garden wholesaler, and as if its location wasn't random enough, inside it's like someone pressed a big button and froze time in 1968. The tables are thick sheets of Formica-like plastic, curving down at the edges, and the chairs are padded with squeaky yellow pleather, the backs like one thick arch of gray, paint-sprayed metal. It reminds me of a retro Wimpy restaurant, or a forgotten Little Chef diner that never got a refurb, and on the wall above where Jack and I are sitting, at a two-seater table that is nailed to the floor, there's a lone, contextless framed portrait of Elvis sweating into a microphone.

"This is . . ." I whisper.

"Mm-hm," says Jack, turning a laminated rectangle menu over in his hand.

"Like, it's . . . I feel like I'm stuck in a dream or something. A movie. Who's that director who does all the artsy, colorful—"

"Wes Anderson." A smile tugs the corner of Jack's mouth. "And I agree."

"It's all the yellow, I think? The yellow walls, the—oh, wow, yellow *ceiling*."

We order—two cheeseburgers and two drinks; a mug of tea for me, an espresso for Jack—from a waitress who looks like my nan, and within moments, the drinks are plonked in front of us as if they were already there, waiting in the wings for us.

I sip; take a deep breath.

This is *a lot*, isn't it? And also, unexpected. Not only me, drinking tea in a (very) wet ruffled lilac blouse Cate convinced me was "really in right now," the puff of the heater in the weird diner's ceiling slowly drying my frizzing hair, but Jack Shurlock sitting opposite me, sipping his espresso, the cup small in his large hand. I'm not sure what this is, really. But I'm grateful to him. The way he stopped for me, the way he asked no questions when Chloe emerged from the café. The way he suggested this place. Warmth, and lunch, but tucked away from everyone else.

"There's only twenty minutes left of my lunch break," I tell him across the quiet table. "Do you think we'll have enough time?"

Jack gives a shrug. "What're they going to do?"

"Erm, fire me?"

"Yeah, well, you're with me, so—we'll just make something up." Jack smiles slowly at me over his espresso cup.

OK, I know he's being all Kind Colleague, but he *is* hot, isn't he? It's that cool, mysterious edge he has. Lin once orchestrated a really poor Mr.-and-Mrs.-style quiz on a charity day, just to quiz Jack on his love life. The whole office discovered, after Jack sat back-to-back with another member of staff—a mere pawn in Lin's game—that he was "single," "dates sometimes," and his last girlfriend lasted four months and he met her when she sat next to him on a train and borrowed his phone charger. He eventually got off the "hot seat" (a computer chair with a printed A4 piece of paper labeled "hot seat" in Times New Roman, stuck to the backrest) when Lin asked him if he'd ever sent a "sexy photo" to someone. He'd laughed, swiped a hand under his chin in a cutting motion, and said, "What sort of game is this?" then, "And for the record, because it's for a good cause . . . *only when asked*," and the whole office floor had burst into laughter as he smirked and walked away.

"Make something up?" I ask him.

"Yeah, I'll just say I wanted to, um . . ." He gestures with a blasé hand. "Quiz reception about the visiting process. Bring it up to date. Get your take."

"Reusable entry passes, if you're asking," I reply. "Like the ones we have, but for visitors."

"Mm. I'm always losing my passes . . ."

"I just think it would be good for the planet and the company."

"Right. Well, there we go then, Millie. We've got a solid alibi." He sips as two men in high-vis jackets bundle in, dripping with rain.

"Long day, John." One of them yawns as the other says, "Yiiiip."

Jack leans back easily in his chair. "So, I found a—forum post?"

"Oh?"

"Mm." Jack always looks at ease wherever he is. The opposite of chaotic rainy, dog-charity-advert me. The way one shoulder is thrown back a little, how he rubs the edge of his stubbly jaw, with a thumb and finger, shoulders always square and open. "It was regarding your . . . technical problem."

"*Technical problem*," I repeat. "Polite way of putting it."

"There aren't many," he carries on, "but this one particular post—a couple of people had the whole email draft thing happen to them. Something similar, anyway."

"Jesus, *really*?" And that makes me feel a little better. To know there are other people out there who might have felt the way I did in the boardroom that morning. I wonder if they're walking around with Nokia bricks, standing in the rain waiting for exes' exes. Maybe we could start a sad little club.

Jack nods. "And I know you didn't want to go down the whole *how* route, keep the whole thing dragging out, but I've forwarded the posts to my coder nerd mate, anyway."

"Oh. Well. Thank you," I say as a low, bubbling sizzle of something cold being lowered into hot oil comes from the kitchen's hatch behind me. "I'm just trying to . . . move on. Right it all, instead. Control what I can control."

Jack gives a tiny tilt of his head to one side. "You said sorry," he states with a shrug. "And the cakes yesterday. They didn't deserve the cakes."

"Steve said good morning to me after the cakes," I tell him. "Although he ignored me just now . . ."

"Millie, Steve spends his working day tweeting creepy stuff to Cheryl Cole or whatever her name is and reviewing IPAs. He should be . . . I don't know, in a *zoo*."

I burst out laughing, and Jack chuckles, then clamps his straight teeth together, like *maybe* he shouldn't have said that.

"Comforting stuff to hear about the head of IT," I comment. "And from the operations manager no less . . ."

"Chief of staff, too, now, thank you, Millie," he says, smiling slowly, a little crescent-shaped dimple prodding his cheek beneath stubble. "Well. That's until they invent something else and add that on too. But hopefully I'll have left again by then."

"Chief of staff *does* sound a bit made up."

"And that's because it is," replies Jack, like he's dropping a well-known fact. "Just made up one day by another person. Another human being. Like most things. Most things in life are just . . . made up."

"*Are* they?"

"Yup," he says simply with a shrug. "You name it."

"So, what, like . . ." I scan the café as the Nan Waitress dumps a balled-up napkin into a large barrel of a bin. "A . . . bin."

Jack cocks his head, a rain-damp lock of his hair, the color of wet sand, dangling over his eyes. "Made up," he says, swiping it away. "Someone went, 'We need somewhere to keep our rubbish so we don't live like pigs,' and they made a box, called it a bin, and now we're like, 'Oh, well, we've *got* to have a *bin* . . .' "

"Is this a way of telling me you . . . don't have *a bin*?"

"No," he replies, meeting my eyes. "I'm pretty prolific on the bin front, Millie. One in every room." And his mouth twitches.

And w*hy* oh why did that make my stomach turn over? Hunger pangs? It must be. There is no situation on earth where discussing bins feels hot, but with Jack it . . . somehow does? It's the ease. The sparkle in his eye, the way he knows exactly who he is.

Oh, what am I doing? Getting a crush on the man who is essentially my boss?

My sexy dream email strides into my brain and says, *Er, you already had a crush.*

Silence expands between us now, and distant, hushed arguing comes from the kitchen. Jack pulls out his work phone, which is vibrating, and he taps away, his serious work face back on, and the tiniest of sinking feelings slumps in my chest as I take in his face. The mouth that's always pouty at rest, the shadow of stubble, the three small, almost-invisible flecks of freckles on his left cheekbone. Because—well, I wish I wasn't *this* person, I suppose. The woman who has publicly made a bit of a mess of her life. Weddings and relationships called off, colleagues gossiping, parents worriedly texting, friends posting about her on TikTok. The woman who was too scared to go into a café so chose to get soaked in the street, despite having a people-facing role to fulfill for another four and a half hours, and is now here with a handsome man, who has actually been briefed about her at work like a plumbing problem, and who feels a bit sorry for her, so has taken her to lunch. How did it all go from quiet and under the radar to weird and complicated? How did *I* get so weird and complicated? One big email glitch, I suppose, is the logical answer, but then, why *did* I have so many drafts? How did I get here? From . . . there.

"Do you think I'm out of my mind?" tumbles from my lips, as if the words have wrestled their way out of my mouth to gasp for air.

Jack's thumb pauses on his phone screen, his eyes flicking up to meet mine. He says nothing.

"You know." I lower my voice. "Writing the emails, yes, but hiding behind Gary Lineker. Chloe. The *cakes . . .*"

Jack watches me for a second with those intense, hazel eyes, then says simply, "No. I don't think you're out of your mind. Not at all. But I do think you're dragging yourself through the mud unnecessarily."

"You do . . ."

He nods, just once.

"But—I sent an email to a man who's about to marry someone, and now he *isn't* getting married. That's *awful,* isn't it? And people at work who used to speak to me *don't,* or they're acting weird with me, gossiping about me like I'm a—I don't know. Dark ogre? You saw them all outside the café—"

"But so what?" Jack shrugs, and it takes me by surprise, that nonchalant, almost harsh "so what?"

I gaze at him across the table and a disbelieving burst of laughter puffs from my mouth. "*So what?*"

"Yep. So what?" Jack looks at me. His eyebrows lift upward, a silent "Well?"

I scoff—a puff of air from my nostrils. "I don't think I've ever felt so what?" I say. "Actually, I think it's that I haven't felt so what for so long that it just *feels* like never. I feel the opposite of so what actually, most of the time, whatever that is."

"And what is that?"

"Like, I . . . need to make sure everything's OK, at all times?" I offer. "Plus, how can I feel at all *so what* at the moment when I'm waking up day to day and suddenly not knowing what to expect?"

"But why do you need to know what to expect?" asks Jack quickly.

"Um." I stare at him across the table, words gathering, jamming in my throat. And I laugh again. With confusion. With amusement at his disarming questions. "I . . . don't know. Because I . . . I've come to *like* knowing what to expect."

Jack shakes his head. "Overrated," he says.

"*Is it?*"

Jack gestures with a hand at us, sitting here at BackDonald's, at this little table, below the portrait of Elvis. "Yeah," he says. "Everything's better when it just . . . happens."

I smile. "Is that why you're leaving again soon, then?" I wrap my still-cold hands around the chunky white mug on the table. "Away from the shackles of Flye and knowing what to expect? Of call sheets and Chatty Martin and being . . . forced to have a bin?"

"*Mute Martin*, you mean," he says with a smile. "And yeah, I— suppose so? It was always temporary, coming back here. Needed the money, and they always have me back, so . . ." And he gives a "So why not?" smile. A total *so what* smile.

"So that's why you're here. It's money to go traveling again?"

"That's the aim, yeah," he says easily. "My mate Enam and me. He's going a bit earlier than me, and I'm meeting him out there. No real plans except Quebec this Christmas, then New Zealand. We're staying on an alpaca farm somewhere actually."

"Seriously?"

"One of Enam's bucket-list things?" Jack laughs warmly. "I dunno.

His thing." And there's love in that laugh. I bet Jack's a good friend. I bet he's all backslaps and hugs and "Here for you, man." "But yeah. Few months on the move, and we'll just—see how it goes. No plan."

"No expectations," I say.

"Zero."

And something coils then in my gut. So much so, I find the palm of my hand moving to rest there, on top of my damp blouse. Is it jealousy? Admiration? To be able to be someone like Jack, who sees work as just money. Life, a game to be played. Someone who's about to go out into the world to explore with no plans, nothing keeping him here. I wonder if he has exes and a story about a broken heart. I wonder if his parents have hopes for him that he's dashing. I wonder if he has unsaid secrets, or whether he's dating at the moment. I wonder if he and Jess have kissed. I keep thinking about how—*energetic* it was between them yesterday. A little spark of that same Christmas party zing between us, maybe. But then, Jack's so free and easy, maybe he just zings all over the place, just has hot one-night stands on beaches or intense weeklong love affairs on mopeds in Italy, full of passionate kissing and "I wish I didn't have to leave you, but the sea is calling me, *mi amore*." I bet traveling with Jack is fun. All ease and calm spontaneity . . .

"So, an alpaca farm . . ." I repeat, shaking myself out of my daydream. "That's pretty niche."

"You know those strange things you just have in your head as wanting to do someday?" asks Jack. A song begins to play in the diner. Something I expect is from the fifties. Grainy, banjo-like guitars, muffled vocals. I almost wouldn't be surprised if we suddenly discovered we'd fallen through time and space itself, here, in Backdonald's. What I wouldn't give, actually, to discover this place *is* a time machine. I'd certainly press all the knobs and buttons that lead back to a life B.E.

"That's one of Enam's things," says Jack. "The alpacas? Mine is . . .

well, loads of stuff. Like, have a regular, bog-standard, family Thanksgiving in the US. Like the movies. Not sure why. Just is."

"Rhubarb farm," I say with a smile.

Jack looks at me, eyebrows raised. "Rhubarb farm?"

"That's one of mine," I tell him. "A—a forced rhubarb farm?" and I'm surprised how easily that just left my lips; rolled out, a whole, solid, rounded truth. Donk. Just like that. One I have never told anyone before. And I realize then that I used to have so many of these things. I'd daydream them up during lectures when I was at university (during the eighteen months I spent really *trying* to make "fine art" and university life feel like "me" before I left) or talk about them with Alexis on our breaks outside in the alleyway when we first met at the pub. She'd smoke, leaning against the heavy, burgundy fire door of the kitchen, talk passionately, hungrily, about how she'd turn everything around for her hardworking dad and younger sister now that her mum had left them, get a permanent position after her sales internship ended, pay off her debt, clear her dad's mortgage someday (and she did, on all counts). And I'd listen, throw lots of things out there, too, like wishes, into the night sky, imagine them wisping off, like her cigarette smoke. See Rome. Kiss someone in the rain. Learn to speak German in Germany. Take a cookery class in France. *Make* something someday that means something to someone. Like Mum does, with the illustrations she creates; children's books and charity campaigns. Just . . . find out who I am. That was the aim. But then came job to job, rent to rent, Owen and heartbreak and . . . life, I guess. The way it sort of sucks you in, sometimes, turns days into years, morphs "someday" into "oh, I *wish*."

"That's an interesting one," says Jack. "The rhubarb. And . . . forced?"

"Watched a documentary on it once. This bloke just walked quietly around this rhubarb farm in the dark with a candle, and it just seemed so . . . peaceful. They trick it into growing? By keeping it in the dark."

"Ah, yeah, I think I know what you're talking about." Jack sips from his espresso. "In kind of—candlelit sheds?"

"Yeah," I say. "I don't know, I just found it really interesting. Cool. I kind of like learning new stuff. Seeing new things. Giving your brain something totally new to chew on, like *Voilà, not seen this before, have you?*" And it feels—*nice*, just saying it, throwing it out there, something Owen used to find a bit "sad," like he often did with recipes I'd bookmark or hobbies I'd want to try, taster courses on Groupon I'd share with him as he'd screw his face up. There was always this sense I should want something bigger. But Jack. He just listens. Accepts it.

"Iceland's one of my places, too, where I've always wanted to go," says Jack thoughtfully.

"Slovenia for me," I remark. "Oh, and Brazil. I've always really wanted to go to Brazil. I reckon you can start again in Brazil. I could have a totally new beginning and change my name there, and everyone is far too romantic and cool to care enough to ask questions."

Jack chuckles huskily. "And why would you have to change your name exactly?"

"Well, what feels like the entire *world* has been contacted by Millie dot Chandler, so . . ."

"Well, maybe you just need a new email address," suggests Jack.

"Chandler *dot* Millie," I say, and I full-on blush then, remembering that email I sent to Jack before he was a Shurlock *dot* Jack. God, can you imagine if he'd got it? *Awful.* I cannot bear even the thought of it. I'd have just had to throw myself into the sea then, two emblematic computer chairs strapped to my feet.

"*Two cheeseburgers.*" A chef in whites and gray tracksuit bottoms places down our food with a singsongy voice. Oh, it smells *amazing.*

Of chip fat and caramelized, charred meat. Oh my goodness, how will I eat this without looking like a barbarian in wide-legged trousers?

"This looks *incredible,*" I say. "And I have"—I glance up at the yolk-yellow Wes Anderson clock on the wall—"precisely seven minutes to eat it."

"No," replies Jack gruffly. "We're having a made-up meeting, Millie. Remember?"

"Oh, yes, that's right. A made-up meeting, with a made-up meal, before we all go back to the made-up constructs of a made-up *office...*"

"Correct," Jack says as I bite into—*oh my God*—the best burger I have ever tasted. "Our place of work: the proverbial bin."

*chapter 11*

**Text message from Owen:** At the Peterboat. Bit drunk. But do you remember we came here and that bloke fell off the ledge into the sea and you gave him your cardigan to keep warm and he left with it? You were gutted. Ha ha. So many memories, Mills. X

**Text message from Mum:** Hello Millie. Cousin Rhiannon said you emailed her a lot of strange letters? Is there something going on with your internet perhaps? I also wondered, has Dad been asking after me? No need to mention it to him, I just thought I'd ask. He does worry. Hope we can see you soon? Lunch, perhaps. Mum x

The following weekend, Ralph has a karate class and then work, like he does most Saturdays, and Cate has organized going to a barbecue at Nicholas's sister, Daniella's, who wants to see Cate, show her there are no hard feelings, and that she will "always be family." Reluctantly, Cate has agreed to go, although both of us did worry for a fleeting dark moment this morning, over scrambled eggs in our pajamas, if it might be a ploy to push them back together. Have Nicholas's head pop up from a bowl of hot-dog rolls or something. "Marry me?" spelled out in chipolata sausages. Because people do strange things when they're desperate or sad, don't they? Plus, families are often the forgotten collateral during breakups. When Owen broke up with me, my mum and Owen's mum, Athena, actually met up to discuss it, as if they could *fix it*—stitch us back together as easily as they hem trousers.

And it was thinking about Mum that made me decide only half an hour ago, as Cate left and the flat fell silent, to jump into my car and see her today; spend some time with her while Dad's on shift on an oil rig somewhere in the Atlantic. There's something about this uneasy, messy life A.E. (After Emails) that makes me crave the safety of dependable things. That intangible soothing anchoring that can be felt only by seeing your parents, even if you are the chaotic black sheep, or the defect Dolly of the brood. Plus, Mum might be pretending it never happened, but as per my Millie Chandler Is Not a Monster to-do list, I need to apologize for the "Do you love me despite having nothing to share about me at brunch" email I sent her too.

I stop at M&S on the way—Mum's favorite—and buy one of those warm, already cooked rotisserie chickens and a selection of obscure antipasti that sound more like spells than food. I also pick up a bunch of sunflowers for her shed office and some fancy tea bags. Mum works as an illustrator—mostly children's books. She's mid-project at the moment, which means her large, paint-sploshed desk will be littered with bunches of bright flowers for inspiration and mugs of different fruit teas, all cold and half-drunk, like cups of beautiful dyes. Mum often has this effect on me. I think about what she'll be impressed by more than what I want. "Millie dropped in with a delicious antipasti lunch and some sunflowers," I imagine her texting to her friends or saying to Auntie Vye, in her huge conservatory. I'm not sure "Millie brought over two Burger King Whopper meals and a crocheted coaster she made that looks a bit like a pig's foot" would suit conservatory convos as much. And I wish I didn't care so much. But the Chandlers are sort of . . . poster-like. Mum a successful, award-winning illustrator. Dad an oil-rig drilling engineer who loves every second of his work. Kieran, a bioscientist living in Michigan with his doctor husband. Mum and Dad, perfect first loves and still so enamored. Mum drummed it into us when we were kids to study hard, work hard, *achieve* hard so we'd never have to suffer like she did, growing up with "not a pot to piddle in." And it sounds stupid, I know, but it's like Burger Kings and messing about with craft projects equals absence of respectable careers and fiancés and ambition and purpose and, therefore, failure. Hers, and mine. Milllie. The Failed Chandler.

I pull into Mum and Dad's road, nostalgic and horse-chestnut-tree-lined, and—*oh*, Mum's Ford Focus is pulling out of the cottage's drive.

Ah, shit. I knew I should've called first. But Mum likes surprises. (And also tiny pots of expensive picnic food.)

"Mum!" I call pointlessly. She's probably going to the supermarket or to the gym. I'll call her. If she isn't going far, I can wait at the house for her to get back, or at least tell her I've sorted out some lunch for us. (And maybe she'll post a Facebook status—a chicken on a plate, among all her friends' grandchildren's birth announcements and lawyer children, a status update of "my thoughtful daughter: absolutely not a disappointment.")

I pull over, take out my ridiculous Nokia. The phone rings, but she doesn't pick up; she just keeps driving, and, well, *fuck it*: I pull off after her.

There are three cars between us now. The phone keeps ringing on loudspeaker next to me on the seat. It turns over to voicemail, again and again. And there's something oddly thrilling about this. I often get the urge when I drive to just keep going, going, going, let the world open up, like pages of a book. No plans. Like Jack said at lunch on Tuesday. What *would* Jack Shurlock say about that, I wonder. I bet he'd say, "Next time you get the urge to keep going, do it. Keep driving; say, 'So what?' And don't look back. None of it's real anyway." But well, maybe this is starting small. Very small. Following your own parent with nothing but antipasti and an apology to somewhere unknown on a Saturday at noon counts, right? Even if it's just a little?

Mum drives, and I continue following, continue trying to call.

It is *strange* she isn't answering, though. Mum always has her phone connected to the in-car screen. Calls cutting through Joni Mitchell or her beloved Absolute Radio.

We pass her favorite little Sainsbury's, then her gym, and then we're into a country lane—one of those narrow, one-vehicle sorts that make you hope beyond hope there isn't another car—or please, God, not a van—coming in the opposite direction. *Where* is she going? And I'm not sure why, but something lands now in the pit of my stomach. Something hot and uneasy. Maybe it's because of their ever-so-slightly weird texts inquiring about each other, the way Dad was asking me about Easter. But all parents are strange, offbeat texters most of the time, right? Isn't that just classic "parents" for you?

Our row of traffic slows as a rusty, rumbling tractor signals into a side road, and ah, fuck it—James Bond, I could never be. I beep the horn. She'd know my little red car anywhere. But all that happens is the man in front of me twists in his seat, bewildered. His lights? His doors? Corpse hanging off the bumper? (Hypervigilant twenty-nine-year-old in a car with an M&S rotisserie chicken melting into a bit of a panic because her mum is simply . . . driving somewhere she doesn't recognize?)

And now Mum is slowing, signaling into a . . . Is that a *country club*?

The man in front is turning in too. And so, of course, I follow.

Why isn't she answering my calls?

I glance at what is starting to become the emblematic chicken on the passenger seat, sweating in its little plastic-handled bag. And maybe it's gut feeling, that hot uneasiness growing inside me. Some sort of deep spiritual knowing Ralph often talks about. The intangible feeling that precedes something going wrong. Because I feel like I want to hold back a little. Or turn around altogether. Pull into a turnoff, eat the chicken on the side of the road, forget I ever came . . .

But I keep going.

Golfers stroll from a huge sandstone estate that comes into view, others straggled on the lawn, pastel blues and khaki beiges; golf carts lined up in the car park.

Then Mum stops; parks slowly by a stout brick building. It's nothing at all like the grand Darcy-esque mansion we just passed. This looks like somewhere you might go to vote, or to attend a small wedding reception. The sort of place that smells like churches and margarine sandwiches.

I pull up, too, switch off my engine.

I should get out. Shout, "Mum! Ha-ha! Hi! It's me! I was coming to visit! I've been following you! What do you say to eating some charred artichokes in artisan dressing in the late-summer sun?" But I can't. Why can't I move?

Mum gets out of the car and . . . she is definitely not dressed for the gym. She's wearing a dress that's very her. Beautiful, strange, and lime-colored. Art teacher meets Woodstock, 1972.

She looks down at her phone, and I wait for her to see the string of missed calls from me, her daughter, and call me back. But she doesn't. She just . . . slips her phone back into her handbag and—

A man.

A man appears. He's tall. Super tall. Six-four, perhaps, Dad's age. He smiles at Mum, and they start speaking. Mum nods, and nods again. She rubs the side of his arm, and he turns, pushes open the glass door of the squat brick building, and she begins to follow. Who even is he? A friend? A new friend I've never ever met?

I step out. Converse shoes crunching on gravel.

"Mum? *Mum?*"

Mum swoops around, an almost-twirl, not even letting a beat pass. And her face—it falls. Her large, bright eyes widening, the corners of her mouth wilting.

"Millie? What are you . . . I . . . What's going on?"

"I was going to surprise you," I call, walking toward her, breeze lifting my hair from my shoulders. "At home, but I saw you drive away. I called . . ."

Mum stares, says nothing. The man has disappeared inside.

"I . . ." She trails off. She's wearing lipstick. She's wearing the necklace Dad bought her for her fiftieth birthday—the owl one. It sits at her heart, flipped the wrong way, eyes shielded.

And for a moment, I hope she'll just say it's the gym. A new swimming pool she takes aqua aerobics at, introduce me to this new friend, say, "For God's sake, darling, your face! What on earth do you take me for?"

But then she closes the gap between us quickly, says, "Does your dad know you're here?" and then, "Look, why don't we go home, Millie? Just so I can explain?"

And something rolls over in my chest, like a boat caught by a sudden wave and overturned.

"It isn't what you think, Millie," Mum says. We're sitting now, as if the last fifteen minutes of Janky James Bond car following never happened, at the old picnic table in Mum and Dad's leafy semicircular garden. And all I can think is a) what the hell is going on? And b) if it isn't "what I think," then why the big drama? Why send me back here, drive in two separate cars back to the cottage to talk, if it's nothing? Nobody sits their daughter down to talk privately if it's just "So, I thought you should know, I've taken up a wee spot of aqua aerobics."

I'd arrived first, burst through the stifling cottage to the garden. And Mum, remote as ever, had said nothing as she crossed the trimmed, football-field-like lawn, and sat down.

"I'm sorry I couldn't explain there," Mum says shakily. "It would've been . . . difficult to. I was seeing someone. Visiting. It's a very— private place."

"Visiting? The . . . tall guy?"

"No." Mum shakes her head, teardrop amber earrings at the side of her head swaying like a clock's pendulum. "No, no, that's . . . that's Jimmy. I was visiting his brother. Julian."

And then there is silence. Strange, empty silence. Mum always thinks before she speaks or *does.* Considers it all, lines it up in her head, like she does with her work—thinks and thinks about a scene before sketching a single line. But right now it feels painful, these considered, careful spaces before her words. Like everything I know about my mum is suspended in midair, and at any moment the rope holding it up could be cut.

Then she says, "Millie, Julian . . . is my ex-husband."

Something drops through my body. A shot put off a cliff.

What? *What* did she just say? Husband? *Ex-husband?*

"Before your dad—"

"*Julian?*" is all that manages to come out of my mouth, because— Julian. Julian. *Julian.* I've never heard her speak about a Julian. Not once. The name isn't even vaguely familiar. And . . . *ex-husband?*

"I've . . . You . . . what?"

Silence.

"You—you never told me you were married before. Before *Dad*?"

Well. She was right when she said "it's not what you think" because Mum. *My mum.* My mum with my dad, her first love. My mum with an *ex-husband*? I feel stuck, like a tripping CD.

"I know," says Mum, her eyes glistening. "I know I didn't."

"But—you . . . *what*? This is . . . You never told us."

And then there is more silence. I could growl with frustration. Do some sort of Heimlich maneuver on her, bring up the words she isn't saying.

"How . . . how long were you married?"

"Four years."

"*Four years?*" I sound slightly hysterical now, but—how could she have never mentioned it in twenty-nine years? Mum is *Dad's* wife. Mum and Dad are two people who just *are*, as one, as if they just manifested on earth, an adult couple. And to think she was someone else's wife once? Before me. Before Kieran and this cottage and everything I've always, always known. And she's visiting him? *Why?* "Does—does Dad know? About being married before?"

She nods, brings a delicate hand to the owl chain at her freckly chest. "Of course he does."

"And does he know about . . ." And I look up at her.

She says nothing. Ah. I see. Of course.

Sweet barbecue smoke billows from next door, and an Oasis song plays. Someone laughs loudly, and there's a splash—a paddling pool probably. A simple Saturday, the last days of summer, playing out next to . . . whatever *this* is.

"Your dad doesn't know I was visiting," says Mum finally, and my heart shrivels like dried fruit. "And I feel awful for lying, Millie, believe me, I do, but it isn't *anything*, and I have not made that decision lightly."

"What is it then? I . . . I don't get it, Mum. If you're not—I don't know, having some sort of, ugh, I don't know. *Affair*"—oh God, that word tastes horrible in my mouth—"then why are you lying to Dad? To actual *Dad*—"

"*Millie.*" Mum grabs my hand. Laughter floats over from next door. "I am *not* having an affair. I promise. Where you saw me," she says, swallowing, "that's a care home. A respite care home that Julian is in. He's . . . very ill. Dying."

And now, I just stare at her. Because—how am I even supposed to feel? I didn't even know this person existed five minutes ago, and now he's dying and Mum looks heartbroken, but all I can think about is Dad. Mum and Dad. Traditional, solid, simple Mum and Dad who fit like tongue and groove. Mum, a creative, loves a silent house, the company of her own mind. Dad, restless, someone who never sits still, can never go a day without *doing something*, needing somewhere to be. A two-person symphony. Dad a strong drum; Mum a soft, subtle melody ribboning the beats. First loves, they always say, "And then we got married and had you both," as if it was just that easy. As simple as a checklist. A Chandler checklist.

Except apparently, it's not that simple. It's never been that simple. And my chest feels empty. Like something deep with strong roots has been pulled from me, the sting lingering.

"He has months, if luck is on his side," says Mum. "And his brother Jimmy reached out to me on Facebook. He said Julian had been . . . asking for me." Her voice breaks a little then, and tears glisten in tiny blobs in the corners of her eyes, yet my heart feels suddenly hardened. "And—well, he's always had troubles. Big ones I thought back then that I could fix. Alcohol. He was destructive . . ."

I pull my hand from hers, cross my arms across my chest. "Dad talks about how obsessed you were with the white dress . . ." I say, trying to hold on to what feels like hundreds of thoughts and memories and anecdotes our family is built upon, before they're gathered up by the wind. "How you'd always been shy, but the massive white dress said otherwise, and . . . Did you have a white dress with Julian?"

"Millie, please."

"Sorry, I just . . . This is all so *weird*, Mum. Like, *so* weird. You're just sitting in front of me and telling me you're lying to Dad, that you had another husband and just *happened* to never mention it—"

"I know—"

"I bought an *M&S chicken*," I blurt, and Mum stares at me, lips parted. "And . . . now I'm here, somehow, learning that—I don't know. Everything you told us wasn't even real?"

And that seems to get her. I almost see it, that crumple of her heart. "Oh, everything was real, Millie. Of course it was real. It *is* real."

"And how long? How long have you been seeing him? Visiting. This . . . destructive ex."

And this feels familiar. It reminds me of rows we'd have when I was a teenager. When I'd sleep in too late, lose homework, wanted to take street dance classes instead of French, like Kieran did; when I quit uni and came home sad and drained. She'd never really say it, she'd even deny it, but Mum carried the disappointment there on her face. And I'd fire things at her as she sat there, calm and stoic and impenetrable. I wanted something—*anything*—from her. To chop it all open like a ripe watermelon, set it free. I sometimes wonder if she's afraid to love me fully. As if were she to love me entirely, as I am, I might stop trying to be the thing she secretly wants me to be.

"Perhaps . . . since the—the spring?" Mum is almost childlike. Like a caught-out teenager. "March."

Oh. March. *Easter.* The email Dad had been confused about . . . "Did you see him on the Easter weekend?"

"Easter?"

"The bank holiday. You told Dad you were with me."

She swallows then. Does a tiny shudder of a nod. Shame drains color from her cheeks. "Millie, I'm sorry—"

"You need to tell Dad. Like, you have to." I feel cold now. As if I'm turning to stone. I'm a university dropout, in a job she never asks about, with hobbies she always seems mildly disappointed by, and yet I was perfect as a pawn to help her craft a perfect little lie. *Let's use Millie as an alibi. She never has anything of worth going on anyway.*

Mum's eyes shimmer in the sunlight, and she reaches for my hand. I retract it, toward my midriff, and she leaves her own where it lands, an inch of tabletop between us, an ant crawling in a crack of the wood.

"I will tell him," Mum says. "I promise, I will . . . just . . . I will soon."

There's a cheer from next door. "Hello!" squeals someone. I imagine the barbecue, families arriving, shirted children with side partings, perfumed people in dresses and sandals and open-collared shirts. Families. Friends. Celebrating a birthday or an anniversary. No lies, no secret lives. I feel jealous. Of their uncomplicated lives. But then—*we* always looked so uncomplicated, the Chandlers, didn't we? Who's to say they don't have all these unsaid things, too? Who's to say they don't have things they're hiding? Ex-husbands and dying lovers?

"I just don't understand why you'd lie," I say. "Dad gets things like this. Dad's a helper, he's . . . kind and—"

She shakes her head rigidly. "Your dad was his friend, Millie. Julian and your dad, they used to be friends back then. He remembers how Julian used to be. What that did to me . . ."

I stare at her, my mother, across the table. I have her brown eyes, her mouth, the pronounced Cupid's bow. We might look the same, but right now, she feels like a stranger. Someone pretending to be my mum. An impostor. "And what, does he still love you?" I ask. "Is that why he asked after you?"

Mum stares at me tearfully. "He says so. But I do not, Millie. I love your *father*—"

"Did you get my email?" And I'm not sure why it comes out then. Something about Mum, of all people, caught in this. The bar she set so high. Another man who loves her. Lying to the man she does love.

"Your email?"

I nod.

And her eyes slide left, then to her lap. She starts fumbling with a flower-shaped button on her dress. "Was it . . . one about brunches?" she asks, a small tight, false laugh in her voice.

"Yes," I say. "I asked if you'd still love me if I continued to be a failure." And I feel I can say anything now. It's like the veneer of everything is cracked and I can see right through.

"I have never said I think you're a failure, Millie," she says, flustered. Then, just when I think she isn't going to say anything else, she adds, stiffening, "But do I want more for you? *Yes.* Yes, I do. But only because I think you're wonderful. I know how much you *could* do. How much you could be."

And I nod. Just once.

I leave after half an hour—feign a pretend dinner with Cate.

When I get home, I drop the entire chicken into the compost bin, throw off my shoes, and sit on the balcony, looking out to sea, eating a tub of charred artichokes with my fingers, no cutlery, getting a mess of oil on my T-shirt. I think of Dad. I think of what Mum said, about what I *could be*, and I let the waves of Leigh drown out the sound of all the unsaid things creaking the floor under our feet, ready to burst through.

chapter 12

**Text message from Brownie Babez:** Your Royal Mail Brownie Babez delivery to Alexis Lee, Canary Wharf, LONDON failed. Reason: code 45: delivery refused

**Text message from Jack:** Hey Millie, if you still have availability, we could really use you at the rugby game tomorrow. 9 a.m. start. No pressure, appreciate this is short notice, but let me know and Petra will forward details. If not, catch you Monday. Jack

This morning, I set five alarms. Yes. *Five* separate alarms, and on the fourth one, Ralph appeared, disheveled, at my bedroom door, pulling his dressing gown around his midriff. "Is everything all right?" he asked. "It sounds like a bank vault's been busted in here." And when I told him I was fine, that I just wanted to be absolutely sure I got up early enough to make the rugby game, in my quest to paper over yet another email-induced crack, he gently insisted on making me some coffee.

None of us slept much last night—Ralph, Cate, and I were up talking until midnight. Firstly, about how Nicholas's family put on a barbecue spread to end all barbecue spreads (and then suddenly assembled like an army and tried to convince Cate to change her mind about the breakup over a toffee cheesecake, Cate's favorite, because Nicholas "wants to be a better man"). Then I'd told them about Julian. Ralph had listened carefully. Cate had hugged me, wanted every detail, asked me over and over, as Cate always does, how *I* was doing. I played it down a little, though, the sinking, weird feeling of betrayal in my chest. I felt a bit like the odd one out. Cate is so close to her two brothers and sister and her parents, and although Ralph doesn't see much of his mum, dad, and three sisters, they're all pretty functional. A solid unit, despite it all. Christmases and meals and birthdays. A family of spidered threads, but all anchored and tied at the center. Yet our threads, the Chandlers, at the moment feel like a scatter of Poohsticks. Separate and drifting. Mum, lying; Dad, oblivious; Kieran, thousands of miles away; and me, spinning in a current, with no idea what the hell I'm doing.

It's why I jumped at the chance of the rugby game. As I sat on the balcony, the sun slowly dipping into Leigh's glittering estuary, all of us nursing cold beers at Ralph's little rattan table, blankets around our shoulders, it had been a little beacon, that text from Jack. A distraction. And something productive, something *brand-new*, instead of sitting feeling shameful, wondering just how calm my life would look had the emails not been sent; wondering how Chloe's feeling, what's happening within the walls of her and Owen's cinema-converted flat; if Alexis misses me. (Or why she refused the brownies I sent to her work.)

And sport and TV may not be where my heart is, like Owen's is, or people like Michael Waterstreet's, but maybe it *could* become so? If I learned enough, if I moved a bit up the ranks, perhaps, found a little drive for it . . .

Although I have to say, this isn't exactly riveting, or what you might expect from glitzy live TV and exciting, important sports games. Because, after parking up in a dusty, hard-grounded car park, I now stand in the grounds of the StoneX rugby stadium itself, and it's . . . *dead.* The angular, brown, wood-paneled building stands tall and quiet, like a community college or a hospital, and although there are a scattering of people at the entrance—fans, I assume—I can hardly see any evidence that Flye TV is even broadcasting here at all.

I dial Petra's number. "I'm here, but I think I'm in the wrong place? I just parked in what is basically an empty, dusty field."

"*Oh,* bloody hell, Millie," says Petra, "you're at the front. Sorry! We're all over the other side, at the back. I know where you are. Stay there, I'll come and get you."

Within five minutes, Petra is strolling up in straight-legged acid-wash jeans, starch-white Converse, and an oversize orange T-shirt, half tucked in, and it suddenly feels a bit "school trip." It's been a while since I've seen Petra in anything except office gear, and there's something a bit exciting about it. A little adventure, in a mini heat wave.

And I wonder if Jack's here. He doesn't attend all the matches he organizes staff for, but . . . I do hope he is. I've thought about our chat at BackDonald's every day since it happened. The ease, the conversation about Brazil and alpaca farms. The "so what?" The gentle hope of it.

"Thank you so much for coming, my love," says Petra, squashing her cheek to mine. "I'm so sorry, I should've said we have to go around the back. With the vans, the lorries, yadda, yadda, yadda. This is the people-facing, nice side. We're out the back with the bins."

"I like your hair band," I tell her, and she smiles, her eyes sliding away from me shyly.

"Ah, Kira got it for me when she was in Frankfurt," she replies, then she points to the fabric squished among her bouncy curls. "It's, um, covered in pickles. She . . . calls me her pickle?" She lets out a little embarrassed groan through a huge grin. "Ah, I dunno, it's *silly.*"

"It's not silly, it's adorable," I say. "Surely all of us want to be someone's pickle."

Petra laughs. "Some people want to be *everyone's* pickle."

"Yes, and they're the ones who ruin it for the rest of us."

Petra leads us through cold, echoey corridors, and I am struck by how *unlike* glamorous sporting grounds it is in here. From the outside, it's all sleekness and shiny stands. All muscular players and cool sportsmen grit. But here it's almost office-like. Bland and gray, the smell of new carpets and vending-machine coffee. The walls are stamped with framed prints of historic matches, between neat signs pointing to "Studio One" and "Player Entrance." It feels like a big machine. A big ol' oiled, shiny machine, just to get a singular rugby match to air, before everyone switches off or goes home again.

"OK, so full disclosure," says Petra, her voice dipping. "And don't panic . . ."

And of course, I panic. It's automatic that you do panic when someone says *don't panic.* "Oh, shit, what?"

"Owen is here."

"Oh."

*Great.*

"But he'll be in the truck the entire time, I double- and triple-checked. This game's a big deal and he's director, so, he'll literally be way, *way* too busy doing his thing." Petra looks at me, wide mink-brown eyes scanning me for a sniff of how I might be feeling.

"Right," I say, trying very hard to keep poker-faced. "Well—"

"And Chloe's finishing in ten minutes," she adds quickly. *Ouch.* Another Band-Aid ripped off with a sting. "She's been here hours, so you won't see her either. She's leaving soon. Triple-checked that too. I've got you."

"Oh. Good," I say, worry simmering inside me like lava. But, well, maybe it's a *good* sign if they're working together. Maybe the wedding's back on? Maybe they've just brushed my email under the carpet as a silly thing that happened, and I can go back to . . . what? Brushing *my own* feelings into the same dark place? What's the plan beyond that? And now I can't remember why exactly I agreed to this at all. Because this was always a possibility, being stuck working with my ex and his maybe-new-wife-to-be. But Owen's been busy with the cricket games, and Chloe was in for a planning meeting about bloody *wrestling* of all things, on the day I bombarded her outside the café. She was not on my radar for today at all.

"These things are so big and busy, you won't see anyone, really," Petra continues, all wide eyes and hand gestures, as if to pull as much reassuring energy into our conversation as she can. *"Especially* out on the field with Marshal. That's where you'll be. With Marshal on camera two."

A silver lining at least. Marshal is one of the freelance cameramen who works for Flye, and I *love* him. In a normal, nonromantic, wish-he-was-my-second-dad way, obviously. In the spring, I assisted him at some events to help Petra out due to some freelancers who had bailed, and he'd been so kind and patient. He taught me how to set up a camera, how to focus, the difference between a good shot (his) and a bad one (mine). He even brought me lunch in on the second day—a little Thermos of the best lentil dal I've ever eaten in my life. Marshal. I will simply stick with Marshal, and everything will be *fine.*

Petra pushes open a door, weaves us left, and just like that, a swarm of warm, September breeze hits us. Fresh-cut grass, a slight tinge of woodsmoke; an autumnal amuse-bouche. And at the end of the arch we stand at the foot of is a huge expanse of green space.

"The player tunnel." Petra grins excitedly. "Cool, huh? We're literally walking down the same path the players will."

And walking through the tunnel *is* cool; the way it opens up its mouth to the wide, green sea of the rugby field. There are people *everywhere*. Crew milling and gathering; people wearing headsets, some holding iPads, others with equipment and cameras and leads and tripods all safely contained inside the borders of the stands and on the outskirts of the safety ropes, warning people off the grass.

Petra's right. This is huge. Even if Owen is floating about somewhere, I probably won't see him.

"Give me a sec, my love," says Petra, tapping away on an iPad. "I just need to send this off to the truck . . ."

"Sure." I nod. "Just let me know what to do and when." Something easy, I think as I gaze around, because I know I'm here to *work*, but I'd quite like to press a big pause button, freeze everyone, freeze time, and wander around. Explore. That's what this shiver in me is, I think. Newness. Like life has opened up a little crack in a door and is saying, "It's been waiting for you all along, you know."

"Right! I'll get your pass from Jack," says Petra with a smile. "And then we'll find Marshal. He'll be delighted to see you."

Marshal *is* delighted to see me, and he even lets out a little cheer that's lost to the breeze as I jog over to the far corner of the field. Marshal's been set up to film by one of the posts, and the entire stadium is in a huge window of sun. I do regret wearing these jeans. It's almost October, but I'm *sweating*.

"Very good to see you!" He beams as I arrive in front of him, and then he does the most Marshal Chandra thing in the universe. He holds his hand up and cocks his head for me to high-five it. I really like Marshal. He's fifty-two, has four sons, and has recently started the most adorable YouTube channel providing camera tutorials. His intros are like something created on Microsoft Paint, and he holds the camera so close to his face, he looks like he's filming into a spoon, but his subscribers *love* him, and he acts like he's won an Oscar every time someone leaves a "thanks for this!" comment.

Marshal is a helper. Nobody is ever bad, just in pain. He's of the mind that people do mean things only because they're hurt themselves. And he's also one of those baby boomers who refuse to be left behind. Last time I helped him, I found him listening to grime music his son sent him. "It's important, you know," he said, "that you keep up with the new things that are being made. Or you simply stop growing."

Marshal and I catch up as I help him set up the camera—he asks me to check that the focus and zoom are working correctly as he sips from a large, handled reusable cup of sugary tea. He tells me about his eldest son, a newly qualified driving instructor, and about how his wife has gone to visit family in Pakistan, and he's been making her a pantry in the cupboard under the stairs as a surprise. He doesn't mention the emails, and neither do I, and instead he asks about me. How am I, how "the flat with the view" is. And then he holds up a finger and smiles.

"Just a sec, Millie. The truck's testing the link." He presses a finger to the earphone on his headset. "Yep, this is camera two, I can hear you." He stares into the middle distance. "Hello? Camera two, Marshal Chandra over, can you hear me? This is Marshal, camera two . . ." Then he sighs, pulls off the headset, checks it over, and puts it back on. "Plastic toot," he mutters. "Hello, hello, this is camera two, can you hear me? Ah, *bollocks.* They—they can't hear me. The talkback's not working. I can hear them, but . . ." He checks his watch, glances around. "Where's Jack when you need him?"

Jack.

A little crackle of excitement zips through me at the mention of Jack being here somewhere. Petra got my pass from him, but I didn't see him myself. And I've been really *hoping* to see him myself. He's been working on location a lot, since our lovely, unexpected lunch at BackDonald's. It's as if Flye is squeezing every last drop from him, holding on to his tail before he breaks free and flies away.

"Can I do anything?" I ask. "I could . . . wait here while you go and look into it, or speak to Petra?"

"Could you let the truck know?" he asks. "It's just out the back. Just through there, you see that gantry? That walkway below?"

"Umm." Oh God, not *the truck.* Anywhere, lovely Marshal, but the sodding truck. Owen is in the truck.

"Argh, time's getting on a bit too . . ." says Marshal, as if to himself. "Always bloody close to the wire, this gaff. Every. Time." Then he looks up at me, dark eyebrows raised expectantly.

"Truck," I say. "Yes, I'll—I'll go to the truck."

"Superstar." Marshal grins, turning the headset over his hand. "Tell them camera two can hear but the talkback's not working, please."

"Right. OK. Talkback. Sure. *Yes.* OK. *Truck.*" I stare at Marshal, who nods back at me. "Now?"

"Please."

"*Sure.* OK! Great. I'll be as fast as I can."

Of course this has happened. *Of course.* But then—it *is* just Owen, isn't it? And this is in a professional capacity. He'll have other people in the truck, too, other workers. He'll be in director mode. He isn't exactly going to say, "Hello, Millie, come on in, shall we discuss how you still have feelings for me? Sorry, guys, talk among yourselves. PS, did anyone else here see Millie's email to all?" No. Plus, time is marching on, and Marshal needs the issue sorted as soon as possible. What other choice do I have? Just grab my keys and zoom home, when the whole reason I'm here is to make a *good* impression, not an unhinged one?

I follow Marshal's directions, pass a little cluster of crew. Their shirts say "ITV." One of them switches on a microphone—one of those handheld ones the pundits hold, with the little square boxes around the edge. Another smiles at me, and I smile back. I must look normal to everyone here, like I'm someone who knows what they're doing. Not someone who feels like they're walking to the slaughter. An OB truck to many, but to me, a fairground haunted house.

I find the truck pulled up on the tarmac at the side of the building, parked across numerous car parking bays. OB trucks are like a mix of a rock star's tour bus and those temporary classrooms most of us had in secondary school. A long, rectangular, windowless metal trailer mounted onto a truck with steps up to a metal door, and while you might expect a shipping container, inside it's more like something from *Star Trek*. Lines and lines of televisions and computers on the walls, desks of mixing decks, the lights low, lit-up buttons and knobs like an arcade simulator ride.

The door to this one is ajar, and I can hear voices. One of them is *definitely* Owen's. *Good.* He's busy, he's talking to someone else, immersed in work. I can just put my head around the door, tell them all what's going on, and disappear again. Professional. To the point. No chance for Owen to regale me with memories of pub outings when we were so in love that I felt like I could have crawled into his jeans pocket and lived there forever.

I knock.

Nothing.

The muffled talking continues.

I knock again.

*Nothing.*

"Hello?"

I pause, peel back the door, and . . . it all happens at once. As I open the door, reveal myself in the doorway, at that *exact* same time, I hear Owen say, "My *mum* helped choose that ring," and a sweet, familiar voice reply, "You really can never see something as your fault, can you? You can never just *hold up your hands*," followed by Owen's deep laugh, and "That's because none of this *is* my fault," as the light from outside illuminates them both, like a giant spotlight on a stage: Owen and Chloe, in the darkness of the OB truck.

Chloe's face drops. Owen stares, but there's something in his eyes—embarrassment? *Amusement?*—and all I can think to say is, "It's Marshal. He needs help!" as if Marshal has just fallen down a well, before I turn and run back down the steps.

**Text message from Millie:** I WANT TO DIE. KILL ME.

**Text message from Millie:** Chloe is here. As well as Owen!

**Text message from Millie:** And I just walked in on them fighting in a truck!?!??!!?!?!? About the engagement ring (I think!?) and I'm going to have to die, or go into witness protection.

**Text message from Cate:** Oh my God, are you shitting me?

**Text message from Cate:** Hold your head up high, baby. You've done nothing wrong remember. They're the ones arguing at work. Unprofesh.

**Text message from Millie:** Yeah well, I went running off to Petra who has sequestered me away in a tiny studio and now I have to ERECT A SET THING!? Alone. I have no idea what I'm doing. So, I'm certainly not winning either!

**Text message from Cate:** Come home.

**Text message from Cate:** You shouldn't have to be doing this shit anyway. #FreeMillie

**Text message from Millie:** I WISH!!!!

**Text message from Millie:** Just tell me it'll be OK.

**Text message from Cate:** Of course it will! You are amazing, brave, and a ball of beautiful energy. They're lucky to have you. You have GOT THIS!!!

chapter 13

*I* have absolutely not got this. In no way, shape, or form. Not in the slightest.

Despite Petra being a kind and lovely friend and tucking me away in a quiet, hidden-away room as big as my bedroom, with the "simple" (apparently) objective of erecting a screen of sponsorship logos that players will be interviewing in front of, I still wish I was anywhere else. I'd even take being in the truck with Owen and Chloe. I'd even take being in stocks being pelted with old turnips over this.

Because I can't do it.

"It just unravels, like a giant scroll!" Petra had explained, all ease and just-that-simple smiles, mere moments ago. "And you then affix the corners at the bottom, and voilà! Job done!"

But I keep doing exactly that and it keeps *unraveling* back up to the top, like a scroll in sodding reverse, like a cartoon blind where the little cartoon character gets gathered up in it too. My hands are completely scratched up, too, from the sharp metal corners, and it is so *hot* in here.

A vent in the ceiling is relentlessly puffing hot air into the room, and I can't find a way to turn it off. I could cry actually. Right now, I could sob, stamp my feet, knock my fists against the carpet like a toddler in front of the one screen Petra completed as a demo, emblazoned with the words "BELIEVE YOU CAN." Thousands of people will be watching this match. Millions, maybe. And yet, the biggest stars of the game will be interviewed in front of a sheet of plastic a pretender like me is in charge of erecting. You'd think that given all the glitz and glamour of TV, this would be a fancy LED screen or something. At the very least, a glossy, ready-made screen. But then I remember Owen and me watching football on TV one afternoon when we were together, him pointing to a screen behind a pundit's desk and saying, "There'll be some poor knackered crew member eating his sandwich behind that right now."

I take a breath. OK. I can do this. Of course I can.

Unravel like giant scroll. OK, done. Affix the edge to— "Fuck!" The scroll reravels back up, a mad flapping sound, like a crazed bird's wings. I slump to the floor. "See!" I shout to nobody. This is impossible. It *all* feels impossible. Everything. Me, trying to be a member of a bloody crew on my weekends, to show the world I am not Bad with a capital B, to fix it all, to appease—who? Is anyone even watching? Does anyone even care? Owen and Chloe are still arguing in production trucks. Mum is still lying to Dad, my actual parents' marriage wobbling on unpredictable ground. Alexis is still ignoring me. Nothing seems to have actually helped. So maybe it's pointless. Maybe it's all just fucked, and fucked is how it just *is*, and that's that.

I gaze up at the one panel Petra did practically with her eyes closed, not a single hair out of place. Sweat beads at the back of my neck. *BELIEVE YOU CAN!*

I scoff to nobody, to an empty room.

"Believe I can what?" I mutter. "Because I believe, little shitty panel with a mind of its own, that *I can't* actually."

I pull the scroll down a little more.

"So, what do you say to that, eh? What if I say to you, *scroll*, that I *don't* believe I can do much at all—"

"All right, Mills?"

I jump—a whole miniature leapfrog. And the scroll goes scrolling on off to the top, because of course it does.

"Sorry, sorry! Shit, did I make you jump?" Owen stands in the doorway with two bottles of water, casually lengthways, in his hands. He weighs them up in his palms. I really hope he didn't hear me talking to myself. (Well, talking to a motivational poster, which I think is somehow worse.)

"Er. Just a bit," I say, getting back to a crouch.

Owen laughs. "Brought you some water. Hot in here."

"Ah. Thanks." I clear my throat, reach up again for attempt number one thousand and fifty-nine because I don't know what else to do with my hands, with my whole body, for that matter, and drag down the screen to the floor again. How did he know I was in here? Does everything get run by him or something? "Did you, erm . . . sort out Marshal?"

Owen crosses the carpet toward me, slim-fit jeans, a close fresh haircut, and crouches next to me. I almost shudder at the mushroom cloud of nostalgia. I could do without Owen today, because I'm feeling wobbly. My resolve, a little weak because of Mum, I think. I feel alone with it. Yes, Cate and Ralph know, but Dad doesn't and he's the one who really needs to know. Plus, even if I told my brother, what could Kieran do, all the way in Michigan from his busy life? It would just be another person in my phone, texting. "Hey, sis, what's happening today?" It would be another thing to do.

"Do you need a hand?" Owen asks.

"No, no . . ." The corner unravels, but Owen catches it with his forearm, me, with my hand.

He turns his face toward me and smiles, placing the bottles of water on the floor one next to the other, like soldiers. "Let me do it," he says. "There's a knack."

Owen reaches over, warm fingertips touching my hand, and I lean away. He smells like Saturday mornings. Post-gym shaving gel and chewing gum. He'd show up at my room share smelling *exactly* like this, in the beginning. The car parked outside, ready to drown me in . . . *stuff.* Stuff that fizzled fast and, if you were to view it on a graph, would have peaked like a spike and then dropped off a cliff. A heart, out of beats. He'd tell me I'd blindsided him—that he never expected to feel the way he felt about me, about anyone. And the "stuff" felt like he'd found a language that expressed it. I remember feeling weirdly relieved when it stopped.

"You pull right down to the floor," he says, "straight down, then as you come up—" He clicks it into place, eyes meeting mine, like two shining pennies. "And there you are."

"That simple," I say, looking away. "To everyone else." I give a fake, stiff laugh.

"Yeah, well. Never your strong point, was it? Manual stuff. Putting things together."

"Oh, I don't know," I say, feeling my muscles tense a little. "I've got better."

"Oh yeah?"

"Mm-hm," I mumble.

And this is what I mean by the uneasiness. I have this urge to just . . . *explain myself.* Impress him, despite knowing I shouldn't want to. I remember the IKEA bedside cabinet. Oh, the bloody IKEA cabinet and how it almost unraveled our whole relationship. Owen had been determined we should move in together, and finally, after four months, we did. And I almost moved straight back out when we had the *worst* argument when the drawer of the cabinet Owen made fell apart, and mine didn't. He swore his cabinet was the one I built. I knew it wasn't, and who cared anyway, it was just a stupid flat-pack cabinet. But he was furious I'd insinuated *his* one was the incorrectly assembled one, and we'd argued about it so intensely, he'd slept on the sofa. We didn't speak until the following night. The ice was broken when I walked into the bedroom to find a bouquet of flowers on top of the cabinet itself. "Rest in peace," he'd said from the doorway. "Also, can we never fight again? We're too fucking hot to fight about cabinets." It's how so many of our arguments went. Big explosion, silence, an easy papering over, and I'd spend the next day exhausted, confused, wondering why on earth I was so uptight about it all; why I fought my corner so hard.

"Studio B, over," Owen says into the earpiece. "Sorry. Truck's chatting. Never stops."

I nod. If I don't look at Owen in the eye, I feel better. More able to say what I want to. "Sorry about walking into that earlier. In the truck."

Owen gives a shrug and watches me, fiddling with the screen. I just want to be at home, out of this studio. The heat of this windowless room, Owen's heavy, familiar gaze.

"Chloe wants to return the ring," says Owen, standing, the words breathing out in a sigh. "And it's stupid, but when she came over the other night, she said she would think about it all. The whole venue deadline getting closer. And . . . *Mum* chose that ring . . ." Owen tips his head back, eyes to the ceiling. "I feel like I've let Mum down. I feel like it's all I do, Millie. I'm all she has."

"Of course you haven't let her down," I say, and the words come almost instinctively. Automatically. Like an old speed-dial button I haven't pressed in years, suddenly pushed. This was an old refrain of Owen's, a story he couldn't let go of. That he, his mum's only child, only family member, was letting her down. "Owen, your mum thinks the actual sun shines out of your arse. You know that."

"Yeah, but she's down, Millie. Since . . ." He trails off, but I know he means my letter bomb of an email. The will-they-won't-they wedding situation. Me and my stupid, stupid sent-to-all words. "And you know how it is," he carries on. "Family. Feeling like you've got something to prove. You know? Feeling like they expect something of you even though they're not saying it."

And there's something about this—us two, like before, talking about things only we really understand. Owen and his mum who thinks he's the golden child, the dad who denies his existence. My mum's expectations. How I always feel I'm disappointing her, especially next to Kieran and his doctorates and handsome husband and literal lifesaving molecular biology research.

So, before I've even thought it over for even a moment, I tell him about Mum. It just comes out.

Owen freezes. "What? Are you . . . are you serious?"

"I followed her," I tell him. "And she was . . . meeting him? The ex-husband? He's ill or something."

Owen moves, like someone ducking from a baseball. Theatrical. Overt. His cheeks puffing out. "*Fuck*, Mills . . ."

"I followed her to a care home. She said it wasn't a good relationship. Alcohol. That Dad witnessed how broken she was after him. He's saying he's changed. He's regretful."

"Well, people can change—"

"Dad doesn't know," I iron over his words with mine.

Owen watches me on the floor, still crouched, still trying to loop the screen corner on the frame. "Jesus. And your dad . . . He's so . . ."

"I know." Owen means traditional. Simple. By the book.

"It'll . . . be OK," Owen says softly, and it disarms me a bit. There's familiarity in those eyes. Memories. Someone who stayed up late on Christmas Eves with Dad, doing father-and-son things. Someone who knows Mum and Dad; knows *me*.

"Your parents are meant to be. Through everything, they're just solid. You know? The dream."

He'd always say that about Mum and Dad; look at them, holding hands ahead of us as we left a country pub on a Sunday late afternoon, say it would be us one day. To be what he never had. He'd planned everything; he even named our imaginary babies. Owen mapped our whole futures. And then—he just left, acting as though he never had. It's why it didn't feel like just a boyfriend I'd lost. At the time, it felt like everything.

"I keep thinking about you," Owen suddenly says, crossing the floor. I'm stretching up for the next scroll, and I freeze, his presence behind me. *Oh, no no no.*

I turn to look at him; move away.

He presses something on his earpiece again. "Those emails. I mean—they've essentially ruined my fucking life." He gives a scoff of a laugh.

My heart bangs and bangs with shame; my hair sticks to my cheek. Why is this room so hot, why is it so small? "Owen, I never ever wanted anything to ruin your life. I would never—"

"But tell me you haven't thought about it. About, like, how good it was. The plans we had, our place, our little flat. Remember how we called it the *cube*?" He smiles, fiddles again with his earpiece.

"Of course I've thought about . . . things," I say, swallowing, but it feels like my throat is corked with marshmallows. "But you left. We did have those plans, and you . . . *you* were the one who left."

"I know, I . . ." Owen's eyes close, thick, dark lashes bristling. "But we couldn't have done long distance, Millie. *I* couldn't have done it and been away from you."

"But it wasn't . . . it wasn't just that."

"Of *course* it was," counters Owen, eyes widening, as if we're disagreeing on which salad dressing goes best and not the ending of our relationship. "I said I didn't want to hold you back, and that's what would've happened if you'd have been here waiting—"

"I was willing to leave my job and come with you," I say, as if he even needs reminding. "You know that. I bought a plane ticket, Owen. Petra convinced work to let me help you set up over there for a month, despite having *zero* training, and you just—"

"Millie." He shakes his head, as if I'm way, way off. "It could never have been that simple."

And this is typical Owen. He makes it all sound so cut-and-dry; like it wasn't *his* decision. When it was . . . wasn't it?

"*OK.* OK. Look." Owen sighs, a hand waving in the air, like he's trying to cut a deal. "Maybe I was just a dumb, fucking, stupid idiot."

"Owen—"

"Actually, there's no maybe about it," he says. "I'll hold my hands up. I've been doing a lot of thinking. I can't stop, to be honest. I know when I've been wrong. And I *know* I messed up."

"Yes," I say. "Yes, you did."

"And I know I was a prick to you."

"Yes," I agree. "You really *were*—"

And like the gods above StoneX Stadium have taken pity on me, gazed down from their seats in the nosebleeds, the door swings open and Owen turns quickly, and in unison, through panic, I stand up, as if to attention, as if I've just been caught doing something I shouldn't be, and as I stand, I let go of the scroll, and *oh my God*—the paneled set is . . . falling. *Actually* falling. I freeze, the panels leaning on me, like a house of cards, and stopped mid-topple only by my sweaty back.

"*Shit!*" bursts out of me.

A hand grabs the screen above my head, pushes "BELIEVE YOU CAN!" off me, stops it slowly crushing me, and when I look up, I see Chloe, stone-faced, headset on, Petra, a man holding an enormous boom mic, and that the hand that is saving me from the screen is attached to Jack.

Jack is still laughing when we're outside in the empty stadium stands on the back row, overlooking the vast stretch of green field, the sky one giant sheet of endless sea-glass blue. It's infectious, Jack's laughter. As much as my face is like a ball of fire and I am *beyond* embarrassed, I can't stop myself from laughing either. It all happened so fast. That door opening, me suddenly standing, like someone electrocuted, and the slow-motion collapse of the screen, my shriek, Jack's arm shooting out, a man standing there with a microphone that looked like Marge Simpson's unkempt, graying head . . .

"I can't actually believe that happened," I say. "Your arm . . . it was like—Edward Cullen or something?"

"As in the teenage vampire?" Jack puts a sneakered foot up on the back of the seat in front of him casually.

"*Yes,* the teenage vampire. I actually can't believe that just happened."

"Well, I for one feel honored," Jack says. "To be able to witness it happen in real time. An organic, unexpected event."

"*Unexpected,*" I say, sitting next to him on a plastic seat. Just us two, among rows and rows of empty mustard-yellow seas behind us and in front. "Right up your street, then."

Jack chuckles and pulls the sunglasses resting on his head down over his eyes.

I unscrew the water Owen brought into the studio for me and sip. A hot-dog-van-tinged breeze cools my skin, gently blows the hair from my hot face. I'd hoped Jack would find me eventually, and although I was *extremely* embarrassed to see him as I was being buried in plastic screens, I felt a sweep of relief over me when I saw him standing in the tiny little hotbox of a studio, looking like something from a spring/summer magazine spread—neat, straight-legged, navy-blue chino shorts, a pressed white T-shirt, his hair short but messy, and his legs—they remind me of footballers' legs. (I really hope he hasn't clocked me looking at them out of the corner of my eye.) And I *like* being with Jack. Jack Shurlock makes me feel at ease. And also a bit . . . giddy? Which feels like a relaxing minibreak away from everything else at the moment. The serious, deep, messy everything of a life A.E. Not least that embarrassing scene with Owen just now.

"Owen laughed, didn't he?" I say quietly as Flye TV crew members mill about below like clockwork ants. The doors open soon, and these seats, this stand we sit high up in, will be full of screaming fans. For now, though, it's like it belongs only to us. Jack and I looking down on a whole miniature terrarium. My Sundays normally look the same. Laundry, long walks, a roast at the Crooked Billet with Ralph, some *Made in Chelsea*. But this up here—this is totally new. And my brain is very happy with that fact. It feels clean. Freshly oiled.

"Owen laughed, but Chloe didn't so much as smile," says Jack.

"Hatred." She'd stomped off, and rightly so, Owen following in pursuit.

"Neither did Petra."

"*Girl code.*"

"And all right, I know *I* laughed," says Jack, "but know mine came from a nice place. A *kind* place."

I turn to him. "Um, you laughed the loudest."

Jack holds a large hand at his chest, tips his head back. "I kept most of it in for when we were out here, didn't I? Away from everyone else. And—*Mr. Kalimeris.*" And when Jack says that, there's a piss-takingness to his words. His eyes are hidden behind glasses, but I just know they rolled. "And those screens are unpredictable, to be fair."

"*Thank you.* Everyone else was acting like they were so easy. *Here, let me help, ooh, look at that, I did it in under a second and all while you were buried in it, how on earth did you manage that!*"

Jack taps the corner of his phone absent-mindedly against his knee. Someone on the field below shouts something through a megaphone, the muffled words lost to us up here. "Unusual, actually," says Jack thoughtfully. "To see him helping."

"Who? *Mr. Kalimeris?*" I repeat, and Jack gives a single nod. "Mm. Really?" I remember all the stories Owen would come home with after an event. He'd talk about how he'd barely had a break to go to the toilet or have a coffee, that he'd been "on the ground with the rest of the boots," supporting the crew, teaching them; how they couldn't cope without him . . . "Have you worked with Owen a lot, then?"

"Not loads," says Jack casually, "but I have, yeah. He's usually in the truck on his director's throne." He gives a smirk.

"Ah, yes, well, I burst into the truck on him and Chloe having a big discussion, so I probably disrupted his throne time, I'm afraid."

Jack shrugs. "Well, they *are* at work, so . . ."

"Poor Chloe looked horrified, though," I carry on. "Looked at me like I was the scarecrow who walks at midnight. But then, she probably feels like she can't escape me. This woman who's the reason she isn't getting married." It's true, though, isn't it? There I am at reception every day, loitering outside cafés like a fan waiting for an autograph, in a tiny room with her fiancé . . .

Jack sighs. "Millie dot Chandler," he says gruffly. And God, I love the way he says my name. I am completely ambivalent toward my name, but when Jack says "Millie Chandler," even with the silly dot in the middle, I'm glad the name is mine. I like the little rumble in his throat when he says the "and" in "Chandler."

"Jack dot Shurlock," I mimic. "Or should I say Shurlock dot Jack?"

He turns his face toward me. "Do you really think you're the reason?" he asks softly, and just as I'm thinking that I'm very glad he's wearing sunglasses because I'd have to be confronted with those playful hazel eyes right next to me, and I'm already struggling to stifle this little crush I have on him, this man who is going to leave for Quebec and New Zealand and alpaca farms soon, he lifts his shades. He eyes fix on mine. Gosh, he's close. "Well? Be straight up."

"Yes," I announce, then I look away, to the rugby field below, "and I think saying it isn't the emails is denial. Of course it was. I said what I said, I wrote what I wrote. Me."

"Fuck the emails," he says almost lazily, and I swing around to look at him in surprise.

I laugh. "Excuse me, Operations Manager slash Chief of Staff?"

"Seriously," he says, his mouth a crooked half smile. "What does it even matter? Really? It happened. It's done. And we can't possibly control what'll happen next, so—"

"Ugh, so, what, *be present*?" and I say the last two words in a stupid, mocking voice.

"Yes."

"No," I say.

He freezes, dips his head. "*No?*"

"No."

Jack laughs out of the corner of his mouth, eyes still on me. "No, what?" He smells like hot showers and clean laundry, and that lopsided what-did-you-just-say-to-me smile does something to me. Sends a shiver through me. And it makes me want to fuck around; be silly. Giggle. It sort of makes me want to lean in, kiss his warm, rough, stubbly cheek . . . Oh, shut up, Millie, you're at *work*.

"I . . . I don't believe in being present," I say, almost like a defiant child. "Well, I might *believe* in it, but I don't think I'll ever be able to do it. I'm just not one of those people. It's like—how can I be present with what's happening now, when so much has already happened and, therefore, more things are *going* to happen, and I can't change what's happened, but I can change what *might*."

"And is that what this is?" asks Jack. "The working here today, all the cake—"

"Oh, why are you so obsessed with the cake?" I ask, and Jack smiles, a glimpse of straight teeth. "But yes. Exactly. It gives me . . . purpose? Like, I might've messed up, a *lot,* but I can fix things."

Jack looks at me and says nothing.

"What?"

"I didn't say anything, Millie," and his eyes travel down my face for just a second, and something stirs in my stomach. Hot and tingly.

"But you want to," I carry on. "Is it the purpose thing?"

Jack gives a deep chuckle.

"So, it *was* the purpose thing!" I say.

"Well, I don't really *believe* in purpose, so . . ." He grimaces, tilts his head to one side. "I believe we're just a weird meat suit, here for ninety years if we're very, very lucky, and everything else is just a game. A construct."

"Ah, yes." I nod. "*Made up.* That's very depressing, by the way. Like, hugely."

"Is it?" Jack rubs a thumb and forefinger along his jaw. " 'Cause life is absurd, though, isn't it? Mad. And we all waste so much time on things that are not going to mean *shit* to us when we're old. Nobody's ever going to be sitting in a rocking chair at eighty-nine, saying, 'Jesus, do you know what, I'm so glad I worried about opening the best ISA with the best interest rate.' "

I gaze at him. "Were you raised by Eckhart Tolle?"

"Who?"

"Or, like . . . Buddha?"

"No," Jack says, then his face . . . changes a little. Seriousness; just a tiny shadow of it, like the passing of a cloud across his features. "I'm a military kid. My mum was in the forces? We never stayed in one place for very long."

And it feels like a nugget. A piece of Jack offered up. And I want to pick it up and hold it with both hands. "*Really?*"

"Really."

"Wow. I sort of expected like—rock star parents or something."

"Rock star parents. I'm just that cool, am I?" Jack smirks, but then that look reappears. A subduedness. A reluctance. A carefulness. "I guess it sort of rubs off? When you move around a lot. Every street, every town, every school is the same. You sort of see through it all in the end. The mask of it? My sister, Brogan, though, she's the opposite. She's got the house, the husband, kids, dogs. *ISAs.*" He meets my eyes then, the corner of his mouth dimpling with a smile. "Yeah, Brogan wants it all . . . locked in. And maybe I should have gone that way. Wondered for a bit if I was doing it wrong by not." He looks up to the sky for a moment, flicks his sunglasses back down over his eyes. "But I dunno. I never did."

"That's because you live in the vortex. The Jack Shurlock vortex." I sigh. "I wish I could do that. I wish *I* could live in the vortex."

"Yeah?"

I nod. "Yup. Just—be that person. Just go off. Do something new."

"You can," Jack says.

"I can't."

"Yes, you can. Just—step inside." And when he turns and looks at me then, his face close, I automatically look away. The way you do when you've looked at something too bright. To shield yourself.

I look back down to the field. I can just see Marshal sipping from a can of something behind his camera.

"I can't," I say. "At least . . . not right this minute, anyway. I've got to go and get everyone's lunch. I promised Marshal a jacket potato, don't you know."

"Just go home, do what you want," says Jack, shrugging. "I'll cover for you."

"You know I can't do that."

Jack doesn't say anything but gives me this look—as if to say, "And why can't you?" A look that's very, very "So what?"

"I just wish the glitch never happened," I say. "*That's* what I want. More than the vortex. More than anything. Then I wouldn't be on jacket potato duty, or being part of the *throne disruption*. Or screen-gate. Up for scrutiny."

"Well, I think you were on the right track when you said you wanted to forget it ever happened. Remember?"

I nod, bring the side of the cold-water bottle to my cheek. I'm so hot. It's the heat wave. But it definitely is also Jack and my little spark of a crush that's burning hotter by the moment. "When I told you not to investigate? Or reach out to a nerd?"

"*Reach out to a nerd*," repeats Jack. "A very important charity, that one."

I laugh as Jack swipes his phone screen into life and starts replying to an email, still smiling.

Silence stretches between us, and we watch for a few moments as, below, crew stand patiently behind cameras, people rush around, meandering in and out. There are a few players now just straggling, taking a look at the field, shorts and shin pads, but hoodies and sunglasses that will soon, no doubt, be removed for the game.

"Did you ever talk to that mate? *The nerd?*"

Jack hesitates, doesn't look up from his phone. He's writing a work email. *Dear Calvin*, it says, *thank you for your email.* "I did speak to my mate, Matt, yeah."

"And what did he say? About the glitch?"

Jack sucks in a breath, lets it out between his words. "Um. Not a lot, really." He continues typing. "Just—theories."

"*Theories?* Like what theories?"

"Just—interference, you know? Being compromised. More *that* than a glitch."

I find myself sitting up in the slippery plastic seat, back straightening. Distant music comes from down on the field, then stops again. "What—what do you mean?"

Jack gives a slow shrug. "Just—I mean, none of this really matters. He can't be sure, and he doesn't work for Flye, doesn't know our systems—"

"But what theories? Like, what *exactly* did he say?"

Jack takes a breath, and there's something in that pause, the way he stops typing, looks at me, that makes my stomach tense with a mini electric shock. "He . . . he said he hadn't come across it before, but he isn't too sold on it being a glitch. Even with the timings of the servers going back on. That if it happened where he works, the most likely explanation he personally would have is that someone sent them. Manually."

The words land there between us like a misfired firework.

"*Someone?*"

Jack nods almost hesitantly, watches my face, as if preparing for me to do . . . *something.* Judder off into the sky like a panicked rocket. Burst into tears? "That's what he said. Not me."

"So, you're saying don't shoot the messenger."

"No, I'm saying if he had to, he would lean more toward a person, not a computer. But you didn't send them, so I feel like his theory falls apart a bit."

I stare down at the field, as if doing an invisible sum in the air. I feel *sick* all of a sudden. Hotter than I was in that tiny room, even though it's cool out here up high with the breeze.

"Millie?"

"So, is he saying—someone else did it? But . . . but who would even do that? Surely you'd have to know my password, unlock my laptop . . ."

"Well, yeah, exactly. Which is . . . *a real reach.* Matt did ask if you could have sent them accidentally. *Unknowingly.* Not on purpose somehow." Jack holds his hands up, showing two palms. "OK, now I'm saying don't shoot the messenger." He gives a small, apprehensive smile, but I don't smile back. "But they're just hypotheses. I would have never said if you hadn't asked, Millie. Because it's just . . . surmising, you know? And what use is that?"

"Yeah, no, of course, I know, I'm—I'm glad you said."

Jack nods slowly, watches me carefully, but I feel strange now. Unsafe. Like I'm suddenly walking on ground that's shifting under my feet, like someone has yanked the curtain back to reveal something unexpected that's been hiding in the wings of my life. Because yes, it might be "a reach," but say if someone *did* press send on my emails. Who would ever do that? And why?

**Text message from Owen:** Nice seeing you earlier. Hope you're OK. And Toni and Mitch Chandler will be all right, Mills. I know it. Trust me. x

chapter 14

**To: all FLYE TV office**
**From: Gail Fryer (PA)**
**Subject: HTG Pictures Summer-Ween party**

Dear all,

   This is a reminder for all those staff members who have been invited to our client HTG Pictures' annual summer party Saturday. As many of you know, the summer party was rescheduled due to CEO Glenn's knee replacement surgery and has subsequently been renamed to Summer-Ween to fit with the time of year. Please find a slightly revised invite attached, but venue and timing details remain the same. A minibus will be leaving from the Flye TV car park on Saturday at 6 p.m. This isn't compulsory and guests can make their own way there if preferred.

   We're sure the party will be yet another enjoyable

evening and will further solidify the relationship between us here at Flye and one of our most important clients.

Best wishes,

Management

"Jeez, look at this. All their miserable fucking faces. Waiting for a meeting, and it's like they've all been given a week to live." Lin gazes through the glass on the other side of the office, a finger hooked on one of the slatted blinds, kinking the middle. She's spying out to the lobby as people start to gather for a planning meeting for a football match tomorrow while we're in here, in a room at Flye that everyone simply calls "Vince's room."

Vince is Flye's repairman, and this cluttered, garage-like office is where everyone drops off broken equipment and Vince attempts to fix it, in the manner of a vet who has been handed an abused animal by the abuser themselves. "This is a *Canon*," he'll say through gritted teeth, "and just *look* at the way it's been treated. But oh, Vince'll sort it, won't he? Vince'll bring life back from the bleedin' dead, he won't mind."

I'm in here packaging up truly-too-far-gone equipment that needs to be posted to the manufacturers for repair, Vince is working silently on a camera at his desk, and Lin—she's hiding because she "wants to avoid the agonizing pre-meeting small talk." Lin sits upstairs at a chaotically messy desk and spends her days chatting to clients on the phone in the same way people talk to their best friends at ten p.m. at home on the sofa. Loud cackles, hand gestures, gasps, sometimes while painting her fingernails, and as if nobody else is in the room.

"Seriously, dude," groans Lin. She has her phone out, checking her blunt-cut, cherry-cola hair in the camera. "The vibe in here continues to be *off*. Corporate hell. It's like we're . . ." She lowers her phone and locks it. "Attending a memorial or something. You know?"

"Mm-hm," grunts Vince without looking up, and I force a smile, make an agreeable "I know what you mean" sound in the back of my throat but carry on filling in the endlessly long returns form for a broken monitor.

I love Lin. Nobody is more suffers-no-fools than Lin. But the last thing I need is to be overheard agreeing that I'm working among people who look like they've just attended a cremation. Even if it's only by Vince. Of course, what I really want to say is that it feels more like a memorial site than you know when people pass my desk these days. I *am* the car crash itself. I'm that receptionist who did that thing, and "Oh my God, did you hear she emailed her ex in front of the whole company and now his new fiancée has left him? Imagine. IMAGINE!"

Lin stares at me, a perfect chalk-blue dot of eyeliner blobbed on the center of each lower lash line. "Millie?" she asks. "*Babe*."

"Yes?"

"What, kindly . . . is *that*?" Her eyes drop to my—*ah*.

"My phone?" I reply.

"*Your* phone?" Lin looks horrified. "Is it really? I thought it might be one of Vince's weird contraptions. No offense, Vin."

"Mm-hm," grunts Vince again.

My face glows hot. I knew people might notice it, assume I dropped my iPhone in the toilet, was using something temporary that I pulled from the depths of my odds-and-sods drawer full of wires and random keys nobody will ever use again. "I changed it out a few weeks ago," I say. "It's a 2010 Nokia . . ."

"It's a relic, man," Lin says with an almost-impressed, wide smile. Lin looks like she should be in a pop band. She's naturally cool; has perfectly square white teeth, high, plum-like cheekbones when she smiles, wears the coolest blend of colors on her eyelids at all times, different every day. "My brother had one of those. I thought he was the *shit*. Oh my goodness, look at the actual pressy buttons . . ."

"They do take some getting used to!"

"And can you have apps?"

"Technically, but the phone's old and it has zero space, so no. No apps. Just calls. Just texts."

Lin looks at me, her head tilting just a tiny bit to the left, as if I'm some sort of strange specimen in a petri dish. "Why, though?"

I freeze for a moment, then give a stiff, unconvincing shrug. "I . . . well, I guess I wanted a little break. A tech cleanse. To—disconnect a little? After . . . everything."

"But—" Lin watches me for a second, her forehead crinkling a little beneath her perfect, dewy foundation. "I mean, I do get needing to instill a bit of a break. My screen-time report said I spent *nineteen* hours on my phone last Monday. I was sort of equally impressed, to be honest. On a working day, too, which I guess says it all." Lin chuckles. "But . . . like, all you did was drop some truths," Lin carries on. "That's how I see it, Millie. Why should you suffer with your grandad's phone. You know?"

Lin is in sales, the sort of person who can sell anything to anyone. She has a podcast with her best friend, which she records on weekends, called *But I Love Me More*, that's about loving yourself first. It's where her unsent-letter idea came from. She suggested it and then linked me to the podcast episode. If I'd have only known it would have ended up like this . . .

"I know," I say. "I know."

"Do you, though?"

"But I've not missed my phone," I tell Lin. "Not really." A . . . half lie, at a push. I'm enjoying the extra time I have, the extra, oh-so-much-clearer headspace without scrolling on my phone for eight hours a day, constantly checking, falling down social media rabbit holes. But

I am missing it too. Fuck, I miss WhatsApp. I miss Instagram and laughing darkly at Love of Huns in bed. I miss ASMR TikTok chefs and hacks I'll never use. I miss the *Married at First Sight* takes on Reddit. I miss memes and feeling . . . *informed.* (Although, yes, most of the time it's misinformed.)

"And that email you sent to Steve about all his bloody fundraising," continues Lin. "Look, I promised myself I wouldn't mention the emails to you, but you are a *genius*, Millie Chandler."

"Ah," I say, wincing. "I really wouldn't say genius."

Vince makes a sound that could be agreement or disgust (or both).

"And the one to *Mark*." Lin slaps her hands together into a clap, then gives a big bark of a laugh. "Nobody deserved it more."

"Lin?" Petra's face appears in the crack of Vince's doorway. "Hey, all." She grins, looking at me, then back to Lin. "Need you in a sec. Sorry."

Lin nods, then looks at me and says, "So, like, don't feel guilty or anything, you know? He *chose* to steal your lunch, and that's just the world of fuck about and find out. The email was the *finding out*." Lin smiles, victorious. Her earrings, two clay pink iced donuts, jiggle. "It holds up a mirror. That's all. We all have stuff we want to say every day and don't. It's why what happened to you cuts too close to the bone for everyone." She shrugs. "And look, I didn't get one, and Prue did, and she deserves it. She's a bigot and a bully and I hate her. Like, actually hate."

"Mm," grunts Vince.

"I imagine her in a hospital bed or something sometimes. To test if it's true hatred. Like, recently, I imagined her buried alive in a desert and managing to find her phone in the coffin or whatever, and calling me and—"

"Did you pick up?" asks Petra, her face dropping, mouth open, as if this is a real-life situation.

"What do you think?" Lin cackles again, and Petra laughs nervously, jerks her head, a wordless "*come on*," and they both leave. And I admit, I'm sort of relieved to get back to my boring, under-the-radar job.

It's been nearly a week since I saw Mum and five days since the rugby, and what has followed has been a—frankly, needed—standard, busy week at work, which I have welcomed like an old (slightly boring) friend. A lot of the bosses—Petra and Jack included—have been on location, and I've been in a big, grumpy, foggy funk I've tried not to be. As Cate and Ralph agreed over dinner last night, Jack's nerdy friend's theory *is* just a theory, with absolutely no physical evidence, but it keeps flitting in and out of my brain, making me wince. That nagging "What if?" What if it was . . . Leona in IT? What if it was Michael Waterstreet himself? What if this is like a *Miss Marple* episode and it was Petra all along, or something absolutely ludicrous? That's what would happen in a Netflix series, at least. It happens all the time on *Selling Sunset.* On *Love Island.* Trust gets severed. Contestants you love turn out to be massive arseholes and chuck a big plot twist into the mix, and you're left questioning your judgment of character. And of course, I know it *isn't* Petra, but the whole thing has left me feeling uneasy. A bit jumpy.

"I think they all deserved it," says Vince. "My two cents."

I glance up. Vince carries on screwing a panel onto the side of a camera, one of those Pixar-style desk lamps, the white paint scratched up like claw marks bent over it.

"Sorry?" I think this is the only time Vince has ever initiated a conversation with me.

"All of them. Can't stand any of them."

"The people who work here?"

Vince grunts. "Those affected," he says grumpily, as if I'm annoying him by not keeping up.

I say nothing; nod.

"Worked with Owen for years," he says and shakes his big, meaty head. "Thinks his shit don't stink. You know? Chloe's all right. Mark, bell end. Michael, prick . . ."

I stare at him.

"Wouldn't trust a soul. Even the ones you think you trust. You— you're decent," he says. "Lin, decent. Jack, decent. Gail Fryer . . . well, more than decent is Gail."

And then I just say it. Vince is smart. Vince would never not tell the truth. "Do you think someone might've done it? Like—hacked me or something? On purpose?"

Vince looks up, the lamp casting shadows across his grumpy bearded face, like someone telling spooky stories by a campfire. "Yes," he says simply.

"Really?"

He sighs, his small, hooded eyes watching me. "I always say, if you think of dark things, there's always someone else actually *doing* those things."

I nod slowly.

"I might think of sabotaging one of them out there's camera, for example. But I wouldn't. Having said that . . ."

"There're people out there that *might* do something like that?"

Vince gives a sharp nod—a composer's bow. "When some people are down, they'll do anything to raise themselves up. Trick in life is finding the ones who wouldn't." He looks back down at the camera. "Hard, though, to come by . . ."

And that . . . is that. He says nothing else, the end of his wise re- pairman philosophizing. Vince fixes the camera as the hubbub outside grows, and I sit on a dusty, scratched-up desk, covered in wires and pens and papers and a pen holder shaped like a miniature wheely bin, packaging up things—a monitor, a light reader—and I think about what Vince said about Owen. Thinks his shit doesn't stink. I mean, Vince doesn't particularly like anyone, so his isn't exactly an impartial view, but Jack said similar. "On his throne" in the truck. Owen never painted that picture. Owen was the one everyone turned to. Owen was the helper, the team couldn't do without him. But then, Owen always has been a bunch of contrasts. He's like one of those days in April. Sunshine and showers and storms, mere moments apart. The flowers, the I love yous, the gestures, the sulking, the withdrawing from me, the leaving, the bloody IKEA cabinets. Sunbeams and lightning strikes.

A knock comes from the other side of Vince's door.

"Yep?"

The door cracks open.

"Vince, my man," says Jack. "*Millie.* Hanging in the magic cottage?" Jack stands in the doorway, and he smiles—wide and warm, that crescent dimple. I love the way his eyes crinkle at the corners when he smiles. I like the way the muscles flex in his forearms as he crosses them at his broad chest. Oh, this crush really is a *crush,* isn't it?

"With the repair genius, yes," I say, and a tiny, teeny smile tugs the edge of Vince's thin mouth.

"Vince, how's the camera?"

"Pile of shit."

"Good to hear," says Jack, his eyes flicking to mine, widening, and it makes me smile. I feel sometimes like all I do when I'm with Jack is smile and smile and smile, like a big, gooey drunk.

"Millie, Petra wanted me to pass on that your vacation day has been OK'ed for Friday."

"Oh. Great. Thank you."

"Mine, too, actually. Any plans?"

Sometimes I wonder if Jack actually wants to know, or if he's just being very boss-like and friendly and all about the morale. We *are* becoming friends, though, aren't we? A friend who I have a little crush on, because who *wouldn't.* "Oh, my lovely friend, shut up, you fancy the absolute arse off him," Cate said when I got home from the rugby game. I'd left at the end of the match, Petra gently suggesting they were fine for crew for packing up. "I know your 'I fancy him' face, and this is *it*. Stone-cold."

"I'm going shopping with my friend Cate," I tell Jack. "We downloaded this app. Helps match you with your skin palette? Which colors suit you . . ."

"Interesting."

"Hoping I find my color and it changes my life. I may return to work head to toe in yellow like a big giant banana. A big squash."

Jack laughs, that lovely, warm, deep chuckle. "I look forward to the results." Jack seems to be down with everything I say. Big bananas. Edward Cullen. Rhubarb farms. There's something . . . addictive about it. I often worry about being enough for people, for the world, just how I am. The Failed Chandler. Tossing random things out there, embellishing parts of myself to see what's acceptable, what strikes a chord, what doesn't get chucked back at me and rejected. With Jack, though, it's like everything I throw out is truly me, and he just takes it. Catches it, doesn't bat it back to me.

"And how about you?"

"My mate Enam's having a leaving thing in town. His mates at the sailing club? I've said I'll pop by. He basically *lives* at that place."

"Ah," I say. "So, you *do* make plans for some people."

Jack drops his gaze to his feet, then back up at me, a glint in his eye, like a pebble hitting water. "Ah," he says. "See, only a select few make the cut, Millie dot Chandler," and when I laugh, I notice that Vince is staring at us like we both just peeled back our skin to reveal grimy, monstrous scales.

Jack clears his throat. "See you at the party Saturday, Vin?"

Vince scoffs. "As if *I* got an invite," he says. "Summer-Ween. Did you see that's what they called it? *Ween?*"

Jack laughs, arms crossing at his chest, and ah—there it is. That lovely dent of muscle, just beneath a rolled-up sleeve. "You up for it, Millie?"

"The HTG party?"

"Yup. Got a plus-one. Fancy dress. Film is the theme, apparently. Creative."

Vince scoffs as if Jack had said, "The dress code is full nudity, except each guest must sport a crash helmet or be fined."

"Michael Waterstreet drunkenly dancing," rambles Jack. "Mute Martin crying over his crush on Gail. Really good food. Narcissists for miles . . ."

I laugh. "*Mute Martin.*"

"Think about it." Jack smiles. "I'll drop the ticket on your desk. No pressure. If you want to use it, use it . . ."

"I will. Thank you."

And . . . *could I*? Go with Jack to a party? As a plus-one? I wonder if he remembers all those Boss Man Michael cocktails we drank together at the Christmas party, those hot, tipsy grins, the chemistry between us, the way he'd asked me to message him . . . But then, he has never spoken of it, so perhaps it really was one-sided, and the amount of rum in the cocktail made me hallucinate? The Boss Man Michael was, after all, a volatile drink. The sort of specimen that should be scientifically studied.

"Good," is all Jack says, and when he leaves, Vince says, "Gail needs a man better than Martin Sachs. Someone respectful. Someone good with their hands," and he holds up a palm under the lamplight and looks at it as if it's marble.

**Text message from Mum:** Your dad arrives home tomorrow. I will speak to him as soon as he comes in. I'm still so very sorry Millie. I really am. X

*From: Millie Chandler*

*To: Alexis Lee*

**Subject: Friday**

Cate and I are going shopping Friday. I know you hate wandering around the shops but you could meet us for lunch after, like we used to? Please unblock me.

chapter 15

*I*f it's just your face that's going to show, you need the face to be, like, *on point.* You know?" Cate picks up an eye-shadow palette and flips it open. "Ohh, *yes.* Subtle. Sexy. The pigment on this stuff is really good too. What do we think? My treat!"

We've been in Superdrug for fifteen minutes, as Cate stops by every makeup stand and looks at every single row, holding shades against my face before putting them back. I wasn't sure whether I'd accept Jack's plus-one—attend a party that will *definitely* be attended by colleagues I may have emailed. But Cate perched at the bottom of my bed this morning holding a black all-in-one catsuit (almost like the things set changers wear onstage so as not to be seen by the audience), and one of those big suit covers with a coat hanger jutting out the top. "Film is the theme, you say?" She'd grinned. "Well, I've had an idea. You're going to be an *actual* movie scene." And then she unzipped the suit bag to reveal a giant rectangle frame you *wear*, like a human photo frame. "I was the Mona Lisa for a work thing once, but I say we paint this frame to look like a reel of *film* and *you* are the star? Plus, when you don't have the portrait on, it's a sexy catsuit-y thingy." And when I'd tried to object, she'd said, "I'm doing your hair and your makeup, and I am driving you to the party. So you have no excuses!" And maybe it was because I knew she was right, and maybe it was seeing how . . . *bright* Cate looked for the first time in weeks. But I agreed. (And actually felt a little excited once I had.)

Cate pays for the palette and grins excitedly when we step out into Leigh town center, making the bag dance in her hand. It's busy in town today. The air cool, tinged with woodsmoke, rap music from the clothes shop opposite floating through its open door, shop windows splattered and plastered with Halloween fake blood and "Do Not Cross" tape. We wander, heading for the footpath that leads to the beach and the route home to our little flat.

"Tea, biscuits, and outfit planning when we get home." Cate smiles. Cate has always had a way of making everywhere feel safe and homely, just by being there. Even when she's sad and mending a heart of her own. Since she moved in, it feels like our own little capsule of a family, back at Four, the Logans, and I'm grateful. Especially that my own family feels flammable. Like the strike of a match could send my parents up in family-shaped flames. And Mum is telling Dad today about Julian. It's why I'm pleased to be here, distracted with Cate, ambling through the beautiful little higgledy streets of our town. It's why Cate suggested the party too. "Something fun for *you*. Remember you?" she'd said.

"Oh, man, would you look at that." Cate beams. There's a wedding party spilling out of the church. The bells are dinging, and guests are scattering on the path, a sea of trodden-on confetti, pastel dresses, and cold, rubbed-at arms.

"There's something so magical about passing a wedding, isn't there?" mulls Cate as we walk. "Being a faceless extra on a day the two people getting married will remember for the rest of their lives, but a day that will fade into total insignificance for you. I don't know, I like thinking about that."

"You're such a romantic." And it's such a Cate thing to say. Despite everything, despite a breakup and horrible Nicholas, who keeps texting, keeps calling her office, she's hopeful. And of course, I wouldn't have expected anything else. Cate is just one of those people—a coper. A doer. A relentless bouncer-backer.

"I love the idea of normal life just . . . lifeing, but, among it all, these amazing moments are happening. Like seeds," says Cate. "Right? Ralph always says that about seeds. You plant a seed, and you're not really sure what's going to come of them. But you know something will."

"Oh, I love Ralph's wisdom," I say, and it warms me through, like brandy, how Ralph is such a part of Cate's life now, and she his.

"His *oblivious* wisdom." Cate smiles. "And me too."

We cut through the shaded footpath, out onto Leigh Hill, a slice of glittering teal estuary getting closer and closer. We cross over onto the footbridge that traverses the train track, and oh, Leigh looks beautiful. So very handsome and dashing. The tide is out, and boats are stranded on the sand. It reminds me of a painting sometimes, this town. A moody canvas of thick, troweled-on paint. One of those souvenir pens, the waves moving every time it's tilted.

"I keep thinking about Alexis," I tell Cate. "I emailed her again about today, and she didn't answer me. And she refused the bloody brownies delivery."

Cate tips her head to one side. "*Babe.* Seriously. You apologized. More than enough times. You know Alexis, she needs to cool off. And there's only so much you can do. She didn't answer me either."

"I know. I just—I feel sick about it all when I think about her. She *did* hurt me, but—she's Alexis, you know? I keep thinking I'll just go there, but if her dad answers . . . I don't know, he's an old man, bless him. He doesn't need the drama. It feels like overstepping." And I don't feel surprised that Alexis has gone full-blown "disappearance." Alexis is very all-or-nothing. Ruthless in what and whom she surrounds herself with. But I hoped she'd treat me, her friend of seven years, a little differently. But then, I suppose she's hurt. (*Did* she really need to post it on TikTok, though?)

Cate links her arm through mine. We crunch through a twirling, circling scatter of autumn leaves. "Look, it'll do you good to forget about everything and concentrate on the party," she says. "Get your hair done, your makeup, wear something a bit daring, a bit funny and lighthearted, something for you. And Jack Shurlock will simply *die* of longing."

"Cate, I don't think I'm really even on his radar."

Cate groans, tips her face back. Her sunglasses almost slide off the top of her head. "Oh, shut the fuck up."

"What?"

"Of course you're on his radar. Seriously, I know these things, Millie," carries on Cate. "At that party, he'll even have to nip off, stick his crotch in the hotel freezer . . ."

I burst out laughing. An old man ambling by in hiking boots with a folded copy of the *Daily Mail* under his arm eyes us suspiciously.

*"Sure."*

"I swear!" Cate beams, and it's so lovely to hear and see Cate so happy. She's had her moments when I can tell she's been crying, or she's squirreled herself away to her room and Ralph has mentioned how he hasn't seen much of her, but lately, she *has* been Cate again. She looks ten years younger. She looks rested. I often get in from work to find her and Ralph in the middle of a puzzle, and it makes me laugh. The creepy steampunk puzzles of Ralph's, among flickering NEOM candles and decorative silver pears. I've never really taken Cate as a puzzle girl, but she always seems so peaceful as she sits there at the coffee table beside Ralph, trying to fit a piece in.

"Even the name's hot, isn't it?" says Cate as I slow on the bridge, peer over the railing because . . . "And that photo on Flye's website, Millie. You can just see he's *bad*—"

"Cate, he's . . . I think he's over there."

"What?"

I stop dead on the bridge and shrink back, away from the edge. "Jack. He's . . . he's there. I think? At th-the sailing club? Oh God. Oh shit."

"Sure, OK, pal." Cate laughs. "Way to shut me up. I was enjoying that. I was genuinely getting turned on. Think I need to up my erotica consumption—"

"No, seriously." I swallow. "Just . . . look over the bridge. He said he was off today. He said he was going to be at a leaving thing. Sailing club and pub or something, but . . . I forgot, and also it's one in the afternoon and I just assumed it would be a nighttime thing and—"

"Oh my God, you're serious? Actual Jack?" Cate lets out a flurry of excited giggles, as if she's just seen the entirety of BTS at a bus stop. (Cate loves BTS.) "*Where?*"

"Outside the . . . the ice cream place. The Mayflower. By the sailing club. He's with—"

"Oh my God, with the bloke and the dog! At the picnic table?" Cate squeals like a dog whistle. "Oh, holy shit, it's like seeing someone famous. Come on—"

"I can't go down there."

Cate swoops around. "Er. Excuse me?"

"No, Cate, I look terrible. I'm only wearing concealer and I've—"

"Hush." Cate removes her sunglasses and plonks them onto my face. She brushes my hair out. She unzips my coat a bit so my raincoat is open, showing my T-shirt. It's baby blue, with a big cartoon strawberry on it (and a teeny-tiny caterpillar on the top, if you look hard enough). "Boobs." She shrugs.

"No," I say, zipping back up. "No, not boobs. Let's just—turn around and walk the other way."

"Are you joking me? We are going down this bridge, Millie Chandler. If I have to drag you by your hood, I will."

"But . . . I'll laugh in his face," I whisper. A woman walks between us, a tiny, woolen-hatted baby sleeping soundly inside a carrier on her chest.

"Why will you?" Cate asks, a hand resting on her hip.

"Because you're with me and you just said he would be dying of longing and sticking his knob in fridges."

"*Freezers.*" Cate giggles. "And you won't bloody laugh in his face, Millie. *Come on.* He is a human being, and you are simply walking home."

I blow out a long breath as Cate loops her arm through mine.

"OK," I say.

"And we have no idea he's there, OK? We're simply walking to our flat because we've been shopping, and this is the way home."

"Right," I say.

"And stop walking like a soldier."

"Right," I say again, and amazingly, right this second, I cannot seem to remember how to walk, despite twenty-eight years of experience.

Cate and I walk in silence, and she cannot stop smiling, which is making *me* want to burst out laughing, and also turn and run away, all at once. Why am I like this? It's just Jack. He's just—a man who works with me, right? A man who is also about to leave the company again and disappear into Canadian snow and New Zealand rainforests. A man who makes my face hot, has such a teasing, dark little smile that it makes my stomach do roly-polies.

"The fact you tried to convince me you didn't fancy him." Cate shakes her head, mock disapprovingly. "This behavior is like—*peak fancying*. Peak crush. And it's about bloody time. I'm excited! It's fun! I've missed Millie having a crush."

And—OK, Cate is right. This is fun. Fancying someone. Giggling with my best friend about it. This butterfly tummy, this alive, electric feeling beneath my skin. Cate's been there through them all. From sweet, poem-writing Darren Smith at school, in the year above, to "Fletch," a cocky, gangly singer in a cover band who used to play the pub Alexis and I worked at. We kissed eventually, about a year before I met Owen, and I called Cate after, as if I were reporting a death, because it was so terrible and tongues-y. (We of course then renamed him "Retch.")

We turn the corner, and now—we're face on with where Jack is sitting, walking directly toward him down the concrete slope. He's with a man who looks about our age; built like a rugby player, heavy beard, and a shaved head. A big Alsatian dog sits calmly at his side, keeping watch.

"Let him see you first," says Cate out of the side of her mouth. "Just talk to me. About . . . I dunno. Erm. Sourdough? Yes, sourdough."

"*Sourdough?*"

"So, what, you need a starter for every *loaf*?" asks Cate, turning to me and raising her eyebrows. "That is truly fascinating, Millie."

"Oh. Erm. *Yes.* Yes, you need to start with something called a sourdough starter, which is super easy to do, actually . . ."

"Is it? How interesting. And could I do such a task at home?" And Cate seems to have slipped into morning TV television presenter mode. (If that TV presenter was talking absolute, out-of-context dross.) Nevertheless, I carry on.

"Oh, yes. All you need is a jar or something similar—"

"He's looking," she says through gritted, smiling teeth. "Like, *actually* looking. He's seen you—"

And I've already "seen" him see me, behind Cate's sunglasses, which I am beyond grateful for, and he's now standing up, his eyebrows rising and a hesitant smile slowly curving his handsome mouth.

"Um. *Hey*," he says, gesturing with his arms, turning his palms out. A mix between a shrug and a "voilà."

"Oh! Hi!" I say. "What a surprise!" And of course, I don't sound surprised at all.

"Yeah! Just a bit . . ."

He steps over the picnic bench, and *ugh*, casual, day-off, autumnal Jack is so incredibly cool and hot that I swallow. He's wearing gray-black jeans, a fitted thin light gray crew-neck sweater, white trainers, and a black gilet. One of those hooded, padded ones, unzipped. And why is the vest so hot? He looks like a . . . hot, smartly dressed farmer or something.

"Jack, this is my friend Cate," I say as Jack stands in front of us. There's that aftershave and also, the smoky, salty October sea air that sticks to your skin. "Cate, this is Jack. He's, um, Flye's operations manager?"

"Excuse me. Slash chief of staff," says Jack, throwing me a smirk as he shakes Cate's hand and says, "Very nice to meet you, Cate," and she says, "Oh, likewise!" in the voice she always uses on the phone to call-center staff.

Jack introduces us to his friend Jonny, who seems remote but warm, and Jonny's dog: Elton.

"Everyone's in the pub," says Jack, "but Elton'd had enough. So had Jonny. He's an unsociable fucker. So, here we are."

Jonny places a meaty hand to his chest against his sweatshirt. "Guilty. And guilty again," he says, patting his dog's side. And as I lift a hand to stroke Elton's head, he licks my hand. A big, giant, Fletch-like, area-covering lick.

"*Elton.* Jeez, sorry," says Jonny, pulling Elton back a little by his collar, but he doesn't shift an inch. His paws are cemented to the ground.

"Ohhh, it's *fine*," I insist, my voice just a little too shrill. "I love dogs! Plus, what's a good lick between new friends anyway?" Cate cackles beside me, and I dig my fingers into her arm. Jack laughs, as he always does, as if surprised; as if he expected something else. And I'm not sure why, but every time I'm around him, I just seem to say what's in my mind, no filter. Things just roll on out, like a tight coil of ribbon suddenly unspooled.

"What've you been getting yourself up to, then?" he asks.

"Just shopping. Nothing exciting." *Except constructing a "look" that hopefully lands you with your crotch in the deep freeze . . .*

"And what's the verdict?"

"The verdict?"

"Your color," he says. "What's your color?"

"Oh!" He remembers. Jack always remembers the little things. "Well. One is coral. And . . ."

"Green," Cate jumps in. "Like, most greens."

"Yes. And one that definitely isn't my color is pastel blue, apparently, so—" I gesture down to my light blue T-shirt. "Good to know."

"Is that so?" Jack smiles, eyes flicking for a second to my T-shirt. Cate is going to pierce my skin with her fingernails (that's if I don't come out in a massive, red-hot, embarrassed rash first).

"So, let's have it." Jonny looks at me, smiling, and crosses his large, tattooed arms. "How is he at work then? He a flake at work?"

"A flake?" Jack laughs. "Fuckin' hell, Jon."

"Yup," Jonny says monotonedly. "The man who spends his life pissing off and leaving us. How is he to work for? You counting down?"

"*Leaving you.*" Jack shakes his head, but something passes over his face. That shadow of seriousness again. The reluctance. "Bit dramatic. You just miss me, don't you?"

"Ha." I laugh. "Well. I wouldn't say flake, no. A very tight ship this man does run." And I am not entirely sure why I'm talking like some sort of Tudor, but what I'd really like to do is sit down opposite Jonny and say, "TELL ME EVERYTHING. Leave not a stone unturned."

"Intriguing," says Jonny. "He's been trying to get me out on the boat."

"The boat?"

Jack nods. "Enam has a boat. *Instinct.* Trying to convince Jon to come out with me on it before I leave. But apparently I'm a *flake,* so I retract my invite."

"Nah, I don't trust you as a sailor, mate. Too cocky to be a sailor. I'm staying here on land. Right, Elton?"

Jack laughs as Jonny ruffles Elton's head. Elton looks delighted. "What about you? Coming out with me, Millie?"

"On . . . a boat?"

Cate squeezes my arm. She's like a human blood pressure cuff.

"Yes, *on a boat,*" Jack repeats.

"With a cocky sailor?" I ask. "I'll, erm, get back to you on that one."

Did he . . . mean that? Was that an actual invitation? It felt like one. And Cate certainly thinks it is. She is practically scarring the skin on my arms. Marks I'll be able to show my children one day, like an injured pirate. "These marks, my little loves, are when your auntie Cate sliced me with her nails because she was very excited your mother was invited onto a boat by a very handsome man in a vest."

"So, will I be seeing you at the party?" Jack asks me, slotting his hands in his pockets. "Summer-Ween . . ."

"I decided to go, yeah. Well, I was sort of *forced* by this live wire because she had an outfit she wouldn't let me refuse."

"Yup. Sorted the outfit to *end* all outfits," Cate says, as if I'm going to be arriving in a working Iron Man suit.

"I'm intrigued," Jack says gruffly, eyes on me.

"Will I recognize you?" I rush out, trying to distract myself, stop the blush covering my body like a rash. "Or will you be, like, stuck in a donkey's arse or something and I'll have to spend the whole night trying to find you?"

"I'm not giving away anything," he says, smiling, "not even to you. So you may just have to check every donkey's arse until you find me."

"So, a—Jack scavenger hunt."

"If you like."

And Cate—I am going to kill Cate. She is grinning so much, it's like she's watching one of her favorite Hallmark movies back at the flat, and I swear Jack has noticed. He keeps looking at her, as if he's not entirely sure she isn't drunk.

We say goodbye—a choir of polite nice-to-meet-yous and single-gesture waves.

"And I'll see you tomorrow," Jack says, leaning in. "I'm glad I could sway you."

As we walk away, Cate and I remain silent, until we are well well well out of sight, when Cate throws herself against the railings by the train tracks and the slope down to the beach and says, "Oh my God. The *vibe* was insane. I mean . . . he so fancies you."

"I feel so weird when I talk to him," I groan into my hands. "Like, I forget how to be *normal*. I do mad laughs. *And I can't believe I said the lick thing.*"

Cate bursts out laughing.

"I said what's a good lick between friends."

"Say that at the party in the catsuit," says Cate, "and you'll be winning, my friend."

Moments later, we barrel, giggling, through the door of the flat. Ralph is polishing shoes. "And how was shopping?" he asks. "Any color breakthroughs to report?"

"Forget the shopping," says Cate. "You just missed *desire*, Ralph. Desire walked up and smacked the whole of Leigh-on-Sea in the face. And it was all for our Millie."

**Text message from Dad:** Millie, your mum and I have spoken. Can't talk now. It's a lot to take in. Maybe I can come and see you. Let me know when you're free? Love you, darling. I'm so sorry this has happened. Dad xx

$\mathcal{M}$aybe this *is* what I need tonight. Not quite the squeezing myself into a jet-black full-body suit with my head in a huge felt frame bit. But the party itself. Because what better way to forget about everything than to get dressed up in something stupid and drink and eat and watch Michael Waterstreet do the worm (which is more like the salt-doused slug) before crying into a miniature hot dog because his wife has left him again.

Plus . . . *Jack.* Jack has a way of making nothing seem like a big deal. Best friend blocking you? No worries. Your mum has been secretly seeing her ex-husband nobody talks about? Happens to us all. Send out all your draft emails? So what? So bloody what?

Cate drives me to the party in Ralph's car, and she is so excited, she can barely contain herself in her seat. "That catsuit is going to change your romantic life for good. I just know it," she says as I get out of the car, and she watches me traipse across the gravel drive like a proud parent seeing her daughter off to prom. She waves and wolf-whistles out the window (until a taxi beeps at her to move).

The HTG Summer-Ween party—*big wince*, and an extra one, in Vince's honor—is being held at a hotel in a banquet hall, and although the doorman barely acknowledges the fact that I'm dressed all in black like someone who is about to break into the British Museum on a wire from the ceiling, the hotel staff smirk to each other when they see me hobble in holding my giant wearable frame.

"I'm a scene from a reel of film," I say. "A frame?"

And when I get into the lift to the basement and get the film trapped between the doors, they laugh even more.

I love Cate, but I do wonder if she *is* right about this costume. Genius, she called it. But then, who am I to argue, given how she's made me look tonight. I looked in the mirror after she'd finished with me, and I could not stop smiling. Using a curling wand and a hair serum that smelled like coconuts, Cate turned my usually pretty standard, frizzy, shoulder-length hair into cascading waves that actually *bounce*, and my makeup is note-perfect. She nailed the nude eyes, and my lips are the most sultry shade of classic Hollywood red I have ever seen. They're full and silky, and I took more selfies on the way in the car than I think I have ever taken in my whole life. Even Ralph looked up from ironing patches onto his new swimming club towel and said, "Well. Bloody hell." So, yes, I may be wearing a giant rectangle on my head tonight, but at least I look "Well. Bloody hell" levels of cool.

The lift opens into a carpeted corridor, where I come face-to-face with a printed signpost. "HTG PICTURES SUMMER-WEEN PARTY." Funny to see the "Ween" immortalized in print.

I follow the arrows, deep, muffled music getting louder. A Katy Perry song.

"Eeeyyyyyy!!!" comes a voice, plus two large heavy hands on my shoulders. "Fuck me, what do we have here?"

*Oh God.*

It's Barry Hendrie, head of field sales, who we only see at parties and the occasional going-away drinks, and he's eyeing my frame like I just walked in dragging a dead body I'd hit on the way here.

"Oh, it's . . . I'm a film frame? A still?" I explain. "Well, the actress *on* the film. The film theme? A take on? You sort of just put your head in it . . ."

He cries with laughter and barrels past me, already stinking of beer, despite the fact the party's been going for only an hour. He isn't in a costume, or if he was, it's been thrown asunder, because he's in a lemon-yellow shirt that's undone at the collar, and sweat has spread all over it from the armpits. I imagine his sweaty Halloween mask split and broken, tossed onto the bar.

Oh, I hope I can find Jack or at least someone *else* I recognize (and haven't pissed off with emails) fast. At least I can always shove my frame on and blend into the background of all the other weird, wacky costumes.

Barry lets the banquet door swing shut, and I have to throw a hand out to stop it smashing in my face.

Well. I'd better enter the fancy dress party *in* fancy dress, I suppose. What is it Cate said? Fun. This is fun. To be a bit silly. A bit frivolous. To forget everything from Life B.E. and A.E. and *remember me.*

I put the frame over my head, push my face through the hole, and shuffle my way in, which is exactly as tricky as you'd expect. This must be how my brother Kieran feels, ducking in doorways. He was six feet by age sixteen, six-five by nineteen, and I always laughed as he ducked into the kitchen at home. I shake away a stupid, little thought that says, "Maybe you'll never see him duck through Mum and Dad's tiny cottage doors again because they're breaking up right this second and you'll see your brother even less than you do now."

"Oh!" And as I push my way in to the party, Barry turns to see me, erupts into laughter, and at the deep, guttural sound, so many people, so many *strangers* in the dark, disco-lit room, turn around to look at me and—oh. Oh no no no no. Am I . . . Oh God, I am. I am the only one in costume.

I am the only one in fancy dress.

Then, as my eyes drift around the hot, heaving room through a crowd of strangers, I see him. Jack.

Or should I say . . . Jack as *Titanic*'s Jack Dawson. Holding a small wooden door.

"I am *mortified*." I have almost finished a glass of white wine, and I've been at the bar only five minutes.

How has this happened? How is it that Jack and I are the *only* ones in fancy dress? I'm dressed like someone who's about to scurry onto the stage of a play and rearrange the props, and he is dressed like a poor *Titanic* passenger, and all while everyone else is, at the very least, in smart dress and, at the most, in dresses that wouldn't look out of place at the bloody *Oscars* . . .

"I am so amused," says Jack, giving the lip of his flat cap a yank. The wooden door and my movie frame are leaned against the bar beside each other at our feet. You can actually *wear* Jack's wooden door; slip your arms through the front so it looks like your chin is resting on it.

"Well, I'm glad *you're* amused," I say to him as he leans against the polished bar with his elbows. "I feel a bit like a tosser." But also, amazingly, it isn't getting to me as much as it normally would. A life A.E., I expect. It has a way of desensitizing you. Turning up in a silly outfit is nowhere near as agonizing as getting emotionally naked in an email and sending it "to all."

"You're a movie star," Jack replies, and he leans forward, pressing an arm to mine. And of course, he smells *even* more amazing than he normally does. "You're not allowed to feel like a tosser."

"If you say so." I glance up at him and notice there are what look like icicles hanging from his hair. I burst out laughing. "God, you look ridiculous," I say. "And also, you've totally nailed it. Like—*perfected it.*"

And he has. He looks truly brilliant. Genius. And I didn't think I could find anyone in braces and a tatty shirt attractive (well, except nineties Leo himself, of course), but I actually can't stop looking at him. What feels like a flurry of baby butterflies are batting away in my stomach and my chest. He has those Jack Dawson eyes too. The piercing, beholding-a-million-things-he's-thinking-but-won't-say eyes. (So hypnotizing, they made Rose pose nude, lest we forget.)

"Whereas I," I say into my glass, "look like someone who might pickpocket someone while hanging from the ceiling during a heist."

Jack grins. "Well, for what it's worth . . . I think you look hot."

*Oh my God.*

Jack. Just called me hot. And . . . this *is* beyond chief of staff stuff, isn't it? He *is* flirting with me. This is not me reading into it incorrectly.

"Well. Thank you, *Mr. Dawson.*" And now *I'm* flirting with him, and thank God for this makeup because I absolutely am, in this moment, full-blown red cabbage face. So red cabbage, I fear someone would stick a rosette to my face: first prize.

"I'm serious," he carries on, as if it's fact. "Plus, you've got the whole catsuit thing too . . ."

"Ah, yes. Well, it isn't *technically* a catsuit—"

"Well, whatever it is," he says, and he gives a slow smile, his mouth closing, as if he's stopping what he really wants to say from coming out, and I laugh (and find myself wishing he'd elaborate).

The music gets louder, and more and more people arrive, and

some in outfits so glam, they only make our outfits look even more ridiculous. There's even a woman with a fur *stole* over her arms.

"So, what actually happened?" I ask over the music. "You *said* it was a fancy dress party."

"Ah, see, I looked at the *old* invite. The pre-canceled-and-rescheduled invite. And we weren't the only ones. If you'd arrived just half an hour before you did, you'd have seen Paul Foot in full *Baywatch*. Like . . . Pamela Anderson–style. Swimming costume. Float under his arm. Blond wig."

"*No!*"

"Oh yeah. He went home to change. *Coward!*" Jack calls out across the dance floor, but Jolly Postman Paul, now in a very anodyne white shirt and trousers, doesn't hear and carries on dancing with Martha, his wife, although neither of them looks like they're having a very nice time.

"And plus, look, we can be the stars of the show now," says Jack, pushing off from the bar. "It's like—it's like Disneyland. You know? When you go to Disneyland, nobody gives a shit about all the normal people walking about. Everyone wants to see Mickey. They want to see Buzz Lightyear. That's us. Buzz Lightyear and Mickey Mouse."

"Yeah, well, you could've texted ahead, *Buzz*," I say.

"Well, that's no fun now is it, Mickey?" He grins, and my cheeks are aching at how much I'm grinning back at him. I actually don't think I'd care if I was dressed like Barney the Dinosaur in this moment. Cate was right. I'm really, surprisingly, enjoying myself.

I order another drink, and a woman appears with a huge platter of canapés. Tiny little brisket rolls, with the cutest, teeniest mini deep-fried onion rings hanging on the buns through a toothpick, like a ring toss. She heads straight for me, and I almost squeal at the sight of them.

"Oh my God, I'm making mini onion rings the *second* I have an hour to myself in the kitchen. Jack, *look* at these."

"Ah, see, we get canapés first. Admit it," says Jack to the server, taking one. "You served us first because we're in costume."

She laughs and gives a tiny shrug, but doesn't say anything.

"We know it. Everyone knows it," carries on Jack. "Just my girl Millie here who needs to catch up."

My girl Millie. *Tingles.*

I take a single canapé (and fall in love again, with a miniature onion ring I'll be trying to replicate the second I can), and Jack and I watch the party from beside each other, as if it's completely normal that a reel of film and Jack Dawson are at a party together: a guest and a plus-one.

"I will get you back for this," I say into his ear, nudging him. "*When you least expect it*, Jack Shurlock."

"Bring it on." He grins, and then his eyes stop scanning on the dance floor. He gestures with a dip of his head. It's Lin, and she's waving at me from the middle of a crowd, mouthing, "Come!"

"Oh! I'm—going to go over. Say hi."

"OK, but you're not leaving the frame behind . . ."

"But I've got to go to the *dance floor*," I protest.

"Tough. We made a pact," says Jack, a hand reaching to pick up my frame. "Unbeknownst to you, when you put that frame on your head, you made a promise."

"What a *sentence*."

"Next party, we can both come as a donkey." He moves so he's opposite me, the frame between us. "I'll let you choose if you want front or back."

"No way. The next party will be the Christmas party, and that is always *super wanky*. I will be in a dress. The dress of my dreams. The opposite of whatever"—I gesture to my body—"this is. And you—you can go full-blown tuxedo." I take the frame from him.

He smirks. "Well, lucky for me, I'll have left by then. Which is good. I hate tuxedos."

"Shame," I say, sliding my frame onto my head. "Call me old-fashioned, but a man in a tux. My favorite. Plus. Even Jack Dawson had a tux at some point. So, you know, it's *in character*. Part of your arc."

I turn and cross the dance floor—yes, with my frame on, because I want everyone to know I haven't come here, without reason, in what is essentially a body sock—meander through strangers dancing, and, of course, pointing and laughing at my bloody costume. I nod, smile, say, "Ha-ha, yes, yes, I know!" but wonder if tomorrow I can gather Cate and Ralph and set the costume on fire in the garden for a ceremonial farewell.

A Dua Lipa song begins. Someone dances into me, their shoulder knocking me in the face, blocking me from Lin. And . . . oh. *Oh.* It's Jess. Good Girl Espresso-in-the-Tank Jess. She stops dancing, drink held high, oblivious apparently to her shoulder hitting my face, and she moves to stand next to . . . ah. Chloe. Argh, why are they both here?

"It's our queen," says Lin. "And she's dressed like a fucking portrait, of course she is. I *love it*."

"It's . . . I'm a film scene?" And I'm not entirely sure why I need to clarify this, standing inches from Owen's fiancée, who turns slowly, looking model-like, and glances at me, drink in hand, like I've just taken a shit on the dance floor.

"Hi, Chloe," I say, and Chloe tips her head just once, a jut of her chin. Jess gives a polite smile. A little more low-key than last time.

"Hi, Millie."

Chloe looks amazing. Svelte and elegant in a white strappy gown. Like Gigi Hadid or something.

Lin fiddles with the side of my frame, thick, feathery faux lashes batting. There are droplets of dried, crystallized glitter on them. "This is genius," she says. "Everything about you is *genius*."

"And you look gorgeous," I say, and Lin curtseys. She's wearing a sheer, floor-length black dress, a dark black bodysuit visible through the lace. There aren't many people who can pull such a look off, but Lin—of course Lin pulls it off.

"Why, thank you, baby. And hey . . ." She leans in, already smirking. Good Girl Jess and Chloe are talking between them beside us on the dance floor, but both with one tentative eye on me, like I might suddenly strip off my clothes to reveal another confession, this time scrawled on my body in lipstick. Another stunt. "What's happening with you and Shurlock?"

*Oh God.* I'm now on fire. A sausage of a woman in a cast-iron griddle. "Me and—Jack?"

"*Yeah*," Lin says. "He's a bit too pretty for me, but—he's smoking hot, and he's just so *smooth*, you know?"

"Is he?" Why do I sound so high-pitched?

"I mean, me? I like my *girls* pretty, and my boys more cage fighters, you know? But fuck. You and him . . . there's chemistry, no? He can't take his eyes off you, and when you're both together, you're super smiley and glowy and *sexy*, I love it—"

"Oh God, no." Chloe and Jess are now both listening, oh Christ. If it were just me and Lin, I might tell her that I like Jack a bit, that I have a (pretty big and getting bigger and bigger) crush on him, that the more I get to know him, the more I think he absolutely would mirror Dream Jack Shurlock of sexy push-against-wall passion—and I really *want* to, deep down. It's so nice, feeling this little fizz in my belly, *liking* someone, that whole mystery dance, wondering if they're flirting back, and Lin is such a cheerleader, she's nothing but a delight to have in your corner. But I feel like a total dickhead flaunting my happy, flirty, little crush on Jack under newly-broken-up-because-of-me

Chloe. Plus, Lin and Chloe are friends. They might gossip about me. *'Nice of her, hitting on your fiancé and meanwhile flirting with Jack—who does she think she is?!'*

"Did you just say no?" Lin's eyebrows are now two confused wiggles. "Are you mad? He's hooked, I reckon—"

"No. No, ugh. There is absolutely nothing going on between Jack and me. Trust me."

"Seriously?"

*"Seriously."* I nod, the giant frame on my head shuddering with agreement too. "I could not be less interested. Not my thing at all." And I wince so much inwardly that I practically shrivel. Because did I really just say that? It's of course a giant lie, but it tastes absolutely horrible in my mouth.

Jess and Chloe's eyes slide from me and back to each other, and Lin starts talking about Paul and his *Baywatch* outfit as she takes selfies with me, and before I can protest, she's posting them on Instagram. Then, somehow—I'm alone with her. The woman whose wedding I called off. Chloe and me, in the middle of the dance floor as people pump the air and dance around us to a Queen song.

"Hi." I give a small smile. "How are you?" I feel like I'm walking on coals or something, on shaky ground, prodding a wasp nest with a stick.

"I'm fine," says Chloe over the music, but she doesn't ask me the same back. "Your costume is . . . creative."

"I—I thought it was fancy dress," I reply, and Chloe smiles, just a tiny, minuscule quirk of her full, coral-pink lips, and it feels like an invitation. A nod from the universe that the army have laid down their weapons or something. It's safe ground. "I love your dress. I like the color. That . . . sort of pearly, creamy . . ."

"Pearlescent." Chloe gives a nod. "Thanks."

There's a long pause between us, and it's strange, being opposite someone who has loved the same man as you. There's a . . . connection. A weird crackle of shared experience between you, even if you'd rather just file each other under "my ex's ex." Does our heartache feel the same? Did he say the same things to her in the beginning as me? Does she think about how "opposite" it ended up? Does she have a version of me in her head that she measured herself against, despite herself? Like I have of her.

"Chloe, I just wanted to say I'm so sorry—"

"Millie—"

"And nothing was going on. Like—*nothing.* I haven't even *seen* Owen for years. Since he left. We didn't stay in touch. He left, we broke up, and the first time I saw him was when everyone got back from India—"

"*Millie.*" Chloe looks uncomfortable, her nimble frame shifting from within the silky material of her dress, but I almost want people nearby to hear me; see me talking to her, see us. If they know I sent that email, they'll think I'm a bad person, they might even think Owen and I were having an affair, and I want them to know just how *untrue* that is.

Petra, Jack, Cate, and Ralph sing, *Why do you need them to know this, though, Millie?* in annoying, choir-like unison in my mind.

"Sorry," I say. "I just . . . feel like I need to explain."

Chloe says nothing, arms folded. She swallows.

"I know what he said to you at the rugby game," she says, large, Bambi-like eyes dropping away from mine. "About how he knows when to put his hands up, say he's wrong. That he knows he fucked up . . ."

I stare at her. Beneath my skin, my blood crawls and ripples. "We . . . we were just talking. How did—how did you know?"

Chloe's eyelids droop to half-mast, a thick fan of dark lashes, a look of contempt and sadness all at once. "I . . . I think he made sure

I heard," she says, the corner of her mouth twisting slightly. "Easily done on set."

Made sure she heard? Does she mean—*the headsets*? Surely people couldn't hear us on the headsets? Oh God, say if they did? Heard me banging on about my parents. What else did I say?

"And without sounding rude, Millie," says Chloe, and her chest rises and falls as if she's having to dig deep right in there to find the words, "it's none of your business where I live or what's going on in my relationship—"

"I—I know it isn't. Of course, it isn't. I just— *Nothing happened*."

"I hear you, OK? I know what you're saying, and I hear you. I just . . ." She draws in a heavy breath, as if it tires her just to simply do it. "The wedding date's just . . . *weeks* away."

I nod.

"We're meant to be meeting tomorrow. He asked me over. To talk. And . . ." She gives a hard, sad laugh. I smell alcohol on her breath. "I'm probably stupid. Leona thinks I'm stupid. *I* think I'm stupid because I . . . I'm ignoring my gut."

"You're not stupid," I say. You're just heartbroken, I think. You just love someone and you're in pain. Your heart is tussling with your head.

We stare at each other across the dance floor, two stills among a sea of moving pictures. I open my mouth to speak to her, but her face changes.

She shakes her head, as if to snap herself out of a trance. "So, listen. Move on, OK, Millie?" she says, straightening. "Because *you* can. But truly, and respectfully, I don't want to talk about this again. OK?"

Startled, I stare at her. A head in a giant box. I nod. So does the frame.

And Chloe is gone. And now Michael Waterstreet is looking at me and smiles tightly, almost sneeringly, the way people might when walking the corridors in a cat rescue center. *"Ah. Poor, mangy idiot. Sad, but I'm not taking you home."* I force a smile on my face. He looks away.

And what did she mean about ignoring her gut? Does she . . . think she's missing something? Like what? Like . . . lying? Cheating? Owen isn't perfect. He might have broken my heart out of nowhere, but—a *cheat*? And I know it doesn't exactly sound like a long shot, but Owen hates cheating. Anyone who knows Owen knows how much he does. He'd wax lyrical about the betrayal of it, the collateral. Because *he* himself was the collateral of cheating, he used to say. Every droplet of anger, of insecurity, in Owen is *because* of cheating. A little boy completely rejected by his father because of it. Him and his mother, isolated because of it.

"I Will Survive" blares out of the speakers, and the DJ announces the dancing competition will be starting soon and for all contestants to gather at the front of the stage. Then, suddenly, Jack is beside me. He takes my arm.

"I've donated forty quid to the charity dance-off," he says into my ear. "Which means we can sit and laugh at the dancers without guilt."

And what is it Chloe said? She can't move on right now. The hurt is too much. And I *know* you can look at it from a hundred different ways, but I *did* cause that hurt. My stupid words caused it. My stupid words that were never meant to be sent, and yet somehow *were*. And if they were still in my drafts, how different would my life look right now? How different would Mum's and my poor Dad's look? *Cate's?* And I know Jack says it doesn't matter, but—say if someone really did do this on purpose? His friend seems to think so.

A sheen of confused tears burns my eyes. Angry tears. Despairing tears. "What do I do next?" tears. I feel so tiny, all of a sudden. So alone.

I want to cry them out. I want to leave.

But instead I nod, say, "Sounds good," as Jack bends to wipe a dusting of dirt from my film-reel shoulder.

**Text Message from Cate:** omg I'm at the cinema with Ralph and he is honestly the nicest man alive, isn't he? He remembered I like strawberry pencils and he's just emerged from the lobby with a whole Pic'n'Mix bag of them for me? He's also just given me his hoodie because I'm cold. Anyway. Hope you don't read this because you're too busy snogging Jack's face off in the shadows. Also, that bodysuit tears easily, lol. Bet Jack'll soon find that out, hahaaaa. Love you xxxx

The dance competition does lift my spirits—just a little. But when Jack gets cornered by a group of drunken, loud men who seem to each take turns in bear-hugging him, I'm happy to slink off, alone with my thoughts, which seem to be riding their own haunted funfair carousel around and around my brain.

I feel confused and sad.

Tired and a bit sick too. Hunger, probably.

I arrange some food in a brown takeout-style box from a long table of buffet food in silver, roll-top-lidded dishes—some mini spring rolls, vegetable tempura, some undisclosed dumpling thingies shaped like seashells—and head outside with it, through large open double doors. Party guests are scattered on the damp, squeaky grass—smoking and vaping, having big, involved deep chats; collars loosened, hair disheveled, words slurred, laughter raucous.

I find a picnic table near the edge of a lake, which looks like a thick, black oil slick in the dark. It's quite mild for October, but the air is damp; the smell of wet soil and cigarette smoke.

I turn my face to the sky; blow clouds upward to the speckles and speckles of stars, feel my heart slow, from gallop to slowing steam train.

My whole world turned upside down, just like that. Its own exploded universe. Everything out of its usual place. And it isn't seeming to settle either. I keep waiting for it all to simmer down, and every time it does, it seems to be kicked up again by a sudden gust of wind. Owen. Chloe's pain. Alexis. My . . . *feelings*, I suppose you'd say about Jack. Jack who is my (temporary) boss. Jack who is leaving. Jack who . . . makes me *feel*. Because he does. I feel things with Jack. Deep, new, scary-but-safe-all-at-once feelings.

And Mum and Dad of course. Let's not forget Mum and Dad— the one unit I always saw as untouchable. That perfect, unshakable love I hoped to find one day myself.

I slide my phone out of my tiny cross-body bag, spring roll resting like a cigar between my teeth.

Nothing.

In the distance, the sound of traffic whirs, like a faraway snowstorm.

I look down at my phone again.

Nothing. *Nothing.*

I miss where Mum and Dad always were; calling me on the sofa on a Saturday night, watching a box set the rest of the world watched ten years ago. I miss Alexis too. Her advice. Her funny texts that are always so *in her voice*, I can hear them in my head. I miss the quiet, simple life. Before—well. Before the truth was set free. And some (Ralph) might argue, why would you want a quiet, simple life if it's based on lies. But I do. In this moment, I do. I'd love a simple life; a lovely little slice of under-the-radar, B.E. life. To feel safe, for a moment, and not like everything is my fault, and I'm alone out here, among the debris of it all. I'd give anything.

"Oh, of course," comes a voice, and immediately I stiffen, brush crumbs from my mouth. He's here. Of *course* Owen was invited. Of course. Top of his game, accolades for miles, awards and a portfolio bursting at the seams, like a rammed-full filing cabinet. "When someone said did you see the girl dressed as a reel of film? I thought, ah, that's got to be Mills. *Surely* it must be Mills."

"Locate the mystery idiot and it must be Millie Chandler?" I ask, prickling. I shut the little lid on my box of food, as if it's a secret, and wish almost instantly I hadn't bothered, because what does it really matter now what he might say? Owen had a thing about food. He'd often talk about how I grazed too much, ate too many "empty nutrients," how I should "give myself the food I deserve," harp on about self-care and food being fuel and not joy. An image of me eating a giant BackDonald's with Jack, a table of napkins, and laughter, flicks into my mind.

"Millie, I'm kidding." Owen chuckles. "Just a *you* thing to do, though, isn't it? Wouldn't want you any other way."

And he would always say that when we first met. That he loved my clumsiness, my chaos, my late-sleeping-in-ness. By the end, though, I felt it's what made him leave. A man weighed down by months of it, who simply needed to release himself of my aimlessness and go and live his real life.

Owen takes a seat beside me, sliding along the bench, both of us sitting the wrong way, facing out from the table to the vast, black mirror of a lake. Instinctively, I inch away a little. A defense mechanism, maybe. Being close to Owen feels scary. Like if I get too close, we'll touch, and the shock will throw me back ten feet.

He looks at me, his wide, lopsided smile fading. The top button of his black shirt is undone, dark chest hair sprigging from the gap, his tanned, stubble-speckled neck. I almost can't bear to look at him. It's that thing again. The nostalgia. The nerves. The unease and fast heart.

"Millie, I'm *joking*. You do know that, right?"

"I know."

"And this catsuit. It's—it's actually *insane*. Like—wow."

I swallow. "It's . . . it's not a catsuit."

"Well, I'm just saying, it's very, very—"

"We talked," I cut in. A movie cut of a subject change. "Chloe . . . Chloe and me. Just now. On the dance floor?"

"You and Chlo?" he asks casually, easily, crossing his arms, slouching back. Old, wet leaves rumple in the dark under his shoes. "And what did she say? I hope she wasn't rude to you."

"No," I say. "No, she was fine. And really, I'd deserve getting *rude*. I was just . . . trying to tell her nothing had happened. Butting my nose in where it isn't needed but—"

"I don't know where her head is," says Owen. "She . . . I dunno." He lets out a long, beer-scented breath. It makes an ice-blue puff in the air. "It all feels fucked, Millie. She's meant to be coming over tomorrow. She—begged to, so. But who knows?" *Begged*. Didn't Chloe say he asked her to go there? I don't know. Plus, it was loud on the dance floor, wasn't it? Maybe she didn't say "begged." "And my flat—it's rammed with wedding paraphernalia. Boxes of it. These—table things she roped me into making for hours on end, some candle tree things . . . loads of stuff. All that craft stuff you like. We made loads of it together. I don't know what to do with it all now. I'm surrounded by it."

"I'm sorry," is all I say, because I don't know what *else* to say. I feel rigid, sitting here like a wooden soldier. I can't stop thinking about what Chloe said, too, about hearing what we said at the rugby game. The way he "made sure" she heard. And her gut feeling.

"Are you?" he asks.

"Am I . . . ?"

"Sorry?" asks Owen. "Are you sorry? Because, and don't get me wrong, my life is *all* over the place . . ." And he stops then, a laugh of disbelief, puffing out of him. "But . . . I don't think I am." 'Cause I've *liked* seeing you again, Millie; talking to you again. And I'm, yeah, confused as shit, but I'm . . . *enjoying* being in touch again. Me and you, Millie, our families. Everything was just—ready-made. Perfect. And I fucked it."

I look out across the darkness, panic rising in my chest. A ripple widens on the surface of the black, shining lake, and upbeat dance music grows louder, flows from the open doors behind us to the cold outside.

"I think about our Sundays all the time. Going to see Mum, or your parents. Your dad and me by the barbecue . . ."

My throat tightens. I can't breathe all of a sudden. And I'd be lying if I said I didn't miss the . . . security of those old days. Mum and Dad, no lies, no bloody Easter alibis. And I miss feeling like I was bringing something to the family too. Like something was happening for me, *finally.* Something to be discussed at brunches. No desperate clamor for rotisserie chickens and hollow approval.

"I texted your dad," he says. "I hope that's OK."

Instinctively, I jerk back. As if the words he spoke made a hand in the air and slapped me. I'm . . . surprised. *Shocked.* I—I don't know if that's okay. *Is it?* "Did—did he answer?"

"Yeah." Owen nods, running a hand through his short, thick hair. He interlaces his fingers in his lap, and I look at them. The scar on his thumb, the silver band on his tanned middle finger that I'd turn in slow circles as we lay talking in bed, the dark hair on his forearms that I'd smooth with my hand. The memories dry my mouth almost instantly, and I swallow.

"I didn't mention anything about your mum or anything, but I told him I'd been to that fishing lake that we went to once. Up in Copt Hall? Me and a mate. And I was thinking about how great your dad was to me, and how shit my own is, and—I don't know. After you told me, I thought, this man deserves the good stuff in life. Good karma. And maybe he needed to hear it. He replied. Seemed OK."

"Right. Thank you," I say flatly, but I still don't know how I feel about it. Owen texting Dad, after all this time. It feels strange. It feels like an overstep. A stride over a barrier. But then, it is thoughtful. Dad probably did need to hear that. "I'm glad he seemed OK," I say. "I'm . . . worried about them."

"I know," Owen says softly. "I understand. And I love your family, and they're not even mine, so I can't imagine how you're feeling." Owen's lips press into a sad arc. "I used to sit up in India, thinking about your parents sometimes, wondering if they were OK. If . . . you were OK. I don't want you to think I didn't." His hand lands on my back, and suddenly I feel suffocated. Like I've just been wrapped too tightly in a blanket, swaddled, and I can't break my arms free. I have waited so long for this. All I wanted was for time to be turned back, to *be* with Owen again. Our plans back on track. And there's a small, still-holding-on part of me that wants to let him hold me. But I also want to run from it. What is it I said to Jack? I like to know what's going to happen. And I do. That scared, small, still-holding-on part does, at least. And I know if I lean into Owen, he'll put his arm around me, and I know already how that feels, but then . . . maybe it'll escalate. And we'll get back together. Let's say we do. I know what that feels like too. And is that what I really want?

I scoot along the bench, inch away from him, but his hand grips my arm. "Holy shit." Owen laughs.

"*What?*"

"Listen."

I pause, tune into the music coming from inside.

Oh God. It's *our* song. Mine and Owen's song. Ben Folds. Who plays Ben Folds at a *disco*? Unless it's been . . . requested?

"We have to," he says, his hand still gripping my arm, tugging it gently toward him.

"No. No, no, I'm not dancing, Owen—"

"Ah, come on, you don't even have to dance. You just need to stand with me, move a bit—"

"No, Owen—"

"It's dark. Nobody's even out here."

"Yes, but—"

"No buts. Just—dance with me." And in the moonlight, his eyes glint, and something passes through me like an electric shock. I remember being at a wedding, trying to find Owen, seeing him laughing with a woman I'd told him made me feel insecure. He wouldn't dance with me. He was "busy." Rolled his eyes to the woman about me. And—

I stand up. And as his hands loop around my waist, I push him away.

"Not tonight," I say, my tone terse. "I'm going inside."

Owen's face screws up; switches under the dark sky, like a lever pulled. "*Right*," he says, his head shaking slowly. "O-K?"

And as I move away, he puts his hand back on my arm.

"I asked you. But you never asked me," he says quietly. "But if you had, the answer would have been yes. Yes, I do still think about you, Millie. And yes, a part of me does still love you."

I say nothing and turn away, walking across the wet grass, long strands seeping rainwater through to my ankles, and when I look up, I see Jack. He stands beside a group of men I don't recognize, Jess at his side. He meets my eyes but continues talking, and I decide then and there: I am going home.

I walk briskly down the corridors, music booming from behind the walls, meandering my way around the hotel, on the hunt for somewhere to hide while I wait for my taxi. I stop where there's an alcove of bare coat hangers, a wooden engraved sign above it hanging from two hooks saying "Cloakroom." It's like something from a nineties community hall; a few coats hang inside, a small wooden stool behind a small pillar of a wooden counter. I assume a cloakroom attendant sits behind it when it's in proper use. But tonight it's quiet, nobody's around, so I take the seat myself, in perfect view of the corridor, watching people stumble out of the party and turn away from me, heading to the exit or to the toilets.

I take a deep breath.

*Ugh.*

I feel like everything is upside down. Like I'm sinking. The only man I've ever loved, the only man I've *ever* planned a whole, entire life and future with, wants to dance with me, and standing there in front of him, *finally,* felt—frightening. Like I wanted to sprint. Race away. Like I wanted to run and run until I found . . . Jack. *Jack.* Because I like Jack. I really do. Because I like how safe Jack makes me feel. And the thing is, that is a another issue, isn't it? Another problem is my sea of A.E. problems. Not only is Jack technically my boss, but he is also *leaving.* For a whole entire year, at the very least. What can even happen? I can't fall for someone and have them leave again. Plus, *does* Jack even like me? Is this just Jack being Jack? All cool and laid-back, without a plan to his name. He was like this at the Christmas party. And: Jess. He was hanging out in the darkness with bloody perfect Good Girl Jess, who he seemed to flirt like a pro with that afternoon in reception, so here I am—what? Sitting in a darkened cloakroom waiting for a taxi because I don't want to interrupt Cate's evening and I also don't know what else to do.

The door swings open. My heart suspends. Barry Hendrie stumbles out. An evening in reverse. He holds on to the wall, swallows, as if fighting against a stream of vomit, then wobbles off down the corridor, the door bumping gently closed behind him.

I stand up. Should I go to the lobby? The taxi will be here soon. The guy at reception said half an hour. "Or thereabouts."

The door squeaks open again and again, a cycle of people leaving, people taking phone calls. And then . . . he appears. He's without his Jack Dawson door, but still in the outfit, one more shirt button unfastened than earlier. For a split second, I watch him, knowing he can't see me. And I realize I really, really do like him. My heart is banging against my chest, like a small rhythmic fist. A hard, undeniable beat of *I do, I do, I do, I do.*

Jack looks both ways, and then—he sees me. Fixes me with those beautiful, playful eyes. And they do something to me, those eyes. *Melt* me. Spark something that sweeps down my body, lighting me up inch by inch.

"Hey," he says, striding down the corridor toward me, and butterflies—butterflies *immediately.* And I find myself wanting to run toward him, throw my arms around him, hold on to him, tightly, freeze time. Instead, I stay glued to the spot.

"What're we . . . trying on a new job?" His eyes lift to the cloakroom sign as he arrives at the little counter and then drop to meet mine. The corner of his mouth twitches.

"Maybe," I say. "Does Jack Dawson need me to hang up his . . . *braces*?"

Jack laughs. "You do realize if I take these braces off, Millie," he says hoarsely, "my trousers will fall down."

"Ha. Yes. Well. I see." Butterflies. I am now solely made of butterflies. "Part of the plan, was it?"

I stand, say nothing, give a big, breathy, flustered smile.

Jack circles the counter, joins me in the alcove of the cloakroom. I find myself slowly moving backward, putting space between us, even though I don't want to. I want to . . . be close to him. So close. The back of my head meets the fabric of someone's jacket, and I let out a mad fake giggle and an "oops," and he smiles, leaves the gap between us. "What're you doing hiding out here, then, Millie dot Chandler?"

"I'm, um, I'm . . . going home," I say. "In about ten minutes or so. Ordered a taxi."

Jack's brow creases, his lips meeting together softly and thoughtfully. "Well, that sucks," he says. "Was it Paul Foot's dancing? Triggering stuff."

I smile weakly. "Maybe."

"Maybe? Did something happen?"

"Sorry, just . . ." I sigh. "It's—everything really. I know you think I shouldn't care, and I shouldn't worry, but I spoke to Chloe, and . . . and Owen, he—"

"I saw him out there with you."

"It was nothing," I rush out; a giant blurt of words with no spaces between. "It was just him chatting and talking about the wedding and everything and . . ." I look up at him; meet his eyes. A sigh heaves out of me. "I saw you with Jess."

Jack gives a single nod. Unreadable. "Yeah. I was going to come over, but . . ."

"I really wish you would have," I say, and the words coming out of me feel like a relief. Because it's the truth. And I feel like I always speak truths with Jack, almost despite myself. I really do wish he had come over. Stepped through the darkness by that table and the dark glass of the lake. And this feeling, with Jack—it's scary and safe, all at once. Like something you know is good for you, but the leap to get there feels vast and wide and scary.

Jack steps forward gently. "I'm here now," he says deeply.

I can't step back now, I'm against coats, the wall of the alcove, and I wouldn't want to anyway, if I could.

And now he's right in front of me.

I can smell him—his hot shower smell, aftershave on his warm skin, and I can feel the heat of him. His warm, muscular leg presses gently against mine, and for a moment I can hardly bear to look up at him, from the opening of his shirt, the taut, ridged skin. His Adam's apple bobs as he swallows, and I meet his eyes, syrupy and intense. He is so close. Heat pools in my stomach, moves lower, and lower. My eyes close for a second, and a vision of me grabbing his hips, pulling him into me, pushing my mouth onto his, holding his bottom lip between mine, barrels its way into my mind.

I open my eyes, and his gaze is already on me—stuck to me. That crackle, that tug between us that I'd felt seeing him yesterday outside that pub, only now larger than ever. A magnetic force, pulling and pulling us closer.

The music blurs into the background and all I can hear now is our breathing; his deep and husky, mine fast, light, like moths in my throat . . .

His hand moves to my jaw, a light graze of rough fingertips, and he tips my face up, to look at him. Jack's lips are so close to mine, I can feel the warmth of them, can smell the whisky on him.

He's going to kiss me. *He's going to kiss me.* All I want is for him to kiss me—

And then the door swings open.

A huge, sudden squeak, and out explodes a group of squealing, screeching party guests, tripping and holding on to each other, like bowing inflatables. More follow. Someone shouts, "Car's here!"

I jolt—*freeze*. We both do. No. *No no no.*

"*Fuck*," Jack whispers, and against him I practically wilt. And against my mouth, he smiles slowly and says croakily, "Another . . . time, I guess?"

And I can't even speak. I just nod, rigidly, my skin surging, pimpling with goose bumps.

"When you least expect it," he says. And before my brain kicks back into gear so I can move, speak, *anything*, he's moving away from me, walking off.

But just before he disappears through the door, Jack turns around and looks at me with such intensity, and a tiny gasp leaves my mouth.

Cate is going to die.

That's if I don't die first.

*chapter 17*

**Text message from Dad:** Hi darling, are you around this
morning? I was hoping I could come over and we could go for a
walk? Dad x

I have never been more grateful for Cate and Ralph than in this moment. The party with Jack last night has left me feeling more giddy,
more *alive* than I have been in a long time, and so far, Cate and Ralph
have spent the entire Sunday morning eating French toast I made
while extracting meticulous details from me about the whole night
(and mostly via Cate, who is interviewing me with such excitement,
it's like I'm a sailor who has just completed a Guinness World Record–
breaking solo trip).

And I'm grateful, really, for the distraction. Dad is coming over,
and I really don't know what to expect. It could be totally fine. It could
be totally not. Look at Alexis's parents. Her mum left her dad—left

them *all*—when her dad, Salv, was in his sixties. She started again; went back to chapter one despite almost being at the denouement of her life. She even remarried.

"OK, so, do it on me," Cate says, jumping up from next to Ralph, who watches, smiling, from behind his black coffee at the breakfast bar. I'm making a flask of tea for Dad and me, like Mum used to when I was young. There are plenty of places to get tea around here, but a flask, the beach—I want the nostalgia of it. To remind Dad when he might need it the most, to remind me, too, of the nice times we had as a family, that of *course* we can get back there, because it was just a stupid lie. A little blip.

Cate positions herself flat against the fridge. "Let's pretend the fridge is all the coats. So, you were here, like this?" Cate is practically juddering with excitement, like a pipe about to burst.

I laugh, pour hot water into Ralph's four-cup flask. I place the kettle down. "Yep," I say, walking over and standing in front of her.

Cate grins at me with gooey, schoolgirl eyes.

"OK, you're too tall for this, you need to crouch so you're looking at *least* at my neck," I instruct.

Ralph chuckles to himself as Cate slides lower. "This?"

"Perfect. OK, and then, he . . . sort of moved closer, and closer, until I could feel his leg against mine . . ." I inch closer to Cate, both of us grinning like deranged Halloween masks.

"I'm aroused," says Cate, and I burst out laughing.

"This is ridiculous, isn't it?" I say, glancing over my shoulder to Ralph. "I do apologize for bringing this into your home."

"Oh, I'm sure he's coping just fine," says Cate, "isn't that right, Ralphie?" and oh my God, he's blushing. I don't think I have ever seen Ralph blush. I'm the red cabbage blusher. Ralph is far too measured and ever level to blush.

"Yes, well," says Ralph. "Far worse things have happened."

"Come on, Millie," grumbles Cate, grabbing my waist. "I'm dying here. Finish the tale. I need to know."

"Sorry, sorry. All right, so, I then looked up, and he went like this." I tip Cate's face to look up at mine, and she grins even wider, and this is all so silly, so infectious. I can't stop smiling. "And it was just . . . what felt like ages and ages, just breathing and *heat*—and then the door opened, and the whole *universe* poured out of the door. I basically froze, then he said, *fuck*, and *then*, he did this really slow and sexy smile . . ."

"A slow sexy *smile*, oh help me . . ."

"Then he said *another time*, and into my ear . . . *when you least expect it.*"

"Fuuuuck," says Cate, sliding to the floor, taking our recycling bin schedule and two fridge magnets with her. We all erupt into laughter, which echoes around our lovely little kitchen.

"*I know.*" I laugh.

"Jack Shurlock is so hot," Cate sings. "I told you he was bad. I can tell. I'm so good at this stuff."

I stride back to the kettle, and Ralph says, "I have to admit, Millie, he sounds like a very cool customer."

"A cool customer," says Cate getting up, dusting a hand down her pearl-pink silk button-down pajama top. "Which doesn't make him sound cool at all."

Ralph rolls his eyes and smiles, and Cate winks at him. Are they—*flirting*? An almost-kiss with Jack Shurlock against a bunch of coats has sent all of us a bit feral.

"So, when do you think it'll happen?" Cate asks.

"When she least expects it," says Ralph as I drop tea bags into the flask. "Clearly."

"Well. That's if he's remembered. He was a bit drunk. *As was I.*"

Cate scoffs. "Why would he *forget*? What, so he'll flirt with you all night, tell you he wants to kiss you, and then erase you from his memory?"

"He's leaving, though."

"Oh, so what?" Cate exclaims. "Do not even tell me you're going to sabotage a kiss with him just because he's going traveling. The two things have nothing to do with one another. I would *kill* for a kiss. I haven't been able to really face that thought since everything but . . . *yeah.* Just a kiss, you know? With someone I fancy who really, really *wants me,* and there's all that hot, sexy, can't-take-much-more longing—"

Ralph bursts into such a sudden coughing fit that it makes both Cate and me jump and swoop around.

"*Coffee,*" he gasps, liquid streaking down the side of his mug. "Wrong . . . pipe."

"Jesus, be careful." Cate laughs heartily. "Too much longing talk for you?"

"No, no," Ralph says, still gasping. He brings his baggy sweatered wrist to his mouth and dabs.

"What can I say? I read a lot of romance. Longing is my currency."

The doorbell rings, and I quickly screw on the flask's lid. "That'll be Dad." A shudder of dread moves through me. Reality, grounding me with a surge. Say if it's—*bad* news? It's one thing having your emails piss your friend off, but it's another having your actual parents' relationship changed by it. I almost don't want to answer the door . . .

"I knew my makeup look would do it," says Cate distractedly as I say goodbye and head for my coat. "And it's that catsuit. I said it, didn't I?"

"You did, Cate," says Ralph. "That you really did."

I open the front door, autumn leaves scurrying across the doorstep, like little creatures caught in the act. With one arm in and one arm out of my puffer coat, I freeze.

It . . . isn't Dad.

"Cate's out," is all I say, as Nicholas straightens in the doorway, slotting a hand into his jacket pocket. In his other is a pile of mail, a fan of white and biscuit-brown envelopes.

"Morning, Millie," he says, as if it's totally normal that he's here; as if he's dropping by for a cup of tea and a piece of French toast. He looks dead-eyed. Tired. His brown eyes slits, his usually smooth, clean-cut face covered in scruffy, heavy stubble. "So, where is she?"

"I don't know." I pull the door closed behind me, a hand gripping the edge. "Shopping, I think. Or maybe . . . yoga? I don't remember."

"You don't remember?"

I point to my face with a lazy finger. "I'm dead, Nicholas. Hung-over, so, no, I don't. You can leave a message if you like, though. I'll tell her."

Nicholas stares at me. Behind him, clouds hang thick, like sodden, inky wool. There's a rumble in the sky—an airplane, or distant thunder.

"OK, then," I say, "is that everything?" and for a moment, Nicholas just looks at me, his eyes suddenly misted over. Then he steps forward, pushes his hand against the surface of the door. "Nick, what are you—" The door opens, but I pull it back, hand burning under the friction of it.

"Millie, what . . . *what* is your problem?" His words are low; spoken through his teeth, eyes closing, like someone trying to keep ahold of himself, to not lose it.

"My problem?"

"I know you're behind—all this." His eyes lift, gazing at the flat, as if that's what's stolen her away. A princess trapped in a castle.

"I don't know what you're talking about, Nicholas. I think you should just—"

"Cate leaving me," he says, voice breaking a little at the edge. He steps back, pulls at the lapels of his bomber jacket, as if ironing himself out. "It came out of nowhere. As if she just woke up one day and decided. And do you know what she said to me the other night? That she doesn't love me anymore. And she hadn't for a long time."

I swallow. He's intimidating. That dead-eyed, intent stare, muscles pulsing in his long, angular face. Cate jokingly called Nicholas her "Stefan" when they first met, after the lead in *The Vampire Diaries*, which she loves. He had the hollow cheekbones, the dark eyes. But right now, he actually *looks* like a vampire. (And not the nice, hot, brooding kind.) "Right," is all I can think to say.

"How can that be true? We were together for *four* years." He grits his teeth together, glances over his shoulder, checks to see if anyone else can hear him. Owen would do the same. Almost as if it wouldn't matter how he was making *me* feel, just that everyone else thought he was a decent person, even meaningless strangers. "Millie, you can't seriously think I deserve this. We have a home—a *life*."

"I'm Cate's friend," I say, my voice wobbling slightly, "and if this is what she wants, I support her."

Nicholas laughs, a hand at his chin, a snarl on his thin mouth. "*You support her*. You—" He looks down at his feet, then back up at me. "You of all people should understand this, Millie. You *get this*."

My heart is racing. He's angry. He's hurt, I get it. But he's making me feel uneasy; shaky on my own doorstep. "I think you should leave, Nicholas. Please. If Cate wants to talk to you, she will."

"All I did was love her."

"Nicholas—"

"Do you know that? All I did was *love* her, and you're all fucking out there, painting me as—"

"Please leave."

And with that, he strides forward, pushes his face toward mine. I jerk back. "You. You have poisoned her mind. It's *my* business with Cate. Not yours. You don't know us. *Me*."

"Please leave," I say again. There's a louder rumble now. Thunder. Definitely thunder. Rumbling, like a temper getting slowly, slowly riled.

"Tell me what I did," he says. I can smell his breath. Coffee. Chewing gum. "Name *one* thing I did that was my fault."

"Did you not download a dating app?" And the words come out wobbly, but hot anger is bubbling up inside me because—how can he ask me that? How can he *honestly* think none of it is his fault? And what I find amazing is that Nicholas has been nonstop texting Cate, calling her, but not once has he said he misses or loves her. Just how irritated he is to have to explain this to people, how *embarrassed*, how he can't understand what he's done, how he's so lost. Him him him.

"Nothing happened!" he says, jerking back, his voice going high-pitched. "Fuck, this is all just—madness. Pointing fingers at me when you can't even look at yourself. Owen was so great, was he? You were so great?"

"I'm not even *with* Owen."

"So you know how this feels, then, don't you, Millie? This." He slams a hand hard against his chest.

"Please leave, Nicholas."

A slow, harsh smirk curves his mouth, but his eyes glisten. Desperation. Exasperation. A man with nothing else to lose. "I walked in on him once, Owen, by the way. Flirting away with Alexis. At one of our barbecues. Remember you left? A migraine or some shit." He rolls his eyes. "The *faces* on them both . . ."

And I know this is Nicholas. That he's spouting spiteful bullshit because he's hurt. But my skin chills at his words. I remember that day. Alexis didn't like Owen. Not at all. But that day, they'd got into a deep chat about parents—Owen and his dad, Alexis and her mum, who'd upped and left the family, including Alexis's sixteen-year-old sister, for a man in Cornwall a few years before. They'd stood in the kitchen together for ages, chatting, drinks in hand, as Cate and I flitted in and out, meandering around them, grabbing food to take outside. I was *delighted* they were speaking.

"And yet I download an app for a laugh," says Nicholas, shaking his head, dragging two hands through his long, messy hair.

"Please will you just *go*."

"I brought her fucking mail."

"*Then give me the mail!*"

My voice echoes around the car park. Thunder rumbles again, and rain starts to pelt the ground, like gravel.

He scrunches up his face. "Do you know what? I tried for her. *I loved her.* I provided for her, yet here I am, and I have—nothing. And do you know what I think? You just want to bring my Cate down—"

"*Me?* I want Cate to be happy. And she isn't *your* Cate—"

"What did you just say?" And he's up in my face again now, but closer. I stand, frozen to the spot.

But before I can say anything else, Ralph pushes past me, grabs Nicholas by the arm, and drags him across the driveway.

Nicholas trips, a long leg folding beneath him on the pavement. He blinks up at Ralph.

"Get off our fucking property," Ralph says slowly and calmly. Then he walks back to me, guiding me gently inside, and slams the door behind us.

## chapter 18

I don't think I've seen Dad this exhausted and wrung out for years. It's the sort of tiredness that runs deeper than not having enough sleep. I know what that looks like on him—the puffy eyes, the paler skin, the sleepy smile. I remember that from when I was seven and would wake him at three a.m. on Christmas morning banging a full-up Christmas stocking on his head. I know that from when he'd pick Cate and me up from the train station at half past midnight when we were eighteen, yawning at a red light, turning to me and smiling, so as to not give himself away, just in case I might suggest I get a taxi. "I can't bear the waiting for the key to go in the lock," he'd say. "I'd sooner come and get you."

But this is a different tiredness. This is red-eyed, gray-skinned, been-up-all-night, all-week, my-world-has-crumbled, dog exhaustion. This is evidence of a lie. A betrayal. A hairline crack down his smooth, protected, nurtured marriage.

The sky is blank and colorless, drizzling a humid British mist. We walk slowly, despite the drizzle, along Grand Parade, toward the steep, grassy ruggedness of the east cliffs. Dad and I traipse side by side in silence, the flask in my hand, two packets of biscuits in my handbag, like Mum always used to have in her backpack. I can still see them so clearly in my memory—the packets wedged next to each other neatly in a row, ready for me to choose, mine and Kieran's fingers running along them, as if it was a library shelf. And I wait with a held breath, footsteps and sloshing tea, until Dad speaks.

"Your mum told me," he says eventually, and my heart drops like a stone, even though I knew that's what he was going to say.

"And are you all right?" I ask, and my voice sounds tiny, like it's trapped in the bottom of a jar.

"I, er . . ." Dad hefts a breath in, and already I can see there are tears in his tired, dull eyes. "I'm not sure, really, darling," he says. "I wish I could say yes, I'm fine, but I'm not quite all right at the moment."

And I hate it. I hate how sad he sounds, his words flat and tone-less.

I nod. "I'm—I'm sorry, Dad."

"You have nothing to be sorry for."

We walk some more. We're at the edge of the steep, grassy mound of the east cliffs now, and the estuary fills the horizon. We wander through the beachy grass on the footpath, the steepness causing us to walk like we're shuffling down the aisle of a moving bus, and as much as this isn't exactly a "happy" trip out to the seaside, I'm grateful for the forceful, unforgiving blasts of cold air, for the sweet, salty smell of the sea. Especially after Nicholas shook us all up; how sorry poor Cate was, as if *she* is the one who should feel sorry. And then there's that thing he said, too, about Alexis and Owen. And something about it—the mulling over of things in my world that might be unsaid and unseen—that makes the whole glitch thing roll into my mind like a chosen bingo ball. The "someone sending it on purpose" thing that is "just a theory." The wondering about if it's true. And if it is, who? Why? And so I close my eyes against the shower of drizzle, let the thunder of the sea and autumn wind drown it all out. Every inch of it.

"Watch yourself, Millie Moo," Dad says, the steep footpath beneath our shoes, but he adds nothing more until we've descended the wonky stone steps and arrived at Cliff Bridge, a winding elaborate bridge that always reminds me of a giant helter-skelter.

"I knew something was wrong with your mum," Dad says finally, sighing. His chubby, rough cheeks are raspberry pink. "And I admit I ignored it, that feeling. My gut, I suppose. What I really felt. Pretended I didn't. Hid it away. And . . . the more I think about it, I don't even know why I'm surprised that this is something she wants to do. Julian. Because your mum, she's so herself. The sort of person who just does what she likes, what she feels is *right*, and that's all the explanation she needs to give in order to do it. And if her heart wants something . . ." He shrugs, shows his palms, as if demonstrating being empty-handed, but there's warmth still as he talks about her. A tiny flicker of a cozy fire in his eyes, because that's what he loves about Mum. "And I even *understand*. I can't stand the man, Millie, but I . . . I do understand the wanting to do it."

We walk over the bridge slowly sloping down to the coastal path. Misty rain dampens our cheeks, and a tiny letterbox slot of sun through the clouds turns the sea to liquid pewter. "What was he like?" I ask.

Dad thinks deeply, as if sifting, trying to find the right words. Then he says, "Just—toxic. I wish I could say a nicer word, but toxic. Julian was toxic."

The word tightens my chest.

"I don't believe he wanted to be. Not deep down. But—the alcohol. It dominated his life in the end. And in turn, your mother's."

I nod. "And she got out?" I ask, even though I of course know the answer. But I feel like a child who needs a happy ending. A crumb of hope on the next page of the book. I can't bear it, imagining Mum, of all people, stuck in a toxic, destructive life.

"She did. I helped her. Another friend of ours did too. And then—" He smiles at me; ruddy windbeaten cheeks, watery, wise eyes that have seen and know so much. "Well. You know the rest."

And I suppose that's what waits on the next page. Dad. Us. The Chandlers. Our family.

"For me," I say, "it's that she didn't tell you."

"That she lied." Dad nods, walking tall beside me.

"Yeah," I say.

"That's it," says Dad simply. "That's what I can't get past. That's what hurts. The intention of it. The lie. Something she carried around and didn't tell me."

We arrive at the bottom of the bridge and to the path that runs along the beach, railings on one side, the train line on the other. Scenes like these are why I love living here so much. It's the contrast of everything. The beauty of the ocean, the vast expanse of sky, the sunsets that look like watercolors; and then the weather-beaten rust on railings, the spiky, overgrown train lines, the boat store, clumsily piled up with peeling, overturned boats with exotic names. Ugly and beautiful all at once, light and shade, rough and smooth. Like . . . life, I guess. Like people. And that's why we hold on, isn't it? Because while we're in the shade, we know the light will come eventually if we just wait a little longer. And as much as my heart aches now, looking at my lovely dad, his thick, black waterproof jacket, the blue checked shirt peeping underneath that my mum would have ironed for him, hung meticulously in his wardrobe, I *know* there has to be a way through this. They're a solid unit. This unwavering, solid unit.

"I said to her," Dad continues, "how much pain, Toni, does someone have to cause in order for you to believe it's just what they do; who they are? At what point do you grant someone no forgiveness? He left her with nothing."

I nod, my heart like a tender exposed wound in my chest. Mum is so strong and together. The sort of person you feel has a lovely clean slate of a reputation; not a foot put wrong, not a single memory that makes you think, *Ach, glad I'm not like* that *anymore*. Like Kieran. Not like me. And just thinking about her putting her trust in the wrong person, being mistreated regardless of her intelligence, her strength . . . It makes me think of Cate. Of me.

I suggest to Dad we sit down and have some tea, and we walk a few yards more until we come to the wooden beach shelter, its panels painted a vanilla custard cream, and the benches a midnight blue. We sit on a bench looking out to sea at the haze of drizzle, water on water, and I pour us two teas into the two plastic cups from Ralph's Thermos. Dad smiles when I reveal the biscuits in my bag.

"You're such a good kid," he says, and I see his mouth quiver, but he hides it with his cup. "Sometimes I worry you don't know that we think that of you."

I nod. "It's OK, Dad."

Dad then gives a stiff shrug. "I think we put pressure on you," he says. "To . . . I don't know. I . . ."

"Walk the line?" I offer, almost too quietly, a part of me hoping he doesn't hear, that my words get carried out to sea instead, but Dad looks at me, almost shocked. And I am, too, in a way, that those words just left my lips. But they *did* put pressure on. Gentle but constant. To do my homework, to get good grades, to have teachers write things like "conscientious" and "polite" on my school reports. To find a conventional path and follow the stepping-stones, one at a time. Even when I met Owen, there was a sort of collective sigh of relief between them. That, OK, I might have dropped out of university and I may have no career, but at least I'd met a nice, ambitious, family man who wanted all the token things you're supposed to want, like a wedding, a house, and savings, and maybe even a family. All things conventional. And I suppose at first I didn't really see it as pressure; more them wanting the best for me. But is it ever wanting the best for someone if you've already decided what that best looks like for them?

"I'm sorry if you've ever felt that, my darling."

"It's—it's OK . . ."

"Well, all the same . . ."

And I don't try to paper over it. Because what is it Ralph often says? Feeling things is what we're *supposed* to do as a human, but not everyone is always going to sit with something you feel and be comfortable with it. And it's not up to you to take that discomfort from them, especially not if it means trading in your own truth for it. "It's OK, Dad," is all I say again, and I place a hand on his.

Dad and I sip tea and eat biscuits. The tide is in, lapping against the concrete wall by our feet. "I stayed at your auntie Vye's last night," he says. "In the conservatory, on a put-you-up bed. Just to get my head together. I thought we needed space from all the talking."

Something sinks in me, hot and heavy. Mum and Dad, in separate houses. No. Not Mum and Dad. Not my safe, dependable parents.

"God," I say. Then, "And also, not that bloody conservatory," and Dad allows himself a laugh. It's bad enough knowing Mum and Dad slept separately, but in the emblematic conservatory of ladies-who-lunch-and-brag-about-hollow-things? It feels like an alternate reality.

"Are you . . . are you both going to be OK?"

Dad swallows. "I hope so," he says, and I want to say, "No. No, not 'I hope so,' say yes. Say everything is going to be OK." "I just need some time," carries on Dad. "She doesn't want to stop seeing him. And I understand that. But I'm just not sure where that leaves me."

Dad takes a deep, shaky breath in, and we sit together, staring out to sea, my heart aching a little. The tide slowly, slowly fades before us, the sludgy sand revealing itself, millimeter by millimeter, water slipping away.

"I think lies hurt more than any truth ever could," Dad says. "Because it turns the person into something else. You start to wonder what else they've been concealing, even if it's nothing at all. It's like someone turned the lights on, and for the first time you can see something you never knew was there. And you have to trust again. Trust that there is nothing else concealed, to see. That's the hard bit."

I nod. It resonates; his words, my heart. Like two magnets meeting. North Pole and South. I think of my emails, all *my* concealed truths, breaking free like birds. The sun, lighting them all up. Out there. Nowhere to hide.

"Mum loves you," is all I can think to say, "she really does," and Dad nods.

And neither Dad nor I says anything else. We watch the tide pull away, the gap between us and the shore, and the waves widening and widening, and I hope that, like the tide, my dad will edge slowly back to shore. To land. To Mum.

**Text message from Millie:** Guess where I am, and who I just saw in the boat store looking very pretty indeed? (Unless there is another green dinghy called *Instinct* hanging out in Leigh.)

**Text message from Jack:** I'll tell him you called him handsome next time I see him. He'll be made up.

**Text message from Millie:** A MALE boat? Rebellious.

**Text message from Jack:** Always.

**Text message from Jack:** And guess where I am. Clue: I'm not in Leigh wandering by boat stores. (Unfortunately.)

**Text message from Millie:** In the vortex?

**Text message from Jack:** Not quite. In a taxi, on my way to the airport. Flye needs me in Madrid. (Then Italy.) Europa League.

**Text message from Millie:** OMG what? For how long?

**Text message from Jack:** Six days, all in.

**Text message from Millie:** Well, that's very unfair!

**Text message from Jack:** Very unfair that I'm in Europe while the UK pisses it down or very unfair that you have to endure a long, painful week of work without me?

**Text message from Millie:** Oh, of course, only the first bit. Who needs Jack Shurlock when I have Cardboard Gary and Chatty Martin for company?

**Text message from Jack:** Mute Martin, Millie.

**Text message from Jack:** Don't make me correct you again.

## chapter 19

**To: ALL office**

**From: Gail Fryer**

**Subject: Flye's Monthly "Dates for the Diary"**

9th—Broadcast Awards Ceremony for those invited

   —South Kensington, London, 7 p.m.

10th—Last date to RSVP to Christmas party

    (invite attached as refresher)

12th—Jack Shurlock's Leaving Us (again!)

    farewell drinks

   —The Peterboat (outside space, booked).

1st—Christmas party

  —glad rags on, folks!!!

**To: Millie Chandler**
**From: Jack Shurlock**
**Cc: Michael Waterstreet**
**Subject: Minutes for meeting—Weds 4 p.m.**

Millie,

I wonder if you are free to take down minutes at our 4 p.m. meeting, Wednesday, when the team are all back from Italy? Please let me know and I'll forward more details when I land.

I was very impressed by your diligent and hard work at StoneX. Especially on the screen display . . .

Thank you,

Jack

Jack Shurlock

Operations Manager and Chief of Staff (cover)

I am sitting in what is probably about to be the most boring meeting ever conducted, with me, thanks to Jack, instructed with the most boring *job* ever. But despite how much I'm trying to pretend to myself that I'm chill, that I haven't even *thought* about him since that moment in the cloakroom at the party, or those texts, and that email that made my cheeks ache, thank you very much, I am buzzing with excitement. Because Jack is coming to this meeting, and I haven't seen him in over a week. It was like Christmas Eve last night, or something. Cate, Ralph, and I watched *Notting Hill* in our pajamas as Cate read our tarot cards (Ralph, apparently, has a secret wild inner animal he must set free, and I have "justice" on my horizon), and we all placed giggly, silly bets on when (or if) the "when you least expect it" kiss might happen.

And I keep thinking about that party. I keep thinking of those eyes on mine, the heat of Jack against me, the way he *wanted* to kiss me, that gruff, sexy "when you least expect it" . . . I stifle the smile wanting to spread across my face, light me up like a spotlight in this stuffy meeting room, and this feels so . . . *nice*. This glimmer among everything. It feels new. But it reminds me of a time before too. Not just the time before the emails, but before everything got so complicated and grown-up. Dates, and crushes, the flirting, the feeling of "What might happen next?" Of course, the too-sensible, too-cautious, keep-your-eye-on-bad-things-you-might-need-to-dodge part of me has its arms crossed and shaking its head, saying, "What are you even doing? He is leaving. Literally *emigrating.* Leaving with a capital fucking *L*." But it's as Cate said last night. "Nobody's telling you to marry him. OK, I did, but also, can't it just be a kiss? A single date? Why does it need to have a linear beginning to perfect, happy end? This isn't one of my romance novels, Millie."

Colleagues file into the meeting room, coffees and teas placed one after the other on the table, scattered around two dinner plates of biscuits that I'd arranged into a nice fan shape but that now look all jumbled, like something from a Cub Scouts meeting. It's one warm box of coffee breath, perfume, and warm ink in here.

A chair scrapes along the carpet.

"Millie?"

I look up to find Michael. He drags the chair, takes a seat ahead of me, casually cool and grumpy as always, but a version of him, in my memory that will likely refuse to ever die, dances madly (and seriously) like he did in the HTG Summer-Ween dance-off.

"Are you using highlighters?" he grumbles over his shoulder.

"Yes," I say. "Petra explained."

"It's just—it helps us single out subjects, projects . . ."

"Totally." I nod, although what I actually want to say is "Yes, I know, Petra is fully capable of explaining something without your aid, thank you very much, you big sexist."

Naturally, he continues to mansplain. "The green is for the immediate issues that need to be addressed—"

"Blue for nonurgent . . ." Although I'm tempted to say, "And pink for all the football players I think are hot. Right? Five doodled hearts for the hottest?"

Michael nods. "Yes, yes," he says, almost astonished. "Yes, that's right."

And really, I can't complain. I wanted this, didn't I? To do extra tasks, put myself *out there* more, show people, like Dancing Michael Waterstreet, that I *like* this company and don't want to destroy it with email bombs. That I'm . . . *more* than what they might think I am.

A warm hand lands on my shoulder, squeezes gently. Electricity fizzles through my body.

"And she even saved me a seat, I see," says a voice, deep and familiar.

I turn to see Jack—meet his warm, playful eyes. And it almost feels strange seeing him. I've thought so much about him, talked about him with Cate and Ralph, about that moment at the party, tried to "logic" my way through the whole he's-leaving-the-country-and-what-if-I-get-hurt? issue over and over in my own mind, that he's almost become someone a little—*fictional.* One of Cate's romantic heroes from her books and Hallmark movies.

Jack takes a seat next to me, swipes open an iPad in his lap, holds it with one hand. He smiles at me—a secret, what's-this-silly-little-meeting-going-to-matter-anyway-once-we're-all-dead? smile. The area on my shoulder he touched with his hand still buzzes beneath my dress.

"Hello, Mr. Spain and Italy," I say.

"Hello, Miss Millie P. Chandler?"

"P.?"

"Just taking a stab at the middle name, there," he says with a shrug, tapping away on the iPad. "Penelope? Petunia?"

"Nope. And nope."

"Am I even just a little bit close?" he asks in a whisper, the top of his arm *just* brushing mine.

"Guess what . . ." I lean in. I can smell his warm skin, his aftershave. "I don't have one."

"What?" He grimaces, looking sideways at me. "*No* middle name?"

"No middle name," I repeat.

"Mm. Shame," he says, going back to tapping on his iPad, nodding quickly to a colleague who ambles in among the hubbub. "I was hoping you'd have a boring one, like me. Mine's *Jonathan*. After my dad. So basic."

"Oh, no, I think that's cute. Jack *Jonathan*. Cute."

Jack laughs, eyes flicking up from the screen to mine. "Cute. She's calling me cute," he utters to himself and makes a disgusted face. "A sad day."

"What's wrong with cute?"

"Where do I *begin*?"

I giggle as Jack, grinning, looks back down at his screen. And people are looking over a little now, eyes sliding away from their hushed, worky conversations, and I feel a little thrill of . . . pride? Like, yep. That's right. I was public enemy number one, and now I'm chatting to Hot Adventurer Jack Shurlock when not so long ago, I was almost fired. He also wants to kiss me when I least expect it. (The disclaimer being: if he wasn't off his head on alcohol and does not remember and said that to everyone because he's just so *smooth*, as Lin said. Maybe Good Girl Jess and even Gail bloody Fryer are waiting for him to kiss them when they least expect it too.)

"I can't believe also," I whisper, "that you mentioned the screen display in the email. And cc'd actual . . ." I jerk my head in Michael's direction, my eyes wide.

"Well, he needs to know how good you were," Jack says, writing something down with a stylus on the screen. His handwriting is surprisingly neat, and *oh.* He's left-handed. *Of course* Jack is left-handed. Of course he rejected the generic, right-handed way of writing made-up letters and symbols. "You're a display pro, Millie Chandler."

"Yes, well, if he didn't sense the sarcasm"—I lean in, whispering again—"he's stupider than I thought."

"Oh, he is," says Jack flatly, still scrawling. "I assure you."

I stifle laughter as people continue to shuffle in the room. One of the freelancers takes a biscuit, turns it over in his hand, then puts it back.

"*Maaaate.*"

George Reckitt, a know-it-all Mummy's boy from Sales, appears behind us and launches straight into whacking Jack's back violently.

"You good?" asks Jack, and when he holds his hand out, George grabs it in that rough, lazy handshake men do, grins at him, says, "My man, my man." I notice this about Jack. People seem to really like him, to want to be his friend, and Jack doesn't really seem to ever be that interested. And I think *that's* the appeal. At least, it often is for me. The more someone doesn't seem to like me, the more I'm likely to prance around to try to make it so. "They like me" equals "achievement unlocked," equals "good enough." I was often like this with Owen, especially toward the end of our relationship. Always trying to enter some sort of correct combination; to get it right. Weirdly, I don't find myself doing that with Jack. If anything, it's the opposite. I . . . show him who I am, and the more he just accepts it, remembers it, holds it, the more I want to share.

"You going tonight?" says George. "Steve's birthday drinks?"

"I don't think so, mate."

"Yeah, well, if you do, just keep me away from the vodka. Ha-ha."

"Ah. Vodka," says Jack, half listening. "Yeah."

"Yeah, we all remember Manchester, don't we? Me and Mark. You and Jess?" George plonks himself down in front of us at the table and laughs. "What a *night.* Carnage."

George takes out his phone, starts scrolling.

"Are you going?" Jack asks casually, turning toward me.

"What happened in Manchester?" I whisper, and Jack taps the side of his nose and smiles, and it thrills me and makes me jealous all at once. *What did you and Jess do? Did you kiss her on the dance floor? Have wild sex with her in the bathroom?* "And no. I've not been invited. Of course." Yes, Jack, calling him a sexist celeriac will do that.

"Lucky girl," he says.

"Am I?"

"Don't you remember the Christmas party?"

And for a moment, I freeze. I do, I want to say. I remember flirting with you. I remember you touching my arm, leaning close . . .

*"S-sort of?"*

"Don't you remember Steve dirty-dancing with Prue and then her husband turning up . . ."

Relieved, I burst out laughing.

George looks over, as if he can't quite fathom why his "man" Jack would be talking to a mere receptionist like me, especially not the tainted one.

"Didn't they *fight?*"

"In the car park." Jack nods. "It was beautiful. A blockbuster. Ties and shoes and bifocals everywhere. And I would bet something along those lines'll happen tonight, and as much as it was fun—I don't think I have the mental capacity post–several Ryanair flights."

We both laugh, and George leans back on his chair, says, "Jack, did you see that notice? From Comms?" and they begin to talk hushedly about something I do not understand.

I doodle on the paper in front of me. Write "minutes" in slow, neat handwriting. Draw a flower for the dot of the *i.*

"So, you're free?" asks Jack, turning back to me.

"Sorry?"

"Tonight."

I nod. "I am."

"Cool," he says, and that—that's *it.* He's a mystery, this man. This "when you least expect it" adventurer who hates plans and human constructs (and also, perhaps, bins).

I open my mouth to say something—I could ask why he wants to know, couldn't I?

But George is talking to him again, and Jack is getting up, following him, nodding, both heading for the watercooler, and then the door closes.

"Good morning, folks." Paul Foot enters the meeting room, trailed by—oh God . . . Owen. Owen is here, and I freeze at the sight of him. And he strolls in. That assured lift of the chin, that authoritative stride, and sits in the seat Jack was in.

"We'll kick off in five, we're just waiting for a couple more . . ." Paul says, moving to the front of the room, a laptop under his arm. He eyes me for just a flicker of a moment but doesn't smile.

"All right, Mills?" asks Owen.

"Hi."

What is Owen doing, just *blatantly* sitting next to me? Boldly, legs wide and sprawled, gum chewing at the side of his mouth. Everyone in this room will know about the email I sent him. That he isn't getting *married* now. And he decides, in front of them, to sit right here.

And now Jack has drifted back.

"Oh shit, sorry, mate, were you sitting here?"

Jack shakes his head casually, but his eyes flash with something. "Not at all. You go ahead."

Owen leans, slaps him on the shoulder, and says, "Nice one," and for just a fraction of a second, Jack catches my eye, and his eyebrow rises; nothing more. He pulls out the seat next to George, two chairs down, places the iPad down on the table, and slowly, deliberately, sits.

"Hey." Owen smiles again. "How've you been?" He smells like his hair wax and the polished leather of his car.

I can *feel* eyes on me. Samira is here, too, Chloe's friend. She's watching; her eyes drop to her phone on the table. What if she's going to text Chloe under the table, say, "OMG, Owen is here and sitting snuggled up with Millie?" I probably would, if I were her. If I was Chloe's friend.

"Um. Good, thanks," I say, suddenly self-conscious. "You?"

I look down at the notebook in my lap then and write "meeting" elaborately (and pointlessly) at the top of the page next to "minutes," and Owen watches me.

"Pass," says Owen, and when I look at him, he gives a tiny, weak smile. "Wasn't expecting to see you here."

"Minutes," I say. "Michael wanted me here." And really, that last piece of information isn't relevant and is not strictly true, but I want him to know. I want him to know I have that something he was sure I didn't have. Ambition. Brains. Being *more*. More than just clumsy, chaotic Millie who gets up too late. He still has this way of making me feel like some sort of clueless sidekick who doesn't really know what she's doing.

"Oh, yeah?" he asks. "And how're you finding it? The game days . . ."

"Great." I force a smile, and so does he. This. Is. *Awkward*. After fleeing from him at the party, after wriggling out of his grasp, I was sure he wouldn't want to talk to me again.

Owen ducks slightly, but he doesn't drop his voice like I expect him to. Not enough to conceal what he's saying anyway. "I hope it's OK, but—I spoke to your dad again. To check in on him." And there's that slight jolt of something again, pinging through me, like a pinball flicked. Unease. That nostalgic, nervous feeling again.

"Did you?" and I do whisper, hoping he will follow suit. But he doesn't. He's doing that thing he does sometimes. That theatrical, slightly performative, almost self-conscious gesturing, his voice slightly more well-spoken than normal. Like he's conscious of being watched.

"He called. We had a nice chat. But I wanted to mention it to you because—I don't want you to think I'm . . . encroaching, or—"

"And was he OK?"

"He seemed it," says Owen with a smile. "In quite good spirits. You know how he is, the old boy, bless him."

"Right. Good." It's weirdly familiar, his language. Like we haven't been broken up for over two years. Like he didn't leave the daughter of the man he's talking about heartbroken and in pain.

"And you know, if you need anything else." Owen's knee touches mine. "We're all adults here, right? Enough water has passed under the bridge . . ."

"Yeah," I say, "yes. Thanks, Owen." But rather than feeling comforted that I have someone *else* in all this who knows us, especially with Kieran, oblivious and cotton-wool-wrapped, oceans away, I feel unsettled. My family is shaken up. Do I really need Owen slotting himself into the middle of it? He may just be trying to help but . . . *is he actually*? I'm sure anyone eavesdropping would agree; say, "Yes, he's being civil. He's being kind. You heard the man, you're all adults." But then, what about those words he spoke at the party, by the lake? *A part of me still loves you.* If I didn't know any better, I'd think he wants people to hear him right now; see us.

"Right! Shall we begin?" Paul claps from the front of the room.

And as I sit up, pen poised, Jack looks over his shoulder at me, then away again.

## chapter 20

**Text message from Jack:** Hey. Still free?

**Text message from Millie:** Haha, well, it's 10 p.m. on a Wednesday night, what do you think?

I'm in bed watching *Below Deck* when Jack texts, and trying to embroider a picture for Cate for Christmas—a cat wearing a Christmas tree hat, although so far it looks more like a little one-eyed goat with a head full of vegetation. And I'm still there ten minutes later when he follows it with a call. I sit bolt upright, like a vampire in a coffin, and stare at the screen. *Jack Shurlock calling...* My cheeks flood with warmth, a Pavlovian (or Shurlockian) response.

"Hello?" I answer, in the way you might when you're sure it's a butt dial.

"Hey," he says, a smile in his voice. "What're you up to?" His voice sounds even deeper, huskier on the phone.

"About the same as what I was up to ten minutes ago," I say. "Expertly screwing up a craft project and watching TV in bed. You?"

"In bed, eh?" he asks. "I'm sitting here on my sofa. Just got home from playing five-a-side."

"In this rain? In the *mud*?"

"I *was* covered in mud, yeah. I've just showered," he says, and I am now, of course, imagining him on the sofa, a towel around his muscular hips . . . "Anyway, if you're still free, I wondered if you wanted to—what is it you said? Step into the vortex?"

I laugh. "And what exactly does that entail?" And for a moment I wonder—is this a . . . booty call? It's certainly the time for it. And do I want to respond to said booty call? (Er. *Yes.*)

"Driving for half an hour," he says.

"Driving?" OK, perhaps *not* a booty call.

"Yup. To somewhere that I know you'll love."

I flip the duvet off my legs. One-eyed goat-cat goes flying in the air, lands on the carpet. "Now?"

"Now, yeah."

"At after 10 p.m.?"

"What's wrong with after 10 p.m.?"

"I . . . don't know?"

"Like I said. Vortex. I mean, no pressure. We can always go another time. Or not go at all, but . . . if you're free, and you want to?"

"I want to," I blurt.

"Cool," says Jack, and I can hear the smile in his voice. "So, I'll pick you up? Text me your address."

And within moments, I'm sprinting into Cate's room into a scene that looks like something from a London basement spa. She's reading by lamplight, a sleep mask on her forehead, her face glistening with skin care, and panpipe music playing. She was off work ill today, with stomach pains she thinks are an early gift from her period.

"Jack is picking me up in twenty minutes," I say.

And Cate, although groggy and dosed up on painkillers, bounces up and screeches, "Just when you least expect it, motherfucker!" so loudly, Ralph bursts in, ready to wrestle an intruder.

It's hard to know what to wear when you have no idea where you're going, and also when it's raining and 10 p.m. in early November. Cate picked out my outfit and practically dressed me (of course), saying jeans were the only option. "You need to look casual, like you haven't really thought about this," she said, and so here I am, getting into Jack's car in jeans, a tucked-in cream sweater, and one of Cate's belted trench coats, which is the *nicest* sage-green color I have ever, ever seen. I don't know how she does this. Cate just *knows* what looks nice. Effortlessly.

Jack leans over and opens the car door. And although I see it often at work, it strikes me in this moment how very Jack this car is. Different. Something you wouldn't expect. It was his dad's, who collects old cars and fixes them up, Jack told me once, and it lives in a garage while Jack travels. It's a red 1974 Dodge Charger apparently (which means absolutely nothing to car-clueless me). It reminds me of the car they drive in *Pulp Fiction*. "It's a silly car, really," Jack once said. "But why not?"

"Good evening," he says as I slide inside the car. The sharp, seaside chill of the night, the heat inside the car, the sight of him, the smell of warm leather, and Jack's post-five-a-side shower and orangey, peppery aftershave make me shiver.

"This is . . . intriguing," I say, "for a Wednesday night at half-ten. But, well, *time is just a construct, Millie dot Chandler.*"

"That's right." He laughs. "Nice impression, by the way. Spot-on."

Jack drives, and the radio plays quietly as rain hammers the windshield. The wipers screech against the glass, and I feel like I need to concentrate on breathing. I have no idea where we're going, and there's something thrilling about it. I feel like I want to hold his hand. I feel like I want to jump onto his lap, bury my face into his neck. I feel like I could let out a little squeal, ball my hands into excited fists. Instead, though, I make small talk, and we chat. And it's unlike Jack and me, really. We don't really *do* small talk. But tonight it feels like filler, the sort of chat you both happily entertain before you know something . . . bigger might happen. And there's something about the darkness of the car, the way Jack's eyes are on the road ahead, one hand on the wheel, the way beneath the makeup, in the dark, Jack can't see the flush on my cheeks, that makes me move onto something that keeps tugging, intrigued, at my sleeve.

"So, what did happen in Manchester?" I ask.

Jack pauses. "Manchester?"

"Yeah," I say. "You and . . . Jess."

"*Oh.*" Jack glances over at me. "I feel like you might be disappointed," he says. "George made it sound way more than it was."

"Try me," I say, wanting to hear but not, all at once.

"Try you," he repeats, and something about the way he says that makes me blush. "OK, so, loads of us went to Manchester for work, and Jess and I, we sang karaoke together," he explains, the L of his thumb and index finger resting easily against the steering wheel. "And Jess being Jess got too drunk and fell off the stage, and I spent the rest of my evening with her in the emergency room with a Domino's pizza. Oh, and I had to carry her back to the hotel—she badly sprained her ankle."

"Ha. Oh. I see." I'm relieved. Just a little.

"And she fell asleep on my bed."

"Right," I say.

"And then she threw up on it." He grimaces. "Lots of Domino's pizza and mimosas. And she was too embarrassed at the reception desk to tell them, so I took the blame for it."

"Wow. How romantic," I say.

"*Romantic?*"

"Yes. Romantic of you. Romantic . . . for Jess."

Jack pauses and glances over at me in the fuzzy dark. "Yeah, I love her to bits, but there's *nothing* romantic between me and Jess, Millie."

I nod. So hard, it's a wonder my head is still attached to my shoulders. "Oh. Cool. Cool."

"Cool?" Jack smiles to himself but says nothing else, and I look ahead, feel his eyes on me, and we both laugh. A flurry of loaded, cheek-aching laughter.

"*OK*." I cover my face with my hands. "OK, let's move on, shall we? Nice and swiftly. Next subject."

Jack laughs. "OK, next subject. Um. Geography? Science and nature? Match these sounds to the animals they belong to?"

We continue to drive, a blur of streetlights in raindrops on the window, just us and the music and this . . . atmosphere. This electric, thick atmosphere I sort of want to bottle; keep as a memory. It's like there is so much unsaid in this car, so many words, but on a frequency only we can both privately feel rather than hear.

Twenty minutes later, we're deep in winding country roads, the headlights of Jack's car our only light.

"Well, this is extremely mysterious, Jack," I say quietly as Jack slows, signals, and turns into a farm track.

"It's meant to be," he says.

A rectangle of a lit-up sign appears among thick overgrowth in the dark.

"Stambourne Farm," I read. The sign is old, blistered wood, but the lettering is freshly painted. We're in a tiny country lane, nothing but thick fields, crops like bristles in the dark. In any other situation, I would feel nervous, want to turn back, but this is exciting. And I feel safe with Jack. I always, always feel safe with Jack.

The car bumbles down the rocky track road in the dark. In the distance, two squares of orange light wobble into view. A farmhouse with the lights on downstairs. To think just half an hour ago, I was leaving my flat, having been in bed with *Below Deck* and my new Christmas project, and now . . . Now we are, quite literally, in the middle of nowhere. An idyllic, slightly spooky country farm. And I wouldn't want to be anywhere else.

"Here'll do," says Jack, stopping at the side of a large courtyard of outbuildings and sheds. The farmhouse itself is huge. Rugged and gray-stoned. The sort of place you'd draw as a kid. A chimney smoking, windows with lead diamonds in the glass.

"We're here, then."

Jack nods. The ambient rumble of the engine now off, the silence in the car between us is almost deafening. I can hear my pulse in my ears. "Any ideas yet?" he asks.

I shake my head. "None. I thought for a minute you might be taking me out on the boat."

"You can always come out with me on the boat." He smiles. "But even I wouldn't recommend a dinghy at night. And that's from a cocky sailor."

Jack flashes a grin and gets out of the car. I open my own door, but he meets me there, opens it the rest of the way, and I step out onto the cold, hard gravelly ground.

Jack smiles down at me. "Still no ideas?" he asks, our bodies just inches apart in the chilly, silent night. No sounds except rustling leaves and a faint whir of the distant, distant motorway.

"Erm . . . immersive *Blair Witch Project* experience?"

"Puking on beds, *Blair Witch Project* . . ." Jack says, closing the car door behind me. "The bar you've set for my romantic ideas is questionable."

*Romantic.*

Is that what this is then? An actual romantic gesture? For . . . me?

Jack puts his phone to his ear, the light of it illuminating his handsome face, turning his eyelashes to spun sugar. "Just a sec."

It smells amazing out here. Of wet, mulched dirt, of woodsmoke, of . . . something fragrant. Mint, I think. Fresh, wild mint.

Something snaps in the darkness. I look at Jack with wide, unblinking eyes and make a comic-book grimace of my mouth, and Jack smiles.

"Where are we?" I whisper. My words make clouds in the night.

Jack holds a finger to his lips, his eyes on mine in the dark.

"You sure it's not the *Blair Witch* thing?" I tease. "You can tell me. I'll try to pretend to enjoy myself—"

"Hey!" he suddenly says into the phone. "Yep. Yeah, we're outside now. OK. OK, great." He hangs up and looks at me.

And before I can even open my mouth to ask another question, there's a creaking of a door, footsteps on gravel, and a woman appears, emerging from the house. She's in jeans and Wellington boots, and she's grinning from ear to ear. She has the sort of face that makes you like and trust her instantly. Round, happy, huge, long cowlike eyelashes. She must be Mum's age, maybe a little older.

"Hello, gorgeous," she says, holding out her arms to Jack. "Couldn't believe it when Ken said you were coming. I even stayed up past eight for you, which is something."

Jack grins, and they both embrace. She's short. About five-one, and Jack, broad, six foot one, give or take, makes her look even tinier. She stretches her arms around his back, patting the black wool of his coat.

"So lovely," she keeps saying. "So lovely to see you."

"Well, I'm honored to be the reason you stayed up," says Jack. He pulls back and looks down at her. He puts his arm around her shoulder, and she puts a maternal hand on his tummy. "Eleanor, this is

Millie. Millie, this is Eleanor Fitch. She owns this place. Stambourne Farm. And she's also my mum's best friend."

"*And* your godmother," she says with an eye roll. "What do I always say, you're never too old for a godmother."

"A meaningless title, though," replies Jack with a grin. "I mean, let's be honest, it is," and Eleanor smacks his arm gently and laughs.

"Millie," says Eleanor, holding out a rough, chubby hand. "Very nice to meet you."

"And you too."

She turns to Jack, a brass key held between her two fingers. "OK, and you remember the drill, Jack?"

"Er. Sort of? Although it's been, like, twenty years?" He laughs.

"It's that one over there." She points to an arched outhouse made of corrugated steel. It's lit by a single square security light above its door, which moths dance clumsily in the spotlight of. "Here's the key. Take a candle each as you walk in. Stay as long as you like, and just make sure the door's locked when you leave. But most of all"—she looks at me and wrinkles her small, round nose, affectionately—"*be good*." She drops the key into Jack's open palm and grins. "You're still coming to see me before you leave? The country, I mean."

Jack nods. "*Might* be OK," he says, and again her eyes lift skyward.

"*Might*," she says. "Just like your mother. Hard to nail down."

And something twists then in my chest. He is leaving. Jack is going to be leaving, and soon. A couple of weeks. Gone. In a whole different other country. And I'll forget slowly his smell, how his laugh sounds, how that deep C-shaped dimple looks when he smiles. I'll forget how . . . *this* feels. Being with him.

Eleanor looks at me. "Bed calls. I have to be up at four."

I nod, smile. "Lovely to meet you," I say, but now I'm backtracking about what she said before. A *candle*? She did say candle, didn't she?

Eleanor turns, disappears down the drive to the house.

Jack and I, again, are alone.

"OK, so what *is* this place?" I ask. "I mean, Eleanor seems lovely and everything, and I sort of want her to be *my* godmother, but for all I know I could be here to have my organs harvested."

"Ha."

"Seriously, when are you going to enlighten me?"

Jack smiles, and leans closer to me in the dark. "Spoken like the woman who hasn't gained any enlightenment from me so far at all. I'm deeply offended."

"Where have you offered me enlightenment?"

"Er, BackDonald's?" he says, his voice low. You could hear a pin drop out here. "That's enlightenment. Right?"

"True. OK, fine, you enlightened me on a *burger level*."

Jack looks at me, cocks his head. "This way, Millie."

We walk together across the hard, crunching ground. Well, it's definitely a farm. That's all I do know. And I feel buzzy, as if my blood is charged with something. Electricity. Stars. And I already don't want this night to end. Even though I have absolutely no idea what this place is or what we're doing here, and it's cold and wet and late, I know that I want all the clocks in the world to stop. Freeze us here.

We get to the door of the corrugated outhouse.

It's thick, wooden, vertically slatted, and painted cornflower blue, from what I can make out in the dark. Jack unlocks it, the key slotting in with a satisfying, deep knock. "Ready?"

"I . . . think so?"

Jack pushes the door open. It rattles, then creaks. And I expect it to be full of light. A greenhouse under low fluorescents or something. White and stark and clinical. But this—this is the opposite.

The . . . beautiful opposite. I actually gasp.

"*Oh my God.*"

The huge space is dark—as dark as the night outside—but the

whole expanse of it is lit by lines and lines of long tapered candles flickering, casting the most beautiful orangeade glow over the room. It's silent, echoing, like a church. It smells like fresh rainwater and compost.

"Forced rhubarb," says Jack, dropping his voice to a whisper, for no reason other than that in a room so large, so dimly, romantically lit, so mutedly quiet, talking any louder than he is would feel almost offensive. "Eleanor's one of the only people around who grows rhubarb like this, and you said it was . . . one of your things, and I had this vague memory as a kid, so." He turns to me, and I'm frozen in the doorway. Words jammed in my throat, like a stuck conveyor belt. "Come on," he says softly, and he closes the door behind me. The handle squeaks and echoes in the silence, but I feel like I can hardly breathe. For me. Jack did this *for me.*

He reaches forward, wiggles a candle free from the rows and rows of them, among the leaves. He hands it to me, folding my fingers gently around the base, holding his hand over mine.

Jack gives a low chuckle. "Millie, are you—OK?"

And I'm glad for the darkness, because tears sit at the edge of my eyes, like a tide about to rise, send waves crashing over the barrier. I nod. "Yeah," I swallow, a teary, watery smile blooming across my face. "Yes, of course. Sorry, just—this is . . . this is perfect."

Jack nods, just once. "Yeah, well, a dark farm isn't exactly classically romantic, but . . ."

Romantic. He's said romantic again. It has to be something. This feels so much like something. And he's looking at me as he says it, as if to test the waters, to dip a toe in, to see how that word sits with me now that we're here, just us two, in this candlelit room, miles from anywhere.

"And this candle here," I say, clearing my throat. Must. Hold. It. Together. Or I'll cry. Or I'll fall. I can't fall. How do I stop myself from falling? "Is it so I can find my way back in the dark? In case of, like . . . witches?"

"Ah, come on," says Jack with a soft smile. "Don't you trust me to protect you?"

It's so quiet, so dark, it's as if everything else has disappeared. That all that exists is us.

"Against all this rhubarb?" I ask, and I look away, sure the tears in my eyes are glistening, unhidden, in this candlelight.

We start to walk in the silence. Water trickles somewhere in the dark stillness, like a leaking tap, and it's like nothing I have ever seen before. It's weird and strange and eerie . . . and totally beautiful. A contrast, like my lovely Leigh. Like everything. So much shade, but so much beautiful, beautiful light. He did this for me. Jack did this for me. But—what is it? What will it be when he leaves? Flies far, far away from me; leaves me behind.

Cate's voice swirls through my mind, like a disgruntled spirit. *Why does it need to be anything besides what it is right now, Millie?*

"This is . . ."

"It's cool, isn't it?" says Jack. "Kind of—bizarre."

"Beyond cool, it's . . . I don't know." And—I don't have the words. I'm overwhelmed. Yes, it's forced rhubarb, and no Paris or Orient Express, but the gesture—it's more than I have ever had in my whole life. And that's why I sort of want to burst into tears. This place is so me. And Jack is right here beside me, *in it* with me. By my side.

"I mean, I don't really understand how it all works," he carries on gruffly. "But—it's clever. The whole tricking thing."

I nod. "They don't allow it to see natural daylight," I say. "They trick it. And because of that, you get this extra-pink, extra-sweet stuff like . . ." I stop, push back a giant, rough rhubarb leaf, which makes a crumpling sound like paper, and hold my candle close. It lights a perfect rhubarb stalk. "See?"

Jack leans next to me, his shoulder touching mine. "I see," he says, then he turns, and his face for a moment is so close to mine. Our lips just inches apart, like they were in the cloakroom . . .

I draw back, stand up. "It's like . . . the color of . . . pink lemonade or something," I say with a laugh, and this between us, this thick static, feels almost unbearable.

We walk side by side together in the dark quiet. I think back to the party. To the awkwardness with Chloe, how torn she was, the bright lights and watchful eyes of the dance floor, that horrible moment by the lake—and I think of Jack, stepping through it all, making me feel like—me. Just me. A woman. A woman worthy of kissing, of desiring, of spending time with. No caveats. And now we're here. By candle-light. In a room that a lot of people might wince at, screw their faces up at; at the damp and cold and dark. But in a room that means some-thing to me. And Jack remembered that. Remembered me.

"Thank you," I say.

Jack nods, strolls slowly beside me down the aisles, each of us holding a candle that lights our way. "I was hoping you'd come. Called Ken, Eleanor's husband, like, how's your rhubarb doing? I might need to borrow your greenhouse."

My laughter echoes. It's huge in here. The size of a tennis court. Rows and rows of sleepy, sweet rhubarb and flickering candles.

"Doesn't make a very good place for a date, Ken said," adds Jack. "And I reckon that's debatable."

And it's like my whole body smiles. Every doubt I've had has just been undone. He said a date. This *is* something. "Candles are very ro-mantic," I say.

"And rhubarb?"

"Rhubarb is the dozen roses for me. You can't make a crumble and custard with bloody roses."

"Ah, well, look at that—I got you, what, an acre?" Jack chuckles next to me, a peep of white teeth, that gorgeous, gorgeous dimple, and—I want to press myself into him. I want to kiss him.

"And thanks as well," I say, "for always . . . sort of, rescuing me."

Jack shrugs and throws me a sideways look. "*Rescuing you?*"

"I don't know. I feel like my whole life got turned upside down when those emails got sent. And you've just . . . been there."

"I haven't rescued you, Millie. You do a decent job of rescuing yourself."

"Oh yeah," I groan. "I have a *great* reputation for rescuing myself. I bake cakes to appease."

"And you volunteer at meaningless rugby games even though they don't deserve you. Fetch jacket potatoes."

"Ugh." I cringe, chomp my teeth together. "I don't want to even think about that rugby game."

"Well, don't."

"Or *any* of it. Or glitches, or the phantom email sender who might be right under my nose—"

"Then *don't*," says Jack again gently, and this time he stops, steps in front of me. "You don't have to think about any of that stuff. It's all shit that's happened, or shit that might. Doesn't exist."

I smile, gaze up at his handsome face. The hazel eyes, the straight nose, the sharp jaw, the slightly crooked, pink, pouty mouth. "I wish I could be more like you," I say.

Water drips. Wind blows outside, branches scratching on the roof, the occasional pop of a candlewick. The hundreds of tiny, teardrop flames dance. And as Jack smiles down at me, hair dangling over his eyes, I'm sure he can hear my heart. It's thumping, like a bass drum.

"You don't need to be like anyone, Millie," he says, putting a hand on the top of my arm. "You're perfect as you are."

I swallow, hard. "I think many would disagree . . ."

"Nobody who matters."

His hand stays there, then drifts slowly, slowly down, leaving goose bumps in a trail, until it reaches my hand. His fingers gently, smoothly slide into my palm, rough fingertips tickling the soft skin. Tingles cascade down my body. He holds my hand, eyes meeting mine. He slowly brings my hand up to his mouth, presses his warm lips to it. Goose bumps tighten every inch of my skin. He lowers my hand, eyes on mine again, loosens his grip, and under my cardigan, his warm hand slides around my waist. My breath catches in my throat as he pulls me gently toward him, and—I want him. Here and now. I can think of nothing else except kissing him.

I whisper his name, tip my face toward his, and he finally leans, his warm lips hovering at first, breathing against mine. And slowly, Jack kisses me. Slowly and deeply.

I close the gap between us, slide my hand around his neck, and oh, he's a good kisser. He grips my waist tighter, pulls me into him; his strong, solid frame. And as my thoughts scramble, melt away, at the feel of his strong hands at my waist, that rumbling moan at the back of his throat, I decide, this doesn't need to be anything more than what it is.

I don't care, I don't care.

What matters now is Jack's soft mouth against mine, hands and arms entwined. The soft light in the middle of darkness, tricking us both into feeling nothing exists beyond this moment, beyond us.

chapter 21

**From: Vince Gudgeon**
**To: Millie Chandler**
**Subject: Email feature**

Hi,

As per what we were discussing in my repair room last week (the theory of someone in this place maliciously sending your email drafts), a thought occurred to me on my commute last night. Back in Feb 2020, our email providers installed a new "scheduled send" feature, which also allows for a bulk/mass email send-out. (Unsure how u do this.) This being accidentally set or switched on could explain what happened to u.

Might be worth pinging IT. Not my area.

Thx,

Vince.

PS—was Gail @ the Summer-Ween party?

*From: Millie Chandler*
*To: Alexis Lee*
**Subject: Fwd: Your treehouse stay**
Just a reminder of our treehouse stay. I've booked us all
on. You, me, and Cate. Please come. I miss you so much.

On Friday, Cate and I walk to work together. Her stomach cramps
have stuck around, and she spent all of yesterday stuffed upstairs in her
bed sleeping, with Ralph and me delivering hot drinks and hot-water
bottles to her door every few hours. She's now changed her theory
and thinks she must've eaten something off, rather than hormonal
cramps, and Ralph has it in his head that it's his fault. That she's accidentally eaten one of his exotic mushrooms, or that she might be al-
lergic to something he put in their lunches last week. (Ralph has taken
to making Cate's lunches, and she his, on alternate days. It's adorable.)
Cate emerged this morning, thinner and tired, but determined to go
to work, and I've used the walk to regale her about my night with Jack
and the rhubarb farm. (For the second time. She insisted on hearing as
much as she could in tiny capsules yesterday, in between naps.)

Cate knocks back two Tylenol like they're Smarties, without so
much as a wince. "I am telling you, Millie," she says, crunching, "this
is the most romantic shit I've ever heard. Anyone can do a candlelit
dinner. Some factory-made one-size-fits-all romantic gesture, but this
was so thought out. So *special*."

"*I know.* And God, Cate, he is such a good kisser."

"I knew he would be," Cate says musically. "Like, you can just *tell*,
you know?"

"We just . . . wandered around this big, beautiful, gnarly green-house with candles, talking, and laughing, and then he . . . just drove me home at midnight. Like it was nothing. Like I'd not just had the most beautiful night of my life. We kissed again in the car. I think we were outside in the car park for a whole hour. His windows actually *steamed up*."

"In total Jack-and-Rose style!" Cate squeaks, unscrewing the lid of her Scottie-dog-patterned water bottle. "Oh, Millie. I'm so happy for you." She chugs.

"And it was simple, you know?" I carry on. "Like, of course it was *exciting,* and I fancy him so much, but it's . . . *simple*." The opposite of anything I've experienced really. How things were with Owen—still *are* with Owen, in a way. Confusing. Hard work. Conditional. *Serious.* And yet this, with Jack. It just feels easy. Easy and at the same time just about the most exciting thing I've ever felt.

We cross over, enter ever-busy Progress Road. A man unloading huge, snakelike vent tubes from the back of a van sings along to a radio and shouts, "Tune!" to his passenger, who, halfway through a McMuffin, holds it high and says, "Tune!"

The sky is low and heavy today, but from behind the clouds sunlight cracks through. It's morphed seamlessly from autumn to early winter, as if someone turned over a page of the world's calendar as we all slept; shook us all up, like a snow globe. And I like winter in some ways. Not so much the head colds and the scheduled, rehearsed stress of Christmas, but I like the cleansing element of it. The crisp, clean air. The glow of lamps behind drawn curtains at night, as I drive home wondering which homes await me in the future, all the places I've yet to visit. I love the way a new flawless year looms in the distance, too, like a fresh, unwritten-in notebook. I hope the weather isn't *too* wintry this evening, though, for our overnight treehouse stay—especially given that it's Bonfire Night and we might have a perfect view of nearby firework displays if it isn't absolutely pissing down. Cate and I have made a loose plan for the evening, and I'm hoping, somehow, that Alexis turns up. An olive branch, up in the trees. A fire roaring, time and space to really *talk*. This is the longest Alexis and I have ever gone without speaking, and it's starting to feel like we might never again. If she doesn't get in touch soon, maybe I *will* just—go there? Drive to her dad's house. But then, do I really want to bring a friendship-in-tatters to her home? Her dad, Salv, is seventy-five now. He's alone all day while Alexis and her sister work. But then, maybe I won't have to think about that. Maybe Alexis will be very Alexis Lee and just show up tonight: explode into the deck of the treehouse, all smiles and "Hello, girls."

"I think you trust him," continues Cate next to me. "Jack. I've been thinking about this, from my deathbed the last few days." Cate flashes a tired, sarcastic smile. "And I think it's as simple as that. You trust him."

"You're right," I agree with a smile. "*I do.* And he makes me feel safe."

Cate stops on the pavement, delicate hand at her giant peach scarf. "Why can I feel a *but* coming?" she asks. "I can, can't I? I bloody hate *buts*."

I groan. "He's leaving, Cate. Next week is his actual leaving party."

Cate smiles sadly, two dots prodding the corners of her mouth. "I know," she says. "I know." And we start walking again. "But I thought we talked about this. You deserve it, Millie, for what it is. For so long you were so sad and—*small*, you know? Too scared after Owen to, I don't know, put yourself out there. A little . . . like me? And I get it. God, do I get it. It just happens, doesn't it? That slow withdraw." Cate reaches out then, touches my arm with a gentle, gloved hand. "But Jesus, please. It can just . . . be what it is. I know we're all about future-proofing and 'must do the right non-scary thing' but look where that got me with

Nicholas. Putting up with shit I didn't need to and felt miserable about for so long. All in the name of 'what you're supposed to do.' " Cate adjusts her handbag and looks up at the sky, a smile on her face, as if seeing something I can't. "Why can't you just—let this be your moment? That story you tell one day. Of the seed that was seeding away, like Ralph says, and grew the lovely little story of beautiful Jack, who kissed you like you've never been kissed before, made you feel everything all at once, in a whirlwind, before he gave you that dramatic goodbye and effed off into this gorgeous, massive world. You can—"

We stop to let a loud, rumbling motorbike cross our paths into a plumbing merchant's. A cut right in the middle of Cate's romantic monologue. A teddy bear is strapped to the front of it with blue rope, like in one of those old classic train movies, and we both laugh.

"Look, all I'm saying is that: you can . . . have that," Cate continues. "Seriously. Remember how nice it was just to fancy someone? Go on dates and just see how it goes?"

"You're right," I say. "I know you're right. You're always bloody right."

Cate rubs my arm with a leather-gloved hand. "And you know what? Enjoy it. The risk of it. Getting roughed up a bit. In more ways than one." She grins.

"*Yes, sir.*"

"And know that your old cramped-up bestie is so jealous, she might die," says Cate. "That's if my stomach doesn't kill me first, which feels quite likely today."

"What *is* going on with your stomach?"

Cate shrugs, places a neat hand flat to the waist of her coat. "I have no idea. I just feel totally queasy and disgusting, and the pain keeps sort of radiating? From my stomach, then to my chest. I don't know, man, it's weird. But I'll live. Probably all that bread I ate on Tuesday with Ralph. We met on my lunch break."

"Really?" I say, and I give her my stupidest shit-eating grin. She doesn't catch it, though.

"Yeah, it was to die for. Gio's? The Italian place? They gave us so much garlic bread. But since then . . ."

"*Us*," I repeat.

"What?"

"Didn't he make you a flask and breakfast today too? Ralph. For your tummy?"

Cate shrugs, tries to stifle a grin, the apples of her cheeks suddenly taut. "Yes. He *did*." Then it's like she gives herself over to it, ducks her head, as if she's revealing a secret she's been dying to share. "Did I tell you he made me ackee and salt fish last week? Just because I mentioned it was my favorite. He followed my actual *mum's* recipe. Got it off her and everything."

"Cate, I think he's probably secretly in love with you," I say, and while I expect my friend to recoil, to deny it, say, "Who, *Ralph*? Bit too nerdy for me," instead Cate smiles.

"Well. That might be nice," she says. "If he . . . is, I mean. He's lovely, isn't he? Like—the loveliest, most interesting person ever. And—have you seen his body?"

I laugh. "Well, he *is* a swimmer. He hasn't missed a session in almost three years. Rain or shine. Plus, all that karate."

"And it fucking shows." Cate laughs. "Couldn't take my eyes off his stomach when he'd jogged back from swimming in the rain and whipped that top off. All that tight rain-dappled skin. Plus"—Cate smiles—"what is it you just said? It's simple."

"You trust him."

"*I do.* And that's hot, isn't it? Or maybe my stomach is just fucking with my head. Who knows?" She laughs, then stops on the pavement to kiss my cheeks. "Anyway, I'd better go. I've come the long way to walk this off, and now I think I might just be plain old late. But OK, a quick run through the plan again. You're leaving work early, you'll go back to the flat, pack the car, come and get me from work at three, then we'll leave for the treehouse bonanza?"

"Deal."

"I can't wait." Cate blows me a kiss as she flounces off down the street in neat stark-white trainers, a maxi skirt skimming her ankles.

I walk on alone, thinking about what Cate said about Jack, about trust, and about doing the thing that doesn't feel sensible but feels right in the moment. Because if I plan this—plan to *not* fall for Jack, plan to withdraw from him, to guard my heart, who really loses? Me. I miss out on the feeling I get when I'm with him. I miss out on memories and stories to tell. I miss out on . . . living.

And so much has changed. I've tried to plan, but really, how far has it got me? I don't really know if my job is any safer, and even if it is, OK, I'm "doing minutes" and the odd rugby game, but—do I even *want* to do those things? And if not, then what was all the planning for? For everyone else? For redemption? For Owen and Chloe? As in, the man who *broke my heart?*

I turn into Flye's car park. At reception's high glass entrance, Chloe stands neatly, talking to Leona. A belted mack tied at her waist. Chloe looks amazing. I'm actually starting to think Chloe Katz might be one of those people who get put into a shitty position and fly. Thrive. Cope by delving into something, like a new gym routine, veganism, or ice baths. But then—weren't they going to meet? Imagine a reconciliation now. What a big ol' strike-through that would be for my to-do list. A big chunk of shame, silenced. A massive win for the life A.E., which, bless it, needs some decent PR.

"Hi, Chloe, Leona," I say, and Chloe gives a small, reluctant smile.

"Hi," they both say, and Leona checks her watch. "I better go in. Almost nine. Coming, Chlo?"

Chloe hesitates, shakes her head. "Nah, I've got five minutes," and surprised, and perhaps even a little put out, Leona says, "Oh," and turns to leave. But then I remember Vince's email. How low-key it was, but how actually, in a very Vince Gudgeon way, it really could be the simple answer to it all. The lovely, non-scary answer that arrived in a lovely, non-scary way. It makes the most sense too. And not that there's anything anyone can do about it, but it's certainly good to know if Vince is right and it can be switched on easily. For *everyone* in the whole, wide world to know, for that matter. Maybe I can get it raised in the House of Commons. Save countless lives while in B.E.

"Oh, Leona?" I ask. "Could I—have a word?"

Leona turns slowly, almost as if irked. She doesn't speak, just looks at me, pushes a die-straight section of mousy hair behind her ear. I don't have a lot to do with Leona. She's a bit too serious for me. She once saw me yawning behind my reception desk and said I shouldn't. "I just think yawning gives the wrong impression, if you see what I mean," she said. "As if you find your place of work boring and unfulfilling. Do you?"

"Yeah?" she asks now, a single, neat eyebrow cocked.

"Um . . ."

She widens her eyes. A wordless "Go on, then." Leona doesn't get the hint of wanting to talk privately, but Chloe does, slips her phone out of her handbag and moves away, gives us a little space, but it's hardly worth the effort. She's still *right there.*

"I wondered—just . . . Vince. Repairman Vince?" I say. "He—he recently told me that our email providers have a scheduled email option?"

"Yeah?"

"Right," I say. "And he said there's a mass-send-out option."

"Bulk," she corrects me. Chloe fidgets next to us, eyes intently on her phone. I now wish I hadn't asked. Her relationship was completely torn apart because of my email issue, and here I am discussing it factually with IT, right in front of her. Not to mention the fact that Leona is being completely cold. I already know this is probably going to be a fruitless endeavor. Probably all that yawning I did. Put her off.

"Okay. Bulk, then," I carry on. "I just thought—my email issue, back in September, might be because of that? Vince said he believes it's easy to switch it on."

"That's incorrect," says Leona quickly, like an AI robot. Chloe's eyes slide to look at her. "The scheduled email option is easy to switch on, yeah. It's a simple hold-and-click, select the time and date . . . But Flye has the bulk option switched off across the board. Pointless feature for a company like this."

*"Oh.* Right. And has it always been that way?"

"Mm-hm."

Leona nods, just once. Her eyes have barely blinked the entire time. She's like a pretty moon, Leona. Pearl-white skin, huge green eyes, small, always-pursed pink lips.

"Is that all?" she asks. "It's 8:58."

"Er. Yeah. That's—that's all," I reply. "Thanks." And Leona twists on her heel and disappears inside. The door slams behind her.

There's silence now, and Chloe clears her throat. "She can be uptight," she says.

"Oh. She's—it's fine."

Chloe looks at me then, her eyes flitting everywhere from beneath those thick, fanlike lashes. Awkward. To the floor, to the heavy, November cloud above us, to me . . .

"So, how—how have you been?" asks Chloe, and there's that something unspoken between us again. That thing that . . . bonds us whether we like it or not. Some sense of "We fell in love with the same man. We saw the same thing in the same person. We have both slept beside the same person. And he let us both down."

"I'm OK," I say. "I think. Besides somehow pissing off Leona." I laugh, try to break the ice.

"I'm sorry she couldn't help," says Chloe, shifting from one foot to the other, like someone trying to get comfortable. "It was shit, really, what happened. The emails . . ."

God, she's nice. I could easily be her friend, latch onto her, meet her for a sandwich at lunchtime, a walk into town. Chloe is warm. I hadn't really realized that about her before, but she is. Even that moment weeks ago, outside the café, it was her friends who were frosty. To Chloe, there's warmth. A hint of vulnerability she wears like a bracelet beneath her sweater cuff. Subtle, but always there.

"Well. Harder for some of those who received them, I reckon," I say. "And . . . you're OK?"

Chloe nods, her arms hugging her small frame. She's built like a ballerina. Petite, strong, elegant. "Getting there," she says carefully. "And I know it's for the best. You know? The man doesn't care about me, and I've learned that now. At least I hope I have."

"Owen?" I ask pointlessly.

"He cares about *him*," she says. "How *he* appears to the world, what *he* can get." A tiny, jeweled heart on a gold chain rises and falls at the hollow of her throat. "He couldn't care less about me or the wedding. It's next week, the date. It's like—there never was going to be a wedding now. Erase and move on."

"But . . . I thought you were going to talk?"

She shakes her head, rosy cheeks balling up with a grimace. "Oh, we did. But—no."

"No?"

She swallows. "No, I felt like I was auditioning or something. It wasn't a chat or a talking-through, it was just . . ." Her words taper off, and once again she just says, "No. But. Well, at least I know now. That this is for the best. That I can empty my parents' house of wedding things. It's like a wedding fair in there."

"But . . ." I can feel my mouth opening and closing. Gawping like a cartoon. "He said his flat was full of wedding stuff—"

"Millie, he's a liar," says Chloe in one mouthful. "He's manipulative. Just writes the story *exactly* how he wants it to be. How it best benefits him."

I stare at her. And I don't know what else to say. Why would Owen lie? To gain sympathy? To . . . what was it Chloe just said? To write the story how he wants it to be.

"Millie, if I were you, I'd just go and live your life and not listen to a single word he says. Even the nice stuff. *Especially* the nice stuff. I'm trying to stick to that myself. I know it's easier said than done, but . . ." She hesitates now, her eyes lingering on mine, almost imploringly. "You and I, Millie, we—we aren't different, we . . ." Her eyes are intense and unblinking, watery now, and I wait for her next word. But it doesn't come. It almost does, but she swallows it down, like a gulp of soup. Instead, there's just a large, weird, loaded beat of nothing.

Then she looks past me, her face transforming with a big smile. People are arriving into work now, rolling in at dead-on nine.

"Morning!" Chloe sings.

"Morning to you too." Samira smiles and side-eyes me for just a fraction of a second. "You all right, Chlo?"

And with that, Chloe turns away and walks inside the office next to her friend, leaving me outside in the cold.

**Text Message from Cate:** Millieeeee! I'm still in pain with this bloody stomach. Called my doctor and they want to see me at 4. I'll meet you at the treehouse. Ralph said I can bring his car. Don't wait around for me and miss check-in. So sorry. Anyone want a fucked-up stomach? Free to a good home. X

## chapter 22

This impromptu trip to pop in and see Mum is not about what I told her it was about—extra deck chairs for the treehouse we absolutely do not need. I'm going to see Mum to check in. Dad is away again on shift, and Mum sounded almost too musical when I called her after I'd seen Dad; too high-pitched to be normal. Like someone pretending to be OK, even when they're falling apart at the seams. Dad had gone home after two nights in Auntie Vye's symbolic conservatory, apparently, but something Mum said, slipped up with, told me he'd slept in the study on the futon.

Mum is already on the driveway with the garage door open when I pull in. She looks tiny in there among Dad's things. When she turns and smiles at me, I can see how sad she is by her eyes. And she looks thin. Gaunt. Gray. Weeks without a proper appetite and Dad's grandiose pizza-oven creations.

"Hello, darling." She smiles, folding a black, pearl-knit cardigan around her.

"Hi, Mum. How're you?"

"Oh, fine, fine. I'm just trying to find the . . . pink deck chairs?" she says with a hollow chuckle. "You know, the ones with the cupholders? These are fine, these blue ones, but the pink ones are much sturdier and easier to carry. Your dad says so. He's probably put them . . ." She pauses then and looks up to meet my eyes. Rain from the overflowing guttering falls over the edge of the open garage like a water feature, slapping the ground. "Gosh, sorry, I'm a bit of a mess at the moment." Then Mum brings a hand to her face. I step forward to hug her. "No, no, darling," she says, a palm up, a gentle stop sign. "I'm fine."

"I can stay for a bit?" I offer.

"No, no—"

"I don't mind. Let me." And it's seeing Mum so small, so lost, among a lifetime of possessions and memories of a life lived with the man she loves that softens my heart like a baked apple.

Within moments, the deck chairs are left leaning against the brick of the house, sheltered beneath the pitched roof above the cottage's front door, and we head inside. I make us a cup of tea and feel heartbroken at the sight of the silent kitchen. When he isn't working, Dad is usually here, marinating something, fixing something, talking at length about the things he's picked up from the local farm shop. Dad isn't home a lot, but this room feels more silent, more empty than ever. It's the absence of him having been home; of normality. He's always calling, leaving meandering voicemails on their old-fashioned answer machine, half-finished projects of his—door handles he's fixed, glued and propped up to set on the kitchen counter, new spices he's yet to open, purchased and ready for a new recipe he wants to try in his outdoor wood-fired oven, on the kitchen shelf. The TiVo leaping into action, murder mystery shows on series link.

"How's . . . how's Julian?" I ask. And Mum's eyes brighten. I've skirted around Julian, not even uttered his name, up until now.

"He's—all right. I . . . I don't know really, Millie. I've—not seen him this week. Or last."

"No?"

Mum shakes her head. A quick, rigid judder. She says nothing else.

"And you. How are you, Mum? Truthfully," I say, and it's like that final word lands between us on the table; she considers picking it up for a while, resists, and then finally grasps it.

"I'm sad, Millie. I'm—really sad. I wish I could say otherwise, but—I'm sad. I'm sad for your dad. I'm sad for doing this; lying in the first place, for being caught up in it. But—did he tell you he's coming over tomorrow? Dad. When he lands?"

My heart bungees. "Is he?"

Mum nods gently. She reaches for the salt and pepper shakers in the center of the table, adjusts the angle of them. "He said we'd talk. And I hope so much that we can talk more than the usual five minutes before he walks away."

"Do you think he's going to come home?"

Then Mum sniffs into a balled-up piece of kitchen towel and squares her shoulders, clears her throat. The quickest gathering of herself. "I do hope so. I . . . I really thought I knew everything when it came to me and your dad, you know." Mum gazes at her hands thoughtfully. Her hands are uncharacteristically clean; no pen, no paint splodges. "That everything had been so easy, so perfect, that there was nothing except more of the same on our horizon." Her lips are a light, faraway smile. "Millie, this has taught me a lot. An awful lot. That nothing—*no one*—is untouchable. That when we make up reasons why the truth doesn't matter, that it isn't important, it's just that. *Made up*. Excuses. Lies. Because the truth *always* matters the most. Even when it's hard or painful. *Especially* when it's painful."

I nod, let Mum's slow, careful, wise words sit with us here at the table, like a soothing song. "I thought you were perfect," I admit. "You and Dad."

Mum laughs then; an almost mirthless laugh. "Nobody is. But I'm really glad you thought that. For such a long time, I was so worried about getting it wrong, like my parents did; always so haphazard, so erratic. I just wanted you to see me and Dad as these strong, able, can-cope-with-anything sort of people. So you could be that too." She smiles, shakes her head. "Strong. Happy. And I think, perhaps in my desperation for that, for you both, I've been misguided. I've not let you . . . *be*."

Silence stretches between us, rain continuing to spit against the kitchen window. The willow tree in the garden, the one I used to sit under on blankets when I was a child, with Kieran and triangle sandwiches and cheese puffs, is leafless and bowing sadly in the wind, its branches skinny, spindling. I'd dream of everything back then. Doing everything. Dancing, singing, grabbing everything and enveloping myself in it. "She's a wild card, is Millie," my grandparents used to say, and Mum, with almost eye-rolling but warm exasperation, would say, "I know."

Where did she go? Where did that Millie go? Before she was too afraid to say everything out loud in case . . . in case, *what*? People didn't love her. So what? As Jack would say. So what?

Mum reaches over and holds my hands with both of hers. "Please tell me things about you. Anything."

I smile.

"Erm. *Well.* I met a guy I kind of like," I say, and boom. There it is. I like him. So much, it's here with me at a table in my childhood home. "That I—really *like* actually. Not kind of. Just—*like*. A lot."

"Well, that's wonderful, Millie."

"He's moving soon, though. Going traveling? He does it all the time. Months and years at a time. He's that sort, you know? And

I . . . well, I'm driving myself insane with it all. I'm in, then I'm out. I'm like—playing . . . the bloody Hokey Pokey."

Mum nods knowingly. "And what's stopping you staying *in*? With this person."

"Jack," I say, smiling at the sound of his name, here with me in this room. "I keep feeling frightened about going any further with it in case it hurts when he leaves. Which . . ." I laugh. "I mean, regardless, it's going to hurt when he leaves, isn't it?"

Mum simply smiles, her eyes glistening. She is always low-key. If anyone is going to cry if I ever do walk down the aisle, it'll be Dad who bawls his eyes out. Mum will simply stand tall, smiling, as if she always knew this moment would come and she is amply prepared. "The age-old fear," she says. "But look, it's a frivolous sort of feeling, liking someone. Don't let all those thoughts extinguish that."

"I know. And he makes me want to be . . . silly too. Giggly. Young."

"And that's what love should be," she says. "At the start, definitely, it should be that way. But it shouldn't be lost to the years. It wasn't that way for Julian and me. But me and your dad—we're still silly. Still bring out the giggliness in each other."

And it brings me hope that Mum is talking like she and Dad are still the same. That it can still go back to how it was.

"Owen and I didn't really ever feel giggly. Or silly. Not really. It was just . . . hard in the end."

"I remember." Mum simply nods again, lets space expand for me to fill.

Rain patters at the kitchen window, and everything feels so strange. As if this could be a scene from years ahead. Jack's right. You can't plan, can you? Not really. Because who would have thought that *this* is how life would look a few months ago? It feels like I'm running out of places to hide. And I think, for the first time in a while, that maybe that's a good thing.

"For a while, I punished myself. Because I thought being with Owen would give me everything. Everything you're supposed to have. But Owen wasn't actually very nice to me. He made me feel less than . . . less than me, for just *being* me. And all under the guise of love." And I think now of Cate and Nicholas. Maybe that's why I could see Nicholas so clearly. The anger I felt was mine to feel. What is it Lin said? "It holds up a mirror." It's that. I could see myself in Cate.

Mum nods. "It's hard to see when you're in it, though. I know that. You don't see it for what it really is until you've gathered enough distance for it to come into view. But nobody, Millie—*nobody* should make you feel like you should apologize for who you are." And I wonder for a second if she means herself too.

Before I leave, Mum helps me pack the boot of the car.

"What if I don't want to be the things you think I can be?" I ask, my hand on the open car door, that first conversation in the garden with Mum after Julian feeling like a hundred years ago now. "And what if I can't, or what if I don't know what I want yet? What if I don't get married, or find a career, or have children, or . . . I don't know. Brunch things. Auntie Vye's conservatory things. What if I'm not what you hoped I'd be?"

Mum gazes at me with round, tear-filled eyes. She reaches up a hand and cradles my face. "Oh, Millie," she says. "You already are."

**Text Message from Kieran:** Millie, Dad told me everything that's been happening at home. I feel like a total shit that I had no idea. Are you all right? We all have our skeletons, but another husband?

One's enough! (OK, too soon?) Please remember I might be miles away, but I'm here. I know I'm rubbish at checking in. We've just finished renovating. I've started lecturing in the evenings. But regardless of time and distance, I will always be your big brother. Mum and Dad will be OK. I know it. xx

## chapter 23

**Text message from Cate:** Mate, I'm not even joking. I'm in the emergency room. I'm OK, don't panic, they think it's my gallbladder. I'm with Ralph and I'm being looked after. I'm so sorry I can't follow you down, but please tell Alexis I love her. (That bitch better show up.) Something about being in hospital that makes you realize what really matters. She's a dick, but I love her. And you. So much. Please stay there and enjoy it. You deserve it.

It started off fine. I called Ralph and said I wanted to turn around, come home, but they both insisted I head to the treehouse and enjoy myself. Cate sounded giggly on pain relief, and Ralph was in full nurse mode, and when I got to the treehouse, I was really glad, in a way, they made me stay. The treehouse is *adorable*, and the view—the view is spectacular. Trees and trees for miles, webbed with endless, endless velvet sky. I had that feeling when I arrived. That opening inside me—that feeling of newness.

But then: the rain.

Oh my God, the rain.

And at first, it was exhilarating. Romantic. Cozy. *I'll pour some wine*, I'd thought, *run a hot shower, get my pajamas on,* enjoy *the peace.* Because what could be so bad about that? I could cook the giant lasagne I'd grabbed from a Waitrose on the way, and all while being surrounded by nothing but trees and sky like those autonomous people do on Instagram. The ones who live in a van for a year and upload pictures of rainy truck windows and cups of steaming coffee.

But very quickly, it went oh so bloody wrong. The storm started. Rain first, yes, and then absolute *hollers* of angry thunder. And it's not the water this time, like it was with the Yurt from Hell. It's the power. The actual *power* went out. And now I sit in darkness with a phone at less than 15 percent battery, no electricity, and rain lashing down so hard, I can't even see out of the window. I found candles under the sink and lit them with matches, but the thunder has ramped up a notch now, which, along with the tree branches scratching the windows, makes it sound like the ceiling is caving in. The sky is a theater, and I am a mere background artist in its show.

I'm trying to enjoy it.

I'm really, really trying.

I *like* new things. I like new experiences. Right?

So I sit by the candles, with a rock star romance book Cate lent me a couple of weeks ago (mainly when I needed somewhere to vent my sexual frustrations after that almost-kiss in the cloakroom with Jack), and try to relax.

*I'll be fine*, right? I am to treat this as a retreat, time to get my head together. Away from the stress of work, of Mum and Dad, of a life A.E.

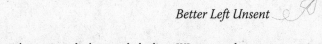

But—it's getting darker and darker. Wetter and wetter, angrier and angrier, out there.

And the more it storms outside, the more alone I feel.

The more alone I *am*.

Cate and Ralph seem to be growing into something lovely.

Mum and Dad are making their way back to each other.

Kieran has texted, but he's busier than ever with his full, grown-up life, thousands of miles away. (I should text him more. I'm not sure why I don't sometimes.)

I keep thinking of Leona, too, bemused by my weird harebrained theories interrupting her busy day. Even Chloe's talking about moving on.

And Alexis—well, she's clearly off living her life without me and isn't coming. Of course she isn't coming. And I really thought she might. Alexis is so much more likely to enter stage left with a bang, a gesture, rather than a small "sorry" text message. But still, she never came. She isn't here.

Nobody is here.

And I don't even realize I'm crying or even panicking as much as I am until I have to speak down the phone. I barely even register the fact I'm calling him until he picks up.

"Hey, you," Jack says happily down the line.

"Hi." I slap on a fake smile in the dark. "I just . . . I just want someone to talk to. Are you—busy?"

"I'm at a bowling alley." He laughs through the phone; a safe, lovely sound that grounds me instantly. "And, er, it sounds like you might be too? Chaz, dude, what the fuck? Sorry, we're getting totally thrashed."

"I'm at the treehouse."

"Oh shit, *yeah*, I remember you saying. That's tonight? How's it going?"

Tears have started almost instantly, my lips quivering, my face burning hot.

"Millie? Millie, are you OK?"

"Um—no," I squeak. "I don't think I am. The power's out. There's a . . . a storm."

"Oh, shit."

"And I'm alone."

"I thought you said you were going with Cate? With . . . with Alexis?"

"Neither of them came. Cate's in hospital. Her—her gallbladder. And Alexis never showed, so . . ." I gaze around the wooden shack, bowing, struggling trees shadowed on the walls. Romantic in the day-time with its beams and slatted floors, its log burners and baskets of blankets like piled-up Swiss rolls, but now, in this storm, it feels more like a glorified, oversize shed that might very well get whipped up like a cow in a tornado, me and my lasagne trapped inside. "It's just me. And there're no lights, because the power's out, and it's sort of in the middle of nowhere so . . . I just wanted to hear someone's voice, I suppose. Your voice."

"Ah, Millie. I'm sorry. Hold on just a sec." Suddenly the line is quiet. He's moved somewhere more remote. I can hear traffic, the solid bleeping of a pelican crossing. The total opposite of me, here in the wilderness, in a literal treetop. "So, you're alone?"

I nod to nobody, to the empty, cold, dark room. The thunder roars outside. The candles flicker, painting halos of butterscotch on the walls. "Yeah," I say in a tiny voice, and I close my eyes, tears falling. God, it reminds me of university. Being alone in a room, somewhere I didn't want to be, everyone else out having fun. It reminds me of when Owen and I broke up, and I sat, shivering, in a horrible house share's box room that smelled like cat poo and mildew, because I couldn't face going home. Until I found Ralph and Four, the Logans. Oh, I wish I was back at Four, the Logans.

"Do you want me to come?" he asks.

"What?"

"I'll drive out."

And relief warms me through, like soup. But how can I ask him to? He's at a bowling alley with his friends. I feel guilty pulling him away. Especially out into the great *Wizard of Oz*–style storm. He'll be leaving the country soon. This might be the last chance he has to see his friends.

"No, Jack, you're busy, you're—"

"No, no, I'm not. I mean—that's if you *want* company. No pressure. I'm not going to gate-crash your holiday." He chuckles.

"No, no, you *could never* gate-crash. I'd really love that, if you came."

"Me, too," replies Jack warmly.

"It's just . . . the storm." I sniff. "It's not exactly safe, is it?"

"It's fine here. Clear as day."

"I'd come back, but I've had two wines, plus it's so mad out there—"

"*Millie.* Just—let me come and be with you. Yeah?"

I smile; let out a tiny hmph of a laugh. "OK," I say. "Yes. Please."

"I can get in the car now, grab some stuff. Can you text me the address?"

And within moments, I hear Jack saying goodbye to his friends, his car rumbling down the phone, his radio burst into life.

"Google Maps is quoting an hour and fifteen minutes," he says. "Hold tight. And don't drink all the wine, Millie Chandler. Save some for me."

Within two hours, Jack is calling me from the little slice of a car park by the forest, and wrapped in a blanket, I stand out on the deck, the phone to my ear, waving in the wind.

Jack moves quickly through the dark, a bag slung over his shoulder, his eyes squinted against the sheets and sheets of rain, and God, he looks *gorgeous*. I, on the other hand, must look like a scared, hiding little E.T. (without the bicycle and small boy).

We bundle inside quickly. The wind slams the door behind us.

"Hi," says Jack breathlessly, raindrops dangling from the ends of his hair. Thunder rumbles outside, like a grumbling dog. "Cool little place."

"Hi," I reply, shuddering. "*Scary* little place." And in one gust, I throw my arms around him. Raindrops from his jacket seep through my sweater to my vest, to my skin. "I'm so glad you're here. Thank you. *Thank you.*"

"Hey, it's OK," says Jack softly into my ear, sending tingles down my body. He draws back and looks down at me. "I mean, it's already a biblical experience, so I think I need to thank *you*. I didn't think the whole rainforest thing would be happening for a few months yet, but life always surprises us."

I gaze up at him in the darkness, just a couple of feet between us, our chests rising and falling, and feel myself crumble a little. "I'm sorry I've dragged you here. To a stormy, dark, and cold treehouse."

Jack smiles, lopsided, a peep of his white, straight teeth. "Ah, come on. Who wouldn't want to be here? We have wine. We have . . ." He steps back and shrugs the bag from his back. "A shit ton of candles. I brought so many. You know what I didn't realize?" He crouches to the bag on the floor, unzips. "How many candles I have as someone who proclaims to not really like them all that much. Look at this one." He pulls one out. "*Peach crumble.* I mean, who the fuck do I think I am with peach crumble?"

I chuckle for what feels like the first time all day, a teary giggle that stings my cheeks. "I think peach crumble is very *you* actually."

"And—oh, wait till you see this. The *masculinity* on this one."

He pulls out a candle that looks black in the dimness of the room. "Tobacco . . . and *musk*. I mean, what even is musk?"

I laugh, my eyes still rimmed with tears. "Wow, what happens when you light it? Do you start mansplaining?"

"Oh, fuck yeah," he says, standing tall, shrugging off his jacket. "And I start getting proper excited about barbecues and screwdrivers. And smashing people's faces in car parks over spaces."

Already, I feel totally at ease. Calm. It's as if I've swallowed a capsule. Gone is the shakiness, the wobbliness I felt, that gaping chasm of loneliness, and now I just feel completely safe. I always feel safe with Jack.

Half an hour later, we're sharing a thick, heavy blanket on the little sofa, a coffee table absolutely packed with flickering candles, the log burner roaring, which Jack got going, flickering orange watermarks over the walls, the weather raging outside. I've even had a text from the treehouse company who say the technical issue is being dealt with, but I almost don't care now that Jack is here beside me, close to me, on the sofa. I'd be gutted if they suddenly arrived to evacuate us. I never want to leave this room. This moment in time.

"I can't believe you drove all the way here."

Jack smiles, candlelight strobing lines across his face. "And why can't you believe that?"

"Just—I don't know. It was all a bit last minute."

"Yeah, but why wouldn't I have come?"

I take a deep breath, look down at the wine in my glass, which looks oil-slick black in the dark. "I don't know . . ." I say. Because I can't believe you think I'm worth it, I want to say. That I'm enough for you to drop everything for. I've never been enough for anyone.

"Well, I'm glad you called me," Jack says softly.

"You're the only person I wanted to call."

Jack looks at me, smiles deliciously slowly.

"Because—well, I knew you had a lot of candles."

Jack holds out a lazy palm—a "Yep, makes sense" gesture. "Plus, you know I can fight off rhubarb. And witches."

"Of course. You were an obvious recruit." I gulp down the wine. The air between us is thick and loaded; impossible to ignore. I imagine it surrounding us, dancing around us, specks and specks of it, like invisible stardust. "It's been a . . . weird night. A big night, really?"

Jack nods, says nothing.

"I went to see my mum on the way here," I say. "We talked about everything. About . . . her lie and Julian. And I sort of realized . . . we all have these unsaid things. All of us. Everyone. I drove away from there and thought, nobody is exactly who they tell you they are. Are they? I spend my life holding myself to everyone else's standards. Comparing myself to everyone else, what they're doing, what they're posting online, what they're saying at brunches or announcing on Facebook. But what I'm comparing myself to a lot of the time isn't even real, anyway."

Jack nods thoughtfully. "You never get the full story," he says. "Really, the only person who ever gets your full story, your full self . . . is *yourself.* And if you're not down with yourself, you're against yourself. And who wants to hang out with someone for twenty-four hours a day who doesn't back you. You know?"

I nod, wine heating my throat. "Well, maybe someday soon I can—*get down* with myself. What do you think?"

"You're not down with you?" asks Jack, then he drops his voice to that deep voice that always makes me melt and says, "*I'm* down with you."

I laugh, heat tingling up up up my body, and I genuinely thought it was impossible to fancy someone *this* much. I feel like leaping across the sofa and jumping on him.

"I feel like I *used* to," I tell him, "but I sort of stopped being down with me."

"Since?"

"Owen," I say, quicker than I think even my brain has realized that truth.

Jack nods slowly as rain pours, and inside the log burner, the fire pops. A neon-orange spark drifting upward, dispersing like a child's sparkler in the night. "Why did you break up?" he asks. "I don't think I've ever asked you. Obviously, we don't have to talk about this shit if you don't want to."

"The job."

"India?" he asks.

"Yeah." I rub a thumb along the rim of the wineglass. "It was his dream. He was in production, working and working toward directing. Like, obsessively. And then he got offered the job to help Flye launch the new channel. And we trundled along for a while, talking about long distance and all that. Then we agreed on a break, which, in hindsight, I know was him sort of *acclimatizing* me to the idea of splitting up. But then Petra offered me some work out there. Only four weeks. Helping set up. She sort of—did me a solid. And then I just thought, well, he's always talking about being bold, being . . . you know, driven? So I used my own savings for an open flight ticket, took some annual leave, and thought, fuck it, I'll make it up as I go along. I'd always wanted to do something different. Something exciting and new. And I thought I'd surprise him. So, I told him just as we were about to go into the restaurant for his leaving meal—he said no. That it wasn't what he wanted. That he was sorry. And he dumped me. Just like that."

Jack looks at me, his eyes narrowing. The reflection of the fire dances in them. "That's fucking shit, Millie."

"I know. Honestly, I don't think I'd ever felt something actually *die* in me before, but in that moment—every bit of truth. Or boldness or . . . me-ness? Just shrank away."

Jack hesitates, his brow furrowing. "I hate that he did that to you," he says, soothingly. "Do you want me to take him out on *Instinct*? Tie breeze blocks to his ankles?"

I laugh. "You're not taking Owen out on handsome little *Instinct* before me, thank you."

Jack smiles. "Just say the word. Although we'll have to make it soon." And I ignore that. The "soon." I don't want to think we're on limited time.

We pour more wine, and Jack gets up, adds two more logs to the fire. I watch him, will time to slow down, so I can savor the moment. The light of the fire, flickering across his serious face, the slow, careful hands, the sweet smell of wood hitting flames.

"Do you think . . . he could've sent the emails?" I ask. And it sounds wild coming out of my mouth, but I've been mulling it over more and more. Especially since Leona disproved Vince's theory this morning.

Jack screws his face up, settles back next to me. He rests his hand on my foot, under the blanket, a warm, safe grip. "Owen? I mean, stranger things have happened. But why would he?"

I shrug. "It's just, it's niggling at me. I wish it wasn't, but it is. Because I do leave my laptop open sometimes, and my desk gets a *lot* of traffic. Maybe it was a prank. Maybe it was . . . I don't know."

Jack sips his wine. Slowly, he meets my eyes.

"Ugh, you're going to go all cakes about it, aren't you?" I laugh. "You're going to say, let it go. That it doesn't matter."

"Mm," he says. "I *am* going to go all cakes about it." He puts an arm along the back of the sofa and, with a finger, strokes my shoulder. "Because why does the how matter? Wondering about it, turning it all over and over, going around in circles . . . Your brilliant brain deserves to be thinking over much better things than that."

I smile, move so my hand settles upon his, at my shoulder. I turn my face toward it, rest my lips on the warm skin of his knuckles. "I can't believe you're leaving," I whisper. I almost say it so he doesn't hear. So my own ears don't hear. I hate those words. I hate that he is going.

"It never feels real until I'm on the plane."

"So, this isn't enough, then," I say, my words quiet. "This. Rainy British forest with no electricity. It's not enough to keep you here."

Slowly, Jack smiles. I was measuring the time left before Jack goes traveling in months, but now it's down to mere weeks—*days*—and I'm tempted to count out in hours because hours sound longer. I can't believe he won't be here. I can't believe he won't even be in this country.

The sky outside roars, as if goading me: *I'm going to take him away, far from here.*

"Almost," says Jack.

"I mean, who couldn't be taken in by all this . . . *gloom*. All this— *cold misery*." And I'm trying so hard to push down this dark emptiness that's opening inside me at the thought of losing him. As if my stupid light tone will cancel it out; this crack slowly, slowly zigzagging the ground at our feet, separating us.

Jack smiles gently in the half-light. "This could sway me," he says.

"The masculine candle?"

"This."

"*In the cold, dark . . .*"

"You."

And that "you" undoes me. I feel myself sink into the chair, my throat tighten.

He squeezes my hand, pulls me gently toward him. My skin tingles, goose bumps pricking the skin.

"You could sway me, Millie dot Chandler," he whispers, and I feel his breath again against my skin, against my lips. Warm and sweet, like wine.

He moves his hand on my foot beneath the blanket, sliding slowly, slowly up my leg. He brings the other hand to my face, his smooth fingers brushing my cheek, and I feel everything. Beneath my skin, like electricity. His lips touch mine, gently at first, as if testing the waters. Soft and warm, and I feel like my heart is going to explode out of my chest. I want him. I haven't wanted someone for so long, and now I remember how it feels. And it's how he looks at me that completely kills me; does me in. He looks at me like I'm beautiful. And I—*believe* him, for a small moment. The way his eyes drop to my mouth, the way I see him swallow, anticipating.

I lean into him, and he closes his mouth over mine softly, his fingertips at my neck, the hand on my leg squeezing gently.

He draws back, pauses inches from my mouth.

"Definitely could be swayed," he whispers as he kisses me again.

## chapter 24

When I wake the next morning, for a moment I could easily believe last night didn't even happen. The room is flooded with hazy morning sunlight, the fridge is rumbling, the air is calm, the trees still, and I can hear the shower. Oh, I hope so much I didn't dream last night. The way we'd kissed (three times on the sofa, and once for about an hour in the bed). The way we'd fussed about, talking about who would sleep where, when I threw my arms up and said, "Look, *of course* we can share a bed. We don't bite, do we?" and Jack had laughed and said, "Only when asked very, very nicely," and that had very nearly sent me over the edge. In the darkness, we'd got into bed together, and I had felt *fucking everything.* The exciting unfamiliarity of the feel of his hands on me, his smell, his lips, and I had wanted so much to have sex with him.

But—and as stupid as it probably sounds—I was trying hard to do damage control. Because there's a part of me that worries a *lot* for my heart. Jack is leaving. He has his ticket. It's going to be hard enough saying goodbye to him, having just known him. Spent time with him. Kissed him. But sleeping with him, having sex with him—that would be the end of me. I'd fall then, being so close to him. And I know it goes against what Cate and I talked about, allowing it to just be what it's going to be, but I'd rather not know how it feels to be so close to Jack Shurlock, if it's still only going to end in goodbye.

Jack emerges out of the shower, a sunbeam streaming through a light box above our heads, lighting him like a spotlight. He's dressed in jeans, but he's topless, droplets of water from the shower still sitting on his tanned skin. Fuck. I can't even bear to look at him. His *body.* For so many months, I've looked at those muscles through his shirt, looked far too long at the angular shoulder blades, at those forearms, and now it's all just—there. And I want to bury my face into him.

"Hi." He grins, those bright, hazel eyes all playfulness. I hide my face with my hands.

"Hi. I haven't got any makeup on."

"What?"

"When you saw me last night, it was dark," I say, voice muffled from behind my fingers. "I haven't got any makeup on. I've just opened my eyes."

"*What?*" Jack says again. "You haven't got any *makeup* on?" He laughs, and I feel the bed creak beneath me, the mattress lowering from his weight, his warm hands reaching up to the hands at my face.

He smells of citrusy shower gel and toothpaste. "I'm afraid I need to see you. Immediately."

I laugh behind my hands. "No."

"No?"

"Honestly, Jack—"

"It's nonnegotiable, Millie."

"No!" I practically squeal, bursting into laughter.

"Or what?"

He pulls my hands away and gazes down at me. A smile curves the corner of his mouth. Oh, his face. Jack's first-thing-in-the-morning face. His freshly showered face. He is so beautiful. I'm toast. I'm totally fucking toast.

"Oh dear," says Jack, shaking his head. "Unacceptable, this face. I really must investigate it further." He leans, lowering closer to me. Droplets of water land on me from his thick, messy hair. I put a hand over my face.

"Not brushed my teeth."

"I don't care."

"I'm gross."

"Don't care." He pulls my hand away and kisses me slowly, and God, my chest, my stomach, my whole body—everything aches. I draw my arms around him, tingle at the touch of his warm skin beneath my hands, feel the taut hardness through his jeans against my thigh . . .

"Jack . . . just . . . oh . . . can . . ."

He moans deep, at the back of his throat, smiles against my lips, his hand lingering at the seam of my underwear, in the crease of my thigh, warm fingertips grazing me beneath the fabric. I don't want him to stop. I don't ever want him to stop . . . But no. No, he's literally *leaving.* Damage control. *Damage control.*

I pull back, our faces inches apart. "I need . . ." I clear my throat.

"*Tea.* Coffee. Or something. D-do you need coffee? I feel like we need coffee."

Jack hesitates, slightly taken aback, I can see, from the sudden change of tone. But he smiles against my mouth. "Erm. Yeah? Always?"

I slide out from beneath him. "I need a toothbrush too."

"If you say so. I'll go and find some sort of hot beverage to assemble, shall I?"

After I've washed my face and brushed my teeth (and *gathered* myself back to human-shaped from a jelloid heap on the floor), I find Jack in the boxy, bottle-green, and shabby-wood kitchen area, sipping coffee at a small, round table. The tabletop is a varnished slice of tree trunk, and the two wooden chairs at it remind me of something from "Goldilocks and the Three Bears."

He smiles at me. "The milk in the fridge is warm from the power outage. But—I managed black coffee?"

"Perfect."

The door to the deck is open a crack, a clean, cold breeze chilling my bare feet. Outside is beautiful and calm this morning, and it's so blindingly sunny that I have to put my hand above my eyes, like a visor, to stop myself being blinded. The rain. The wind. The storm. It's all gone. The world's cobwebs, blown away.

"Can you believe the brass neck?" he says as I sit. "We were basically blown into oblivion last night, and now . . ."

"I know. And now this," I say, and I take in his thoughtful gaze. The sun hitting the smooth skin of his face, the breeze ruffling his shower-damp hair. He chews the corner of his mouth in concentration, watching the trees gently sway outside, breathes into his mug as he drinks, kicks up a puff of steam. Oh, I wish he wasn't going. I wish he was staying. Forever. A forever of last nights. Kissing and hands sliding over my hips. A forever of chatting on our sides in the darkness, both laughing so much, the bed shook.

"So . . . are you all set?" I ask tentatively.

"All set?"

I nod. "You know. To jet off. To *pastures new*?"

Jack smiles thoughtfully, looks down into his coffee. "Er. I think so? Everything's ready to go into storage at the flat, the new tenant came and measured up yesterday. They want to put a four-poster bed in the bedroom, so."

"Bloody hell. How . . . alluring."

Jack's head tips back, and he laughs. "Ah, I don't know about that, Millie. He was all about beer fridges and putting his flatscreen in the bedroom for the boxing when we chatted."

I smile. "I suppose anything is alluring in the right circumstances."

"Depends who you're with." He flashes me a smile then, full of cheek, and my stomach flips.

Oh, I don't want to leave. I don't want to leave this forest, or for us to get into our cars, drive away from each other. *Give it a couple of weeks and he'll be flying away,* says a little voice in my head, and I shake it away. Because how can that even be true? How can it even be *fair*? This is just. . . starting. It's like watching two amazing episodes of a twelve-part series and never, ever watching them again.

"So, you remember Jonny?" he says. His bare foot touches mine under the table as he moves in his seat. Neither of us shifts.

"Certainly do. He seemed nice. Cool."

"He said the same about you," he says. "Because apparently if Elton licks someone, it's a good barometer."

That moment with Cate on the bridge feels like so long ago now, despite it not being that long at all. I had no idea back then that I'd be kissing Jack in a candlelit shed, or here with him in a treehouse. So much has changed, but in the most natural, smooth way . . .

"Well, he's a pastry chef. Runs this amazing, tiny Turkish bakery place in Chelmsford. And he's been approached by this company—they run events and stuff? It's all about being able to try new things without, like, signing your life away before you even know if it's for you? Anyway. They want to work with him, for him to run and teach classes on, I dunno, how to be a Turkish bakery genius, I guess?"

"Classes?"

"Yeah, like, a limited course, accessible to everyone?"

"That's amazing," I say.

"Well, I was actually thinking of you," Jack says, and the words land there in front of us in the sunny kitchen. "I know you like learning new stuff, and . . . I just thought of you and the *rhubarb*. The cake. The—goaty-cat thing." He grins. "One starts after Christmas. Runs for, like, eight weeks, I think? Evenings?"

"Oh." And it's sweet. It's so sweet. Because Jack knows me. He remembers; remembers all the little things about me, collects them like keepsakes. And the classes with Jonny is definitely something I'd like. It *is* so very me.

But something hurts too. That Jack is so easily, breezily, discussing me doing something away from him. That without any sort of sadness, he's handed me something to do with my life, when he's out there, living his own. Both of us, separate.

Obliviously, he hands me his phone. "So, this is Jonny's stuff. His food. His art, I'm sure he'd say. And if you go on this profile, you can see the stuff on the classes. The *coming soon* post . . . Battery's almost dead, but there's enough."

It feels weird to have Instagram in my hands again. Everything pricks up. Ears, eyes, longing to scroll. Like a switch flicked, my fingertips tingling. It's like a drug. I suddenly want to spend a whole day scrolling.

"Take a look," he says and stands up. "No pressure, but I told him I'd suggest it to you. Throw it out there. You can throw it back at me if you like. At my head and everything." He laughs. "Anyway. I left my charger in the car. I'll dash down there, have a look . . ."

Jack pads through the treehouse. I hear him pull on shoes, grab his car keys in the next room, and the exit close.

I have *so* missed my phone. This alone makes me miss it, Jonny's kaleidoscope of photos. And Jack is right. He *is* a genius. Beyond talented. His food does look more like art. Lime greens and fuchsias and utterly perfectly piped creams in things I have never seen before, let alone eaten. I watch a video of him kneading dough to a SZA song; there's a beach in the background that is *definitely* not anywhere around here. And now my stomach feels like it's being kneaded too. With . . . yearning. Envy. Jonny just out there, living his life fully. And I don't know if it's this that I want—but it is *something*. I really do want something else. I'm just not sure what. But it feels closer than ever at the moment. As if my fingertips are just centimeters from touching it.

I scroll and scroll. Then I have no idea what I've done, the layout has changed since I gave up my phone, but I'm accidentally on Jack's main grid. "Ah, shit," I say, but Jack is still out. And then it pops up. A looping video of a pair of running shoes on concrete in a perfect slice of sunlight. Caption: *Never want to run. Always glad I did!* \*sun emoji\* *Good morning everyone. If we keep expecting things to get better, they will. This morning's mantra.* \*praying emoji\* #postbreakup #movingon

Posted by Chloe Katz ten minutes ago.

And it's all too easy—all too deliciously close, in the palm of my hand. I press onto her main profile. I watch her stories. A share of a post from a friend's baby announcement. A quote about new beginnings. A flow chart of how to—truly—ask how someone is. "Talk to your Friends," says the infographic. There's a dog meme, then a dark, line-drawing post leading to a carousel of "signs of covert emotional abuse." I scroll. I press. There are still some photos of Owen on here. Not many, but some a lot farther down her page. Owen-and-Chloe selfies. A close-up of their hands, holding each other's. India sunset after India sunset. Looped clinking glasses.

And then I find Owen's account. I've of course looked before. An open, nonprivate account, of course. For all to see. All his posts are artsy, with one-line captions, interspersed with distant, posey photos on beaches or him at work, hunched over a camera, silhouetted. But then there's a photo of him in the IT office. It's been filtered to fit with his feed, but it's him, Leona, and Steve, and the table is littered with pizza boxes. *When it's all hands on deck and IT hold you hostage with fast food*, says the caption. *#workinglate*.

And the date . . .

The date is the day the servers were down.

The date is when my emails were sent.

I stare at the screen.

But . . . Owen said he wasn't there. Owen said he was in Manchester. He did, didn't he? I remember so clearly that's what he said that evening we talked in the rain.

I close down the app. Lock Jack's phone and put it on the table, as if it's a firework about to go off.

The door behind me closes again.

"Got it," calls Jack. "So, what do you think? See anything you like?"

*chapter 25*

"So, what're we saying?" asks Cate, folding her legs beneath her on the sofa. "Owen's a little lying freak?" We're in our living room at Four, the Logans, somewhere I've been dying to be ever since I saw that post. Jack had to get back, a visit from his landlord, and sitting alone in the treehouse, in silence, the creaking of the trees holding me up, I felt something just heave out of me. "Perhaps it was your last fuck to give," Cate had texted back earlier, and I'd gazed around at the trees, at the thick, thick forest, shielded from everything beyond it, and wondered if she was right. But I think it was realizing . . . I really don't love Owen anymore.

There I was, in this safe, honest bubble with Jack.

And there in the center of it, like a stain, was Owen. His profile. Beautifully curated photos, perfect captions, and all posted while his life apparently imploded because of my email . . . it's like I suddenly saw it. His profile an emblem of him; how he lives his life. Perfectly fake. A story he's peddling. And that pizza-box IT picture. He could still be telling the truth, of course, but I suddenly realized—why wouldn't he lie? What evidence in his life—work aside—is there that he is the perfect, rounded, and purehearted human being he portrays himself to be?

"I don't know," I say. "The whole thing just left me feeling cold. His profile. It was all just so . . . *him.*"

"And he was in a photo *in* the office?" asks Cate. "That night?"

I nod. "Brazen as fuck. Him and Leona. And Fundraising Steve. This caption saying *it's all hands on deck here tonight.* And they'd ordered pizza, and I *know* they ordered pizza the night the emails were sent because I remember boxes the next day. In the kitchen. Classic IT, they never clean up."

"Maybe he meant he'd been in Manchester earlier in the day?" asks Ralph measuredly. "Oh. I'll take that." Ralph jumps from the armchair, grabs the huge mug of steaming mint tea from Cate's hand. "Don't want you moving around."

She smiles sleepily at him. "Ralph, I'm fine. Really," she says, and he gives her the smallest of knowing smiles. A doctor at the hospital diagnosed Cate with gallstones. She has keyhole surgery in a few weeks but has been signed off for a week for rest and given painkillers she has taken to calling "her babies" because of how much they're helping. She's snuggled in a blanket, her hair scooped up in a bun that would make me look like I had an onion for a head, but on Cate, it looks so neat and purposeful. I'm so glad she's here with us. I'm so glad she's okay. And it was the only place I wanted to be today after driving home. Here with Cate and Ralph, our little flat by the vast November sea.

"Plus, there's what Nicholas said," I add. "About him being a liar. About the flirting."

"Oh, don't listen to bloody Nicholas," tuts Cate.

"I know," I say. "But also, what Chloe said. She said he's

manipulative. That he . . . writes his own story, pushes *that* narrative. He'd told me his flat was bursting with wedding stuff, but Chloe had no idea what I was talking about."

"Mm." Ralph nods. "Well. It's certainly a very interesting theory."

"I don't know what to think." I snuggle up next to Cate. I would normally feel elated after the night and morning I had with Jack. Every time I remember it, heat zooms down my body, and I feel like I need to dunk myself in ice. But I feel weirdly flat and confused and shamefully, almost grateful to be home, as much as it means being away from him. Because my head is jammed full. Of Jack, mostly. About the fact that I like him, and he'll be moving countries for the foreseeable and we'll have to say goodbye. "Ever since I found out that someone probably pressed send themselves, and it's probably *not* a glitch, and not the bloody scheduled thingy, I just feel like I'm missing something." What is it Chloe said? About her gut.

Cate and Ralph exchange looks. Cate giggles. She always giggles with Ralph.

"Well, it wasn't me." Cate laughs. "Just saying."

I laugh. "A groundbreaking twist *that* would be."

"And are you sure it wasn't Ralph?" Cate grins at him. "Did you break in? I can just imagine you in a spy outfit. All black. Sunglasses."

"I once broke into work," he says, leaning for a cauliflower floret. He's roasted a huge tray of them in olive oil and salt and arranged them in a big bowl the way someone would do with popcorn. He read online that Cate should stick to alkaline foods until her surgery and has taken the information and instantly, as is the Ralph way, soaked it up and become it.

"*Did you?*" Cate laughs. "Well, holy shit, Ralph Nobleman."

"Never told anyone," he says, chewing. "Used the code for the fire door. Borrowed a jiffy bag."

"Is that so?"

*"And two* stamps."

Cate reacts like Ralph just told her he bent an oak tree with his own bare hands. "Erm. Wow. And that's legal fucking tender."

"Certainly is." Ralph winks and we all laugh, Cate giggling into my shoulder.

"Anyway, screw it, do you know what?" she says, straightening and loosening her bun. "I would just ask Owen. Like, you'd know if he was lying, wouldn't you?"

"I . . . think so? I certainly don't really trust him to tell me the truth."

And slowly Ralph smiles at that, like he's just witnessed his own child take their first steps. He has a look on his face of "Well done, I knew you could do it."

"What?"

"Nothing," says Ralph. "But—well, it's just nice to hear you say this sort of thing. It's progress. And from the state of you when you first stepped through that door—I could never trust a person who made someone like you into someone as fragile as that."

Cate nods vigorously, then shifts, loops her arm through mine, her dressing-gowned arm warm, lavender-scented cushioning be-tween us. "You were always infatuated with him," she says softly. A candle dances on the coffee table. "I know Alexis used to bang on about that, but he had this . . . hold over you, you know? Where you had him on this pedestal. Like you couldn't believe he was with you. And he'd sort of perpetuate it? It was almost like you were nervous of stepping wrong. In case he left." She looks up at me then, her face just inches from the side of my face. "And I can see that, because I was the same with Nicholas. They make it that way. You become only who you are through their lens."

I let the words sink into me, bittersweet, like lemon syrup. Be-cause I can't argue with it. I know it's true. I did worship him in a way, and I hated myself for it. A feminist. An independent woman. Someone with all this energy, all these *things* I wanted to try and see and do. And there I was, trying to impress my own boyfriend, feeling grateful when he'd pay me a compliment, even though he paid plenty to strangers on Instagram or women he'd meet at the gym who were strictly "just workout buddies, why don't you trust me?" Owen made me feel like I needed to be something, to hit the right notes, for a prize.

"And then enter Bad Jacky Shurlock," says Cate, giggling next to me.

"*Bad Jacky Shurlock?*" I laugh. "You make him sound like a wrestler."

"Well, he had you pinned down, didn't he? *One! Two! Three!* Oh, it seems poor Millie Chandler is all shagged out and can't get up."

"Cate, we did not *shag.*"

"Yet," Cate says, pointing at me. "You have not shagged him *yet*. Maybe it'll happen on the boat. When's that happening again?"

"Wednesday. And it's almost December, Cate. My coat's staying on."

"Killjoy," says Cate.

Ralph chuckles to himself, shaking his head, picking up yet another piece of cauliflower.

"What?" says Cate smilingly. "Look, just because my gallbladder is screwed does not mean I no longer need to get laid."

"Hm," says Ralph. "Well, sex is at least an alkaline activity."

"*Ooh.* Well, aren't I lucky?" scoffs Cate. "Cauliflower and sex. What else can a girl ask for? Might not bother having it removed."

## chapter 26

**Text Message from Jack:** Half-day approved here. Think they'd approve anything I requested, mere days from leaving.

**Text Message from Jack:** Mute Martin acting as my desk for 24 hours.

**Text Message from Jack:** Seven hour lunch breaks.

**Text Message from Jack:** A golden goose shitting out golden eggs right onto Michael's head.

**Text Message from Millie:** Hahaha. Mine's approved too! Tell Instinct to gird his loins.

**Text Message from Jack:** No need. Instinct is always ready.

**Text Message from Millie:** Instinct is such a hunk.

I'm on a boat. I am *actually* on a boat. The jetty behind us is getting farther and farther away, like one of those old moving sets they'd have in the olden days, a man pedaling a bike to make it move. And oh, it's so lovely to be drawing farther and farther away. Something eases inside me; breathes.

"Oh God, we're swaying . . ."

"Yep," says Jack, concentrating, pulling the lever to one side, straightening us as we drift farther out to sea. The boat rumbles quietly, sloshes through the water, and Jack stares straight out to sea, eyes on the horizon, both of us zipped up in coats.

"I'm on a boat."

"You are indeed," says Jack.

"On a Wednesday afternoon," I repeat like a mantra, so it sinks in, "here I am, *on a boat*."

Jack chuckles. "Call him by his name, Millie."

"*Instinct*." I laugh. "OK, I am in the sea, on . . . OK, hang on, is he a mister?"

"He's actually a sir."

"*Sir Instinct* of Leigh-on-Sea. The only male boat for miles."

"That's right." Jack laughs, and as the boat speeds up, the front of it rising a little, a little scream escapes my mouth. It's *wild*. I have lived here for years, but this is the first time I've been out here like this, beyond swimming. I see them all the time: dinghies bobbing, people rowing, chatting, beneath the sky. One of those things that I thought belonged to other people and not me.

It's beautiful out here. It's one of those cold, but high-skied, blue winter days that make you want to ponder; to wonder. And after earlier, that cringe-inducing conversation with Leona, I almost feel like I don't want Jack to ever turn around. I want to just lose myself to the sea. Lose myself with him.

"And you . . . definitely know what you're doing?" I call out over the sound of waves, the whirring of the motor. "It's just . . . the water is probably ice cold."

"Mm-hm. And why do you feel the need to ask me that?" says

Jack, pretending to be offended, a hand at his chest, the other hand wrapped strongly around the boat's steering lever. He's of course briefed me on the official names for things—rudder, motor . . . something else that I keep referring to as "a stick."

"Just . . . cocky sailor?" I offer reluctantly, and Jack shakes his head. "Which I'm finding very sexy, I have to say. Just not very reassuring."

"My cockiness does not affect my ability to pull levers, Millie," he says. "Plus, it's easy. You can come and have a go—"

"Nope. I am sitting right here, thank you very much, Jack Shurlock. Every time I move, I feel like the boat moves—sorry—*Sir Instinct* moves. So, I'm going to remain rigid. If that's all right."

Jack smiles that gorgeous smile over at me, the high autumnal sun lighting his hair golden. He gives a one-shouldered shrug. "Fine by the cocky sailor."

The boat rumbles on and on across the teal surface of the water. It really is so beautiful. The briny, sharp, and sweet smell of salt water, the distant bustle of Canvey Island on the horizon, Leigh getting farther and farther away. I know I needed this—I needed nothing more than to be away from work. I needed to *literally* be away from land. I think even a doctor themselves would prescribe this. If I sat and explained everything, plus "Oh, and it turns out my ex was lying about his whereabouts, but who am I to judge, I ruined his life. Oh, and I really like a guy—the first guy I have liked in years—but he's leaving the country for the foreseeable," I am pretty sure a doctor would say, "Oh, Millie Chandler, what you need is a boat. A boat maneuvered by a handsome man with delicious arms."

We sail and sail for a while, both of us quiet, almost taken and speechless by how lovely this is; how *escapist*. The salty air drying out my hair, the sound of waves and wind in my ears, the cries of seagulls, the whir of the motor. People getting tinier and tinier on the beach. It looks like a toy town. It looks unreal. *Made up.*

After a few moments, Jack kills the engine. "How's this?"

I nod thoughtfully, gazing at the skyline. "Perfect," I say. "Are we allowed to just—be out here?"

"Who's coming to get us? The boat police on a ship brimming with grannies telling us to keep warm." Jack grins. "And of course. Perfect conditions, perfect tide . . ."

"No sharks. Or slimy eels?"

"No sharks," he says. "No eels. In here with us, anyway. We're all good."

The sea surrounds us. The boat bobs gently. I turn my head toward the dome of the sky. And I suddenly feel something build inside me, rise in my chest. I breathe it out. A huge, meditative sigh.

"Ahh, this . . . makes me feel things," I say. "Do you know what I mean? All this water. Sky. Life. All this world."

Jack gives a singular nod. "Makes you feel insignificant, you mean," he says, the boat rocking slightly as he shifts, sits on the little ledge opposite me. Our knees touch. "And it should be disempowering, but it's . . . the *opposite*?"

I meet his hazel eyes, the pearly, sunlit-edged clouds behind him. "I'm not sure if I agree."

Jack smiles. "Oh yeah?"

"It actually feels a bit scary to me, all this world. Pressure to . . . *make something of it all.* And yet, we're all sort of stuck. In systems, in routines, in what's expected of us, all of which ensure we *aren't* making something of it all." I look up at Jack, shake my head. "Sorry, I'm just . . . thinking. About recently. About what it all means. I feel like a jaded old man holding up a bar." I give a fake laugh. The sort of laugh you give when you want to trick yourself into not feeling as though you could cry at any moment. He's leaving. *He's leaving.*

Jack says nothing; watches me carefully with those deep, glinting eyes, and for a moment, I wish so much I could freeze time. Take a screenshot I can keep in my brain somewhere, safely tucked away, to look at any time I forget how this feels. I never want to forget how this feels. He looks so beautiful. The sky looks so beautiful. Life, for this moment, feels so beautiful.

"I just think, we're not *nothing* or insignificant, are we?" I ask. "Because, how can we be? In a world where . . . all *this* exists. We're here for just a blink. And yet most of the time, what we're reduced to is, I don't know. Doing the same thing. Going in the same circles. Letting *other* people, other things, make us forget how important we actually are."

Jack nods thoughtfully. "That's why I live in the vortex," he says.

I smile at him. "So, what, if you live in the vortex, you don't let those fuckers in?"

"Precisely," he says quietly. Waves slosh. A seagull above cries, like a soundbite from a "beach sounds" playlist. "And I advise it. Any fuckers who take up your headspace . . ."

"What, tie breeze blocks to them and hand them to *Instinct*? Proverbial breeze blocks, of course."

"Of course, proverbial," he says with a smirk and turns, gazing across the water quietly, as if taking it all in one last time. The boat bobs. A plane bumbles overhead, unseen behind the clouds. Jack's phone bleeps once. An email.

"Jack?"

"Mm-hm?"

"In the interest of . . . *proverbial breeze blocks*," I say tentatively. I want to ask, because Jack, chief of staff—he'll probably know the answer. But I also don't want to. I don't want to bring everything out there in here, with us. And yet . . . "What your nerd said. Your coder nerd."

And Jack sags. Just a tiny, tiny little bit, almost undetectable, but I see it and the shame makes my ears go hot, despite this sharp, cool, salty air, the raincoat zipped up to my neck.

"Right," is all he says.

"It's just . . . the night it happened, Owen said he was *in* Manchester. But I don't think he was. I don't even know, but . . ."

"Manchester for what?" asks Jack.

"Cricket?"

Jack rubs his stubbly chin with his hand, thinking. A seagull swoops and lands flawlessly in the water. From elegant bird in flight to rubber duck.

"Cricket," he repeats. "Yeah. Yeah, he would've been."

"But could he have come back from Manchester?" I ask. "In time to *send* the emails? They were sent on a Thursday."

Jack presses his mouth into a downward arc, his stubbly chin dimpling. "I mean—yeah. It was a packing-up day, so the day was shorter. But he *was* in Manchester. Exact timings, though, I wouldn't know."

I stare at Jack across the boat, watch him watching the horizon, November sunlight glinting in his eyes. But I suddenly feel like there's this . . . edge between us, here, miles from land. A deflatedness. And looking over at Leigh, small and rustic and higgledy in the distance, knowing my flat is right there, work is right there, Owen is right there, my whole world right there, and here I am, with someone who is about to be nowhere near here . . . I feel like my chest is going to cave in.

"I know I sound like some sort of cut-rate detective," I say shamefully. "But I want to ask him. If he lied. If he was here when it happened."

Jack looks down at his feet for a second, gives a lazy shrug. "I don't think Kalimeris will ever give you the answers you want, Millie."

I say nothing; nod. The boat bobs and bobs, and it's as if there's an invisible cloud between us both; swelling and swelling with things we want to say, things we don't know how to, bearing down on us in this little boat. *Don't leave me. Please don't leave me.*

"We could just keep going," Jack says softly.

"Go on then. After you. You know all the levers and buttons and stuff."

Jack gives a deep chuckle. "Yeah, not sure how far *Sir Instinct* would get us."

"Or you could just stay here?" I say. "That's always an option. Stay here, continue to work at the proverbial bin . . ."

"Ah." Jack laughs. Then he stares thoughtfully out to sea. "Or you could just leave."

"*Leave?*" I feel frozen now—like a fish in a net.

"Yeah, we can just . . . do this," he says. "But. Everywhere else."

"Me, you, and Enam and the alpacas?" I say, my whole face, my whole body, going hot.

"Why not?"

"Ha. So what, eh?"

"Yeah, so what? Come."

And he reaches a hand up to my face, traces a warm finger down my cheek. I look down at my feet, and now I want to cry.

"I can't just be like you," I say.

"I'm not asking you to be me, Millie," he says. "I'm asking you to be you."

And that final sentence—those last words—unravel me. Because this, the boat, the sea, the sky, adventure . . . it is me. Or at least was me. Until I landed here, my feet stuck in the mud.

I hold his hand. He squeezes.

"But . . . money. And . . . responsibilities and . . . I don't know. The same reasons, maybe, that you won't stay put? In a way."

Jack nods, but something that looks like sadness scrunches the lines at his forehead, narrows his eyes.

There's silence now. We watch a tanker on the horizon skate along, lazy and slow, pearly pink clouds above us in the dimming sky.

Jack releases my hand and slowly brings it to my face, tips my chin. "It's never been hard to leave," he says. "I'm not used to it being hard to leave. But this time . . ."

And as his sentence disperses in the air between us, as tears sit at the waterlines of my eyes, and as rain starts to fall in unison, I close my eyes, and Jack kisses me, slow and careful.

And I make a wish—like I used to, imagine it wisping off like smoke into the universe. I wish that I will be somewhere with him like this again someday. And he won't have to leave me.

**Text to Alexis:** You probably won't get this because you've blocked me, but I miss you so much. I wish I had you to talk to. I feel like I'm in a mess. I feel like I'm falling in love and it's an impossible situation. You'd know what to say. You'd know what to do. Please, if you get this, let's talk x

Message delivered.

*chapter 27*

It's Jack's leaving drinks at the Peterboat, and I am *dreading* it. He officially doesn't leave the office forever until Friday and doesn't actually leave the country until Wednesday, but I am dreading it. This goes against the rules. This goes against what I decided. That I would just enjoy being around Jack, kissing him, *feeling* all these things, without the need to attach meaning to them, but . . . how is that possible when you start to really feel things? Have it root itself into you, grow? I like Jack. I really like him. More than like. And . . . God, I wish in a weird way I had never called him at the treehouse. Something happened that night, looking into his eyes; feeling his heart beating against me, close and snuggled, beneath the sheets. I stepped off a ledge. I . . . *fell*. Or am falling. Oh no, I cannot be falling. I can't can't can't. He is leaving. He's even trying to set me up with a *job* here. He is certainly not falling. I don't suppose Jack really falls.

I look at him across the pub. It's freezing outside. The sky is black and hollow, in the way it can be before snow, and lights glisten on the water, like smudges of liquid gold. Flye has booked the outside area under a marquee and surrounded by the glow of orange heaters and dancing electric tea lights in jars on tables. Leigh always has so much atmosphere. The endless blackness beyond the balcony of the pub, the warmth of the heaters, the cobbled, dank streets, the puff of happiness and chatter on pub windows. As always, a perfect contrast. And me—a perfect contrast too. All I want to do is be with Jack. But I also don't want to be here. Because being here means Jack is leaving, and I can't bear the thought of not seeing him for a whole entire year. Or . . . *ever again*? And let's say I wait. I know how that one ends. He could meet someone else. Fall in love. And where will that leave me? Here. Waiting again.

"Here we are." Petra sits next to me at one of the tables and places a glass of wine in front of me. We're on the outside edge of the marquee, the glass partition to one side of us, the sea and lit-up distant docks jutting out like an island ahead of me.

"Thank you," I say, picking up the glass, condensation striping the side of it.

Petra smiles at me sadly. "Going to be weird without him, huh?"

"Ugh, yes. A lot of people'll miss him, I think."

"And you?" Petra touches the top of her arm to mine. "Will *you* miss him?"

My eyes lift to meet Petra's, and she smiles warmly, all glowing skin and peach lips.

"I can tell by the way he looks at you," she says. "And I know you well enough by now to know that . . . you at the absolute least . . . *really like him*?"

I hesitate before a defeated groan pushes its way out of me. "*A lot*," I say. "Like a lot, a lot, a lot, Petra." And we both in unison look over at him, like synchronized dancers in a musical.

"He's so lovely," I say.

"*So lovely*," repeats Petra.

Jack stands among a crowd of Flye colleagues in deep, smiling conversation, the collar of his shirt open, arms straining against the cotton of the sleeves, that lovely edge to his jaw I wish so much I could run my finger along, beside him in bed, like we did at the treehouse. My heart aches. He looks . . . so happy. So . . . *living his life.* I just want to be with him, talk to him, listen to his stories, those little nuggets that make Jack, Jack. Squeeze everything out of him like an orange.

"And I'm sort of torn, you know? Between being so happy I had the chance to get to know him before he leaves. To feeling . . . *this.*" I hold my hand to my chest. "This horrible, tight golf ball of *doom*, right here."

Petra swallows and nods, her own hand drifting to land on her own chest. "I get it. Wishing you could've somehow dodged it, saved yourself the heartache?"

"I always seem to get the heartache."

"Oh, I used to say the same." Petra flicks her hand in the air, as if shooing the false thought away. Petra finds my hand under the table. "I used to retrace my steps with Maria, calculating the absolute best time it would've been to walk away. But . . . I don't regret Maria."

Her hand lands on my back affectionately, presses my dress, hot from the heater behind us, against my skin.

"I mean, I thought I did for a while, but . . . I've come to realize, now I've found Kira, that Maria taught me how to be vulnerable. And also taught me what *real* love is. Because it wasn't what she gave me."

"God, Petra, I'm going to cry now."

"Drink!" Petra says, ushering my glass to my mouth. "Do the healthy thing and drown it all out."

We both drink, but then stop when someone behind us drops a glass that smashes (and then, of course, as per pub law, causes a cheer to erupt).

"Don't regret Jack," Petra says into my ear over the noise. "Because I don't think he regrets you. Not for a moment."

"But I don't think Jack regrets anything, Petra," I say. "He's . . . different. He doesn't follow the crowd, he doesn't really lay down roots and . . . he's all about adventure and living life for life's sake."

Petra smiles.

"Like you."

I smile. "*Me?*"

"Uh, *yes.*" Petra knocks her arm to mine, then pauses, a warm smile spreading into her cheeks. "Millie, when I first met you, when I *hired* you, you told me that temping worked for you because it was a stopgap and you weren't ready to hang your hat on anything. Do you remember?"

I nod hesitantly, but sometimes I struggle to remember the girl who walked into Flye's offices almost five years ago. "I do. It *was* meant to be a stopgap. Some bloody stopgap that was."

"I remember you opened up about university and how disappointed your mum was. How you wanted to save some money and think about what you wanted to do. That you'd never really found out. I remember you were reading—"

"*Eat Pray Love,*" I say, smiling. "Oh my God, I read that book so many times."

"I think you're a hibernating adventurer, Millie." Petra smiles widely, and there's something about that phrase that makes me laugh, but also that opens up something in my chest. Something in bloom. A seed, sprouted. "And maybe . . . maybe Jack"—she glances over at him now, a bottle of beer in his lovely, tanned hand, listening intently to an extremely already-drunk Paul Foot—"taught you to remember who you are when you finally emerge again. Wake up. Go out into the spring, you know?"

And it feels right. Petra's soft, warm, loving words feel right.

I watch Jack for a little as Petra and I drink. I rest my head on her shoulder. "Was I happy?" I ask her.

"When I first met you?"

I nod.

"*Yes.* I mean, you were a little lost, like we all are in our twenties, but—you were excited. Hungry for whatever life had to give."

"And then what?"

And I feel her take a deep, long breath in, and she turns to me. I lift my head. "Heartbreak," she says.

"Owen," I say.

Petra nods and looks ahead again, leans her head against mine. Someone behind us cheers, and I hear Jack laugh. I could pick that warm, husky laugh out of a lineup. I'll miss that laugh so very much.

"He blew out your fire," says Petra. "And it's like you've kept to a small flame ever since. So that it's not seen, or so it doesn't grow, or set fire to something, illuminate you."

I close my eyes, and a tear tickles the corner of my eye and plops out onto Petra's sweater.

"And I know this because *I* have done it. But is that living, Millie? I don't think it is. So, what, because you're afraid of getting hurt, you never jump, hope for the best? Living is being bruised. Living is *feeling* everything the heart can. The pain, the ache, the good and bad. You can't have one without the contrast of the other."

A warm hand lands on my shoulder. "Hello, the queens of my heart."

I twist around to see Kira. She leans and kisses the top of Petra's head. She's still wearing her paramedic's uniform. Her big brown eyes are lined with a flick of turquoise liquid liner.

"Hi, Kira."

"Ah, my love, you made it," says Petra, and her whole face transforms. Lightness. Sparkle. Softness.

"Of course." Kira smiles, tipping her head to one side, the tight curls of her Afro bouncing. "They're playing Fleetwood Mac."

"I can hear that."

"And they're dancing in the next room."

And Petra nods, gives her a big, beaming smile. "Is that a big hint?" She turns to me. "Do you mind?"

I grin at her. "Go! Dance to Fleetwood Mac!"

And as Petra starts to walk away, Kira's hand on her back, she ducks back to me and says, "Time to step out, Millie. Meet the spring."

A hand slides around my waist as I stand at the bar, and I melt almost instantly at the touch.

"And where've you been hiding?" Jack's deep, hot voice speaks into my ear, and I smile, turn to face him.

"Talking to Petra. Oh, and under a blanket next to a heater out there listening to Chatty slash Mute Martin talk about his verruca." I smile. "You?"

"I was going to ask if there was room under the blanket for me." Jack grins. "But also, I do not need to hear about the verruca."

"You don't know that for sure, Jack dot Shurlock."

"*Oh*, I do," Jack says, his hand sliding away from my waist as he comes to stand next to me at the bar. "I got a fuckin' verbal dossier on it yesterday."

I laugh. "What a leaving present."

Jack chuckles and says, "What're we having then?"

It's weird. We haven't been in front of colleagues in a social situation since . . . all of this. The rhubarb farm, the treehouse—and oh, God, I can't even think about the treehouse without my entire body turning to jelly. Maybe Cate is right. Memories of the treehouse will stay with me for the rest of my life. The hours we talked, how safe I felt, and Jack's soft, skilled kisses. I keep thinking about those hands, that sexy rumbling groan, the way it was so hard for us to stop touching each other. Ugh. He's leaving he's leaving he's leaving and I am at his farewell party and he seems really happy actually, and really fuck-ing ready to sign me over to a bakery class countries and countries away from him—

"Millie?"

I clear my throat. "Oh! Erm. No. It's fine. I'm getting it."

Jack cocks an eyebrow. And what am I doing? Being scared to accept a drink, stay with him, drink beside him in front of everyone in case it means, what? I fall in love with him? It's all too late. Everything is too late. Damage control. What damage control?

A barman appears, tired but smiling. "Same again," says Jack, hand-ing over his glass. "And?" He looks at me, and the barman does too.

"A white wine," I say. "Spritzer." I look at Jack shyly. "Thank you."

Jack gives a small smile, then he scooches closer to me, his warm, strong arm touching mine.

And God, I can't even bear to look him in the eye right now. My chest feels heavy, like it's full of not one, but hundreds of heavy golf balls of doom. I don't want him to leave. Everything I feel for him—it's too much.

"I can't believe you're leaving."

Jack nods softly, a wave of his hair dangling, as ever, over his fore-head. I reach up and touch it. He smiles slowly. "As I say, it always feels like it might not happen until I'm on the plane."

"Ugh."

Jack laughs. "What? What is it?"

"Don't leave me," is what I want to say. "I know it's not been long, but please don't leave." But instead I say, "I just sort of wish you weren't going. Just yet, anyway."

Jack smiles gently, then says, "Really?"

"Why do you say 'really'?"

Jack pauses, shakes his head. "No real reason," he says. "Got some-thing for you later, though."

"*Have you?*"

"It's nothing too exciting," he says, then he leans in and says hotly into my ear, "It's a new email address."

"What?" I laugh. "Seriously?"

"Made you a new one. A whole fresh slate—"

"Hellooooooooo, people!"

Oh no. Oh fuck.

"Hey, Owen," says Jack.

"Bro," Owen says, raising a hand. Then he leans in and says, "Mills." It's meant to be a hug, but I don't move, and he clumsily presses an arm around me. It feels like a hot, lead weight.

"Hi."

"And *how* . . . are you?" And he is drunk. So drunk. I can smell it on him, feel the heavy limbs, the hot skin beneath his shirt. I remember this so well. I hated him getting drunk. I hated how he said horrible things. I hated how sometimes the only time he said nice things to me was *when* he was drunk.

"Good," I say. "You?" Shifting closer to Jack. He doesn't move. He's like a muscular statue. A guard. Immovable.

"Oh, me? It's my wedding day. Congratulations to *me*." He lets out a guffaw, but the grimace is followed by what looks like literal pain. A scrunch of his whole face, like someone stepping on an overturned plug.

He knocks back a sip of beer. "*My* wedding day. Today was meant to be my wedding day." He looks at Jack. He has a flicker in his eye. A goading spark. "Happy leaving day."

Jack fixes him with a completely unfazed look and says simply, "Thanks."

"You're doing the right thing," he says, sliding closer, his arm on the bar, gliding across my midriff. I move closer to Jack, feel his hand slip around my back. He stands taller. "Getting away from this shithole."

"Wouldn't call it that."

"No?" Owen makes a face, a childish, wordless "Oooh!" "Why're you off then?"

Jack's brow furrows, and a tiny irritated smile tugs at the corner of his mouth. He says nothing.

"I should just piss off, too," Owen says. "Like I did to India. Fucking loved it out there, man, I really did. And then you have to come back here, to this." He throws his heavy arms upward. "Show: *over.*"

"Owen, do you think you should have some water?" I ask.

"Aww." Owen puts his hand on my arm, then glances up at Jack. "She always looked after me, this one. She's like that, aren't you? My little *nurse.*" He grins at me, all dark, slitted eyes.

"Back off, eh, mate?" says Jack, words sharp, piercing the air.

Owen lifts his hand off my arm. "Sorry, Mills. Sorry, you know it's just me, yeah? You know it's just— Fuck." Owen loses his balance.

Jack pulls me closer to him, swaps places with me, pushes me behind him—and oh God, this can't be happening. Owen is drunk. Owen is emotional. And Jack is ready to . . . what? Fight him?

Owen holds a palm up. "It's all good," he says. "Sorry. I'm sorry if I scared you."

"Me?" Jack laughs. "Nah, I'm good as gold. Thanks, though."

"I was talking to Millie."

"Owen," I say. I step in between them. "Owen, do you need to sit down?" And I look right into his eyes pleadingly. It worked sometimes. This softly-softly kind approach. Like I was appealing to a small child. To calm him down, to defuse him. I don't want him to ruin tonight; ruin Jack's party.

Owen looks at me. And he sighs, like he's deflating. Shame drags on his face, and it falls. "I'm fucked, Millie," he says defeatedly. "I'm . . . I dunno what to do. My mum. She's at home, alone. She . . ." Then it's like he sobers up for a second. "Your dad. I need to call him. Maybe we could go there? See the old man. I miss them."

I swing back and look at Jack, whose face has changed. It's all hard, rigid lines, a muscle pulsing in his neck. "He needs to go home," I say. "He's wasted."

"I'll get him an Uber," says Jack coldly.

"What did he just say?" slurs Owen.

"I'll do it," I say. "Owen, why don't we go outside? Get some air?"

Jack turns and looks at me as Owen closes and opens his droopy eyelids and nods. "Good idea, Mills."

"I guess I'm going outside then," says Jack as if to himself, and his tone is irritated. Flat. Something blooms on my cheeks. Why do I feel responsible for this? Why does this feel like my mess?

"No, no, it's fine—"

Owen stumbles, and I put an arm out to steady him. Owen laughs and stands. "Fuck."

"I'm going outside, Millie," Jack says again.

Outside, it's bitter cold and dark, the air damp. The sea roars behind us like a caged animal, and Owen leans against the brick of the pub. Muffled chatter and music emanate from inside.

I scroll through my address book. I'm sure I have a taxi company's number in here.

Jack stands by me but away from me, his hands in his pockets, the atmosphere hanging over us all like thick bonfire smoke.

Owen gets his phone out. "I can order myself an Uber, I'm not a child." He holds his phone, realizes it's upside down, starts laughing.

I don't have Uber. I don't have *apps*. And for a second, it's like everything freeze-frames. Me out here, a stupid phone that barely works, Jack who is leaving, Owen who left me, slumped and drunk on what should have been his wedding day, me trying to keep it all tick tick ticking over as usual . . .

"Booked," says Jack, slotting his phone into his pocket. "Ten minutes."

Owen raises a thumbs-up. "Appreciate it, Shurlock." Then he laughs, groans, places his hands over his face, and says, "God, Mills. I'm fucked."

"You need sleep," I say.

"I need something."

Jack stands like a guard silently, then steps back toward the door. "Safe journey, mate," he says flatly, then he looks at me, a silent "You coming?" on his face.

I look at Owen, broken under the glow of the streetlight, drizzle starting to drift from the sky, like dust. I think of today. What was meant to be his wedding day. Before he got my email. And all the mess following Jack into his final farewell.

"I'll wait with him."

Jack stares at me in the darkness. Then nods. "OK," he says. "Right." And then he turns and opens the pub door.

"My Mills . . ." Owen slurs, and Alexis's voice is suddenly in my head. *Er, what're you doing, MC? Seriously, what are you doing?*

Oh, I miss her. I miss her so much.

I stride to the door, grab it before it closes. "Jack?"

He turns, looks at me.

"I'll just wait until the taxi comes," I say. "He's . . . he's really drunk and messed up, and it feels wrong to leave him. He'll just cause a scene inside."

Jack hesitates, and I can hardly bear to look at him. Those hazel eyes, that look sad for the first time ever, that expression full of things he wishes he could say . . .

"Millie, it isn't my business what you do," says Jack.

"I'll come back in. As soon as he's in the car—"

"Millie." Jack pauses, then his eyelids close slowly, as if steeling himself. "Did . . . did you say you weren't interested in me?"

"Wh-what?"

"Jess said something. Said someone talked about me and you sort of . . . recoiled. And—Jess can be a bit negative. Bit skeptical. But *did* you say that?"

Oh my God. I did. At the Summer-Ween party. Weeks ago. But I did it for Chloe's benefit; I didn't want her to think I was out there having an amazing, zingy time with someone I liked when her life was falling apart because of *me.*

"*No.*" I step forward toward him. "No, I didn't mean—"

"Jess said you said you weren't interested. Not your sort of person, not at all—"

"Jack, honestly . . ."

"So, you . . . *didn't* say that?" Jack looks at me. "Why would Jess tell me that, then?"

I swallow, look at him in this tiny, dimly lit lobby, the door behind Jack keeping the noise, the pub, what feels like the rest of the world, out. "Look, I did say that . . ." I admit sadly. "But Jack, I didn't mean it. I didn't mean a word of it. Just, Chloe was standing right there and . . . it was ages ago—"

"Chloe . . ." he repeats, his eyes sliding skyward. "So you said that for Chloe's benefit?" He looks at me then, despair sagging his shoulders.

"I know," I say. "God, I know. I'm a fucking idiot. But she looked so sad, and I was so happy to just be there with you, and . . . what was I supposed to say?"

"The truth," says Jack. "For your benefit. Not mine, not Chloe's. The truth—"

"*Mills?*" Owen calls from outside. "Millie? Ah, shit, my phone . . ."

Jack shakes his head. "Millie, I really don't have the headspace for this. I . . . This is my leaving party, and I'm standing here, with fucking Kalimeris outside making a scene—this is . . . this is not me."

"I'm sorry," I say. "I really am. I should have never ever said it." But the "this is not me" stings. As if *I* am drama. As if *I* am not him.

Jack nods, pulls open the pub door. "I'm going inside. Let me know when the taxi's taken him home."

And then he, too, is gone. And I stand between the two doors, both inside and outside, as if in a tiny cell. A tiny purgatory. What am I doing? *What* am I doing?

I open the door, step outside. I pull my jacket around me.

"My Millie." Owen smiles.

"Did you find your phone?"

"Nope." Owen laughs. "Fuck it. I don't care."

"Don't be ridiculous," I say. My eyes drop to the pavement, and I see it immediately, between the arch of a pub chalkboard stand. I bend and pick it up as it vibrates in my hand. "You've got a text," I inform him. "Multiple." I hand the phone to Owen, but I see the names on the screen. Hannah, Niamh (Hinge) . . . and *Leona*? As in . . . Leona in IT? Chloe's friend?

He takes the phone, smirks down at the screen. "Shurlock's a bit pathetic, isn't he?"

"Be quiet, Owen."

"Are you friends then?"

"What?"

"Are you and Jack friends?" asks Owen. "Or are you fucking him? You wouldn't go for him, would you? Not sure you're his type. You're definitely my type, though. *Fuck*." Owen stumbles closer to me. I stride back. My foot lands in a puddle, splashing my ankles. My shoe squelches, and I suddenly feel like a tight coil popping undone.

"Did you cheat on Chloe?"

"Did I—what?" He recoils, like I've just attempted to slap him.

"Did you cheat on Chloe?"

"No. No, why, what has she said?" Owen stares at me across the darkness. "Seriously, Millie, why are you asking me this right now? Jesus, my head is *spinning*—"

"Yes or no."

Owen looks at me, his jaw tense. "*No.*"

"I think you're a liar," I say, and Owen's eyes are suddenly wide circles, unblinking, but I feel like something has burst. Something is coming out of me, a concealed box broken open. "I think you are a cheat and a liar and someone who breaks people's hearts and shits all over them and doesn't think twice about it. So long as you have a supply chain of other people, stoking your fire." The women lighting up his phone. The unsuspecting women on his phone, like I was once. Like Chloe.

"Millie, are you fucking kidding me?"

"Did you send my emails?"

Owen laughs then. Deeply and scoffingly. "Why the fuck would I do that?"

"I don't know, but—you're out here, playing the broken jilted fiancé, and yet your phone's blowing up with girls' names and . . . this is what you did to me. Played this anguished, sad, 'I don't want to do long distance' boyfriend, all the while setting up some sort of new life without me. New job, new girlfriend."

"She's got into your head, hasn't she?" Owen says angrily. "She's got into your head, like she's trying to get into *everyone else's* . . ."

A car sloshes along the wet ground and pulls up on the cobbles.

"Nobody is in my head," I say to Owen. "I can just see clearly."

The window of the car slides down.

"Uber?" says the driver.

"Him," I say.

And as I walk away, Owen calls, "None of this is my fault, Millie. Millie?"

I don't turn around. I just keep walking across the cobbles, until I'm on the path home.

*chapter 28*

Dear all,

The Peterboat have been in touch to say an olive green cardigan was found on a chair in the marquee after our get-together there last night. If it belongs to one of you, you're free to pick it up from their lost property box at your convenience.

Thanks,
Gail

Whoever it was must have been v cold or v drunk (or stupid) to leave without it, ha ha ha. Also, ur looking v pretty today xx

**From: Vince Gudgeon**
**To: All LEIGH office**
**Subject: Re: Cardigan found**
Sorry. Didn't realize I sent to all.


**From: Gail Fryer (PA)**
**To: All LEIGH office**
**Subject: Re: Cardigan found**
LOL Vince. Thank you. xxxxx

Fundraising Steve actually *smiles* when he sees me this morning, although I can't help but notice his shoulders slump when I push open the door. Something happened last night on the way home from the pub. A hot, angry fire bubbled up within me as I ran and ran over the moment with Jack in the pub lobby. His face. The disappointment on it, that crushed my heart like a squashed tin can. And then Owen's phone, lighting up and lighting up. And lying in bed, at home, staring tearily and shakily at the ceiling, it continued. Everything from the last few months, flipping through my mind, over and over, like a looping videotape. The emails, Owen and Chloe, Mum and Dad, the fallout of everything.

And then I thought of Jack's friend's theory. That niggle that won't stop tugging at me; that niggle that won't stop buzzing around my mind like a trapped bee in a beer glass. And I realized last night, alone in my bed, that I *do* want to know the truth about it, if I can get my hands on it somehow. Because I want to move on. Just like I've avoided looking my feelings in the eyes for so many years, just like I avoided so very many things I wanted to say but was too afraid to speak out loud. And maybe they won't even be able to tell me anything, these nerds in IT, but I'll at least be able to look them in the face, in the office I probably should have thundered into, all those months ago, and ask them. Back myself. *Get down with myself*, as Jack would say.

"How are you?" I ask Steve.

Steve nods. "I'm all right," he says tentatively. "And . . . you?"

"OK. Sort of."

"Right."

A clock ticks on the wall, and a fan whirs in one of the computer towers. "Listen, Steve, I wondered if I could talk to you? About . . . the whole email thing."

Steve hesitates and nods. He's wearing a Christmas tie. Tiny little reindeer, with shiny red pom-pom noses.

I close the door softly behind me, and he looks up.

"I'm sorry about my email to you," I say. "About the . . . fundraising."

"It's nothing." He clears his throat, a large hand in a fist at his mouth.

"I think all the charity stuff you do is great," I say. "I really do. But . . . I did mean what I said. The sexist comments and stuff. I really think you need to consider—"

"I have," he says quickly, his long oval face flushing powder-paint pink. "I've . . . I've been thinking a lot about it. About how I conduct myself."

"Oh."

"My wife and I. We're . . . seeing someone. A, um. Couples therapist?" And it's like it has cost Steve the *earth* to divulge this to me. He's almost sweating, as if the words themselves choked him on the way out.

"Oh. I see." And I can't help but soften. "Wow. Well. I . . . hope it helps you, Steve. I think that's a brave thing to do. Really."

Steve nods again. The gelled prongs of his hair not moving at all. And it all makes a little more sense now. It's like Marshal says, isn't it? That some "bad" people, aren't bad, just in pain. His comments about my body, about the temp's marriage. It was never us. It was him. Steve and his unsaid struggles with his own marriage. His own image. His own sense of self.

"Look, I know you're limited to what you can do," I say to him, "but I just . . . I need to know at least *something.*"

"Millie, if it's about the emails, I can only do what I can do."

"But I know you must know more than I do. In fact, I know you do. And Jack says—"

"Jack Shurlock?"

The sound of his name makes me want to cry. I have never seen him so resigned as last night. The "this is not me" comment keeps swirling around my head.

"Yes. He said I need to make a formal complaint, and if that's what I need to do, fine, but I don't want to cause drama, and I know you can't go around telling me things because it's private and all that, but . . . I just want to know what I can."

He sighs. A big humph of a sigh that smells like instant coffee. "OK . . ." Steve stands up, brushing a hand down his chest. "Look," he says. "We don't have a definitive answer for you, Millie. And by that I mean nobody has walked in here, hands held high, and said, 'Yep, it was me.' So, until you complain, we as a company, as an IT department, are just to assume you did it—and before you say anything, I know you didn't. But on paper. Shitty emails get sent. Perpetrator denies it. But doesn't want to complain . . ."

"I know."

"And to be honest, we had no evidence of you signing out of the office either . . ."

"I always forget to scan if someone is going out in front of me," I say.

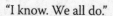

"I know. We all do."

"What . . . what about CCTV?" I ask.

"Deleted after thirty days." Steve sighs. "Only certain staff members have access, and I am not one of them."

"What, so . . . that's it?" I deflate. Now what?

Steve shrugs. "I'm sorry," he says. "We can only find what we can find in these situations. Which computer, what time, who signed out." He walks out from behind his desk and fixes me with a stare, unblinking. "When the servers came back on." Then he circles the desks. "I'm going to make a coffee."

"N-now?"

He whisks past me and through the door.

I glance around. Ah. *AH.*

He's left his computer on purposely, to help me. At least, I *hope* that's what it is.

I scoot around to his desk, all the while looking over my shoulder, being careful not to be seen. Although it's early, most people aren't taking any notice, they're still half-asleep, finishing coffee and cereal and messy, crumby breakfasts at their desks.

I glance at his screen. It's a mess of open windows. But there is one window in the corner that looks like a log of some sort. And on the screen is a list of names that signed out after the servers came back on. The people who were in the office when my emails were sent at 10:07. And three lines down, the only name showing next to reception is:

Signed out via reception: 22:14—Jack Shurlock

Jack said he wasn't at work that night. He definitely, definitely did. Why would he lie? He said he left at six. He made a point of saying he left at six that night, I remember it. I feel sick. I feel genuinely *sick.* But no—come on. This is Jack. Why would Jack . . . what am I even saying? That *he* sent my emails? God, I don't know. It sounds ridiculous, but— well, look at Mum. I'd have thought Mum lying to Dad and having a total secret history was ridiculous not so long ago. Nobody is safe.

I don't wait for Steve to return. I just pick up a random Post-it note and walk out of the office so it looks like I've been in for something banal. Not that I'd notice people looking at me anyway. I'm dazed, my eyes tunnel-visioned, everything sounding loud and quiet all at once.

I head straight for the bathroom, sit on the toilet seat where I did all those months ago, when my emails were sent, my chest rising and falling. OK, so, what? Jack. *Jack sent the emails?* Is this what I've been missing? Why would he do that? Especially given we weren't even really friends at that time, weren't really *anything*. And I close my eyes, and all I can see, all I can feel is his lips on mine. All the times he told me not to press, not to go looking for the answers. Why? This is why. Because he sent them. Really? Would he really do that? He has no reason to want to do that.

Then why did he lie and say he wasn't here?

I saw it. Saw his name with my own eyes. I stand up and feel red-hot with anger. Why do people feel they can take me for a ride? Alexis. Owen. My own mother even. And now . . . Jack? Jack who I feel safe with. Jack who I have grown to care so much about. Jack who I . . . trust. Trust. Was I wrong to trust him? Before I have even decided, it's like my feet have already made the decision. I am storming out of the bathroom, the cubicle door slamming against the wall as I leave, the bathroom door causing my hair to feather out, like some sort of angry dinosaur. I storm across the office floor, all fluster and heavy footsteps.

"Ah, Millie, I was wondering—Millie?"

I whisk by Chatty Martin, my eyes fixed on Jack's office door. He's in there. I can see him through the glass on the phone, his mouth in a huge smile, that mouth I kissed over and over. It's his last day today. His final day working here. And then he's off. Going. Good. *Good.*

And I don't knock, just burst in there, and his face drops when he sees me, his mouth for a moment freezing in an O shape.

"Can I . . . can I call you back, Carrie? Yep. Yep, no, that's fine. Thank you." He places the phone down and holds his arms out at his side. "What's up, are you OK?" He eyes the Post-it in my hand for a second. Why am I still holding the decoy Post-it?

"Did you lie to me?" And my words blurt out almost hysterically, and echo. It's bare in Jack's office now, in the way bedrooms are the night before moving house.

His familiar, beautiful hazel eyes widen. "Did I lie to you?"

"You said you weren't here the night the emails were sent."

"Right?" He stares at me, his mouth still frozen open, his eyes unblinking. He crosses the floor and closes the door behind me, but I don't move. "Millie, what is going on?" he asks calmly.

"You were here."

"I was . . . what?" He looks confused; worried about me.

"You were here," I say, and I can barely speak. My words are so dry in my mouth. "That night. You were *in* reception around the time it happened, and that's where my laptop was."

"What? Millie, I'm sorry, but where are you getting this information from?"

"IT," I say. "I saw the log. It said your name, it said the time, and it said you were here."

"But I wasn't," he says calmly.

"Are you not Jack Shurlock then? It literally says *your name*." And I suddenly feel like I'm juddering with it, this righteous anger at how people lie to me. Do it to my face. Like Owen did, like my mum . . .

"And I'm literally saying, I wasn't here." And now he looks pissed off. He straightens, his shoulders squaring. "Are you kidding me, Millie?"

"Is that why you've been so nice to me?" I say, deflating, suddenly feeling like one big open bruised wound.

Jack sighs and shakes his head slowly. A wave of hair moves, dangles at his forehead. "What do you think the answer to that question is?"

"You barely paid me an ounce of attention after you spoke to me at the Christmas party, and then my emails get sent and you start talking to me and . . . Why would you lie? Why would you say you weren't here when you were?"

"I feel like a lot of this you need to say to other people, not me—"

"I don't know who to trust," I blurt. "My life was upended and someone did it, and *you*—"

"I can't believe you think—" Jack's nostrils flare. He rubs at his chin roughly, stubble beneath his fingers. "I started talking to you, Millie, because I like you. I liked you then, too, before I left the first time. I just wasn't sure you liked me back. You were still hurt. Owen had . . . done such a number on you. I thought it was only right I left the ball entirely in your court. Then I got your email . . ."

"My email?"

"It was delivered," he says. "I have a new email address, but the ones to my old address get forwarded. Rerouted."

Oh my God. Jack got the sexy dream email. Jack got the flirty "I like you and wanted you to kiss me" email. I stare at him. My mouth opens, like a fish dropped on the shore.

"But . . . it says you were here," is all I manage to say, pathetically, meekly.

"I have a million things to do today before I leave," Jack says. He steps behind me and pushes the handle down. "And I need to make a phone call."

"And that's . . . it?"

Jack nods. "Yes, Millie," he says deeply, like an authoritative teacher. "That's it."

Jack stares at me then, and I see him in those eyes, that man I spent a whole night wrapped around, melting into. I step over the threshold.

Behind me, Jack shuts the door with a calm click, and silence falls over the office.

**From: Petra Kairys**
**To: Millie Chandler**
**Subject: My office**
My love, can you come to my office at five thirty, before you leave for home please?

I am shaky and teary by the time five thirty rolls around. I saw Jack about five minutes ago with a box of his stuff, like people in movies have, the only thing missing a plant spilling over the side. He walked wordlessly past my desk, and I'd almost wanted to shout after him. A big "fuck you." A big "come back." A big "How could you do this to me?" Because after having a day to mull over it, I'm no clearer. Jack's name was on Steve's log. And he denies being anywhere *near* the office, and I feel I trust him and believe him, but also, what else am I supposed to think?

By the time I enter Petra's office, I am ready for anything. I am ready to resign. I am ready for a warning. I am ready to be fired. For all of it. I have let go. Except perhaps not in the way my friends wanted me to. Maybe I've let go so much, I'm throwing fireballs into everything, burning it all down like some sort of reckless, lawless receptionist with nothing to lose.

Petra closes the door quietly behind me, shuts the blinds so we're in a tiny boxed cocoon in the middle of the office, and says, "Champagne?"

*"Champagne?"*

"Well. Prosecco." She slides out a miniature bottle and two straws from her bag.

I smile weakly. I suppose you know you've fully crossed over to madness when your boss and friend is offering you alcohol in the office. "I'm good. I'm driving, so . . ."

Petra shrugs and puts both straws into the bottle. She sips from them and laughs. "I have two of these in my bag."

"Is . . . this a cry for help, Petra Kairys?"

Petra laughs, then slowly, slowly raises her hand from behind her desk. A small gold band sits on her finger, a small, square-cut diamond in the center. "I'm engaged."

"Oh my God! When—did this happen? We were literally together just—"

"I know, I know." She sips. "Kira proposed last night. We were walking back from the pub, and the stars were everywhere, and I'm eating *cockles*." She laughs. "And she just says it. No down-on-bended-knee proposal or anything. But she just says it. Will you marry me, Petra? And I stand there, my fucking hair like seaweed, seafood hanging from my mouth, and she just . . . says it. And—I froze. I . . . I never thought I would freeze, Millie."

I nod rapidly. "I get it," I say. "I think it's almost too huge to even consider being like, yes, sure!"

"Yes, exactly! So Kira being Kira—"

"The best girlfriend who ever lived," I add.

"Gave me the ring. Told me to think on it. And if I wasn't comfortable, we didn't need to do anything right away. Or ever."

My eyes fill with tears. "God, Petra . . ."

"I know. And it was a yes the second I opened my eyes this morning really. But it was a lot to say yes, you know? To sort of . . . look it in the eye. This risk of yes, I might get hurt again. But if we don't risk it, what's the fucking point of living? You can't live properly without risk."

I nod as Petra sips some more. My heart is thundering in my ears. I've been unsettled ever since that moment in Jack's office. I don't know what to feel or what to think, and now it's all coming out in tears. Happy tears, confused tears, sad tears, what-the-fuck-am-I-going-to-do tears.

"Congratulations, Petra," I say, and she sniffs too.

"Don't start me off."

"Sorry." I laugh.

"I can't even tell her yet. She's on shift till bloody midnight."

"She's so lucky," I say. "You're so lucky."

Petra smiles at me, reaches for my hand, squeezes it.

"I saw you earlier," says Petra, and I make an "mm" sound, a signal to Petra of "God, you don't need to remind me."

"I'm so sorry if I made a scene, I—"

"No, no, do not apologize. That's why I emailed you. I wanted you to see my ring, of course, but I want to know you're OK. And if you're not, to know it *can* really be OK. Things can turn around. Look at me. And things have been starting to turn around for you lately. *Change.* I've been secretly hoping for you to hand your notice in actually." She laughs.

"It doesn't feel turned around now," I admit, my shoulders sagging. I feel like I'm melting into myself, disappearing. "I'm . . . I don't know. I don't know what to do."

"What happened earlier? With Jack?"

"I somehow found out that Jack was here when he said he wasn't on the night it happened."

"Oh." Petra blows out a long gust from her glossy lips. "Jesus."

I nod.

"But—Jack wouldn't lie. Why would he do that?" Petra asks. She chews the corner of her lip, shaking her head. "OK, he's super smart and everyone fucking loves him. But work drama? Jack? Getting involved in that stuff? I don't think he would do anything like that. Plus, he *helped* with the investigation. When it happened, he just wanted to help you."

That hurts. A little nettle sting on my heart. "But why did he say he wasn't here?"

Petra takes a long sip and then leans back on her computer chair. She looks up at the ceiling the way a philosopher might and says, "I *wish* I had access to CCTV," with a groan. Then she sits up. "Oh. *Oh.* You know what we could do? I have access to the car log now. So I can see vehicles check in and out of the car park? I can see *registrations.*" She pauses, stares at me, and a shiver runs down my spine.

"Oh my God, really?" I rush out.

"Yep."

And I'm reluctant, even though I've wanted clarity on this, this thing that's changed my life in numerous ways for months. It's almost like I'm scared to know. But I want to know more than anything, all at the same time. I want to let go. I want to move on. I want to know what happened the night they were sent, once and for all. Regardless of the answer.

I swallow. "Do it."

Petra turns to her computer, cupping her hand over her mouse. She clicks her tongue. "OK, so . . . hang on . . ."

Petra taps a few buttons, then presses print. The printer next to me starts to spit out a page of registration numbers. The paper smells warm and sweet, and it almost turns my stomach. If it really wasn't a glitch, the answer to who was here that night, and who could've sent my emails, is on *that page.*

"I've printed between 6 p.m. and midnight. We can see who leaves late. See if anything jumps out at us."

I take the page from the printer, my heart racing, as Petra sips and sips on the miniature bottle of prosecco, her wide eyes staring at me across the desk, like she's waiting for the reveal at the end of a film.

I scan the list. Jack's registration checking out of the car park at 6:34 p.m. I continue down the list to see if his car checks back in. It doesn't. My heart sinks but blooms all at once. Jack wasn't here. Jack told the truth. Of course he told the truth.

"Jack checks out."

"What time?"

"Super early."

"Before emails were sent—"

And then I see something. Owen's car checking in at nine and leaving at 10:27 p.m.

"Owen was here," I say into the silent room. "He said he was in Manchester. I asked him, and he *swore* it."

"Jesus," says Petra, releasing the straw from her lips. "Fucking people. I hate people. M—Millie, where . . . where are you going?"

And now I'm standing, limbs surging with hot rage, as if I've been injected with it. He's lied to me. He continues to lie to me. "I'm going to Owen's."

"*Now?*"

"Now."

"Hang on," she says, standing. "I'll come with you."

Petra dashes after me, and I walk across that same thin, ribbed carpet I walked across, shamed and nervous and sick, just mere months ago. And all the while . . . all the while, Owen was sitting there, feeling as though he was—what, getting revenge on Chloe? Showing her he meant it when he said he could get whoever he wanted—and "Look! Stone-cold proof my ex is still in love with me and I was moving on!"

We push through the exit—Flye's car park dark and lit by streetlights, the sun long set, the air cold and smoky in that November way.

And as I get to my car, I see Jack, packing up his trunk, two cars along from mine. Boxes. Bags. A helium balloon that bobs in the night, the streetlamps casting a shadow over the words on the foil: "We'll miss you!"

He stares at me.

He's leaving.

He's *leaving*, and this is it. This is his last day. The last time he will probably ever drive out of this car park.

This could be the last time I see him again. And I've ruined it. I have ruined this beautiful, perfect thing I had with this beautiful, perfect person.

"Oh. Jack," says Petra.

"Hey," he says.

"All packed?" She sips her prosecco and holds up the bottle. "I'm engaged."

Jack smiles then. A small, but genuine, warm smile. "Congratulations, Petra. That's really awesome."

"Hope it doesn't go horribly wrong!" she says in a giggly singsong. Then she stumbles and holds a hand out, steadying herself on my car. The prosecco remains steady in her other hand. "Oops . . ."

I press the fob to unlock the doors on my car. "You can get inside, Petra."

She does a tiny salute with an index finger and gets into the passenger seat.

Jack looks at me, and I look at him. I can't believe I ever doubted him. I hate myself for it.

"Where are you going?" I ask.

"Jonny's," he says. "Seeing some friends before I go."

I nod. And all I want to do in this moment is throw myself at him. Fold my arms around him, breathe him in, beg him not to leave. Say, "Don't go, Jack. Please don't go. I'll come. I'll come *anywhere* if you're there." And the words—they sit so close to my lips . . . But I can't. I can't say them again. "Jack, I'm so sorry about earlier. I'm just . . . I'm so sorry."

Jack nods sadly, drops his eyes to the pavement. "I know," he says.

"It's not OK."

"I know," he says again. And there is something so pained, so resigned about it, that it makes panic rise in my chest. I feel like I've lost him. That he might be standing there, but he's already gone. A ribbon connecting us cut, and I'll only notice when he's too far to ever get back to. "Where're you going now?"

I swallow. "Owen's," I say shamefully. And then I rush out, "Petra checked the records, and Owen's car was here."

Jack nods, a barely there bob of his head. "Well. Good luck," he says, shutting the boot of the car and circling to the driver's side.

I stand, rooted to the spot. Good luck? I think of the rhubarb farm. I think of the treehouse. His kisses, his touch. I feel like someone has shoved a dagger into my heart.

I turn on the damp concrete, my trainer soles crunching on the hard ground.

"Millie?"

I swing back to face him, tears in my eyes. Hope sparks in my hard. Like a single, struck match.

"Yes?"

And he says nothing.

There are so many thousands of things I want to say and want to hear. "Don't go. I'll stay. Come with me. I won't leave you. I'm so scared to say goodbye. I can't do this again. I think . . . I love you."

He shakes his head, looks down at his feet. "Look after yourself," he says gruffly, and a flash of images go through my mind like a flipbook. Pulling me to my feet, Jack Dawson, on *Instinct*. All that time we had together, and now . . . now he's going. Now he's as good as gone.

I nod. "You, too," I say as a tear slides down my cheek.

"Bye, Millie."

"Bye, Jack."

Petra sits sipping prosecco in the passenger seat, and she is still sipping when we pull up in the car park of Owen's flat block.

She straightens beside me. Owen's car sits in front of us; the same car listed on the printout. "The little knob is home, then," she slurs, craning her neck. "Shall I come in with you?"

I shake my head. "No, no, it's fine. You stay in the car." Although there is a part of me that wants her to see, wants *everyone* to see. He would hate that. As Chloe said, he's a manipulator. He wants everyone to see him in a perfect light. But I want to do this alone. Stand in front of him at last, unafraid and alone.

I open the car door. "Are you going to be OK?"

"Me? Absolutely." Petra smiles. "I'm going to listen to a podcast and drink my prosecco. But if you need me, Millie, you just shout, yeah? I'm right here."

I nod.

"And are you sure you're going to be OK?" she asks.

"Of course." And I hope those words seep into my soul, like warm wax, harden to a truth. Because I don't feel like I'll be OK at all. I have to confront him—Owen. This time last year, I would have given anything for him to just *look* at me again. Now I'm about to walk up to his front door. To call him out. To face him. See him exactly as he is for the first time.

I walk up the path, legs shaking, kneecaps feeling like they're held together with panna cotta and jelly. A little yellow light beams inside through the frosted slot of a window next to the communal front door. My heart thumps as I press the speakerphone. It rings inside, a two-beat chime that repeats and reverberates through me.

It's going to be OK. I have every right to be here, I don't even need to accuse him. I can simply say, "You were there the night my emails were sent, and I believe you did it. What do you have to say to that?" But you know—less detective-y.

The speakerphone crackles.

"Hello?" I say. Silence. "Hello, it's me. Millie."

Silence again.

Then a door squeaks inside, somewhere out of sight in the lit-up hallway.

And then—

Chloe.

Oh God. I had not planned for this. I was never expecting Chloe. They've broken *up*. I have spent the last few months begging Chloe to believe I had nothing to do with the email being sent, had not been having an affair with Owen, didn't want him back, and here I am on his doorstep on a Friday evening, while people go to their homes for the weekend for baths and takeout. To pubs. To clubs. To friends', like Jack has, for his leaving dinner.

Chloe stops on the other side of the door when she sees it's me. She looks pin-faced—flushed. Her hair is tied back, and she has her sleeves rolled up. Like I've interrupted her doing something. Cleaning?

She opens the door. "Millie?"

"I . . . I . . . Sorry, is . . . I wasn't expecting you to be here."

Chloe looks haunted at the sight of me. "He isn't here. I was collecting some of my stuff."

"Oh. Right."

"He's at the gym," she says tonelessly. "What did you want?"

"I just wanted to talk to him. Tell him I know it was him. The emails . . ."

"What . . . what do you mean?"

"I looked through the registration logs of that night," I say. "The car logs? And Owen was there when the emails were sent. I'm going to tell IT. Make a formal complaint; finally . . . I don't know. Hold him to justice—"

"Millie, don't do that."

And I feel sad then, looking at Chloe. Because I would've laid down in front of a bulldozer for Owen. Because it's what he does. He makes you think you're lucky just to get *looked at* by him. And even though their relationship is over, even though she talks about him like she hates him, she's still trying to protect him. Owen the bloody king Kalimeris.

"I'm sorry, Chloe, I really am, for everything that's happened to you, but I have to."

Chloe stares at me. She's frozen on the spot. And I recognize it. Those worried eyes. That flushed skin. It took over two years for me to be "over" my breakup. And Chloe is only months in. She still feels that hold, that grip. She closes her eyes.

"Millie. It was me."

I freeze now, both of us like two mannequins, one in the doorway, one on the threshold, two people on either side of a looking glass. A mirror image.

"Sorry? *Wh-what* was you?"

"I sent the emails, Millie," says Chloe. "I'm so sorry. It was me."

## chapter 29

I'm meeting Chloe at the end of Avenue Road, where there are two benches and endless uninterrupted views of the estuary. She told me she was at Owen's picking up the last of her things. "I can't be here when he gets back," she said. "Neither can you."

Petra's true crime podcast plays as we drive. "Her heart was found outside her body," says the ominous voice through the phone. "And her family were quoted as saying it was a betrayal she could have never seen coming."

All Petra does is shake her head. "Chloe?" she keeps saying, over murderous details. "Chloe?"

Minutes later, I stand in front of one of the benches, the metal balcony in front of me. Wind whips through my hair, salted, iced air. Chloe pulls her car behind mine. She gets out and approaches me nervously, the way you do when you're too scared to walk too close to the edge of somewhere steep. She looks like she might burst into tears. Behind us, the sea is black.

"I'm so sorry," says Chloe, the wind carrying her words away. "I really didn't mean to hurt you, Millie."

"I don't understand," I say. And it's true. I've been playing Chloe's words over and over in my head as I drove here, but I still can't work them out. How is this happening? Why on earth would Chloe do this? I've spent weeks trying to convince her; to *fix* this. "Owen's car was there," I say weakly.

"I drove Owen's car," she says simply. "I've been so scared you'd find out. That *someone* would. I worried what everyone would think of me, that I'd lose my job, that—"

"*I* have been worrying about those things, Chloe," I call over the wind, the low, rumbling waves unseen in the darkness. "I have had months of my life consumed by it. I've been driving myself crazy with it all and all the while . . . I don't understand."

Chloe's chin dimples, bottom lip wobbling, like a child's. "I know. Oh gosh, Millie. And it was really never meant to happen like that. At first, I was just going to send one. The invitation reply. And then I thought, well, that would look so suspicious, wouldn't it? So, I panicked and just sent loads. So it looked like some sort of *bug* or something? I know I sound unhinged. Believe me, nobody is more ashamed than me."

I stare at her. Wind lifts our hair from our faces, and Chloe clutches the coat around her like it's the only thing keeping her standing upright.

"Why did you do it?" I ask, my own voice wobbling now. "I never did anything to you."

Chloe's close eyes, her nostrils flaring. "Because I wanted out, Millie," she says. My heart stills. What? "We'd broken up. It was horrendous. Just fight after fight, him . . . *gaslighting* me. Doing things and denying it, *laughing* at me, pretending I was going crazy, and I left. This was about . . . three weeks before we got engaged. But then he came back. Tail between his legs. And God . . ." She brings two hands to her face now, lets out a sound that's half cry, half exasperated, angry growl. And all I can think is, this is what he has done. This is what Owen has reduced her to. Us. "Millie, he was *so* convincing," she cries, dropping her hands from her face. "He had a ring. A ring he'd gone out and chosen with his mum. She was there. The whole family was there. His and mine. And he proposed. On one knee and everything. He'd got my cousin to video it. They even put it on YouTube." She winces—something that looks like a mix of pain and dark amusement. "And I really thought it was it. That he was genuinely changed, and—I loved him so much. I . . . *still* love him so much."

"God. Chloe . . ." I don't know what to say. Words fail me. I stand, empty, in the wind, no words, no clear thoughts. One gust, and I feel like I might be carried away into the blackness of the sky, like a paper bag.

"So, of course I said yes. And my family . . ." She laughs. "I was engaged before. A few years ago. A nice enough guy, but I was young and—you know how it is?" She swipes tears away roughly, goes back to hugging herself as if she daren't fully let herself go. "But my family, they're very . . . traditional. They hated that I called an engagement off. Embarrassing, isn't it? I'd broken up with him just before I came to Flye. And it was a new start, and I was convinced everything would be OK. Then I moved departments and . . . became friends with Owen."

I swallow.

"I remember."

Chloe nods. "I know. And—Millie, he painted this picture. That you were hard to live with, that he wasn't happy, that you weren't like me."

That hurts. Really hurts. That I was probably trundling along in love, and he was out there telling a story. *His story.*

Chloe screws her face up. "I hate thinking back to that time.

How naïve I was. But the thing is with Owen, he always makes it out to be other people. When we broke up, before he proposed, he made *me* apologize. For pushing him. For pushing his buttons. And everyone sort of gave me this look. This '*Phew*, at least you didn't push him away entirely' look, because what a catch! Because he does that. People like Owen. He's charming and clever. They look up to him."

Someone walks by in the darkness, talking on the phone. He's holding an open bag of chips, and the pungent smell of salt and vinegar hangs in the air like vapor. A nice smell. A homey smell. But right now, it smells ominous. Everything feels ominous.

"And as soon as that ring was on my finger, as soon as my mum and dad were booking the bloody golf club all my brothers have been married in, I . . . Millie, I couldn't breathe. I knew I'd made a mistake. Because I knew he was—manipulative. Abusive. And I knew he was cheating on me. And I thought it was with you."

"*Me?*"

"I know it wasn't now," implores Chloe, and she steps toward me, boots scraping on the path. "I don't know who it was. But he was texting a lot, and he stank of perfume after coming back from the gym once and he kept talking about you. Deliberate, I think. Keep me on my toes. And the more the wedding things were getting booked, the more nervous I was getting, but I thought—how can I call it off? He'll vilify me. Everyone will think it's me. Oh, here she goes, calling off another engagement. And how could I face my family again? All my friends, everyone I *know*."

"But are you even sure he was cheating? Were you even remotely sure before you used me? You put me in the firing line, and—"

"He's done it before," says Chloe wobblily. "With me."

She lets her words hang there, like fog between us. And I know. I know exactly what she's talking about. The thing with Chloe—it moved fast because it had started long before I even realized. Owen cheated. On me. Of course he did.

"I'm so sorry," says Chloe. "I'm so sorry, I never, ever wanted you to get hurt, but I was . . . lost. Completely, completely lost."

Chloe starts to cry then, and I don't know what to say. I'm furious. I'm sad. And somehow—free all at once. Like someone's cleared the fog, tuned the frequency, and I can finally see clearly.

"How did you know my emails were there?"

"I didn't," she says. "But he said he was in Manchester, and he wasn't answering his phone, so I'd gone to the office. Driven there."

"To check up on him?"

Chloe nods, her arms a tight, nervous belt around herself, as if it's keeping her in one solid piece. "Sounds crazy, but I wanted to check he wasn't hanging back with someone in the office or something. With . . . you." She meets my eyes shamefully. "Then IT—my old team. They roped me into helping. And . . . it was too easy. Your laptop was just *there*."

"But—Owen was there too. I—saw a photo. On Instagram. Him with IT, with pizza."

Chloe's brow furrows. "That was—no, that was for the new equipment tracker thing Steve's trying to set up. Leona called Owen for his help. His forte, she said. That was . . . I don't know. A month before?"

So, it was just uploaded late. A photo that got taken and not shared and passed around until weeks later, maybe. And of course Leona called him in to help. She's probably with him right now.

"And the password?" I ask. This whole thing still feels unbelievable. I was sure. I was *so* sure it was him. Had the story in my head: the beats, the beginning, middle, and end. It made sense. A fitting dark end for the man who broke my heart. A man I could finally, finally see clearly. But this . . .

"Owen has the same password," she says. "For one of his

streaming things you shared together. He still has your profile. He'd . . . tease me about your profile. Kept it on there for just that reason really."

I stare at her. Rain sprays our faces; my cheeks are numb with cold. I'm searching my head. Unpicking the story I had stitched together, rearranging it, putting it back together, like a handmade quilt.

"Did you use Jack's pass?"

Chloe shrugs from within her thick parka coat. "It was in the kitchen." Simple. That simple. A memory of Jack joking about his lost passes flickers into my mind. Of course it was that simple.

My heart drops. "Right. And then what? You—thought you'd make me the villain."

Chloe swallows, her eyes glistening as rain starts to fall. "God, Millie, this was never about you. Please know that. It was about me. I knew if I could just allow that email to be seen, people would see. They'd choose *my* side, see him for what he is, and I'd be . . . free. I wouldn't be flighty Chloe who's called off another wedding. I'd be poor Chloe. Who got out of a shitty relationship in which her fiancé cheated on her and talked about her like she was just a passing thought. My *parents* would hear me, and not him. They wouldn't blame me."

I stare at her, raindrops starting to sting my neck, landing on my eyelashes. I think of Mum. I think of her disappointment when we broke up. I think of how it weighed on me; another failure. Failed university. A so-called dead-end job. A failed relationship. And I understand. I've felt that invisible pressure; the invisible shame.

"I'm sorry you went through what you did," I say, and my words are clipped, flat, but I mean it. But I also, above everything, want to go home, crawl into bed, and cry. Weep away this lonely, dark shadow that seems to be clouding me, the longer I stand here, in the cold dark.

"Nobody is more sorry than me, Millie. I'm so sorry he cheated on you. I'm so sorry that I did what I did. You don't deserve it."

I nod. "I know," is all I say. "Just—don't tell Owen I was at his."

"Of course. And I know you don't owe me *anything*, but—"

"I won't say anything . . . about the emails. About you."

And then I turn away, walk to the car. Waves crash angrily behind me, as if they find it so easy to express everything that's thundering silently inside of me.

"I'm so sorry, Millie," Chloe calls again, but I don't turn around. I get into the car, buckle myself in.

"Millie?" Petra asks worriedly.

"Time to leave," I say, my voice wobbling. "It's done."

And as we drive away, Chloe just stands staring in the shadows, alone, watches us disappear.

## chapter 30

remember once the comedian Russell Kane saying everyone at some point has a kitchen-floor reset. Where they find themselves on the floor, a crumpled mess, crying, feeling as though they'll never, ever recover. Rock bottom. And that's what I feel right now.

I tried to make a pavlova. I woke to a silent house, stood in the quiet of a new morning, then I thought, I'll make a pavlova. I'll make a giant wispy pavlova like I saw on Food Network last week. I'll decorate it with loads of berries, lose myself to the project of it all. Distract myself, *immerse* myself. But as the food mixer whipped on, tears built up in me like water in a hose, and I slumped against the counter and cried.

And now the mixer above my head continues to whir, like a dutiful pet, and I sit in the dark kitchen as the sun tries to make itself known behind the blinds I've yet to open, sobbing. I don't know where Ralph and Cate are. Ralph's probably at work, Cate at yoga.

I'm angry at Chloe. But more so at myself. For turning on poor

Jack, the only person who has completely stood by me, my trust slowly eroded by Owen, and I couldn't even see it. And he's leaving. He's leaving and I'm here alone, with a bowl of egg whites. Alone, alone, alone.

I hear the kitchen door click, and although a part of me wants to scrabble up to my feet, proclaim to whoever it is, "I'M FINE!" I don't move. Because I'm not. I'm not fine. I'm not bloody fine.

"Millie?" The under-cupboard lights flick on, and Cate stands between the counters of the kitchen and looks down at me. "Oh my God. *Millie?*"

She clicks off the whisk above my head. I'd told Cate and Ralph everything last night when I got home. I'd talked so much, for so long, my words starting to slow, to slur, that I'd fallen asleep on the sofa. Ralph had covered me with a blanket, and Cate had said gently, "We'll talk tomorrow," and clicked off the floor lamp.

"Baking disaster?" Cate asks worriedly.

I shake my head. "A me disaster," I say. "An *everything* disaster. I am a disaster."

"Don't say that," comes a voice.

From behind Cate, footsteps scrape against the kitchen tiles. Black chunky Doc Martens, red laces, thick, black, diamond-patterned tights . . . My eyes drift up to meet hers. "Oh my God, Alexis."

Alexis's round, blue eyes are full of tears. "Oh, Millie. I'm sorry," she says. "I'm so sorry."

"*I'm* so sorry."

And then both of us burst into tears. Alexis hides hers behind her hands, like a mask.

"Oh, this is good!" Cate is saying, clapping her hands. "This is really, really good! We all need to cry and let it all out. And then we can talk. Ralph? *Ralph!*"

Ralph comes rushing in from outside. "Sorry, but someone is mixing the recycling again in the bin store—"

"Sod the bins. Did you check the whereabouts of that Starbucks order?"

"Oh. No," he says, fishing out his phone. "Did you do it on my Deliveroo? But, er, Cate, I'm not sure coffee cake really falls under alkaline—"

"Cake, Ralph," is all Cate says. "You're lovely, but if I hear the word *alkaline* again . . ."

Ralph smiles, defeated.

"I'm having my cake. Gallstones or not."

"Gallstones or not," he repeats, and he says it with such warmth, it almost sounds romantic.

After ten minutes, Ralph has flicked the lights on, opened the blinds, and put soft music on. Some sort of weird, echoing Siren-y tune. Ralph always finds obscure artists at folk festivals and buys their homemade CDs. I found Cate listening to one last week as she brushed on an avocado face mask.

I sit at the breakfast bar between my two best friends—between Cate and Alexis—and I feel held.

Ralph spoons the overwhipped egg-white mixture onto a baking tray. I have no idea if it's even salvageable, but he's going to try, and if not, it's going into the compost bin outside apparently, which Ralph seems equally excited about. "It's always interesting seeing how long sugar keeps things preserved for."

"Cate called me last night," says Alexis, fiddling with the hem of her chunky-knit black sweater. "I've been wanting to . . . ring you. But anyway, Cate picked me up this morning and . . . Millie, I'm so sorry. I'm so sorry I'm a stubborn little fuck."

"You're not a stubborn fuck," I say. Because it doesn't matter. All that matters is she's here now, when I need her. And I have missed her. Regardless of everything, I have missed her so much.

"I've been in a rotten place, Millie. Like . . . so rotten."

"I—I had no idea. You never said—"

"I know." Alexis sniffs deeply, as if to stop tears falling, keep her chest open and puffed up, shoulders strong as always. "But even I had no idea. Until your emails. And then everything just . . . came into focus. Horrible, horrible bloody focus."

"Oh, Alexis. I'm so sorry."

"No." Alexis shakes her head, the thick, straight edges of her bleach-blond bob swaying bluntly, like the rigid edge of a broom. "And I should have just spoken to you. But I . . ." Alexis dabs at her dark, fox-like eyes. "I wanted to just . . . cut the world off. You know? I realized I was lost. Miles from myself. Miles and miles, just . . . working sixty-hour weeks, obsessing over commission, like a *dick*. Sleeping pills to fall asleep, caffeine pills to wake me up, just . . . lost. And I realized when your emails came that I was. That I'd been deeply unhappy for a while."

"Lex, I wish you'd spoken to me. I really, really do." Alexis. Unhappy? But she's always so together. And when she's not, she maps out the route to "together," lights a fuse up her arse, and goes exploding off until she reaches it. Alexis never stops long enough to feel anything. She just—goes. Like a rocket. Like that amazing, inspiring rocket I met all those years ago.

"I wasn't in any fit state to talk to anyone, really. Well. Except a psych. I've been to a . . . retreat thing?" Alexis's chin drops to her chest, as if the words can creep out only if she isn't quite looking at them. "Like a . . . argh. Brain rehab, if you like. I went a month ago. Got back two days ago. It's been . . . good. Four grand a week and you get all the therapy you want, a dish of avocado for brekkie, and a fuckin' little cuddle here and there." Her eyes drift up to meet mine. She stifles a laugh, her big explosion of a laugh that I love so much, sarcasm a dark little flicker in her eyes. Then she sags in her seat. "It's just when I'd see you . . . you and Cate. You reminded me of everything I wasn't. I realize now that I felt completely left behind by you both."

"*Left behind?*" I ask, softly. "Alexis, you're the most successful person I know. Look at everything you've done. You started at the very, very bottom—"

"Absolutely," agrees Cate. "Literally changed your life."

"And now aren't you, like, the highest-paid salesperson in your entire department? You've won *awards*, Lex. You paid your dad's mortgage off. Changed your dad's, your sister's lives. I remember how determined you were when your mum left to turn it all around for them."

"Yes, but who am I, Millie?" asks Alexis unsteadily, voice now a sad whisper. "Like, really. Besides some sort of machine who works and makes money and is everyone's fucking *tree* to lean on. Everyone's rock." Alexis swallows, looks down at her nails, fiddles with a silver ring on her thumb. "And I'd think, Cate is so . . . *Cate*. You know? And I know the bloke's a dick, but Cate, you had Nicholas and Christmas Lane and I'd think, she's just one of those people, Cate. Enamored of the little things. And I don't even know how to even *access* that part of myself."

Cate gives a watery smile but shakes her head. "I'm hardly a poster girl for normality, Lex."

"And Millie, you, you were fucked over. Owen was the *pits*. Put your heart in a blender and drank it for his breakfast. And you're still—*gentle*. You know? Brave but soft. In a nice way. You heaved around this heartache and pain, but you still . . . carried on. Happy here, with Ralph and the sea. Just that. The sea. And your crochet—even if they all look like human organs." Alexis gives an affectionate smile. "Whereas I'm just walking around like this woman made of steel. Acting like *nothing* hurts me, that I don't need what everyone else needs. I don't need *anyone* else. And actually, I'm a . . . fraud."

"Alexis, you're not a fraud," I say.

Alexis swallows. "All this shit I preach. Money and motivation and life on my terms. Every time I saw you both—Cate with her cleaning schedules and happy face and you with walks around Leigh, despite having a broken heart—I just felt jealous. Because for someone who preaches self-love, I don't love myself at all. I don't honor myself at all."

I reach over, hold her hand.

The doorbell rings. "Ah. That'll be the cake," says Ralph. "I'll get it."

"I couldn't look, though," Alexis continues. "It's so much easier to look at other people, isn't it? Make them out to be weird or wrong so you don't have to look at yourself; face yourself."

"Lex, we all have things we want to say and can't," I tell her. "To other people, yes, but most of all to ourselves. That's the hardest of all." A tear slides down my cheek. Alexis catches it with her fingers, and meets my eyes. They're warm and familiar. "I'm so happy you're here," I say.

"Oh, me, too," she says, bottom lip wobbling, and as if she just hands herself over it, she cries too. "Oh God, my makeup is so screwed. This is the new Fenty . . ."

Cate laughs, dabs a tissue at Alexis's eye. Alexis goes to take it, as ever self-governed, won't be fussed or cared for, but . . . then she stops, her hand drifting down to her lap.

"Argh," Alexis groans tearfully. "I wish I'd just stopped being so angry and sad and just said . . . *help*. Say, 'Hello, girls, I'm jealous of you both because you both seem to know who you are and I do not.' "

"I don't!" I say. "I really, really don't!"

"Shit, neither do I," Cate adds. "I mean, look at me? At where I am now, versus where I was. Nobody ever has it all together. Even if we appear to. And in my opinion anyone who seems OK from the outside needs to be approached with caution. It won't be all it seems. We all have stuff beneath the surface."

"You never get the full story." I nod, and my heart aches then. Jack. Jack says that. I wish so much I'd told him the whole story of how I felt about him. Before he left.

Ralph arranges the cake on a plate shaped like a toadstool, dishes out the coffee, and Alexis tells us she's signed up to volunteer at weekends at a dog rescue center, that she's filed a request for sabbatical leave to live off her savings. Rest. Have a holiday. Think about where she wants her life to go.

"Alexis?"

She looks up at me, a tiny piece of carrot cake between two fingertips, matte-gray polish chipped.

"Nicholas said Owen and you—he saw you once. Walked in on you?"

I wait for Alexis to screw her face up, say, "Er, *what*?" But instead she nods, just once, a giant sigh deflating her a little. "Owen would say things to me, yeah. Hit on me. Flirt with me. Make . . . comments. Out-of-line ones. He messaged me a week before you broke up. 'Heard you were going to Goa.' Wanted to meet up."

"Oh my God."

"The guy's a weapon, Millie," Alexis says. "I made the mistake once about telling him about Mum. How she just—struts around with her other family, like we only exist on Christmases, if we're lucky, and he . . . swept right in there. And at first, I felt chuffed. Do you know what I mean? Like, Mill's found this nice guy who gives a shit about her friends, and ah, look at him, listening, he *understands*. But . . . then he—" She screws her nose up, closes her eyes. Two thick, perfect eyeliner wings. "Put his hand on my leg."

"*Oh my God.*"

"I know. He's disgusting. But I didn't know what to do. I know you think you *will* know what to do in that moment, when it actually *happens* to you, but . . . anyway, then you broke up. And I was like, *Thank fuck*. Because you never had to know. I never had to hurt you."

"But it wasn't you, Alexis," I say. "It was him."

"I know. But I'm your friend. It's up to me to protect you from horrible things. Not deliver them to you."

I dab my eyes with tissue as music floats from Ralph's little speaker. Gentle piano music this time.

Owen the villain. Sometimes there are heroes and villains, and he is just one, isn't he? Always was. A *covert* villain. The worst kind. The kind that sucks you in, all sleight of hand. But then—there are the overt heroes. The gentle, kind, oblivious heroes, like Ralph, who hands out our drinks, who places cake on little plates for us, who puts my dodgy meringues in the oven.

"Well, you don't need to present perfect to me," says Cate. "And I mean this to, well, everyone in this room. You can be flawed, you can be a bitch, and show me all your ugly bits—"

Alexis laughs. A reluctant, oh-go-on-then Alexis laugh.

"And I will still love you."

"Same," I say.

Alexis nods. "And *same*," she says tearfully. "Although I don't think a living soul has ever seen my ugly bits. Not really. My ugly bits even have secret ugly bits. You want those, too, Cate?"

"Erm. Could I possibly show you something?" Ralph interjects. "I've been working on it for a few weeks."

"The fungus sweater? Did you start?" I ask. "Oh, Ralph found a fungus sweater knitting pattern he wanted me to take a shot at," I tell Alexis. "Sorry, Ralph, it's just—we were talking about ugly bits. And, well, that sweater . . . no offense."

Ralph smiles and shakes his head. "No. I mean, none taken, but no, this is even cooler." Ralph grabs his laptop from the counter, taps away on the keys. "Here. Take a look."

And when he slides the laptop across to me, I'm greeted with a baby-blue screen. "OneNewMessage.com," I read. "What . . . is this?"

"I created it. A website. Sort of . . . inspired by Alexis's TikTok."

"Oh yeah." Alexis grimaces, the downward tug of a lip. "I'm sorry about that, Mill. But I mean, you did go viral. So, you're welcome, I guess?" She laughs and then pauses. "Except you probably didn't want to go viral on top of everything—"

"What?" I sit up, and laughter bursts out of me. "I went viral?"

Alexis goes wide-eyed. "Er, totally! People started sharing emails they wish they could send. They took sides. And . . . well, most people sided with you. Which, well, it handed my arse to me, really. The internet *does not* hold back." She laughs, then gives a shake of her head. "Anyway. Sorry, Ron. Do go on. I never shut up."

"Ralph," says Ralph. "But Ron. Ralph. Don't worry about it. It's all swings and merry-go-rounds really."

And over Ralph's head, Alexis mimes to Cate, "OK, I love him."

"So, yes." Ralph clears his throat. "People go here—so it's got a sort of email interface, but it's fake. And you pop who it's to here, so, for example: my shitty ex-boyfriend Owen." He looks at me and smiles. "And then *from*, Millie or Me or whatever you want to appear as. And then you type in what you really want to say."

"Fuck you, tosspot," says Alexis. "Just a suggestion. Happy for you to edit it a little."

Ralph types it smilingly. "And then you press send. And it appears . . . here. On a sort of online fake Outlook email program that everyone in the world can view if they so wish."

"Oh my God. *Ralph.*"

"Do you hate it? Sorry, it was just something I was playing with—"

"No, I *love it.*" A big, warming, cheek-stretching smile almost bursts my face. "I think it's genius."

"Do you?" Ralph beams. "It's already had some entries. Someone shared it on Twitter, and we've been getting lots of traffic. And really, people are just *inspired*, Millie. They feel understood. *Seen.* Because everyone's got them, right, things they wish they could say? And this will be a place people can come to say them. What they really want to say but can't. And perhaps question why they can't." Ralph smiles gently.

"Oh my God. I'm actually going to cry—"

Alexis and Cate envelop me in a hug.

"Have you seen at the top of the page? See where it says, 'Inspired by Millie Chandler'?" Ralph says gently.

"I didn't really do anything, though."

"Yes, you did," says Ralph. "You said what you said, held your head up and you looked it all in the eye, even though you were scared. That's brave, Millie."

Cate starts crying then. Ralph interjects with a leftover Easter-themed napkin, and she takes it. "God, Ralph, you are so . . ." Then she grabs the sides of his face and kisses him on the lips.

Ralph looks like he might explode. His whole face looks like a shocked emoji.

I let out a little scream of delight.

"Well, excuse me?" says Alexis.

"Oh. Um. Oh. That w-was . . ." Ralph stutters.

"A shock?" laughs Cate.

"Awesome," says Ralph, open-mouthed. "Very awesome indeed."

"Yeah, well, there's more where that came from." She grins, and I burst out laughing.

"Well, I guess that sort of answers a question I've been trying to find a way of asking," I say. "Although I thought you were already—I don't know. *At it?* After the whole . . . gallbladder thing."

Cate cackles. "Oh, my gallbladder, the babe magnet."

Ralph laughs. "Well. Let's just say we're on a promising trajectory," he says, and we all laugh as the screen in front of us blinks every so often with "one new message"—a stranger sending their secrets out into the world. And it makes me think of my own. How much there is I want to say, and do, and what I should no longer hold back.

FLIGHT STATUS—QE4302—Quebec—departed: 10:44 a.m.

## chapter 31

**Text message from Mum:** Dad lands in the morning. Everything is OK. Would be lovely to see you for brunch if you're around. I love you Millie xxxx

When I enter my old childhood home, I'm hit by a warm, cozy smell of nostalgia and safety. Furniture polish, fresh coffee, and breakfast cooking. I can hear Mum humming and muttering under her breath, "Now, where has that gone?"

Mum turns, sees me at the kitchen doorway, and she looks like she might burst at the sight of me. "Oh, darling. You're here. You *came*."

"Of course I came. Plus your cooking. I miss your cooking . . ."

Mum smiles. "I've gone a bit overboard. But now that you're here, you can help me. I've lost the bacon."

I laugh, setting my bag and coat on the back of the kitchen chair. The house is spotless. Mum would've planned for this ever since she put the date in the diary. It has the feeling of nostalgia in here. The Christmas tree twinkling through the frosted glass doors leading to the living room. Pringles and chocolates in neat piles on the side; cupboard overflow. To think Mum would have been buying ahead, as she always does through November and December, not even knowing if Dad was coming back, if they would be OK . . .

"How does someone lose bacon?" I ask, fishing through the fridge.

"God only knows, Millie," she says, putting the kettle on. "I bought some this morning."

"Farm shop?" I say, taking a seat at the table. Mum and Dad are obsessed with the farm shop.

"Yep. Two packs. Both— Oh, blimey. They're here. On the counter. Under this towel." She pulls a grimace, then laughs, an embroidered Christmas-pudding tea towel in her hand. "Worrying, that is. My poor mind." Mum's excited. But she's also nervous. She's like this before one of the books she illustrates is released. Excited it might fly, worried it might not, all the emotions curdling in one big giant pool of jitters.

Mum chops mushrooms. I make coffee.

"When's Dad due?" I ask.

"In"—she checks her watch—"any minute now. And how are you, Millie?"

"I'm all right," I say. "Things are better. You know when you just feel—clearer?"

Mum nods, leans to crack open a steamed-up window. "I do, love. Yes."

And I do. Even though Jack is gone—his flight on time and taken off, and now probably off on other adventures, taking people thousands of miles from people who love them, I *do* feel clearer. Missing him every minute of every day, but clearer. Like one by one, I'm throwing a bottle into the sea. Slowly, slowly letting go.

A clatter comes from the hallway, a jangle of a chain, and the front

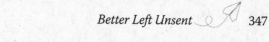

door swings open and slams again. Dad stands in the doorway. He's holding two bunches of flowers wrapped in brown paper, and from behind them, he smiles. A lovely, freckly Dad "Surprise!" smile.

Mum freezes at the chopping board and turns. "Mitch?"

"Hello, you two," he says softly in his lovely, familiar, warm Dad tone. "How are we then?"

"Hey, Dad!" I stretch up, reach my arms around him, and Mum simply stands, her hands at her apron.

He hands us a bunch of flowers each—white roses for Mum and a spray of heather and lavender for me. "I thought it looked different," says Dad. "And I thought that was perfect for you."

A few minutes later, we all sit at the little round table in the kitchen with cups of coffee, sausages in the oven, the bacon still out and un-opened, bread lined up in the toaster, ready to be pressed down.

"Millie, I'm sorry if anything that happened put any strain on you," Dad says.

I nod, don't deny that it did.

"We had a . . . hiccup in the road," he continues, "a hump, a hurdle, if you like. But we are right here. Solid as a rock. Because that's just life, isn't it? That's just . . . well. Love." And when he says this, his words are all warmth. All him. All I've ever known Dad to be.

"I'm so glad you're here," says Mum. "Both of you."

Dad swallows, and he shifts on the chair. He brings out his phone. "And . . ." he says, and he spends far too long going in and out of apps until he loads up FaceTime. He presses Kieran's name.

"Oh," Mum says as it starts to ring, and Dad props his phone up against a salt mill. The three of us squish together in the frame. A mis-matched family portrait.

Kieran's face flashes onto the screen. "Hello, family." Kieran laughs, and the screen is a sea of smiles. His hair is graying at the tem-ples. He's had a haircut. Those long, floppy curtains he had all the way until we dropped him at the airport and he left for MIT, when he was eighteen, long, long gone.

"What's for brunch then?" he asks. His accent is only *just* a little lost to an American twang. "Sausages in the oven?"

"Of course," Mum says. "Links you call them, don't you?"

"Oh, we have snow!" Kieran grins, not hearing Mum. The screen jitters. "Hold on, let me just show you. It's still a little dark but you should be able to make it out. Jennings has gone to work with actual chains on his wheels."

Kieran swipes up his phone, takes us around his beautiful home, to his snowy "backyard." It blurs on the camera, but it's pillowy white for miles.

"Oh, I love snow!" I say, and Kieran brings the camera to his face.

"Then come," he says. "Come and see your big brother."

"I wish," I say.

"What's stopping you?" He settles down on his sofa and yawns. His dog, Mango, sniffs the screen. "Well, beside the fact we send each other really crap text messages, weeks apart and half-finished, and can't even answer each other about what we've had for *dinner*, let alone venture into invites and plane tickets?" He does that Kieran thing. Where his face is die-straight, in mock seriousness, then breaks into a massive, clowny, Dad-joke smile.

"Um. *You're* a shitty texter," I say. "Not me, thank you."

"I am such a shitty texter," he admits. "I prefer the phone. Like, actual landline. Forces me to sit down."

"Sure, old man." I laugh. "And an abacus. Do you prefer an abacus over calculator too?"

"Do you know," says Kieran, "I love an abacus."

And my cheeks are aching so much, talking to him. We've sunk straight into our brother-sister dynamic. Kieran self-deprecating and old before his years. Me the lighter, younger, piss-taking sister. And

I'm struck now by how much I *get* Alexis in this moment. I think talking to Kieran was . . . painful. That's why I haven't stayed in touch as much as we've got older. Kieran held up a mirror to me of all the things I wasn't and thought I should be. And I've missed him. I really, really have missed him.

"Millie," Dad says, shifting in his seat. A calm Dad voice, breaking up the sibling silliness at the breakfast table. Ocean or no ocean. "We, erm. We wanted to give you something. Didn't we, Toni?"

Dad places a debit card on the table. Silence falls across the room for a moment. I stare at it. "This—this is for you."

I look at Dad across the table. "What? What is it?"

"We saved a lot for you both, as you know."

I nod, looking from one to the other. My smiling, watery-eyed mum. My smiling, watery-eyed dad. "For . . . for a wedding. For a house, you said."

Dad swallows. "And that was selfish of us. To assume that's what you want. To assume getting married is who you are. It might be. It might not be. But . . ." He stops and looks at Mum.

"We've had a lot of time to think, Millie," she says. "And so much of what you said—I'm so sorry if we've ever made you feel less than for just being who you are."

Tears sit at the edge of my eyes.

Kieran smiles from the screen, a hand slowly stroking Mango's round little head.

"It's your money. We worked, we saved for *you*. And it's yours. Kieran had his for what he wanted."

"Wedding. House deposit. Jeez, how did I get so basic?" he asks, and I laugh through my tears.

"Therefore," Dad adds calmly, his speech ready to go and rehearsed (on the plane, I bet), "it should be spent on what *you* want it for. For who you are. Take a holiday. Pay off your student loan. Go and . . ."

"Be Millie," says Mum, and that moves me. Turns my heart to warm syrup.

"Oh my God, are you . . . are you sure, though?"

"Don't start with that, we'll take it back." Dad chuckles, warmly, color in his lovely round cheeks once more. I think about him on my doorstep. I think about him drinking from Ralph's flask on that drizzly bench. A contrast to right now. "It's yours," Dad says. "How could we not be sure?"

Mum passes me a tea towel, which I laughingly dab at my eyes. I take the debit card, turn it over in my hand.

"Just so you know, I resent you all for making me cry." Kieran laughs, and he gets up in search of a tissue and carries us to the kitchen. "I am a Brit in an emotionally engaged country, and you are ruining my rep," he says, his voice quietening as he riffles through his kitchen drawers for a napkin.

"I'm sorry you felt you couldn't tell us you wanted something different. That you felt things you couldn't share." Dad swallows, his eyes glazing over with tears. He turns to Mum. "And . . . Toni, how is Julian?"

Mum looks at Dad, her eyes shining. She gawps for just a flicker, then of course gathers herself. "He's—he's . . . he's OK."

Dad nods. "I know I'm an old man, a soppy old man. But my life is nothing without you, Toni. You, Kieran, Millie. And so much of my life was and is happy because of you all. You have *made* my life. Messy, stressful, painful sometimes, but . . ." He brings a chubby, large hand to his nose and sniffs. "It's been a wonderful life. Because of you. And if on his last days, Julian needs some of that, then . . . I understand. I do."

He holds mine and Mum's hand across the round table. Mum holds the phone, Kieran's face cradled in her hand.

And together we sit, a family, at that little wooden table. Having spoken our truths, having made a mess, a tangle, and unteased it again. And like the tide, we made our way back.

**Text Message from Millie:** I miss you Jack.

**Text Message from Millie:** I miss you so much.

## chapter 32

**Text Message from Alexis:** OH MY GOD I think I just adopted a dog!!!!!??? The process is long af, but Millie, let me tell you, this dog has one eyeball and black patches around his eyes like Robert Smith. He was a stray, found around the back of a McDonald's. I have found my soulmate. Once and for all. Which means today is a lucky day. Perfect timing for tonight. Good luck, my brave friend. Knock it out of the park. Xo

**Text Message from Cate:** Remember you're saying this for you, and nobody else, Millie! This is your moment. Say it all out loud and PROUD. Let the whole world (ok, whole function room) hear it. Oh, and don't rush home tonight. Me and Ralph are going out for pulled pork and then home to watch Dirty Dancing. Not a euphemism. (But also, absolutely a euphemism.)

The Christmas party is out in pure colorful swing. There are so many fairy lights and Christmas trees, it's like a nineties Christmas music video—like the actual North Pole itself, with an added vibe of a nineties boy band's Christmas video. Flye always goes all out, which Petra has always found laughable, considering so much of their top secret data is held on an Excel spreadsheet. "Well, we may have to put petrol in the PCs to make them work, but at least there are fillet steaks and cocktails named after the directors at the Christmas party," she often jokes.

As promised, I am wearing the dress of my dreams. No fancy dress for me this time. Cate helped me choose it (with guidance from the palette app, of course). A-line. Silk and elegant. Ocean green that falls to the floor, a split up one side. A far cry from my frame-head catsuit (which now hangs in my own wardrobe, for memories' sake).

"Baby," says Lin, coming up behind me. "I mean—can we just . . . Twirl for me."

I laugh and twirl, the skirt of the dress lifting a little as I do.

"You look incredible. Like a Hollywood star. But also, I'm going to have to break your legs. One at a time."

"Why?" I laugh.

"Pet says you're leaving. You're not, are you?" asks Lin, feathers from her grapefruit-pink dress brushing me in the face.

"I am," I say with a smile. "End of the month. I'm going on holiday with my friends Alexis and Cate. Just for a week. And then to visit my brother Kieran in Michigan, and then . . ." I trail off.

"You don't know?" asks Lin smilingly.

"Nope," I say. "And I'm fucking terrified, but I also can't *wait*." And it had felt like a slow, but fast decision all at once. I'd sat on a bench by the estuary with Cate, watching Ralph swim with his group, scarves and hats and keep-cup teas, and watched boats in the distance disappear, watched clouds morph and change and skid by in the sky, and I'd just known. It unraveled in front of me. I'm ready for change. And on Monday, I'd given notice in the same boardroom I was reprimanded in just months ago. Petra had clapped excitedly as if on fast-forward, Paul Foot had told me warmly I would "certainly be missed," like a true jolly postman, and Michael of course had extracted a nose hair.

Lin hugs me and says, "I'll miss you, you weird, bad bitch. Plus, who will I moan to once you've gone? Cherry won't let me whinge. Brings her vibration down, apparently."

"Write it in an email," I say, "and just don't send it."

Lin throws her head back, laughs, feathers whacking me in the face once more. "The thing with me, though, Millie, is I *always* fucking send it." And I think, perhaps that's the best way after all.

I drift around the party, a cocktail in hand. This one is named Paul My Finger after Paul Foot. (Yes, really.) Only marginally better than last year's, "The Foot Spa." (Which was made so much worse by being swamp *green* in color!)

I drift around the room, gaze at the people I have shared time and space with for the last five years of my life. Despite it all, I am out the other side and everything is OK. And like my parents, like my friends, like Chloe and Owen and every single person on this planet, they all have their own shit going on behind closed doors. Nobody is perfect. Nobody has it all figured out. We all have shadow parts, as Ralph said. I just happened to show mine. And now there's a website out there, inspired by the moment light was shone on my shadow parts, where everyone feels safe shining a light on theirs. And there's safety in vulnerability. If you show yours, the right people are inspired by it and feel safe to show theirs. Like Jack had shown me his.

I wish so much Jack was still here.

But he's gone. Would've landed in Quebec by now. There is a part of me, though, that hoped he'd be here tonight, somehow. Coming back, like my family did, around that table. Like Alexis did. Like Cate, who came back to herself. Stupid, I know. But I allowed myself a little daydream. Jack in a tux, under the glow of Christmas lights, that gorgeous smile, his safe, safe arms . . .

"Well, hello," says a voice. And I wish so much it was his voice. But it's not. It's Fundraising Steve in a suit that looks too small for him. "No picture frame for your head tonight? Heard about that."

"Maybe if you're lucky I'll stick it on my head later," I say as a Mariah Carey remix erupts from the PA and someone cheers. "Give you all something to talk about."

"You just need your partner in crime," he says. "Jack Dawson, wasn't he?"

I nod. A warm, sweet sadness spreads across my chest.

"Good for a laugh, is Jack," says Steve.

"Strange without him here," I remark.

Steve shakes his head, one of his weird, gelled prongs moving like an insect's feeler. "Do you know, I saw him at the airport."

"*Really?*" Oh my God. Is he—was he coming back? Everything lifts in me. As if I've suddenly been attached to a thousand helium balloons.

"My Mary. She was coming back from Krakow. Some hen do thingy with her mates. I went to pick her up. And there he was." Steve holds his hands out in the air, carrying an invisible boulder. "Backpack as big as his body, the lot . . ."

My heart sinks. Sinks so much, it's like it's in my feet, turning to liquid. I knew he'd gone. But hearing about him actually leaving is harder.

"It was nice to see him actually. Say goodbye. Offered to buy him a pint, but he had to go. Flight to catch. Such a lovely fella, that one."

I nod, feel tears collect in my throat. Someone pushes past me, says sorry. "Right. Yes. He is."

Gone. Backpack as big as his body.

Gone. I wish he was here. I wish so much he was here. But the truth is, he's as far away from me as he could possibly be. I haven't heard from him. He talked about roaming packages for his phone, new SIM cards, how he often switches his phone out when he's camping and in hostels to something more robust. But then, I don't blame him not contacting me even if he can.

"A shame," says Steve. "I thought you two were a thing. I told him that too. I said, 'I don't know much, but I thought you two matched.'"

I'm going to do this. He might not be here, but I'm doing it for him. For *me.* I want to stand in front of hundreds of people and face my biggest fear. Not only talking about how I feel, but talking about how I feel in front of everyone I know. Show my little bruised, nervous heart that needs to know it's OK to reveal itself. Because *So what? So what?*

Petra takes to the stage first. The music fades, and she taps the microphone once and then twice, like she's watched way too many movies where this is how speeches start. "Hello, hello, people of Flye." She laughs, and she pulls her teeth into a tight grimace.

Kira smiles back at her from the floor, gives two proud, loving thumbs-up, and it makes me smile. Petra, who had once been like me. Battered, bruised, and scared of love, she has pushed through and out the other side, standing in a proverbial shard of light.

"It's so nice for us all to get together for the night, to be out of the office, off location, here as people instead of emails, humans instead of phone calls and video conferences and orders barked during halftime. But it's more to say thank you for your hard work, and for all of us to remember that we are all people, with hearts and lives and hopes and dreams and fears. We aren't just our jobs."

Everyone claps, and nerves creep up my skin, as it'll soon be my turn to speak. I take a deep breath. As long as I don't trip over, domino it off the stage, what could go wrong? Cardboard Gary Lineker's snapped neck blinks into my memory. Going out the same way Cardboard Gary went would be symbolic.

"And while it seems sometimes time doesn't move when we all come into work day after day, same routines, same lunch breaks, same mugs and small talk at the kettle, time goes on. People arrive and people leave. Every year I stand here and say goodbye to certain people. We have recently said goodbye to Jack Shurlock, who has flown to pastures new, miles and miles away, the cheeky bastard." Laughter. Again. "June Briggs retired, fittingly back in June, and George Reckitt has gone to get his PhD in . . ." Petra pauses and checks her hand, which is scribbled with black ink. "Geotechnical engineering. Wow. Well. Anyway. It hasn't been the same without them, but we of course wish them the best. But someone here tonight is going to be leaving us and has become a sort of . . . office celebrity, shall we say, in her own right. Millie Chandler will be leaving at the end of the month after five years with Flye."

People clap, and I'm pleased to report not a single rotten tomato slaps against me.

I step forward into the spotlight. This is it. Here I go. I feel as good as naked up here, all eyes on me. Petra puts an arm around me. "Do you still want to speak?" she says into my ear as people whoop.

"Yes," I say, "yes, please."

And here goes nothing.

"Hi, everyone," I call into the microphone. Feedback squeaks from the PA. And is that really what my voice sounds like? "What a year. What a *five years,* I should say, but . . ." God, there are so many people out there. So many faces, so many eyes on me. But not his. Not a single pair of the eyes in this room are those warm, hazel eyes I wish so much I could see. "And if any of you didn't know me, you certainly do now, thanks to something called *my email drafts.*" Everyone laughs, thankfully. A titter that travels around the room, like a soft wave. "I've learned so much working at Flye, most of which I learned the moment those emails were sent and landed in so many of your inboxes—and inboxes across the land."

Lin, in the crowd, smiles at me, phone poised, filming me. She's invited me onto her podcast to talk about the emails, and I've said yes.

"Since that moment, my life has changed. I've learned to look things in the eye. I've learned to honor how I feel. And I've learned . . . we're all a bit messed up actually. That's why you all panicked. Panicked because what if it happened to you?" Everyone laughs—nervous laughter, but laughter all the same. "Because we might put on a front, pretend we say everything we want to, that we mean what we do say, but . . . we all have unsaid things. Things we wish we could say or know we never will. To think you do, and nobody else does, is a lie. We are all the same."

"Yes!" shouts Lin, and someone whistles.

"I don't regret a single moment working here, and OK, I wish I could say I don't regret a single email sent, on my behalf or not. But there is one email I regret. One I never wrote or sent. But I thought I'd say it instead. In front of you all, knowing he's a million miles away, so this is even cringier, even weirder. But I'm telling the truth. Out loud. I just wish you were here to hear it, Jack. And in that tux you told me you hated."

There is a poised, warm, open silence. One that's loaded with wanting to hear what's next, and also an undertone of "Might she be having a breakdown?"

"Jack Shurlock," I say. "I know this is too late. I know I should have said this before. The whole time I was worrying about all the things I said, and you were trying to convince me I shouldn't, I should have been worrying about the unsaid things I wanted to say to you. Jack Shurlock, I am in love with you." I swallow, my hands shaking, the words landing there, in the room, floating like haze in front of me. Nowhere to go but *out there*. "And I would stand here in front of crowds, in front of stadiums, in front of . . . *the entire world* and say it, even if you never felt it yourself, even if you never said it back. Even if you never heard me. Because it's my truth. And although I wish very much I could live forever in your vortex, you have taught me that I hope I live until the end of my life in my own."

And for a second, there is silence. And then—people clap. People whoop and cheer. Lin shouts, "KNEW IT, BABY!" Some people stare at me like I've just crouched naked on the stage, and others aren't even listening. They're too busy pushing steak canapés into their mouths. And that alone is an emblem of the world, really. Nobody's really watching. They're too busy worrying about themselves. (Except Petra and Kira. Petra is crying, and Kira's eyes are closed, holding her like she's at church.)

"And I know you got that email by accident," I carry on. "But I should have sent it back then; sent it myself after that Christmas party, minus the embarrassing bits. So here it is. Sending. To all. *In front* of all. At *this* Christmas party. 'Hi, Jack, hope the hangover isn't too nasty. I had such a nice time talking to you. When you get back, do you fancy going out sometime?' "

I step off the stage and feel twenty feet tall, albeit, slightly wobbly with adrenaline. Because I did it. I faced my biggest fear, looked it right in the eyes, and said, "So what?" And the world didn't implode. I just wish Jack was here to have seen it. I wonder what he'd have thought, seeing me up there onstage. I wonder what he would have *said.* Maybe he would've turned me down; said, "Nah, you're all right, thanks, Millie. You're too much drama for me." But it almost *doesn't matter.* What matters is I said it. What matters is that I feel it; that I feel *alive.* That I'm being Millie. No hiding, no quashing down. Just Millie. As I am. Grown in the dark, ready to step into the light.

People I've never spoken to pat my back as I move away from the stage. A waiter proffers a whole tray of what look like miniature fish heads at me, in a scatter of pink edible flowers. Then someone takes my arm in the darkness.

"Millie. That was amazing."

It's Chloe. She looks incredible in a butter-yellow tuxedo. I would look like a walking banana in such an outfit, but she looks like something from London Fashion Week. And something in her face is different. She glows. She looks so much better than she did when I last saw her on the bridge, in the foggy darkness, and I almost want to hug her. I feel like we've been through so much, me and this woman who exploded my life.

"Hi," I say. "And thank you, I was *unbelievably* nervous."

"Seriously. I'm in awe, Millie. It was so romantic."

I pull my mouth into a grimace. "Really? Well, my biggest fear was that I would pass out and break my nose on the fall, so the alternative wasn't romantic at all. Nothing romantic about a squashed, bloody nose."

Chloe gives a smile, glossy, white-toothed, then hesitates. "I'm so sorry again. I know I keep saying it, but I am."

"Don't." I give a small smile. "Really."

She nods, sadly, eyes dipping to the floor, then looks up at me. "It was Leona," she says, almost defeatedly. Of course. Of course it was. "They're seeing each other apparently."

"I'm sorry," I say. "I'm really sorry, Chloe," and she lifts a stiff shoulder.

"I'll be OK," she says. "Plus, I'm sure she'll be saying the same to me in a few months. Just like I was saying sorry to you. A horrible, dark cycle."

"Chloe, it was actually the best thing that ever happened to me," I say.

Her eyes brighten under the lilac disco lights. "Really?"

"Really." I nod. And I'd have never seen it like this in the beginning, but now I can see everything was leading to this. To breaking free not only of Owen, but of all the barriers I put up, in the name of protecting myself. Barriers that kept me safe but kept me stifled too. And without those emails being sent, I'm not sure when I would have got here. Or if I ever would. "Chloe, I feel like you set me free."

Chloe's eyes glisten under the spotlights. "I feel like you set me free, too," she says, and she reaches forward, folds her arms around me; a curtain fall. A page turned. That when she pressed send, she was releasing us, like birds.

After a few moments, we say goodbye, and Chloe moves into the crowd. I realize I haven't once looked for Owen since being here. I don't care if he heard me, what he'd make of it, what he'd be thinking. I really have totally let him go. I let that version of Millie go too; put it all into a bottle, watched the waves take it away. Because I'm the Millie I've always been. The one who wanted adventures. The one who wanted new things. The one was ready to find out who she was. And she'll help me find the Millie who'll come to be too. And . . . it's exciting. I'm *excited.*

"Can I help?" says a barman as I approach the bar.

"Oh yes." I pick up a small plastic stand of a menu from the wooden surface. "Can I have a Petra-Fying, please?"

"Sure."

I sit as the barman shakes a stainless-steel mixer, pours out a bright green cocktail, places down my drink. "Nice speech."

"Oh. Thanks."

"I'm sure he'd be over the moon," he says, running a thumb and forefinger down his dark mustache, like a pincer. "The man in the tux."

"Oh." I sip. "Well. I suppose we'll never really know. But I like to hope so."

The barman nods. "There're quite a few tuxes here, actually," he says. "Not that I'm saying any other man in a tux could replace the man who passed—"

"Oh God, he's . . . *not dead*," I say. "My man in the tux, he's . . . he's just in *Quebec*."

"Oh! Oh, well, blimey! Phew, eh?" The barman laughs, and so do I.

Jack would laugh too. "Killing me off, are you, Millie dot Chandler? Well, that's all well and good, but just make sure nobody sings any of those made-up hymns at my funeral."

"Thought it was a bit sad for a Christmas party," says the barman. "Lost opportunities with a dead man who never got to wear his tux."

"No! No, he thankfully is very much alive. I just . . . fucked it up a bit."

"Ah." The barman smiles, close-mouthed. "We've all been there. Oh, damn. Did you want the pineapple slice in the Petra-Fying? I forgot to add it."

"Ooh yes, if you like."

He reaches beneath the bar with tongs, his eyes darting up. "And ah, told you. Knew there were other tuxes floating around here." And he nods behind me. "Nice seeing a tux. Don't see so many these days. Even at weddings."

"Agreed. *Classic*," I say, and I turn around.

And it happens in a blur. I see the tux. I see the glinting hazel eyes. Standing there . . . is *Jack*.

Jack.

Jack Shurlock is actually here.

Everything leaves my body. Air. Words. *Everything.*

"Oh my God," leaves my mouth, shaky and tight.

I stand up, barely even feel my feet on the ground. It's like I'm floating. Levitating. And I'm pretty sure I'm not hallucinating, or even drunk. I've not had a single sip of Petra-Fying yet.

"Jack," I say, my heart hammering, hammering. "You're . . . *you're here.*"

Jack smiles at me. That slow, sexy, familiar smile that makes my skin tingle, my stomach roll over. My hands fly to my face, flat to my cheeks. "I'm here," he says simply.

Then he moves in front of me.

"You're actually here," I say again, my voice barely a whisper.

"I couldn't leave," he says softly. "I couldn't leave you, Millie."

"Are you . . ." Tears gather in my throat, prickle my eyes. "Are you serious? Are you seriously here?"

Jack nods slowly, his soft, gold-green eyes glinting. "Went to the airport. Sort of hoped you'd come screaming through the barriers, to be honest." The corner of his mouth lifts amusedly. "Slo-mo shot of you sliding between the security guard's legs . . ."

I laugh, my eyes stinging with tears. "Oh my God." I throw my arms around him, and I close my eyes, breathe and breathe and breathe him in. Jack. My Jack Shurlock. And he's *here.* He didn't go. He didn't leave.

"I never had a reason to stay," he says. "You're right. I never knew what it was to *want* to stay anywhere. Until you. You're the reason I want to stay, Millie. Nowhere feels like anywhere without you."

He pulls me into him, and I can hardly breathe as he pushes his lips gently to mine in a kiss. A kiss that feels like a slow promise.

"I swayed you," I say, inches from his lips, and he laughs, that sexy, low chuckle.

In a whisper he says, "You swayed me."

And people are looking. People have surrounded us, actually. All eyes on us. All eyes on *me.* And I feel nothing about them. It's like they're not there. Just me and Jack, in our vortex.

"I did a speech earlier," I say, drawing back and looking up at him; at his gorgeous, gorgeous face. "You'd have loved it, I reckon."

Jack raises his eyebrows, then leans in, warm lips close to mine. "Saw it," he says. "And loved it. Although . . ." He pauses. "You didn't have to do that. The whole get-up-onstage thing. The whole asking-me-out-in-front-of-everyone thing. You could've just checked your emails."

I laugh. "My *emails*?"

Out of his pocket, he gives me a square of paper. On it is an email address—a Millie dot Chandler email address. And a password. "The new one I set up for you."

I take the paper from his hands.

"And by the way, the answer is yes. With you, the answer is always yes."

And surrounded by hundreds of people and watchful eyes, I kiss Jack Shurlock, the man I truly love. I live my truth out loud.

107 new messages

> **From: Jack Shurlock**
> **To: Millie.Chandler**
> **Subject: Good morrow**
> A new email address. Just so you don't have to move to Brazil, change your name, etc. A lot of admin, I imagine.

> **From: Jack Shurlock**
> **To: Millie.Chandler**
> **Subject: FYI**
> Dear Millie,
>     Nobody looks as cool as you with a screen leaning on their back.
>
>                          Jack (the teenage vampire)

**From: Jack Shurlock**
**To: Millie.Chandler**
**Subject: Any color is your color**

Hi, just me, saying I just saw you at the sailing club and I appear to be slightly jealous of Elton? Being jealous of a dog is not a good look for me, Millie Chandler.

**From: Jack Shurlock**
**To: Millie.Chandler**
**Subject: Cloakroom**

I have never wanted to kiss someone as much as I wanted to kiss you tonight. Well. Perhaps, since the Christmas party. Why do we always get interrupted?

**From: Jack Shurlock**
**To: Millie.Chandler**
**Subject: Someone asked me once . . .**

If I ever have moments that I know, there and then, I'll remember forever. I told them forever was a stretch.

But I'm pretty sure that smile you gave me when we first walked into the rhubarb barn was one.

**From: Jack Shurlock**
**To: Millie.Chandler**
**Subject: Swaying**

I just left you at the treehouse and thought you should know something. Despite myself, I think I'm falling in love with you, Millie Chandler.

**From: Jack Shurlock**
**To: Millie.Chandler**
**Subject: Tomatometer**

Also interested to know whether my Tomatometer rating is the same in real life as it is in dreams, or whether it's affected by a) reality, b) being in a cold treehouse, c) while in the presence of a tobacco-scented candle.

I'd like to find out. (Again.)

**From: Jack Shurlock**
**To: Millie.Chandler**
**Subject: Instinct**

I thought you should know I was very tempted today to keep on sailing and sailing, until we reached anywhere that wasn't here. I don't want to leave you, Millie. I don't know how I'm supposed to. Fuck.

**From: Jack Shurlock**
**To: Millie.Chandler**
**Subject: Driving**

Driving away from you tonight was the hardest thing I've ever had to do.

**From: Jack Shurlock**
**To: Millie.Chandler**
**Subject: Swayed**

I just left the airport. Got to the plane door and turned around.

I can't leave without you.

I don't want to be anywhere without you.

You are my reason to stay. I'm sorry I took too long to realize that you always were.

I love you, Millie Chandler.

(And now I guess I now have to go and find a tux . . . see you soon.)

*epilogue*

**From: Millie.Chandler**

**To: All**

**Subject: An update from us—can you believe it's been a year?**

Hi everyone! Good morrow!

I thought it was time for an update because Jack and I realized tonight (while nighttime sledding, would you believe? Pictures attached!) that tomorrow marks a whole, entire year since we left. An entire year since I stepped out of my little snuggly safe hollow, waved goodbye to Leigh-on-Sea, and got on a plane with my boyfriend, Jack Shurlock.

A year on, we're here in Lake Bohinj in Slovenia, and OMG it's like a hidden winter wonderland. I'm talking amazing, mirrorlike frozen lakes, I'm talking actual Fox's Glacier Mint–style ice-capped mountains and cabins with smoking Santa Claus chimneys. (Again, pictures attached!) And before you get all jealous, from your desks and Tesco aisles and drizzly UK streets that could never compare, I hope it helps to learn that I write this from inside a ski jacket while wrapped in multiple duvets in a creaky wooden cabin bed. I can't feel my feet, and all because Jack has lost the fire lighters for our little log burner. He's actually gone to smooth-talk the couple in the cabin next door for theirs. (A couple we have named Mr. and Mrs. Costa del Sol because all they have said to us since arriving is, "This isn't like the Costa del Sol. In the Costa del Sol, you can get two beers for four euros. In the Costa del Sol, they play *Emmerdale* on screens in the bars.")

And I'm aware I'm not even updating you all. Just rambling chaotically about random shit I'm sure all you *really* miss me spouting in real life. And I really do miss you all. So much. Especially you, Ralph, Cate, and Alexis. (You, too, Fundraising Steve, if you're reading. I'm sure you asked Jack to be added to our "all" list, and I don't want you to feel left out. I miss you all in fact. And I know even Jack does, in his own Jack way.)

Oh, I don't know what else to say. Seems it was easier writing emails when I was in emotional turmoil, ha-ha. But what I totally do know is that I've had the year of my life. With—and I say this, watching him through the window, traipsing back across the snow with, HURRAY, the Costa del Sols' fire lighters—the actual love of my life. I'm happy. Even freezing cold and wrapped in blankets by a frozen lake, I'm so happy. I didn't know I could even be this happy. Be this free.

We've been to Quebec (and discovered I find alpacas

very unnerving). We've been to New Zealand (a place so beautiful I started writing ACTUAL (terrible) poetry because of it). We went to visit my lovely brother and his husband in Michigan (hello, Kieran and Jennings!), and from there hired a Winnebago, which at first was so romantic . . . until Jack got us so lost in Texas in the wilderness that I cried and called him, in my angry panic on the side of a dusty road, "a very dangerous man." A name he has, of course, adopted and insists I call him by now whenever he finds himself doing something very undangerous. (Helping an old lady with her luggage, roasting corn at our little fireside, neatly hanging out my stupid Kermit the Frog pajamas from the washing machine. "Oh yes," he'll say, "a very dangerous man indeed.")

And I don't know where we'll go next. We're just . . . making it up every day, planning only as much as we need to right now. But we think about you all often (and yes, OK, I text a lot of you every day, because a Bear Grylls I will never, ever be). We're actually thinking of coming back for Easter, though. Mum, Dad, can we stay with you? I guess there's always Auntie Vye's conservatory, if not.

Cate and Ralph (and my lovely, lovely Four the Logans)—OMG, I live for your updates. Your selfies, cuddled up on the sofa, your hilarious swimming updates where Cate texts me "I'm in hell" and Ralph texts, at almost identical times, "I'm unsure but she seems to dislike it"—they're like hugs from home. (PS, Cate, the mushroom sweater looks hot on you, which is completely unfair. You are supposed to look ridiculous. Not stylish. How do you *do* that?)

And Alexis, how is Robert Smith? I still believe it to be the coolest dog name of all time (and he, the coolest dog. Oh, and Elton, of course, Jonny. Both equally cool.). Good luck this afternoon with vet man, too! Both Jack and I agree, he really does have a touch of the 2003 Ethan Hawke about him. (And of course, I expect a full 1,000-word first-person statement via WhatsApp tonight, post-date. No pressure.)

PETRA AND KIRA! Please accept this as our official RSVP! We will be there. We would not miss your wedding for the world. (And did I read this right? You actually have a wedding band called "The Pickles"? I LOVE IT SO MUCH.)

Lin, I MISS YOU. That is all. (Oh! And you'll be pleased to know that my Granddaddy-phone is now back in the garage where it belongs.)

Oh, and Steve—put us down for £5 a mile for your Bath race. Jack requires more details on how the bath *moves*. Does it have wheels? Will you be dragged down the street by a car? A horse? Jack really wants it to be a horse.

Anyway, everyone out there, I'd better go. Jack needs the iPad. He promised it to Mr. Costa del Sol later in return for the fire lighters. (He wants to watch *Emmerdale* and the DIY SOS special.) Plus, I've just been informed I have an hour to get ready. Jack is taking me somewhere—sorry, *Dangerous Man* is taking me somewhere. It's a surprise. Nothing changes (and everything changes)!

Stay tuned for the next update, I suppose!

Love to you all. Love to Leigh. (Oh, and give our love to *Sir Instinct*, too, if you find yourself passing. We hope to be out on him again sometime, someday soon.)

Millie and Jack xxx

# acknowledgments

Ahhh, how lovely to be at the acknowledgments stage with *Better Left Unsent*, the lightning bolt of an idea that's been my fictional escape for two years now. Because sitting down to write acknowledgments means the book is finally finished. All the worry and doubt, all the jiggery-pokery, all the turning puzzle pieces to make them fit, all the late-night, should-be-sleeping thinking is done. The book is its own solid, three-dimensional world with its own beating heart and wings, and acknowledgments always come when it's the time to let it go. *Fly*, so to speak. The writer's gentle guidance (and, ahem, sometimes *forceful wrangling*) is no longer needed. It exists. And it doesn't need you anymore. And that is both lovely and anxiety-inducing! It's comforting to know, though, that it is now with you, the reader. Because *you're* who this is for. You're why I get to do this. So, firstly, and most importantly, thank you so, so much, from the bottom of my heart! For reading, for reviewing, for reaching out with your beautiful messages. I hope you've enjoyed living fleetingly in Millie's chaotic world. (I hope it doesn't make you worry too much over your own email drafts, though!)

A huge thank-you to my unstoppable powerhouse of an agent, Juliet Mushens at Mushens Entertainment: Part human, part The Flash. I am forever grateful for your honesty, hard work and loyalty, and for always, always believing in me and the stories that live in my head. Thank you for always jumping aboard with me. (And for forgiving me, and laughing at, the absolutely off-the-wall references that make it into my emails that should perhaps, stay in my own drafts, never to be sent . . .)

Thank you to the always incredible Mushens Entertainment dream team, and coagents, and to the utterly brilliant Jenny Bent at The Bent Agency, New York. You truly are the dreamiest of dream teams.

To my US editor, the amazing Emily Bestler at Emily Bestler Books. I am so grateful for your guidance and your belief in me over the last few years. (And I always say it, but it'll never not be true that your editing notes will always be my fave.) Thank you to Lara Jones and Hydia Scott-Riley, Zakiya Jamal, and Holly Rice-Baturin as well, of course, as the whole incredible team at Emily Bestler Books, Atria, and Simon & Schuster. I'm so grateful to you all.

To my whip-smart UK editor, Melissa Cox, thank you for your hard work and your insight (and for making Ralph a lil bit sexy. I owe you. So does he, ha ha.) To Sarah Bauer, Misha Manani, Salma Begum, Sophie Orme, and the whole amazing team at Bonnier Books/Zaffre. I'm excited for all that is to come . . .

There were lots of little technical details I needed to get right for this novel, and that would not have been possible without Liv Matthews, and the supersmart Matthew Whitehead, who put up with lots of emails about technology I will never be clever enough to understand! Thank you to Becky Williams, and to the kindest soul,

Holly Chubb, for giving me a window into the world of sporting broadcast and television, and of course, my brother, Bubs, and my Dad, for answering all my broadcast and cameraman-y questions.

Thank you so much to Fiona Cummins and Charlotte Northedge for being so generous with their time and answering my Leigh-on-Sea queries!

To Gillian McAllister (uppercase!), thank you for seeing through all the fog I create in my own mind and showing me that this was the book I should write. Without you, I might still be flailing around saying, "Two years, and I've still had no book ideas." And of course, thank you always and endlessly for your friendship.

Thank you to Beth O'Leary, for always listening and reminding me that there's no such thing as having "too much fun." Thank you to Holly Seddon, Lindsey Kelk, Stephie Chapman, and many more of you who make this solitary job feel less so. It's an honor to call you friends.

To Amanda and Alison for showing me where my bravery lies.

To Grace, Sally, Emma, and Toni for being those mates I always hoped I'd be lucky enough to find. (And for listening to what is essentially, one thousand words of whining per day about school dinner admin, Mum guilt, and how very tired I am.)

Mum and Steve, Dad and Sue, Bubs, Vicky, Ani, little Lottie and Max, Nan, Grandad, Alan, Marl, Libby, and Patricia. Thank you for all the boundless love and support. (And for the endless quirky, hilarious material. My favorite thing in the world is laughing with you all.)

And finally, to my beautiful babies, and to my Ben: thank you for loving me for everything I am. You are my everything. You are my home.